A Double Death
on the
Black Isle

Also by A. D. Scott

✖

A Small Death in the Great Glen

A DOUBLE DEATH
ON THE
BLACK ISLE

A Novel

❧

A. D. Scott

ATRIA PAPERBACK

New York   London   Toronto   Sydney   New Delhi

ATRIA PAPERBACK

Atria Paperback
A Division of Simon & Schuster, Inc.
1230 Avenue of the Americas
New York, NY 10020

ATRIA PAPERBACK and colophon are trademarks of Simon & Schuster, Inc.

Manufactured in the United States of America

ISBN 978-1-61793-187-1

To Martin Scott McNiven

AUTHOR'S NOTE

Although the majority of this book is geographically accurate, some of the places in the town and on the Black Isle have been deliberately obscured, others invented. Many of the names are commonplace to the Highlands of Scotland but none of the characters are based on people living or dead. This is entirely a work of my imagination.

A Double Death
on the
Black Isle

ONE

Cycling across the suspension bridge over the wide, fast-flowing river Joanne Ross glanced down—no, no bodies. She looked up at the pink-red castle filling the skyline and the town circling around it—no, no ambulances, no fire engines, no accidents. On the last few panting yards up the cobbled steepness of Castle Wynd she looked towards the police station and courthouse, hoping for anyone, anything of interest. Then she caught herself.

What are you? Some kind of ghoul? Wishing for death and drama so you can have a scoop on the front page of the Gazette? *So you can impress your editor? So you can be somebody?*

It was Tuesday, the day before deadline on the *Highland Gazette,* and the weekly anxiety was always the same: Would it be the same roundup of the same stories of the same place and people, with only the date changed? Or would a real news story break in time for deadline?

Joanne arrived in the office before the others—as usual. She wriggled onto the high chair; pushed her thick, nut-brown hair behind her ears; rolled a small piece of copy paper into a huge typewriter; flexed her fingers, readying herself for the battle with words and machine.

Rob McLean, the other reporter on the *Gazette,* clattered through the door in an icy mist of semi-arctic air. It was April and despite the calendar and the daffodils and the spring blossoms, winter had yet to leave.

He threw his scarf on the desk; Joanne threw it back at him. Keeping his motorbike jacket on, he parked himself on the desk.

"Where are the others?" he asked.

"Probably trying to find something of interest for the front page," Joanne replied. "As should you be. Deadline? Tomorrow afternoon? Same as every week? Remember?"

He looked down at her green-eyed brightness, "Aye, I remember."

They grinned at each other and Joanne was reminded why Rob was her friend.

When she first met the self-styled star reporter, just out of his teens, ten years her junior, darling of girls ages three to one hundred and three, the only son of one of the most illustrious solicitors in the county, her initial reaction was distrust; men who were this good-looking—men with wheat-colored hair and startling blue eyes and a wonderful, cheeky grin—should be untrustworthy. Or so she had believed until she became friends with Rob McLean.

The telephone rang. Rob leaned across the reporters' table and grabbed the receiver.

"*Highland Gazette.*"

"There's a fishing boat on fire in the canal! Right next to the bonded warehouses. Maybe the whisky will explode!"

"Really? Can I have your name?"

"It's me, Rob, Hector."

"Not you!" Rob's groan made Joanne stop typing and listen.

"Suit yerself. I'm away to take more photos."

"Can whisky explode?" Rob spoke into a dead receiver.

"There's a boat on fire down by the whisky warehouses." He jumped off the table. "See you later." He was out the reporters' room like a rabbit with a ferret on its tail.

Joanne thought for all of two seconds. "Wait for me." Three steps behind, she raced down the stone stairway.

"I've a feeling this is the front page," Rob said as he bumped the motorbike off the pavement.

"You'll be more unbearable than usual if you're right."

My mother-in-law can tut all she likes, but thank goodness I'm wearing trousers, Joanne thought as she swung onto the back of Rob's bike.

Before she had a chance to button her coat, they were off in a red streak down towards the river, across the bridge, off to investigate the fire. Rob's overlong, straw-yellow hair caught her in the eye and the straight stretch of road—like any other road leading out of any other town, bleak, mean, and littered—went by in a blur. They flew past a school, a long row of grey council houses, past the Caledonian football grounds, up the slight rise to the canal, coming to a halt in the queue of traffic held up by the half-raised, articulated bridge. It had opened to allow the boat to pass through to the flight of locks to begin the slow, spectacular process of being lifted from sea level to the much higher canal to continue the journey to Loch Ness and beyond.

Three cars, one lorry, and two cyclists were waiting on the town side. More vehicles were queued up on the opposite side of the canal. A small group of spectators were chattering away, excited by the fire. Clouds of thick, black, oily, acrid smoke blew hither and yon, fanned by a capricious North Sea wind, blotting out the distant hills and mountains. The fishing boat was well alight.

Joanne glanced towards the canal locks. She looked quickly away. The memory of the small boy found murdered there last year made her desperately sad; the memories of the suspicion that stalked the town, of the betrayals, and most of all of her own guilt, still hurt.

I believed the word of a monster. I chose not to believe the obvious. Never again will I close my eyes and ears, and ignore my children's stories simply because they are children.

In spite of being a single mother escaping from a violent marriage, Joanne Ross was determined never to repeat *her* loveless childhood with her girls.

A waft of smoke enveloped her, breaking her reverie. She started to cough. The smell irritated her nostrils; a cloying mix of burning rubber and incinerated herring, it would take days to get out of her clothes and hair and put her off fish for a good while.

A scurry of firemen were scrambling about, shouting, dragging hoses, trying to find a way to reach the drifting boat, all the while knowing it was a lost cause: the herring smack was as ablaze as a sacrificial Viking longboat at Up Helly Aa.

"Look at that!" Rob elbowed Joanne, mesmerized by the frantic scene below.

They watched the uniformed figures dancing along the towpath, their cries and shouts borne in the wind like the cries of squabbling seagulls. Two firemen were pulling a reluctant hose, another dropped a hand pump into the canal, others were using long pikestaffs to stop the boat from drifting and at the same time keep it away from shore, away from the bonded warehouse holding a good portion of the whisky of the Highlands of Scotland.

The canal basin was mirror-still, making a double image of the fire and the centuries-old, stone buildings along the towpath. At the far end of the tongue-shaped waters, she could see the Black Isle crisp and clear, its lower slopes delineated in violent yellow gorse. With the distant hills, the topmost snowy tip of Ben Wyvis, and infinite blue sky, the setting was so picturesque that the oily smoke belching from the fire seemed a desecration.

The harbormaster stood rubbing the top of his head in

frustration, unable to do anything about the disaster jamming up his precious canal and preventing the bridge from being lowered. His shouts at no one in particular were completely ignored.

Spectators from the neighboring village of Clachnaharry, the site of one of the many mostly forgotten battles in Scottish history, gathered on the opposite bank of the canal. The spectacular inferno set them hooting and skirling like Saturday-matinee Red Indians, the cries even louder as a bright burst of flame shot up, sending showers of sparks heavenward.

In the midst of the mayhem, Hector Bain, camera wielded like a weapon, was taking pictures. In and out of the crowd he ducked, stopping still for a second to take a shot, darting off for a different angle, feverishly trying to round up some of the firemen for a better composition, working the scene like a border collie with a panicked flock of sheep.

It took Joanne a moment to realize that this multi-colored miniature of a person with two cameras and what looked like his schoolbag round his neck was not an orange-haired troll. It took the morning for her to realize that Hector Bain was Rob McLean's nemesis.

"Let's get closer." Rob was off.

Joanne needed no encouragement. There was something elemental about a fire. They hurried down the towpath to join the mêlée. The massive iron gates that guarded the warehouses and guarded the bonded whisky for the taxman were open for once. As they got nearer it was obvious the boat was doomed. The bridge and wheelhouse were gutted, the engine room well ablaze. Joanne spluttered. Another gust sent a swirling stinking black cloud of fumes in their direction. Her eyes watered, her nose now hurt.

"Over there!" Rob pointed and grabbed Joanne's arm. They made for the lee of one of the bond warehouses where Hector, or

Wee Hec as he was usually known, was winding on a new roll of film. Then, eyes focused like a bird of prey, he popped out, took a series of quick shots with his second camera, stopped, surveyed the scene, and, absolutely sure of his judgment, crouched down and shot another series from a different angle.

A dull *whoomf*, more an implosion than an explosion, then a shout of "she's going down" brought an anguished cry from a fisherman standing on the edge of the towpath, oilskin leggings and wellie boots streaked with oil, face blackened with soot, his hair singed.

"This your boat then?" Rob asked going over to him.

"Get lost!" the man snarled.

"I'm from the *Gazette*. I just want to ask . . ."

Hector swung his camera towards the fisherman, clicking furiously. Two others from the crew, young lads, were coming up fast behind their mate. The three, legs akimbo, stood in a menacing line. Rob backed away, hands up.

"Okay, lads. Okay. I can see now's not the time. Maybe later, aye?"

He went to step forward, to offer a cigarette, but the skipper was after Hec.

"Get that bloody camera out o' ma face."

Wee Hec stepped behind Joanne, trying his best to hide. The man reached around her, snatching at the precious Leica camera.

"Leave him be." Joanne tried smiling.

Too late. The fisherman had Hector by his Clachnacuddin supporter's scarf. Joanne kicked Hec's assailant hard in the ankle. He let go and turned on her, more in surprise than in anger.

"Give him the film, Hec," Rob shouted.

The man stopped.

"You only need the film, not his camera." Rob was holding his hands up, attempting to placate the fisherman.

"I'm no giving up ma film." Hec was trying to hide the camera inside his duffel coat.

"Then you'll no mind your nosy friend getting a dooking." The man was on Rob in an instant.

"Give him the film, Hec. Give him the film."

No chance. A huge shove, a yell, a splash, and Rob was in the canal. It was deep even at the edge, but his leather jacket, his pride and joy, was soaking up the water, pulling him down. His waterlogged bike boots didn't help. And to crown it all, Hec whipped out his camera and started taking pictures of the floundering reporter.

Hearing the clicks, the man turned back towards Hector. Joanne moved fast. Later, she and the skipper were to wonder where her strength came from. Straight at him, the high kick landed right in the stomach. With a loud "ooof," he doubled up, more winded that hurt, more surprised than angry. And Wee Hec was gone, running up the path, his stubby legs pumping, his coat flapping, running towards the firemen and the shelter of the shiny red engine.

"Never. You didn't."

McAllister interjected at all the appropriate moments. Encouraging. Amazed. Amused. Trying hard not to laugh. The editor-in-chief of the *Highland Gazette* more than admired Joanne, and he loved the way she told a story with her face, her whole body describing the action.

"Where did you learn to defend yourself like that?"

My marriage, she thought. "In the ATS during the war," she said.

She could never explain that she had joined the women's army to escape her mother, only to become trapped by a husband.

"But go easy on Rob will you?" she asked.

"Well it's not every day you get rescued by a lassie."

"That's what I mean."

Joanne looked at McAllister. She saw a resemblance to a bust of a French philosopher; she noticed the touch of grey at the temples and thought, not for the first time, *what an interesting face.*

"Half-drowned by some fishermen. Rescued by a lassie. Pulled out by the Fire Brigade . . . I've half a mind to print the account."

"Don't you dare! Rob would never forgive me for telling you."

"Sorry. I'll try to restrain myself." He smiled. "But what was all that about? Not just an accidental fire, you said."

"No, no accident according to the firemen."

McAllister leaned back in his chair; Joanne opened her notebook and explained.

She had been at the fire station for the previous hour, talking with the chief fireman and some of the crew.

The firemen cheered Joanne when she walked in. They'd seen the fracas with the skipper, watched as he tried to get his breath back—not injured but severely embarrassed. Now, as they were cleaning and stowing their equipment, the men were quite happy to talk to her—along with some teasing.

Not that Joanne told McAllister this. What happened, no one knew for certain, she told the editor, but these men are professional firemen, they know their business. Two of them had been in the worst fires of the war—in the Clydeside blitz.

"It was what we call an 'incendiary device,'" one fireman told her.

"Any clearer than that?" Joanne had asked.

"A petrol bomb in a milk bottle to you, dear," an older crewmember said, and he knew a thing or two about those weapons. He had been a member of the Billy Boys gang in Glasgow in his youth.

"Do the police agree?"

"The police take their report from us and we know our business."

"Of course." Joanne flushed slightly, not meaning to question their professionalism. Looking around her, seeing the men, the machines, the efficiency with which they treated their equipment, she knew that if the firemen said it was a petrol bomb that had started the fire, a petrol bomb it was.

McAllister heard Joanne out. "So, a Molotov cocktail, eh? The anarchist's favorite weapon."

"I bow to your extensive experience in those sort of things."

"Aye." He shook his head and sighed. "I've seen the damage a simple Molotov cocktail can cause. It was a favorite of the International Brigade in Spain. But not very usual in these parts." He thought about it for a moment. "Anything more?"

"It became a bit scary towards the end," Joanne replied. "I know the skipper was distraught about losing his boat, but why so angry over a few pictures? And why would someone burn down a herring boat? Another thing, the boat is from the Black Isle, the skipper too, so the harbormaster said. So why were they going through the canal, all the way through the Great Glen to Fort William, with a full hold of fresh herring?"

"Why not to her home port you mean?"

"Exactly. And then there's the mystery of the crewmen, they're from the Isles."

As McAllister was listening to Joanne, as the different strands of the story mounted, his night-dark eyebrows, the only part of him that betrayed his thinking, rose or wriggled with each complication.

"Why does a local skipper have strangers for a crew?" she asked.

His eyebrows signaled, "Why?"

"Fishing boat crews are like families. So if they're not family members, it's usually men from the same home port. The skipper on this vessel—*The Good Shepphard*—is from the Black Isle; the crewmen, they're not even from the east coast—they spoke Gaelic."

When she finished, McAllister looked at his scrawled notes and saw how much information she had collected in only a few hours. *For a woman who had been the typist on the newspaper not three months since, she's come a long way.*

"This is a great front-page story. Let me have your article by the end of the day."

"Me?" Joanne stared at him. "But I'm new in the job. I've never done a major story."

"I've been waiting weeks to launch the newly designed *Gazette*, you know that." He pointed at the notes he had made. "This is the best news story we've had in a long while—it's dramatic, mysterious."

Joanne looked down at her hands, nervous, excited, trying hard not to blush. *I'm too old to blush,* she told herself, "I'll do my best," she told the editor.

"I wouldn't ask if I didn't think you were up to it," McAllister was impatient with Joanne's lack of self-belief, "and don't forget, with Don McLeod as subeditor, most of what *you* think is your best writing will be cut by that ruthless red pencil of his. So, get the sequence clear in your head, then don't think too much, just write."

As Joanne left the editor's office to cross the four steps to the reporters' room, she hugged herself.

"My first real story," she muttered, "my first front page."

✦ ✦ ✦

Hector Bain, part boy, part man, part troglodyte, with a more than passing resemblance to Oor Wullie, that well-loved cartoon character from a Scottish Sunday newspaper, trudged through the promise of a spring morning. In a land where winter was said to reign for eight and a half months of the year, brisk would best describe the weather.

Such an innocuous word, "weather," a word that only a native of the Highlands would use to describe the cloud-scudding, bone-crushing, ear-piercing, gusty wind that blew straight from the North Sea, down the Firth, down the Great Glen, over a succession of lochs, where it met the gales of another wind that arrived, unencumbered, three thousand miles from the wastes of Labrador. Locals would call these half hourly blasts of horizontal rain "showers" and outsiders would describe them as a "deluge."

Not that Hector noticed. Trotting through the town, smiling at acquaintances, grinning at contemporaries, answering inquiries about the health of his granny with, "She's great," or, "She's brilliant," or, "She's grand, thanks," up the steep cobbled wynd that clung to the lee of the castle, head down and coat held tight to protect his precious cameras. A right turn—he arrived at his destiny. Only the semi-spiral stone staircase in the tall, narrow building to climb and he would be there in the sacred lair, there in the reporter's room, the heartbeat of the *Highland Gazette*.

"Cripes, it's Oor Wullie!" Don McLeod said.

"No it's not. It's a gnome from my mother-in-law's rockery." This came from Joanne.

"You're both wrong. It's Horrible Hector," Rob declared with an uncharacteristic scowl. Addressing the cocky figure standing expectantly in the doorway he asked, "So, Wee Hec, what the heck are you doing here?"

The apparition stepped into the room proper.

"Hiya Rob. What like?"

At five foot two inches short, wearing clothes for an eleven-year-old and with two cameras round his neck, he looked like a wee boy dressed up as a photographer for Halloween. But the cameras round his neck were serious. Together, their net worth would buy a motorcar.

His red, sticking-up hair and his turnip lantern grin gave Don the Oor Wullie joke, but, so far as anyone knew, the cartoon character didn't have the orange freckles with matching sodium light hair.

Joanne's guess at garden gnome came from the lime green knitted woolen tourie—far too big for Hector's head and weighted down to one side by an enormous bobble. A black and white Clachnacuddin Football Club supporter's scarf completed the outfit. Hat and scarf had been knitted by his granny who could never find her glasses, and it showed.

Still grinning at the threesome sitting around the reporters' table, Hec waited. When it became obvious that neither Don nor Rob were going to introduce him, Joanne spoke.

"We weren't formally introduced yesterday. I'm Joanne Ross, I'm a reporter here. This is Don McLeod, deputy editor. You know Rob."

"I know." Hector continued grinning until Joanne decided this was the natural state of his face.

"So," Joanne asked since her colleagues continued to ignore the apparition, "what can I do for you?"

"It's more a case of what I can do for you, Joanne."

"Mrs. Ross to you, boy," Don growled at the newcomer.

"Here's ma card."

He handed the offering to Joanne. She peered at a hand-cut, hand-printed rectangle of cardboard the color of spam.

"Hector Bain. Photographer. The *Highland Gazette*."

Rob reached over the shared desk and snatched the card from her.

"Did you use your wee sister's printing set?"

"*Highland Gazette?* What's this about?" Don's frown made the lines on his fifty-maybe-sixty-something-old face resemble a relief map of his native Skye.

"Morning. I see you've met our new photographer." McAllister stood in the doorway, enjoying the consternation.

"Him? We're to work with him?" Rob poked a finger at Hector.

"I've heard of some daft things in my time, but this takes the biscuit," Don McLeod told the editor.

McAllister shrugged. "You asked for a photographer. I got you a photographer."

"Aye, but what else is he besides?" Don replied. "I know you're keen to get the new *Gazette* launched, and yes we're desperate for a photographer, but not that desperate." He narrowed his eyes, squinting through the smoke of his fifth cigarette of the morning, which dangled from a corner of his mouth.

McAllister checked the clock. "Let's get on, we've a paper to publish."

Don spread the new-look layout over the High Table, his blasphemous term for the square table used by the reporters. Five large typewriters took up one end and the layout filled the other. The gap between table and walls made a passage just wide enough for two to pass if they were good friends.

Joanne leaned over and took a look. "Don, you're an artist!" she exclaimed.

"Oh my, Mr. McLeod, this is wonderful." Mrs. Smart, the office manager, had come in and was looking over Joanne's shoulder.

"It's certainly different," Rob contributed.

"Not bad at all," was McAllister's opinion.

Don McLeod's chest swelled like a wee bantam cock about to chase the chickens. He opened his mouth to explain more, stopped, stared, looked at the gangling figure in the doorway—six foot three would be Don's guess—and said, "Dr. Livingston, I presume."

It was the nut-brown face and the plus fours and the tweed deerstalker hat, which could have easily been a pith helmet, that made Don think of the legendary explorer.

"Mortimer Beauchamp Carlyle, actually. But please call me Beech. Everyone does. How do you do?"

"Fine, thanks," an awestruck Rob replied.

And like a character out of a Boy's Own Adventure novel, darkest Africa chapter, the gentleman stuck out his hand. Rob took it and immediately, in spite of at least fifty years between them, they became fast friends.

"Beech will be writing our new Countryside column," McAllister explained.

"Oh really? And who's doing Town?" Rob had meant this as a facetious remark and nearly fell off his stool at the answer.

"Your mother."

This time McAllister had consulted his deputy and Don had agreed with him. Margaret McLean was as well informed about goings-on in the town as Don McLeod, but in an entirely different social strata. Birdlife and nature, on the other hand, meant nothing to Don—nor to most of their readers. Don cared little about farming practices, but anything that stirred up the farming gentry was fine by him. The final argument on the hiring, McAllister wanted kept secret. But Don knew. Beech was on the board of guardians, that obscure body that oversaw the finances of the newspaper for the investors.

"'Town and Country!' 'McAllister's Mischief,' that's what it should be called," Don was to remark later over his usual pint and a half. And as usual, he was not wrong.

With Don McLeod as deputy editor and chief subeditor; Joanne Ross and Rob McLean on reporting duties; Hector Bain the photographer; McAllister the editor-in-chief, writing the leader and obituaries; and Mrs. Smart overseeing the finances, they were all set to revamp a newspaper essentially unchanged since 1867.

Later that afternoon McAllister was sorting through the photographs of the fire. They were spectacular. He finally chose one showing flames shooting up through the decking, an oily black cloud of smoke ascending towards heaven, the name of the boat, *The Good Shepphard*, clear, the whole disaster showing in duplicate on the flat-calm waters of the canal basin. And in silhouette, to one side of the picture, his body conveying his anguish, was the skipper—Alexander Skinner of the Black Isle.

"Great front page for the new *Highland Gazette*," McAllister murmured, happy at last. "Let's hope this story runs for weeks."

Two

*

The bruising on Joanne Ross was invisible. Like a peach with the flesh discolored around the stone, she seemed untouched. But the shame of "having to get married," that understated euphemism for the rush to the altar, followed by a six-month pregnancy, marred her own marriage and caused her parents to disown her. Ten years on, they had not relented; they had never forgiven her for shaming them, never met their grandchildren. The pain has softened but when asked by friends, by her children, she made excuses about never visiting—the price of the train tickets, her parents being too elderly to have young children around, anything other than tell the truth.

She was aware that she was a quarter-step ahead or behind the beat of the community. Her mood often depended on the weather, her opinions seemingly influenced by a mischievous imp hovering somewhere in the region of her left shoulder. A tune, a song, a poem could change her walk. Her wide-open face showed the bloodlines of a true Scot. But her cheekbones were on the edge of too strong, her mouth on the side of too wide, and her skin too freckled to be considered beautiful.

She knew her husband was ashamed of her; he'd married a woman who would never fit in, in the Highland town where respectability was all-important and being "different" was a sin.

"Stubborn," her husband, Bill Ross, called her. "Too much schooling" in her mother-in-law's opinion. "Stuck up" was the phrase one of the mothers at the school had used. *A mind of her own*, McAllister thought, but he meant that as praise.

Joanne shook off thoughts of her failed marriage and went back to typing. She worked steadily, her athletic shoulders wrestling with the heavy, awkward typewriter as easily as a cowboy with a steer, plowing through lists scribbled on scrap paper, typed notes, scrawls on the back of an envelope, and one that just said "repeat last year's." They were all notices of the holidays and events surrounding Easter.

She glanced at the clock, one surely stolen from a railway station waiting room, and noted she had five minutes before anyone else would appear. She made tidy piles of the bits of copy paper, the finished work ready for Don's pencil. Then she would retype it all over again. How she could continue with all this, plus her new job as full-time reporter and her new status as a single mother, she hadn't yet worked out.

Ask for help, Rob had suggested. But she couldn't. Not wouldn't, couldn't. Silly I know, she told herself often, recognizing in herself that trait that seemed to be one of mothers and women in general, that catchall phrase used when help was offered—I can manage. Yes, she could manage, but only by being first in, last out.

"Blast," Joanne spoke out loud. "Five minutes more, that's all I need." The phone kept ringing. "Double blast." It wasn't going to stop. "*Highland Gazette*." She sighed.

"Just the girl I'm after."

"Patricia Ord Mackenzie—you are psychic. I was about to call you." A small white lie—Joanne *had* been meaning to call Patricia, but first she needed to don an armor-plated carapace of confidence to deal with her oldest friend.

"It's all that water from the Fairy Well I've been downing—makes me psychic," Patricia laughed.

"We're looking forward to this Easter holiday." Joanne meant it. Holidays away were not something she could afford, but she was looking forward to a few days away—as long as they didn't have to spend much time with Patricia's mother. "The girls are driving me crazy with questions about the Black Isle. Are your parents prepared for the onslaught of two lively children?"

Patricia laughed again.

"The house is big. We can avoid them as much as possible."

Joanne wholeheartedly agreed with her friend. As much space as possible between her, her children, and Patricia's mother would be a very good idea. The Ord Mackenzie family was very grand in an estate-owning, ancient-name, Highland-gentry way. And Mrs. Janet Ord Mackenzie made certain that everyone showed due deference to her as the lady of the estate.

"Anyway," Patricia continued, "I've called to ask you to come early. The eight-o'clock ferry. I've something special planned."

"Eight on a Thursday? It'll mean a rush. Everyone at the *Gazette* usually goes out together on Wednesday night, and this week is special as we're . . ."

"I'll pick you up at the jetty and we'll go straight there."

"Go where?" Joanne was intrigued.

"A surprise. I've some really good news."

"So have I. We're launching the new *Gazette*, and I've been given the front page, my first big story. It's really exciting, it's about a fire and . . ."

"Wear your glad rags tomorrow," Patricia interrupted. "It's a special day."

"Now you've got me really curious." She caved in—as Patricia knew she would. "Fine then. Eight-o'clock ferry."

Joanne hung up the telephone. "Patricia Ord Mackenzie," she muttered, "what are you up to?"

Feeling slighted, she looked up at the ceiling, and shaking her head, said, "Thanks for listening to me too, Patricia. Thanks for being interested in *my* life."

Although they had met when they were seven, and had been at boarding school together for the whole of their education, Joanne was never sure if they were close—there was a touch of the bully in her friend. Perhaps it was their family circumstances. Patricia came from a wealthy, landowning family; Joanne was a daughter of the manse. But, Joanne acknowledged, in their years in a bleak, Scottish boarding school, where crying singled you out as a baby, they had formed an unlikely friendship, a friendship of girls who never quite fitted in with the clique. Or at least Joanne assumed it was a friendship. *So why do I always feel inferior when I am with Patricia? Why do I always give in?*

The noise on the stone stairway interrupted Joanne's reverie. Everyone seemed to materialize in the reporters' room at the same time—a difficult feat given the width of the stairs.

"I declare the news conference open. All aboard and correct and ready for D-Day?" McAllister looked around the ensemble, taking in the nods and grins and ayes and the shrug from Don. "Mrs. Smart?"

"I'm pleased with the response from our advertisers, Mr. McAllister. Most have taken more space. There is also a full page from Arnotts advertising the latest televisions."

"Well done, Mrs. Smart. Don?"

"The printers and compositors are ready." He didn't mention he'd promised them a bonus of a couple of bottles of whisky if they got the new edition out on time. "The expanded sports pages are looking good," he continued, "Countryside column too. The only problem with it is the length of Mr. Mortimer Beauchamp Carlyle's name. Maybe we should give him a pseudonym. . . ."

"Five shillings for the best suggestion," McAllister declared. "On the subject of new columns, I'm instituting one, the title is 'For a' That.' It will go on the opinion page, I'll use it to stir things up a bit."

"Only if it is checked by a legal eagle," Don told him.

"Naturally. Rob?" McAllister asked.

"I've a report on the plans for the new bridge across the river. I did a vox pop as you suggested. A surprising number of people are concerned that another bridge would fulfill the Brahan Seer's prophecy and bring disaster to the town."

"Don," McAllister turned to him, "a heading stating a threat to the town from a seventeenth-century seer would be great. Joanne?"

"I've written up the fire and covered the meeting with the fire chief. I think that's everything."

"I see." He was busy and brusque and wanted Joanne to stop looking nervous every time he asked her a question. "Did you call the fire chief for an update? The police? The procurator fiscal's office to ask what the charge will be? Do you have a quote from anyone in the fishing village in the Black Isle? This must be a big event for them. The west coast connection, what's that about? Have anything to add to turn this into a front page to remember?"

McAllister hadn't noticed Joanne getting pinker and pinker and squirming on her stool as he counted off the phone calls yet to be made, facts yet to be ascertained, opinions yet to be canvassed. But Don did.

"For heaven's sake, give the lassie time to draw breath." Don pointed his finger at Rob. "You, you talk to the polis seeing as how you're so pally with Woman Police Constable McPherson. You, McAllister, call your new pal Beauchamp in the Black Isle; see if he's heard any gossip. Me, I'll talk to my contact in the procurator fiscal's office *and* I'll call our man on the west coast, see if he can find out anything, and Joanne," he turned to her, "call the fire chief, ask if he's finished his report and ask if you can have a sneak look at it. Use your charms. Then, let's say . . ." he glanced at the clock, ". . . eleven thirty, we'll get together and see where we're at."

"Yes, Mr. McLeod." Rob laughed.

"And you," he pointed to his boss, "in your office now, I'd like a wee word."

Don carefully shut the door of McAllister's office, well aware that Rob and Joanne would be waiting to hear the explosion. But he wasn't going to give them the satisfaction.

McAllister sat down, lit a cigarette, and waited for Don to do the same.

"This fire is a big story," Don started. "It's not every day you hear about Molotov cocktails in the Highlands. It's a great front page to launch the paper." Don's tone changed to a low, pre-bark growl. "But for heaven's sake, just because you fancy the lassie and are getting nowhere, stop taking your frustration out on her. I'm not having it. Right?"

Don left, closing the door behind him before McAllister could recover enough to reply.

The meeting later in the morning to pull together the story of the firebombing was productive. Joanne had written five hundred words from the point of view of the firemen. She also had a brief account from a neighbor who had been waiting in her car to cross the canal when the fire broke out.

"Good lively stuff, Joanne," Don commented as he took his wee red pencil to the more extravagant quotes.

Don read through Rob's report on the comments from the police. "The usual 'Saw nothing, heard nothing, know nothing,'"

Don called it. "The procurator fiscal's office would only say 'The accident inquiry is in progress,'" Don added, "so not much there."

"No, but this story is looking good. It has legs." McAllister was happy. "One, we have a great picture," he started, counting off the points with his fingers.

"Don't tell Hec that, or we'll never hear the end of it." Rob was still smarting at Hec being made a full-time member of the team.

"Two, this is a good description of the fire, Joanne—colorful but succinct." McAllister went on, "I like the interview you did with the firemen—you got the balance between the facts and the human interest just right; your interview with the witness who saw it all from the beginning is sharp and newsworthy."

"I had trouble getting off the phone, the woman blethered so much." Joanne smiled and blushed at the praise.

"Three, the whole mystery as to why the boat was making its way to the west coast rather than home. Graham Nicolson, our stringer in Fort William, will investigate. That should give us something for the next edition."

"I think this story will run for at least a couple more editions," Rob interrupted. "The police are completely baffled as to why anyone would firebomb a fishing boat. They have no suspects, no clues."

"'Police Baffled.'" Don was delighted. "A favorite headline of we hacks in the newspaper trade."

McAllister rolled his eyes and held up his hand again. "Finally, Beech has heard rumors of a family feud involving the owner of the boat."

"I like it," Don agreed. "Family feuds—great copy. But keep that for the next edition."

"All right, let's put this together, we only have five hours." McAllister paused, "Joanne, everyone, thanks—good work."

Mondays, news meeting; Tuesdays, two days to finish the paper—the routine was busy, but steady busy. Now it was Wednesday, and Wednesdays were for panic, a noisy late afternoon panic, but controlled like the panic of sailing—quiet stretches, then a burst of weather to keep everyone on their toes.

This Wednesday, with the deadline for the new *Gazette* looming, tension came early to the reporters' room. It had an almost visible presence. The dust motes, in a beam through the north-facing window, seemed thicker than usual. The low, churning, industrial noises of the presses in the bowels of the building had started earlier than usual. Even the typewriters seemed heavier.

Joanne and Rob were attempting to type in quick time instead of waltz time, so the machines jammed more often, the paper disappearing into the jaws of the monsters. A carriage stuck. A ribbon unwound. Sometimes this happened at the same time. Joanne spoke sternly to the Underwood with ladylike expletives. Rob thumped his.

Don moved up and down the three flights of stairs to the presses more briskly. McAllister popped in more often, asking more questions.

Five o'clock, the tempo accelerated to real time. Don was to and from the reporters and the typesetters, bringing copy, waiting at the stone, signing off on pages. McAllister, his jobs done, was hovering around like an expectant father outside the maternity ward, getting in everyone's way.

At six o'clock, Don returned with some finished pages.

"They look good, no, they're great," pronounced McAllister.

Rob and Joanne leaned back from their machines, their part of the process finished at last. Simultaneously they stretched their arms out, glanced at each other, and grinned.

Rob looked around the room. "Station Hotel?" he asked. It was the only safe place to take Joanne; her reputation would be seriously besmirched should she be seen in a public bar.

"You two go," McAllister said. "Don and I still have a lot to do."

"Sorry Rob, I need an early night." Joanne regretted her promise to Patricia; she would have loved to stay with the others. "I'm off to the Black Isle for Easter and have to catch an early ferry tomorrow morning."

Rob decided to stay on at the *Gazette* office. The excitement of waiting for the first pages was infectious.

Eight thirty—another hour, maybe less, and the first edition of the new *Highland Gazette*, Easter 1957, would be printed. This is history, McAllister realized, the first real change in a hundred years.

The abiding fear of an editor of a small-town newspaper was to print an article, a headline, destined to become one of the notorious legends of newspaper lore, one of the stories relayed to journalism cadets in every newspaper in the country. He remembered one apocryphal story. An Aberdeen paper, the day the Second World War was declared, ran a front page devoted to the local Agricultural show—"Local Man Wins Prize for Biggest Turnip," or did they say neap? He wasn't quite sure.

Eight o'clock came, and he couldn't wait any longer. Walking downstairs, he cheered immensely. This was the sound and the smell of a newspaper. Normally Don, the father of the chapel, and the comps would chase everyone, even the editor, out of the hallowed ground of the stone.

But tonight was different. The comps and printers nodded silently as McAllister joined them, understanding his need to be there. The noise from the press, the clanking, the whirring, the steady industrial hum, filled the basement. The very walls, carved from solid stone, seemed to vibrate.

Rob joined them, hovering by the big machine, mesmerized by the cogs and flywheels and conveyor belts all awhirl, clanking out copies of the broadsheet pages before they went shooting off to be sorted and folded into a tabloid format, then shunted to a man who would stack them and tie them into neat bundles of newspaper.

Forty-five minutes later, the first copies rolled off the press. Don had already reviewed individual pages, but this was the first neatly folded copy of the newspaper, ink fresh and barely dry. A printer lifted one from the growing pile and ceremonially handed it to McAllister. McAllister grinned. They shook hands.

Don grinned as his copy was handed to him. Rob waved from across the shop floor and came to join them. There were more handshakes, a slap or two on various backs, the father of the chapel and the printers joined in, grinning, before turning back to nurse the fickle machines.

Rob left. The roar of his motorbike echoed through the empty streets as he sped home to share the new *Highland Gazette* with his parents. He debated whether to take a copy to Joanne, but decided it was not the done thing to arrive late at night on a quiet suburban street at the house of a woman who had walked out on her marriage.

McAllister took two more copies, one to dissect, one as a souvenir. Don joined him on the steps of the *Gazette* building. They looked at each other.

"It's a start," came McAllister's verdict.

"Aye."

And the two men, who from a distance resembled a reverse Laurel and Hardy—the skinny one tall, the fat one short—strode off in opposite directions into the dark of the town, both trying vainly to keep a grin of satisfaction from breaking out, frequently.

THREE

~

The Black Isle, a peninsula surrounded on three sides by the Cromarty, the Moray, and the Beauly firths, was an island of the mind rather than geography. Picturesque in parts, forbidding in places, it was quite unlike the surrounding glens of heather and lochs. Hilly country, less than twenty miles in length and eight miles across at its widest, a high ridge of forest ran through the middle, the farmland on either side broken by shallow fissures made by healthy burns. The abundant woodland had more oaks and beech and birch than the usually coniferous Highland forests. There were sacred wells, prehistoric standing stones, a castle or two, the remains of Iron Age settlements, and a history teeming with stories and characters.

Each village had a different character, the inland ones insular and isolated, the fishing villages insular, packed with working boats, pleasure craft not encouraged. The cliffs on the south side were studded with fossils and caves and were the haunt of summer birds. The northern shoreline—stony, seaweed strewn, was overshadowed by the upside-down pudding shape of Ben Wyvis. And Wyvis made the weather sun-snow-rain-wind-four-seasons-in-a-day weather.

Like a series of nesting Russian dolls, each village and farm kept to itself, aware of neighbors, but not particularly hospitable to those a few miles over the hill.

The name Achnafern came from the Gaelic words for farmland and woodland. Achnafern Farm looked prosperous, and it was. Surrounded by arable fields and pasture, a neat row of four, single-story stone farm cottages stood facing a large cobbled square with byres and barns and milking sheds completing the other sides. A little way off, nestled in the lee of the woods, looking towards distant hills that still showed a deep mantle of snow, stood a substantial, two-story farmhouse, also built of stone.

A half-mile away, Achnafern Grange, an elegant Georgian manor house—multi-windowed, three-storied plus attics for the servants, home to generations of the same family—reigned over most of what it surveyed.

Allie Munro was born in one of the farm cottages to a family who had been on the estate for generations. He was now foreman, as had been his father before him. His grandfather had been head plowman in charge of the teams of horses. Now Allie; his wife, Agnes; and their sons Fraser and Alistair lived in the big farmhouse.

Even though it was a tied tenure, the house gave him a distinct feeling of pride. Not that he would ever let anyone know this. For all the inconvenience, the drafty hallways and the five bedrooms and a study used as the farm office, it was the status of the place that mattered. Now that was all about to vanish.

Agnes Munro had hung out the washing, had tidied up the breakfast, had finished making broth, and was now baking a cake and trying to keep herself fresh and tidy before the big event. Her son Fraser, sprawled in the chair, feet up on the hearth rail, doing nothing but getting in her road, was ignoring her.

"Now don't be making arrangements over Easter," Mrs. Munro was doing her best to keep her annoyance with her eldest son out of her voice. "I need you to help me clear out the house. We've too much stuff, and it's a wee cottage we're flitting to."

"She's a right cheek thon madam, ordering us out of the house we've been in for years."

"Don't go talking of your betters like that."

"Ma, Patricia's no better than you or me."

"She's the laird's daughter."

"She's a stuck-up tart."

At that his mother exploded.

"I'll no have yer smutty talk in my kitchen. You know nothing. You come back here after ten years, and you're none the wiser for your time away. She's a good lass thon. And as for stuck-up, who's the one who helps me out? Patricia. Who takes me to tea when we go to town? Patricia. And to the Black Isle Show every year? Patricia. She buys my eggs every week and pays fair. She's right generous at Christmas, and never forgets my birthday. Unlike some!"

Fraser Munro had the grace to look shamefaced, but an apology was not in his character. "It's still no right. She canny just up and tell us we have to leave."

"It's the estate's house, and well you know it. And I'm warning you one last time . . . it's none of your business." Mrs. Munro did not want to talk about the move. It upset her.

She bustled around the Rayburn, banging pots, piling more wood into the fire, making an already hot kitchen almost unbearable. "We have a perfectly nice wee house to move into—much less work for me. You'll be off back to the regiment soon enough, so with only your brother at home there'll be plenty of room in the cottage for the three of us."

She didn't catch his look. He had yet to tell them, but the army had had enough of Fraser Munro's insubordination, his drunken sprees, and his fighting—this from a Highland regiment notorious for fighters.

The clock in the hallway struck the half hour. Agnes Munro started to panic. She hadn't picked the flowers.

"The cake will be ready in three quarters of an hour," she told him. "Mind and take it out the oven." She had her doubts this would happen. "I'll set the alarm clock to remind you."

"For heaven's sake, Ma, I'm no that useless."

She didn't say what was on the tip of her tongue, but hurried upstairs, threw off her apron, dabbed some powder on her nose, smudged on a dab of lipstick, smacked her lips, put on the single strand of river pearls Allie had bought her for their silver wedding anniversary, put on her best coat, then, on top of the new home perm, she perched her best Sunday hat, hoping it would stay put because it was often windy down by the old cathedral.

When she left, Mrs. Munro pulled the back door shut as quietly as she could.

It's ridiculous I should be hiding from my own son, she thought as she went into the garden. There was not much available, spring being late in the Highlands. She selected lily of the valley for the matron of honor's corsage. She snipped narcissus and jonquils, filling out the bridal bouquet with ferns. Not her choice, but it was what Patricia wanted.

Patricia's wedding day, not how I pictured it, but as long as she's happy. Mrs. Munro sighed with her whole body. It was hard for her to hold back her disappointment at Patricia's choice of husband. He was a man Mrs. and Mr. Munro hardly knew, but they had heard about him over the years.

Mrs. Munro would never have voiced her thoughts, and only her husband knew how much she loved Patricia.

After the babies were born, Mrs. Ord Mackenzie had been sent to a private hospital in Edinburgh "for her nerves" the doctor had said. The baby girl had been given to Mrs. Munro to look after. Since her own son Fraser was seven months old at the time, Mrs. Munro had suckled newborn Patricia until she was weaned, and the girl had lived with the Munros until she was nearly three.

It was only when Mrs. Ord Mackenzie became aware of the gossip about their only child being raised in the farmhouse that she had taken Patricia to live in Achnafern Grange.

"By then the damage had been done," Mrs. Ord Mackenzie told her daughter—often.

When Fraser Munro heard the toot of the horn and the squeak of the garden gate—one more job he hadn't done—he stirred himself from the chair to go to the window. Like the beast of prey he was, he was always alert for his mother's vulnerability.

He stood, the rush from his hangover making him swear. He watched Patricia get out of the Land Rover, hug his mother, take the basket of flowers, and put it in the back. She made a quick, neat three-point turn, and they were gone.

"Now what the hell is that all about?"

Glad of the peace with no mother to nag him, ask him why he wasn't helping his dad, give him jobs to do around the house, or tell him off for getting in her way, he fell back into the chair and dozed. He became aware of the smell of the cake. He ignored it. At first it was a slight scent of burning—he ignored it—then a full-blown blast of incinerated sugar and butter and eggs. Eventually the smoke forced him out of his chair. He opened the oven door; grabbed a tea towel; took out the cake; and chucked the cake tin, tea towel, and burnt offering into the sink. He left the smoke-filled kitchen and grabbed his coat and cap, deciding to make for the village, then, remembering he would have to walk, remembering he was furious with his father because he would not let him borrow the farm Land Rover, remembering he would have to help with the flitting this weekend, he was transfixed by a surge of rage, a sudden, blinding, red rage.

"Thon bitch."

Yet somewhere within him, if he had had the slightest desire to examine his soul, he would have recognized that the sight of his mother and Patricia hugging was what did it. His rage was a rage of bright-green jealousy.

"Hurry up! We'll miss the bus! And the ferry!"

Annie had run ahead to the corner and was jumping up and down as she watched for the bus. Joanne, dragging Wee Jean by the wrist, was trying to run in high-heeled shoes, to carry the bags, to keep her hat from flying off.

"It's coming!" Annie shrieked. But she had the good sense to stop the bus, telling the conductor her mother was just around the corner.

With a "sorry, sorry," Joanne scrambled onto the platform. At the station, they ran for a second bus and caught it just as it was leaving for the ferry.

When she saw the billboards outside the newsstand, she realized that she hadn't picked up a copy of the *Gazette*.

"Double blast!" she muttered.

Annie overheard, as usual. She glared at her mum. Joanne's hair had escaped; her nylons had a run; and she was pink from frustration from the early start to collect the girls from their grandparents, from the running, and from not being there with the others to see the new edition roll off the presses. Now she was frustrated at not having the newspaper to show off to Patricia, to at last show her friend that she had achieved something, was someone.

They made it to the ferry on time and walked up the car ramp. It was a short crossing, took only five minutes. In bright sunshine, with deep blue skies, the pier on the Black Isle side was clearly visible, the whitewashed cottages along the shoreline, the bright yellow gorse on the hillside, and the sparkling waters of the firth made the setting picture-postcard perfect—a rare event.

Because the passage connecting two wide firths was narrow and the tidal race deep and fierce, the ferry set off on a forty-five-degree angle to reach the other side safely.

Halfway across, Wee Jean shrieked, jumping up and down in the prow. "Look, look, porpoises!"

The exuberant mammals danced and frolicked alongside the boat. The crew and passengers smiled at the sight of the pod. Arches of miniature rainbows flew off their skins as they leaped and corkscrewed, racing the ferry.

"It's a sign of good luck, you know," Annie pronounced.

"It is that," a passing crewman agreed.

For some, thought Joanne. The dolphins cavorting in the pellucid waters of the firth reminded her of an incident a few years ago on a previous ferry crossing.

"Look," Bill, her husband, had said to Annie—Wee Jean was too small to enter his horizon—"porpoises."

"Actually," Joanne had pointed out to Annie, "they are dolphins, bottle-nosed dolphins."

"You're such a bloody know it all." Bill had been furious, "Up here we call them porpoises."

Joanne shivered at the memory. I don't blame him, she thought, I shouldn't have contradicted him. I only wanted Annie to know the correct name. And there was no need for him to elbow me so hard in the ribs I could hardly get my breath.

The ferry docked on the north side of the firth. There was no sign of Patricia. Joanne sighed—all that rush for nothing. The girls had run down to the foreshore and were busy trying to skim stones across the water.

"Did you see that, Mum?" Annie called. "Mine did six skips."

Wee Jean was no good at the game, so she busied herself gathering seashells while Joanne meandered along the high-tide line.

Memories of other holidays in the Black Isle returned as she crunched her feet over the bladder wrack, popping the dried seaweed pods. With her sister Elizabeth, they had rented adjoining caravans in the village of Rosemarkie some fifteen miles away. It had been a week of sun and freezing winds and morning haar with the foghorns blasting across the firth, shaking the thin, aluminum shells of the camper, which terrified the children when they first heard it. It had been a week of walking to the Fairy Glen, of roaming beneath the cliffs searching for fossils, of picnics in the sand dunes, and of grilling fish on fires made amongst the rocks on the foreshore.

Of the rest of the Black Isle, the hidden north side, the dark forest covering the spine of the land, Joanne had only passed through, never explored. She thought this peninsula called an island was a mysterious place. *Perhaps it is the history*, Joanne thought, *perhaps it is the standing stones, the fairy wells, the castles, the ruins.*

The persistent peep of a car horn made Joanne look around. A slightly battered Land Rover pulled up, and there was Patricia, waving.

"All here, how wonderful! And all dressed up and ready to go. Jolly good."

The girls were suddenly shy at Patricia's exuberant greetings. But the "jolly good" stuck in Annie's mind, and many times over that bizarre weekend she would whisper "jolly good" in Jean's ear, in the exact tone with the exact timing, then collapse in giggles at her own wit. Joanne, overhearing the joke, was hard-pressed not to giggle with them.

"Thank you for the gift. You really shouldn't have."

Joanne was embarrassed by the money her friend had sent.

The envelope had been addressed to Miss Annie and Miss Jean Ross. Annie had pounced on it, read the card, and danced around, waving a postal order made out to her saying, "Look, Mum, for me. One for Jean too. All our own money." It had taken a long argument to persuade Annie she couldn't spend it all on books and to tell Jean, no she couldn't have a new dolly.

"The girls bought new coats and hats."

"Thank you, Aunty Patricia," they chorused.

"Sorry about the Land Rover, but it's clean," Patricia said as the girls piled into the back. "Mummy hates me using her car and refuses to buy me a car of my own. Probably a none-too-subtle hint that I should be off and married with a husband to provide for me."

They drove through the countryside and villages and rattled past the Ord Mackenzie family estate, only slowing as Patricia pointed out what was left of the Italianate mansion on a hill-side facing the firth. When Joanne had last seen it, there was a deserted, but nonetheless magnificent mansion dominating the farmland, woodland, and hillside. A staircase to nowhere and an unsightly scar was all that remained of the extravagant building.

"Granny Ross, my mother-in-law, is related to the game-keeper on the estate there," Joanne explained, "as well as being a cousin to Mrs. Munro, your housekeeper."

"I know. Mrs. Munro keeps me up-to-date with the family goings-on."

Does she now? Joanne thought and was not comfortable with the information.

At the next village, they turned off and parked in the precinct next to the red sandstone ruins of the cathedral. Surrounded by thick walls and copper beeches, horse chestnuts with sticky swollen buds, and oaks as yet bare of leaves, the substantial remains of the cathedral were a striking sight.

Patricia was looking around, searching. The children, picking up on her anxiety, followed her gaze, puzzled as to what they should be looking for. Joanne made towards the wicket gate set in a lichen-covered archway.

"There's Mrs. Munro." Patricia waved. "She's waiting for us. Yoo-hoo."

Joanne watched in bemusement as her friend took a wicker basket from Mrs. Munro, then stooped to pin small corsages onto the children's coats.

"And, ta-ra, this one for my matron of honor."

"Matron of honor?" Flabbergasted would be too mild a word to describe Joanne's face.

Patricia beamed. "Yes, my wedding. Here and now." She pointed to the building on the other side of the cathedral precinct, the registry office. "I'm to be married in, let's see, twenty minutes. Now you know why I wanted you to dress up."

"But I didn't even know you were engaged."

"Skipped that bit. Bun in the oven." Patricia patted her stomach and giggled, from nerves or bravado Joanne couldn't say. She was desperate to know more, but was aware of Annie avidly hanging on to every word.

"Why don't you go with Mrs. Munro to see the cathedral?" Joanne shooed her daughter off. She watched Annie join the housekeeper, who was already hovering over Jean like a broody hen, her nervousness at being here, deceiving her employers, momentarily distracted by the running, jumping children.

Even though Patricia had insisted on her being at the wedding, Mrs. Munro would do anything to avoid the fury of Patricia's mother, Mrs. Janet Ord Mackenzie.

"There will be trouble," she sighed to herself, never anticipating how great the trouble would turn out to be.

"I want an explanation, Patricia Ord Mackenzie. Now." But

Joanne couldn't help smiling. This was so typical of her friend, announcing an intrigue or a plan or an escapade at the very last minute, making it impossible for Joanne to refuse to join in.

"You're the only one I could count on," came the shrugged apology. "After all, the same thing happened to you."

Joanne winced at the tactless honesty of the remark.

"I've known Sandy for forever. Well, at least five years." Patricia lit a cigarette before plowing on. "These things happen. He's a local. I met him on the farm. A handsome devil, that's what I first noticed . . . along with many other local lasses no doubt. . . ." Patricia laughed. "Then we started seeing each other . . . you know how it is . . . but it had to be secret because . . ." Patricia hesitated. She couldn't remember why it had to be secret; she was not ashamed of her romance with a working-class man. "When I became pregnant, Sandy was really pleased. He proposed, I accepted, and here we are." She threw away her cigarette and searched in her bag for a lipstick.

"I see." Joanne didn't really, but was stuck for something to say. "Do your parents know?" was all she could think to ask.

"Absolutely not. I'd be packed off to a nunnery or whatever one does in these circumstances. No, best get it over with and present them with a fait accompli. She can rant and cry all she wants, but if it's a boy, and I'm certain it will be, Mummy will forgive me anything."

"I can't see your mother crying," Joanne commented, recollecting her own nightmare. Their mothers were both of the same school of steely resolve.

"No," Patricia agreed. "Tears would turn to ice as they left her eyes." She looked at Joanne and the pink flush of vulnerability, or was it pregnancy hormones, softened Patricia's face. "I'm sorry to deceive you. It's going to be hard, so I need your support. And I want you at my wedding."

Joanne leaned forward, wrapping her arms around her friend in reply. Patricia held on tight, a slight sob of relief escaping through all the held-in emotion.

Over Patricia's shoulder, Joanne saw a vaguely familiar figure stepping out of a car. In his buttonhole was a red carnation—for a wedding, presumably. His companions, on either side of him, wore white carnations, identifying them as part of the wedding party. They came towards the women, shuffling slightly, as though their shiny suits, *hired*, Joanne thought, were scratching them. But perhaps they were just embarrassed.

Joanne stared at the weathered, brown faces; the flattened-down hair that held the indentation from seldom removed caps; and it dawned on her that she did indeed know these men.

Patricia turned. "Darling." She rushed forward to the oldest of the three. "You should be inside. It's unlucky to see the bride before the wedding." But laughing, she took his hand. "Come and meet my best friend and matron of honor—Joanne Ross."

Smirking, his hand held out, he said, "Pleased to meet you at long last. I've heard a lot about you." His hand enveloped hers, squeezing her hand until Joanne almost cried out in pain, all the while staring, daring her to speak out, taking his revenge. She could read it in his eyes: "That's for humiliating me." Another quick squeeze and she was sure her wedding ring had broken the skin: "That's for kicking me."

"How do you do," Joanne gasped, staring straight into the eyes of the skipper of the herring boat.

"This is ma' friends."

The two crewmen stepped forward. Looking sheepish, they touched their foreheads with a cocked forefinger. Patricia noticed nothing, dizzy with emotion—part elation, part fear, and a mercifully mild bout of the usual morning sickness. The clock chimed ten. The meager group gathered at the foot of the registry office stairway.

"This is it, then." Sandy offered his arm to his bride. "At long last."

Joanne followed. At the top of the steps he turned to her. "Fancy that eh . . . me marrying into the Ord Mackenzie clan." Then he winked.

As he turned to go into the registry office, Joanne had a sudden sickening premonition that this was not going to work out, and that this would happen sooner rather than later.

Four

Joanne would later recall that weekend in small episodes. Like a film director, she would try to organize the memories, but they refused to fall into chronological sequence—a fragment of farce alternating with a scene of excruciating embarrassment, moments of real pleasure ending in sharp pain, the pain that only families can inflict on one another. And Joanne felt herself clearly, vividly, hovering above, looking down on those scenes; she saw herself, lips tight together, waiting on tenterhooks for the next revelation, the next disaster, the next episode in the drama.

The friends walked in the woods, primroses and wood aconite and wild garlic carpeting the mossy banks along the swift-flowing burn, the girls with small bags of salt "to shake on rabbits' tails," Patricia had explained. It was an old joke, but a good one, and even though Annie saw through it she played along for her sister's sake.

The girls went riding, Annie going solo, Wee Jean happy to be led on the fat pony. In the afternoon, gathering driftwood and shells on the beach at Rosemarkie, Joanne and Patricia chatted about anything other than the subject foremost in their minds while the children ran to and fro between the breaking waves and the women, anxious for a small phrase of praise for each shell, each treasure gathered from the tide-line. Across the firth, the ramparts of Fort George loomed grey and sinister, a fitting backdrop. When the day ended, both women—and to a lesser degree

Annie—were glad that not one word had been said about Patricia's wedding, nor of Patricia's new husband.

On the Saturday evening, Mrs. Ord Mackenzie insisted on the torture of dinner in the high-ceilinged, long, dim, and echoing dining room of the Georgian mansion. The table setting was formal, with enough linen, dishes, glasses, and silver cutlery to sate the appetite of any burglar. The temperature was that of a seldom-used room. The atmosphere matched.

Mr. Ord Mackenzie sat at the head of the table, his wife on one side and his daughter on the other. Annie and Wee Jean were down from Patricia, and Joanne sat a safe gap from Janet Ord Mackenzie. The remaining six yards of table was empty. Joanne prayed that the girls would not disgrace her.

Great Expectations, *that's what it feels like*, Joanne thought.

"More vegetables, Joanne?"

"Would you pass the mustard, Daddy?"

"The primroses are everywhere this year. So bonnie."

The conventional questions were asked: Joanne's health and welfare and her parents' health, even though Mrs. Ord Mackenzie knew that Joanne was excommunicated.

Patricia and Joanne were just at the point of self-congratulations on an ordeal endured when Wee Jean, in all her innocence, ignited the touch paper.

"Aunty Patricia, can we go to the shops sometime? I want to get some sweeties with the half-a-crown your friend gave me."

"And what friend is that?" asked Mrs. Ord Mackenzie.

Wee Jean was scared of Mr. Ord Mackenzie. His coat, his knickerbockers, his shambling slow shape, his moustache, and the hair coming out of his ears made her think he was made entirely from tweed. But his wife—her skeletal body, her silent walk, her grey hair so immaculate Jean was sure Mrs. Ord

Mackenzie took it off at night—terrified the child. She suspected the woman was a ghost, so all the cajoling, bribery, and warnings to stay silent were forgotten, so mesmerized was the girl at being spoken to directly.

"The friend Aunty Patricia married."

The sharp intake of breath from Joanne and Aunty Patricia's fork clattering onto a plate started the tears.

"I don't mind his name." She started to cry. "I'm sorry."

"Patricia!" Mrs. Ord Mackenzie elongated the name into three syllables, the final "a" roared as loud and as fiercesome as a battle cry at Culloden.

Wee Jean's tears turned to sobs. Annie, sitting beside her, took her wee sister's hand.

"Excuse us," Joanne stood, "I must take the children to bed. It's been a long day."

"I'll help." Patricia stood, holding on to the dining table to steady herself. "Mother, Daddy, we'll talk in the drawing room later." Shoulders squared, she led the miserable troop from the room.

Her father watched in bewilderment.

"What was that? Who's married?"

It took a while to settle the girls. Joanne read Wee Jean three stories and Patricia read a chapter of *Anne of Green Gables* to Annie.

"Isn't too grown-up for you?" Patricia asked. But no, it was currently Annie's favorite.

When they were walking down to the drawing room, Joanne brushed against her friend and was surprised to feel her trembling.

"I don't feel up to this, but it has to be faced sometime," Patricia whispered. "I'm so glad you're with me."

"Let's pretend we're being summoned to the headmistress's room for late homework," Joanne suggested.

"Far more serious than that," Patricia said, "more like being caught with a boy in the rhododendron bushes."

They were still smiling as they entered the room.

"Mummy, Daddy," Patricia started in a bright kindergarten schoolteacher placating a difficult parent voice, "can I pour you another drink?" She held up the decanter. "No? Well, Joanne and I will have a wee dram." She poured two healthy slugs then sat on the sofa as outwardly calm as Mary Queen of Scots awaiting her execution.

"On Thursday morning, I married Alexander Skinner," Patricia announced.

"You are getting married?" Her father beamed at her. "Jolly good."

"I presume you are pregnant," her mother said.

"He is a fisherman," Patricia continued. "From the Black Isle . . ."

"A fisherman?" her father asked. "I must look out the salmon rods. Been a while since I've had a spot of fishing."

"Penniless no doubt," her mother commented.

"On the contrary, Mother, he has his own boat. . . ."

That shocked Joanne. *Sandy hasn't told her.*

"You will meet him on Easter Monday," Patricia told them.

"Jolly good," said her father.

"You always were a stubborn, difficult, and not particularly bright child," Mrs. Ord Mackenzie said. "But this is completely unacceptable. I will consult our solicitor. I will not have a common fisherman marrying into my family."

"Too late for that now," Patricia told her.

Mrs. Ord Mackenzie stood. The conversation was over. As she passed by without saying goodnight, Joanne could have sworn she felt an icy draft in the woman's wake. *Don't be silly*, she told herself, *you've been reading too many faerie tales to the children.* But she felt herself shiver nonetheless.

"Well, that wasn't so bad, was it?" Joanne smiled at Patricia.

"Just wait. Mother will make my life miserable one way or another," came the reply.

"Well, well, will you look at this?" Fraser flapped a copy of the *Gazette* at his mother, but didn't bother to rise from his chair. "See," he said, "the boat that was burnt to nothing, *The Good Shepphard*, it belongs to Miss Stuck-Up's fancy man."

"Let me have that." Mrs. Munro grabbed the newspaper out of her son's hands and stared at the front page.

"I was reading that." Fraser stared in surprise at his mother, but she was out the kitchen door, with the newspaper, before he could react.

She squeezed past packing boxes lining the hallway. She was out of the farmhouse and into the kitchen of Achnafern Grange, sitting at the kitchen table, one ear cocked for the sound of footsteps, reading the front page of the *Gazette*, leaving Fraser to wonder what on earth was going on.

Mrs. Munro read the whole article, twice over, fearing, not for the first time, what her dear lass Patricia had got herself into.

Joanne too had been thinking about the *Gazette*. She was desperate to see a copy. But that would have meant asking Patricia for a lift into the village. She would have to wait until Tuesday. Don often quipped that today's newspaper is tomorrow's fish and chip wrapping. He was right, there was something very sad about old newspapers.

The distant chattering from the girls as they helped Patricia sort through her childhood collection of books, ready for the move to the farmhouse, made her smile. Annie would choose so many of Patricia's discards it would be hard carrying them home. Wee Jean was thrilled when Patricia gave her five dolls.

"No," she assured them, patting her tummy, "I won't be needing them. This is a boy."

Joanne walked through the house into the kitchen.

"Can I help with anything, Mrs. Munro?"

Mrs. Munro gave a start. She was so completely engrossed in the newspaper, she didn't have time to hide it.

"Is that the *Gazette*? I was so rushed on Thursday morning I didn't pick up a copy. May I see?"

Joanne took the paper, stared at the front page and understood only too well why Mrs. Munro looked nervous. The picture of Sandy Skinner, although in profile, was clear and distinct. In the background, the image of his boat, flames shooting skyward, looked spectacular. But the visceral pleasure in seeing her first assignment as a journalist, there, on the front page, overwhelmed her.

"This looks great!" Joanne exclaimed. "I wrote this, you know. It's my first real story." She looked at Mrs. Munro. Mrs. Munro was looking over Joanne's shoulder.

"Let me have a look." Patricia was by her side in a flash. "You clever thing. You, a journalist, who'd have thought it? Goodness, is that my Sandy? It is. Goodness! What's this?" Patricia skimmed the story. "Joanne! Why didn't you tell me?"

Why didn't Sandy tell you, more's the point? But Joanne didn't say that. Instead, she muttered, "I'll explain all I know—which is only what is in here," she tapped the newspaper and thought, *why couldn't I get to read this on my own and enjoy my wee moment of glory?*

✦ ✦ ✦

Sunday morning was taken up with church. Joanne and the girls joined the Ord Mackenzie family, neighbors, and tenants in the Easter service. Afterwards, the congregation milled around on the church steps, on the path through the graveyard, murmuring greetings, shaking hands, catching up with the news, the gossip, women examining one another's new Easter bonnets, men predicting the weather.

Another walk after lunch, this time along the ridge of the Black Isle, with views across the firths on both sides and the looming Ben Wyvis shadowing their every step.

"When is the baby due?" Joanne asked.

"Six months from now." Patricia smiled. "I want you to be godmother to my son." They began the descent down past the overgrown garden of an estate, the grand house in ruins.

"Tomorrow Sandy will be at the Easter picnic. Perhaps you can stop him and Mummy coming to blows? You can borrow my old hockey stick," Patricia teased.

Joanne could take no more evasions and bright, false smiles. "Is that why you invited me? So you could confront your parents with me there, thinking there would be less of a scene?"

"Joanne."

There was that too-wide smile again. That patronizing way Patricia had of saying "Joaaanne."

"Don't be silly. You're my best friend. I wanted you at my wedding. I thought you could help me be brave. You must have gone through a similar scene with your parents." She turned to Joanne, shaking her head at her lack of understanding. "If anyone has a right to be cross, it's me. You really should have told me about that article in the *Gazette*."

"What did Sandy say?"

"I haven't had a chance to talk to him." Patricia went slightly ahead as the path narrowed. The downward path was as taxing as the climb. "A fine honeymoon this is. No husband and my parents, at least my mother, outraged. Next week Sandy and I will be in the farmhouse and out of my mother's way, but Joanne, please, help me through the rest of the weekend."

"Of course I'll help." Joanne felt a pang of guilt that she doubted her friend. "I'd love to be godmother to the baby. But you should have told me, not just dropped me in it."

"I could say the same."

Patricia had the last word, as always.

Easter Monday, the children awoke late to the sun shining through a delicate lace of ice on the inside corners of the windowpanes. They ran down to the kitchen, still in their pajamas, where Patricia and Joanne and Mrs. Munro were having tea and preparing the picnic hamper.

A distant bell rang and rang, giving every indication of not letting up until answered.

"Now who could it be that uses the front door?" Mrs. Munro wiped her hands on her apron before taking it off. It was two minutes before she came back with Sandy Skinner.

He edged Mrs. Munro aside, grabbed Patricia, and was kissing her just as her mother came in to ask who the visitor was. Mrs. Ord Mackenzie stared. No one else knew where to look. Except Annie—she too stared. The dogs were more than staring—the two older spaniels were standing, pointing, hackles raised, barking furiously at Sandy. No one could quiet them. The third dog, not much more than a puppy, was cowering in her basket under the kitchen table. Wee Jean crept into the basket, put her arms around the dog, and stayed there, safe.

The picnic was absolutely awful, Joanne told Rob a few days later.

Joanne, the children, Mr. and Mrs. Ord Mackenzie, Patricia and Sandy Skinner, and the dogs, had walked through the woods to the boathouse that belonged to the demolished mansion. The jetty, sitting out over a dried-up, reed-strewn lakebed, was a well-loved family picnic spot. The sun came out in fits and starts, and it stayed cold. Joanne and Patricia opened the hamper, laid out a gingham tablecloth, and arranged the plates and cutlery and food and the painted boiled Easter eggs ready for the girls to roll down the banks.

No one ate much. The farce of a family outing was held together by dint of good manners, and the presence of guests and children. Sandy was included in the former category; to Joanne, the idea of him being family seemed absurd.

Sandy teased Patricia, making her blush, making pointed remarks about the boathouse. It was where they used to meet, he announced with a wink at Joanne.

"You told them, have you?" he asked, nodding towards Mr. and Mrs. Ord Mackenzie. He was aggressive when he spoke, his local accent hard to understand.

"Told us what, my dear?" her father asked.

Patricia took too long to answer. Her mother got in first, almost shouting.

"That she's pregnant, married, and moving into the farmhouse," she pointed a long, bony finger. Wee Jean mistook it for the pointed finger of the witch in *Sleeping Beauty* and burst into tears.

"With *him*," Mrs. Ord Mackenzie finished.

Joanne stared off into the distance, wondering how she could get to the ferry without transport of her own. Buses . . . probably only twice a day at the end of the half-mile driveway, and then maybe none on a public holiday. Maybe I could find Mr. Beauchamp Carlyle, he lives not far away. Or Mr. Munro might take me to the ferry. Or call McAllister, he'd come over. . . .

No, she decided, enduring was the only option.

Mrs. Ord Mackenzie had not finished. "It's all too ridiculous, Patricia. Look at him."

They all did. There was Sandy Skinner, skipper of the fishing boat—now no more than wreckage at the bottom of the canal. He was cocky, defiant, full of himself in his shiny suit and his white socks and his slicked back Brylcremed hair. Star of the front page of the *Gazette*, leaning back on one elbow, smoking and grinning, he was the picture of a man who knew he had come up in the world.

He lazily blew out a breath of cigarette, completely aware of all the consternation he was causing. In that moment, Joanne caught a glimpse of the animal attraction, the bad-boy film star brooding sexuality of the man. "Not sure about the farmhouse." Everyone turned and stared at Mr. Ord Mackenzie.

"Allie Munro and the wife and kiddies needn't be put out of their home. Why don't you two young things move into the east wing? Plenty of room there."

The star of Joanne's first feature article burst out laughing.

"Great idea! Don't you think, mother-in-law?" He put an arm around Patricia, staking claim. "Who'd have thought it? Me in the laird's big house wi' the laird's daughter. Grand that, eh Pat?"

Joanne saw Patricia flinch, but whether it was from being called Pat or from the thought of still living in the realm of her mother or from a glimpse into a future with Sandy Skinner, Joanne couldn't decide.

All she could think was—*thank goodness Mr. and Mrs. Ord Mackenzie read the* Ross-shire Journal *and not the* Highland Gazette. *I couldn't take any more scenes.*

FIVE

Easter or not, Don McLeod didn't believe in holidays; he was away to the west coast to follow up on the story of Alexander Skinner and the fishing boast. He could have done this by phone, but he fancied the trip and the company of an old friend.

A copy of the new *Gazette* lay on the passenger seat. He would glance at it from time to time and grin. Not that he would ever let anyone know, but he thought it was "grand"—his word, the Highland word of highest praise.

The road through the Great Glen Don knew "like the back of ma hand." But familiarity did not lead to any degree of contempt. Every twist, every turn, every view over loch and hill and distant mountain, he relished. The easy run out of town; the first glimpse of Loch Ness; the haunting remains of Castle Urquhart, halfway down the chain of lochs; the former army fort built to house soldiers, there to quell the Highland clans; Ben Nevis snow deep on its slopes and folds and crevices, were familiar sights, yet still sights that made his heart glad.

When he arrived in the town on the sea loch at the end of the glen, Don made straight for his friend Graham Nicolson's shop. The building was long and low and whitewashed and consisted of a general grocery; a newsagent; an attached cottage; and a shed out the back for the hardware, timber, animal feedstuff, and coal.

The *Highland Gazette* covered a huge geographical area and stringers like Graham Nicolson were invaluable. He was proud to be an occasional correspondent for the newspaper. His appearance helped—friendly eyes, ginger beard and hair that always needed cutting, he looked like a shaggy highland cow, minus the horns—and people talked to him.

"I have to congratulate you," he said to Don as they shook hands. "The new *Gazette* is a fine job." They spoke in Gaelic, being men from the Isles. "We sold out by ten in the morning."

"No, it's us has to thank you," Don replied. "Your stories from the west coast are much appreciated. Sorry we don't pay much."

"I'm paid enough for the occasional dram. Not too early for you?"

They grinned at each other, the question only a matter of form—it was never too early for a dram.

They settled in round the kitchen table to talk. On the second dram, they got on to the mystery of the firebombed fishing boat. Graham Nicolson's information was interesting, but made little sense.

"So," he started, "this Alexander Skinner, Sandy he's called, all I know for sure is he is not well liked. And everyone I spoke to is curious as to why he's selling his catch here instead of on the Black Isle. When you consider the cost of sailing down the Great Glen, through all the canal locks, it must add a fair bit to his fuel bill, not to mention an extra day's wages to the crew. I heard he owes the two lads money; I haven't been able to track them down yet, but I will."

"I've no doubt about that," Don laughed.

After they had finished the stories and the reminiscing and the bottle, Don realized it was fortuitous he had been invited to stay for the night. He wouldn't have far to stagger to bed.

Mortimer Beauchamp Carlyle spent most of the Easter weekend perched on a shooting stick, binoculars at the ready, gazing down to the mudflats of Munlochy Bay, watching the birdlife. It was a crossing point of the seasons, the migratory species only just beginning to reach northern parts for their summer holidays. Waders and seashore birds were what Beech most enjoyed. Elegant, long-legged, ballerina-stepping, clumsy in take-off, delightful of flight birds—Beech seldom tired of watching them.

A blast of cold wind as the sun hid behind an ominous cloud decided him—a pint of beer, then home.

As he was passing the sweet clearwater spring known as the Fairy Well, he stooped, cupped his hands, scooped up water, slurped at it, drips falling from his chin, down his jumper, onto his jacket.

"Magic," he pronounced. "Never had water like this in the Sudan."

He strode up the steep farm track, where his shooting brake awaited on the other side of a locked, five-bar gate. At the top of the track, there was a three-hundred-and-sixty-degree view. The southern aspect, framed by the headlands of the bay, was of the firth and the distant southern shore. To the west, the bright-yellow, gorse-clad cliffs were dotted with sheep. To the east another view of the firth, farmland, and the main road, the northern view too was of fields and farms and woods. A stately house dominated the rise to the northeast, Achnafern Grange. *Haven't been there in a long while*, Beech thought.

He drove into the village, parked by the harbor wall, glanced at the fishing boats neatly moored in the small refuge, and made his way to the pub. The locals noted him as he came in. He was not of this village, but his family bones were Black Isle. They nodded in greeting. He nodded back and the landlord poured him a pint.

"A fine day," Beech said.

"Aye, it is that."

That was all that was said, but that constituted a conversation in these parts.

Beech settled by the window, enjoying his beer, the quiet broken only by the slap of dominoes on a table in the far corner. He closed his eyes, listening to the hush of men busy doing very little.

A commotion from the snug bar startled him.

"Out!"

The landlord opened the serving hatch to see what was happening. Beech and the others listened in. It was like a scene from the Saturday night play on the Home Service.

"But I am old enough, I'm twenty."

"You're never!"

"I have a driving license, but it's at home."

"Without proof of age, I can't be serving you."

"I only want a half of shandy." There was a pause. "Look, here's ma card." He handed it to the barman. "See. I work for the *Highland Gazette*. I'm the photographer."

The barman studied the card and the realization crossed his face as obviously as a thundercloud obscuring the sun. "So you're the one responsible for that photo on the front page of the *Gazette*? The one wi' Sandy's boat on fire?"

"Aye, that was me."

Hector had barely finished the sentence when the landlord was through the door to join the barman, and the sound of Hector's protests were loud and clear and enjoyed by all.

"Out! Now!" Two younger men went through to join in the fun. Beech saw he would have to intervene.

"Hector," he called out, "can I give you a lift?"

"I have ma car."

"Hector!" Beech commanded.

The landlord dropped Hec's arm. The others stopped and stared. Beech had Hector out the door and across the road and down to the harbor before anyone could think.

"This your car?"

"Aye. Not really. It's ma granny's."

"Follow me to my house. We'll sort all this out there."

Hector looked back, saw a gathering of young men, one of them pointing at him, and decided to do as he was told. For once.

Rob's Easter week had started with a phone call. The news editor at the Aberdeen daily newspaper had rung him. "Robert McLean, please," he had asked. "The very one," Rob had replied. "There's a position open on the paper, would you be interested?" the editor had offered.

"Yes, of course."

A well-known, well-respected, big-circulation Scottish daily paper phoning me, asking me if I want a job, Rob was so flattered he didn't stop to think.

"Can you come for an interview on Easter Saturday?"

"No problem."

It had taken a whole day for him to come down to earth. That he might not be offered the job never entered his mind. But every time the future of the *Gazette* was discussed, which was almost constantly, a dirty puddle of guilt, viscous like nasty, well-used sump oil, sloshed around the pit of his stomach. To make it worse, the fire on the boat was shaping up to be a great story.

It's only an interview, I don't have to make a decision immediately, he told himself, *besides, nothing may come of the Sandy Skinner story.* Aberdeen—the city held no attractions for him, as he did not know it well. His girlfriend, Bianca, was at the Glasgow School of Art. It was when he thought of her, which was often, that he faced the reality of how far everywhere was from the

Highlands—how big the mass of the Grampians, how long and occasionally dangerous the main road south, how expensive the trains, how exorbitant an aeroplane flight.

But Aberdeen? It's a city. It's cold. The newspaper is good; the people there may not speak English, but they can read it.

Easter Monday being a holiday, the *Gazette* news meeting was postponed till Tuesday morning. With only two days to produce an expanded edition, Joanne was trying to type up her notes as fast as possible, wrestling with her conscience almost as much as she wrestled with the typewriter.

How much can I write about the weekend without being disloyal to Patricia? The phone interrupted her struggles with her sense of loyalty.

"*Gazette.*"

"Good morning."

"Patricia." Joanne laughed to cover her guilty conscience. "I was just this minute thinking about you. How are you feeling?"

"I'm well thanks. Joanne I called because . . ."

"I'm sorry, Patricia, can we talk later? I have a meeting in a few minutes. I need to organize my thoughts."

"Oh I'm sure you will wing it. You always do."

Joanne wondered if there was an implied criticism in that remark.

"Joanne, I need your help," Patricia continued. "Sandy asked me to call. He is really angry about his boat being on the front page of the *Gazette* in such a sensationalist newspaper article. Now the Aberdeen paper has picked it up and they keep phoning this house for an interview, so Mummy is furious as well. Please tell Mr. McAllister the boat is gone, end of story."

"I can't influence the editor, Patricia. Maybe Sandy should talk to him."

"He won't talk to anyone, not even me."

"Are you and the baby well?" Joanne tried bright and chatty. She didn't want the discussion—"sensationalist newspaper article" indeed.

"I'm healthy enough. It's everything else. Daddy is still insisting we live here, in the same house as my mother. Sandy agrees."

"I'm sure she will come round when the child is born."

"Your mother didn't." And with that remark, Patricia was gone.

Sandy Skinner had been eavesdropping on his wife's phone conversation.

"That your friend, the interfering one from thon *Gazette* rag?"

"That was Joanne, yes. She's promised to do her best to help."

"That'll be the day."

Sandy knew instinctively that this was not the time for a quarrel. But he was furious.

None of his plans were working the way they were supposed to. He had charted it all as carefully as the route to a new fishing ground. He kept note of her cycle for a good twelve months, he knew when she was ripe. He had bedded her, made her pregnant, married her, and now he wanted his due.

He lit a cigarette and stared out of the windows across the fields towards the firth, which showed up on the horizon as a grey strip of light.

The loss of the boat was a huge blow, financially and otherwise—he'd learned everything he knew on that boat. He would have said he loved her if he knew how.

Who'd have known a milk bottle and paraffin could sink a boat? He'd deal with the eejit that threw the bottle. He knew there would be no help from his family, even though the boat and the business was rightfully his. He was the firstborn son after all.

No one in his village would help after he took on those west coast boys as crew instead of locals.

The Church would be no help: he'd been thrown out of the Brethren, all for a harmless drink or two.

Then there were the debts. Wriggling out of that situation was proving impossible.

I should've taken Pat to see the bank manager. That would impress him, show him what I've married into.

Missus Ord Mackenzie should have been a man, he thought, *cold auld bag with no tits on her. There hasn't been a son in their family for generations, all inherited down the women of the family. But I'll put that right, and ma son will have it all in due course.*

It might be fine for my boy, but me, I hate this farming catastrophe. Filthy places, farms, loads o' stupid animals and even more stupid fellows running around wi' tractors an' all, doing the same thing year in year out, never leaving the land, never going anywhere. Me, I'm a hunter, out on the high seas, out in all manner of weather and danger. Thon landsmen are cowards, not real men. They huddle round their fireside the minute a wee storm threatens.

Thinking is no goin' to get me anywhere, he said to himself, *Patricia will have to get me out of this. I can twist her round ma wee finger. Just have to get her away from her ma. What was it she was bleating on about? A honeymoon? Complete load a shite, that. But still. On our own, I can work the charm. Then she'll see sense.*

He put the cigarette out in his teacup and spoke.

"I've been thinking. Maybe we should go away for a few days, a wee break, eh? Sort of a honeymoon?"

Patricia's face said it all.

"Sandy, what a lovely idea. But not too far please, I get really carsick at the moment."

"Somewhere along Loch Ness, maybe?"

"Perfect."

Well done, Sandy lad, he told himself. *It'll all work out. Her stuck-up friend from the newspaper will tip her the word on any developments. I'll squeeze the money out of her father somehow. The old duffer won't refuse, it being for his grandson and heir, after all. Aye,* he thought, *me, Sandy Skinner, I'll be the laird o' this place afore long.*

"The cheek of the woman . . ." Joanne spoke aloud just as Rob arrived in the newsroom.

"What woman?"

"Patricia Ord Mackenzie. I was there for the Easter weekend . . ."

Rob wasn't listening, his own weekend still tingling in his veins. He felt guilty about the job interview. *I can't keep it secret; I'll have to tell her.*

"Joanne, I went to Aberdeen for . . ."

Don and McAllister arrived. Rob said no more. Mrs. Smart came in and joined them at the table. Hec snuck in last, like a dog unsure of his welcome. He was the *Gazette*'s photographer, but was he part of the team? He had his doubts about that.

The newsroom buzzed with a morning-after-holiday energy. McAllister spread out last week's pages on the big communal table.

"Right, let's get started. Overall impression?"

There was a babble of "great" and "very good" and "like it" and "very happy" and "smashing." The last word was from Hector. It was currently his favorite word, and he used it for everything and anything.

"Any phone calls?" McAllister asked Don.

"A few" was the reply. "Well all right, more than a few. On Friday I did a ring around the newsagents and shopkeepers. They like it."

"It sold out at the station," Rob said. "I tried to buy a copy and they were all gone by ten o'clock."

"Sold out in Fort William by lunchtime," Don added.

"On Saturday morning, not usually a busy time for me, I took bookings for advertisements," Mrs. Smart told them.

"My parents-in-law think it's easier to read," Joanne contributed. "That means they like it, and my mother-in-law is not one for changes." Joanne turned to McAllister. "You haven't given us your verdict."

"Early days yet."

There was a spontaneous groan.

"Sorry," he laughed. "This edition is good, but we have to keep it up, every week, every year. . . . So, next edition? Front page? Anyone?"

"Last week's lead story is still good for a follow-up," Don said, looking at Rob. "Any more from the police?"

"They've still no idea who threw the petrol bomb."

"Maybe I can use my 'Police Baffled' headline this week." Don glared at McAllister, who had changed the heading to a more innocuous, "Police Search for Information."

"I've done a think piece for page five," Rob continued, "the state of fishing, small boats being squeezed out by the big trawlers, intense rivalry between ports, Icelanders trying to keep all their fish for themselves, that kind of thing. Some are even saying the herring won't last forever."

"I've some smashing pictures of fishing boats," Hec contributed.

"Talking of which . . ." McAllister nodded to Joanne, "the

fishing boat story. Have you found the skipper, what was his name? Skinner?" McAllister was looking at her, but she couldn't meet his gaze.

"I *did* meet the skipper of the boat."

"And?"

"What I found out is not really relevant to . . ."

"I'll be the judge of that."

"I was in the Black Isle for Easter, staying with Patricia Ord Mackenzie, an old school friend and . . ." She paused.

"*And?*" McAllister was getting impatient.

"Patricia was married on Thursday, I was her matron of honor, her husband is Sandy—Alexander—Skinner, the owner of the boat that went on fire."

"Did you get an interview?" asked McAllister.

"An Ord Mackenzie married a fisherman?" Don.

"Can I take their picture?" Hec.

"I bet she's up the spout," Rob.

"Goodness me," Mrs. Smart.

All this was said all at the same time, simultaneously, overlapping, leaving Joanne flustered and guilty and completely lost as to how to reply to any of the questions.

"Order." McAllister thumped the table. There was a momentary hush.

"Joanne, firstly, there is no 'went on fire.' The boat was firebombed. That's a crime in Scotland. Second, this is a sensational new twist to the story—you should have told us immediately." McAllister caught the warning glower from Don. "Sorry, I know it must have been awkward for you, but does this Skinner fellow know who threw the bomb?"

"Sorry. Sandy didn't speak to me much."

"Did you ask?"

"Sorry, no. After seeing the front page, I doubt he will give an interview to anyone at the *Gazette*, especially me. Patricia Ord Mackenzie called first thing this morning. She said her husband asked her to ask me to ask you to drop the story."

"And?"

"I told her Sandy Skinner should speak to you himself."

"Joanne," he looked at her carefully, "do you have a conflict with this? Can you continue working on this story, no matter where it may lead?"

"I don't know. Sorry."

She was seized by the sensation that she had somehow failed. On her first story, she had not been professional, had not taken the opportunity to question Sandy, to do her job, to grab a scoop, as Rob would have done.

And as the buzz of the newsroom continued around her, as stories were discussed, assignments agreed upon, she felt she would never measure up to the standards of a professional like McAllister.

The meeting over, Joanne and Rob had the reporters' room to themselves. Joanne was trying to decide how to approach Sandy Skinner for an interview.

Rob was reading the report from Graham Nicolson. "It says here that Sandy Skinner was in Mallaig a couple of months ago, looking for a crew. I bet they had to be Catholic."

"Oh really?" She was not that interested. She kept starting a sentence, hating what she wrote, and tearing the paper from the machine, scrunching it up into a small ball and throwing it at the top-hat-cum-wastepaper-basket that sat under the only window in the room.

"Catholic crews can fish on a Sunday, or leave on a Sunday night, to get to the fishing grounds before the others. It's been a source of tension for years. You see, many of the families on the east coast are Brethren, strict Sabbatarians."

"Sandy Skinner can't be religious, he married Patricia in the registry office."

"Maybe that's what this is all about, a religious dispute," Rob speculated.

"Maybe." This time, as she ripped the copy paper from the typewriter, Joanne's fingers caught the ribbon, which unrolled into a fankle of black. As she tried to thread it back into the spool, the ink stained her fingers, the desk, and the cuff of her best white blouse.

"Blast and double blast!" This was as close to swearing as Joanne got. "Blast this machine and blast this story!"

"I'm happy to take over the story, but you'd be sorry if you give up. It could turn out to be very interesting," Rob said.

Joanne gave up on the typewriter ribbon. She went to stand in the window. *Rain is not far off*, Joanne thought, peering through the grimy panes to an equally grimy sky, *knowing my luck it will probably sleet.*

"It never occurred to me that friendship could get in the way of a story." She spoke to the clouds, not wanting Rob to see how upset she felt.

"We can work on this together," he offered, "and whenever it starts to get hairy, blame me."

"Thanks, Rob, but I have to learn to stick up for myself. Patricia is my oldest friend, but . . . I don't know what it is, but I sometimes feel . . . used."

"I know. She's not my favorite person. We were forced to spend holidays together when I was a child, our fathers are friends." Rob didn't elaborate; it would all sound so petty. "Speaking of friendship, I have a confession."

He told her about the job offer.

"Never! You can't!" Joanne looked at him, at his cheerful face, his dandelion hair, the way he had of never standing but always leaning in a casual film-star kind of way, and she felt the hot sting of almost tears. "Oh Rob, I'm sorry. I didn't mean that. It would be great for your career, but I'd miss you."

"I'd miss you too . . . and all this." He gestured round a room so tight you could almost touch the walls opposite. "It's flattering to be asked, and I haven't made a decision. The idea of a good job on a big Aberdeen newspaper is all very fine, but . . ." he grinned at her, "their accent is so thick I can't understand a word anyone says."

At lunchtime, and only because Don told him to help select a shot for the front page, Rob met Hec at his studio, also known as his granny's washhouse.

Ducking under the clothesline, where negatives and proof sheets were dangling thickly from wall to wall, crisscrossing the tiny space, Rob noted, and was impressed by the custom-built cabinets stretching from floor to ceiling, all neatly labeled according to a classification system known only to Hec. It was then that Rob realized he was in the lair of a true professional.

"Here, take a pew, we'll sort through these." Hec handed Rob proof sheets and negatives.

They looked through dozens of, to Rob anyway, very similar shots of fishing boats, and a harbor.

"I can't do this, Hec, I can't tell anything from a negative."

"Fine. I'll look through the Black Isle negs, you look through the prints."

In his own kingdom, Hec was different—not such a pest. He was confident, good company. Rob selected about a dozen of what he considered the best shots, then looked at them again. He stared at one particular photograph. He found another similar shot, but the figure was farther in the distance.

"Hec, can you make this bigger? Maybe blow up a part of it?"

"Easy peasy." Hector looked over the shot. "That one's no good." He leaned over Rob, patronizing, a man who knew best. "See, here, the angle's all wrong, the boat's only just caught alight, there's no drama in the composition."

"So who's this then?" Rob pointed to a figure on the left of the frame, running along the canal towpath, away from the fire.

"Oh aye, him. I saw him. He was running towards the lock keepers' house at the end of the canal basin. You know, the locks that lead into the firth."

"Hector!" Rob didn't realize he was shouting.

Hector immediately turned defensive, his shoulders hunching, his eyes blinking. "What?"

"Don't you see?" Rob shook the pictures six inches in front of Hector's face.

"See what?"

"I give up. You're hopeless, helpless, and useless." Rob knew there was no point trying to get sense out of Hector. Instead he gathered up the prints and the negatives and the magnifying glass and drove back to the office where he dumped everything, including Hector, in McAllister's office.

"You can sort this out," Rob handed the photographs to the editor, saying, "because if I stay, I'm likely to do him damage."

McAllister took the prints and the negatives, saw what Rob had seen, then sent Hec home to print out some blowups. It was late afternoon before Hector returned.

The police station was a short walk from the *Gazette* office. Tucked beneath the castle walls, the too old, too small, too narrow building, its walls imbued with the scent and sound of misery, cast a spell on all who entered. Wee Hec was terrified. McAllister was scared too. Scared that Hec, who was only at the police station because he had been ordered to, would reach up and hold his hand.

"Detective Inspector Dunne, please."

They were shown into an office, not an interview room, McAllister noted and approved. This inspector was shaping up to be a huge improvement on the previous detective inspector with whom McAllister had a traumatic history.

McAllister had already told Detective Inspector Dunne of the photographs. Now he handed them over and he and Hec sat in silence as the policeman examined them.

"Thank you for bringing these in." DI Dunne's tone was formal, all business. "I'm intrigued by this particular picture," he pointed to the shot showing a person running along the towpath. "But before we go on to look at these in detail, Mr. Bain . . ."

Hec took a quick look round to check if there was another Bain in the room.

". . . It's been eight days since the fishing boat was set on fire. Why didn't you show these to us until now?"

Hector looked down at his hands and said nothing.

"Answer the Inspector." McAllister poked him in the arm.

"Because they're no good, the shot is the wrong angle." Hec gave an exaggerated sigh, treating DI Dunne as he had treated Rob earlier—as someone who was a complete ignoramus about art. "The pointy bit of the boat is straight on to the camera, so you get no idea of the size of it, and there's no smoke or flames. . . ."

"Hector." McAllister's growl terrified Hector.

When he continued, Hec's voice had gone up an octave, so he sounded as well as looked eleven years old, "Mr. McAllister said I had to give you these pictures."

"Do you understand why?"

"No, sir. I mean, yes, sir."

"These photographs could help us find a criminal." The policeman was patient, interviewing Hector as he would a child. "They could be important evidence."

Hector was listening now.

"What I don't understand is, why didn't you mention this to the constables at the scene of the crime?"

"The sergeant doesn't like me."

"Which sergeant?"

"The fat one. He says I'm a peeper."

"That must be Sergeant Patience." A most inappropriately named man, Detective Inspector Dunne always thought. "Is that why you didn't come in earlier? You'd already spoken to the sergeant?"

"No, he saw me and I saw him, so I hid."

"He only wanted to take your statement about what you saw."

"Why me? There were plenty other folk there. He's always picking on me."

The Inspector tried again. "You saw someone running away from the fire?"

"No, I never."

"But I thought you did."

"I never."

"Hector." McAllister knew it was time to intervene.

"What? Rob found this picture. There is somebody running. But how was I to know they wis running away from the fire? Maybe they wis going to the lock keeper's house, or the swing bridge on the railway line 'cos the other bridge was closed—I mean open. Maybe they wis late for work, maybe . . ."

"You took his picture," Inspector Dunne said.

"No, I never."

"You took a picture and in the picture was a man running. . . ."

"No."

"No?"

"I'm not sure he wis a man."

"Hector." McAllister nudged him.

"I was taking pictures of the fire. The person happened to be there. I happened to take this photo. I didn't pay any heed 'cos I was that busy taking that many shots. Rob saw the picture. Then Mr. McAllister told me I had to come here and show it to you. So I'm here."

McAllister guessed where the conversation might lead. "I apologize for not getting this photo to you sooner," he spoke to DI Dunne in a formal, official manner. "We only found out about its existence today. The *Highland Gazette* would never withhold evidence."

"Apology accepted," DI Dunne said. "I'm glad you didn't go ahead and publish before showing it to me."

No, thought McAllister, *I won't tell him that I was sorely tempted. Better to keep on the good side of the police.*

"Hector, thank you for providing the photographs." DI Dunne was once more the formal policeman. "But in future, if you have anything that will help us in our inquiries, try to get it to us sooner rather than later."

"Yes, sir." Hector was so relieved he jumped off his chair and was out the door before McAllister or the inspector could say another word.

As he walked back to the office, McAllister thought of the new detective inspector with respect, admiration even; how the man refrained from reaching across the desk, grabbing Hec by the neck, and throttling him, he would never know.

McAllister was about to leave for the day when his phone rang.

"McAllister."

"Angus McLean here."

McAllister knew from the tone that this was a formal call.

"The Ord Mackenzie family and Achnafern Estate on the Black Isle are my clients," Mr. McLean explained.

"Yes."

"I am giving you the courtesy of a call before I write to you on behalf of Mrs. Alexander Skinner née Ord Mackenzie."

"And?"

"She asks that you stop publishing articles about a private family matter. If you do not do so, she will be forced to take further steps."

"A fishing boat set alight by a Molotov cocktail, in a public waterway—namely the canal—attended to by the fire brigade and the police and subject to an inquiry by the procurator fiscal, is hardly a private family matter."

"I've told her that."

"Thank you, Mr. McLean, I will note that you called and I will make sure that we do not publish any story that could be deemed as private family business."

"Thank you. I will draft a letter accordingly."

"Yes." McAllister knew the formalities were over and dropped into the not-for-publication, friendship mode, "But Angus, just so you know, I have no intension of being bullied by any member of the Ord Mackenzie clan."

"Quite so."

McAllister could hear the smile in the solicitor's voice as they said their good-byes.

Threaten all you want, Mrs. Skinner née Ord Mackenzie, McAllister thought, *but your husband's affairs will be on the front page of the next edition and there is nothing you can do about it.*

Six

꧁

Chiara Kowalski née Corelli was the one person with whom Joanne felt she could completely be herself.

"We're both outsiders," Joanne joked. "I may be Scottish, but I could live my whole life here and I'd still be an outsider."

Not much younger than Joanne, Chiara had come to the town with her aunt to join her father, Gino Corelli. He, as well as hundreds of other men released from prisoner-of-war camps throughout Scotland, had decided to make this country home.

Gino Corelli started with a mobile fish and chip van, and now his café and chip shop was as much a part of the town's landscape as the castle.

Living in the north was a mixed blessing for the Italians. Highland regiments had served in Messina, Sicily, at the battle for Monte Cassino, and many other skirmishes on the long march through Italy. Flesh wounds healed, but memories didn't. Many remembered all too well that Italy had been on the side of the Germans initially. Joanne's mother-in-law, Mrs. Ross, was one. Being called a turncoat was one of the milder taunts Gino had had to put up with.

But Italians had been a presence in Scotland for centuries, contributing to the life of the community with not just cafés; they were citizens as much as any native-born Scot. Then the war came. Men were interned in freezing barracks in desolate parts of the countryside, leaving the women and children to run the businesses. When the war ended, they remained and rebuilt their lives. Keeping to themselves mostly, the bright ice-cream parlors, the cafés, the chip shops, and vans with "O Sole Mio" jingles were welcome—as long as no one mentioned the war.

Chiara had been a teenager when she and her aunt had left Italy to join her father. After a journey that she never spoke about, through a desecrated Europe, they were reunited; she attended the local convent school, studied, made friends, and married another of the war's casualties—a Polish aristocrat who, along with thousands of his compatriots, had escaped in the weeks before the occupation.

Joanne remembered a February evening in the Corelli home, when the wind was fierce outside, the curtains shifting as it penetrated invisible cracks around the window frames. Chiara put another log on the fire, complaining that she'd never been so cold.

"My darling," Peter had said to his now wife, "you have no idea of real cold. Before I came to Scotland, I was used to freezing Baltic winds, but a winter in the Hebrides showed me what real cold is."

Peter Kowalski had survived both the war and the Scottish winter of 1944–45 flying over the Atlantic from the island of Benbecula with the "Land of Silesia" Squadron of the Polish Air Force, then on Coastal Command.

Joanne loved hearing the stories of the Corelli and Kowalski families. She loved hearing there was a big world out there, a world she knew she would never know. But most of all she knew that Chiara and her family cared for her, and their affection and laughter and teasing came without strings.

Unlike Patricia, Joanne sometimes thought.

The café down by the river was full when Joanne arrived. The lunchtime crowd was tucking into sandwiches and tea with the occasional daring customer trying something more adventurous. Like spaghetti.

"Some Scots say they don't like Italians, but they like our cafés," Chiara had told Joanne.

The friends were settled in their favorite window seat with a view of the castle and the bridge.

"Have you heard from Bill?" Chiara was the only person who ever asked Joanne about her husband.

"We've been separated nearly four months," Joanne started slowly, thinking through her situation. Why she hadn't seen or heard from Bill Ross puzzled her as much as it puzzled Chiara. "And I haven't seen him once."

"Has he seen the girls?"

"He saw them at their grandparents.'" Joanne was reluctant to say more, even to Chiara. She knew her husband was not really interested in the children, or perhaps it was that he was not interested in daughters, and she didn't want to say, but the longer he stayed away, the happier she was.

Chiara noticed the way her friend was fiddling with the salt-shaker as she talked. It was as though Joanne thought that in avoiding talking about her husband, she might be able to forget his existence. But Chiara knew he was not a man to let his wife leave without taking revenge. She also knew when to change the subject.

"So, tell me more about May Day in Scotland," Chiara asked. "What's all this about dancing around a phallic object for fertility?"

"I was only teasing." Joanne looked around to see if anyone had overheard her friend. "You don't really believe all those May Day superstitions, do you?"

"Of course, I'm from good old Italian peasant stock." Chiara pulled back her thick, black hair so it was tight against her skull and did an impression of an ancient crone. "No," she laughed and shook her hair so it tumbled in a thick, black curtain over her shoulders. "In southern Italy where we come from, superstition is deeper than even the Church. The fertility rites over there predate the Romans. Peter and I so want a baby that I'll try anything."

"How long have you been married? Six months? Just keep on trying is my advice."

"Oh, we do that all right."

Gino looked through the steam of the coffee machine at the sound of laughter coming from the window table. He beamed at his daughter and her friend.

Half past four o'clock the next morning was early for Joanne and Chiara and very early for the girls. Chiara drove her father's fourthhand but beloved Wolseley, the leather seats making a comfortable bed for the children. Chiara's Aunt Lita had decided to join them and she sat in the middle of the backseat, with Annie snuggled against her on one side, Jean's head cradled on her lap on the other.

Faint whispers of grey along the horizon forecast dawn. The pearly light was soon lost as the car descended to the river valley. They followed the murmur of the fast-flowing water towards the site of the ancient burial mounds and standing stones.

The grove of oak, beech, rowan, and birch sighed expectantly, waiting for the arrival of the sun. The larch and pine joined in with a seashore sound. The river running over gravel and stone added darker notes. Distant bleating of sheep added higher notes. With a caw or twenty, the rooks awoke. The blackbirds and thrush and tits and other invisible hedgerow birds sang the high-register trills, arpeggios, and soprano solos until the glade echoed with the sound of the dawn chorus.

The women and girls had to walk a little from the road along a well-trodden pathway leading to the stones. The smell from late hawthorn was not as strong as it would be if the sun was up. Wild garlic was another smell just distinguishable amongst the scent of vegetation. The bluebells were not yet out, the primrose not yet open, the pink blooms of Herb Robert were plentiful, and Joanne knew that in summer this woodland hedgerow would be thick with dog roses.

The children were nervous, sensing the night creatures departing with the dawn, sensing the spirits that never left, day or night, not quite knowing why they were here or what to do.

"Wash our faces in the morning dew," Joanne whispered through the silence. It almost seemed sacrilegious to talk in such a setting. This grove of the ancients is a natural cathedral, she thought, far more sacred than any church.

The children looked around, remembering the ritual from previous years. "Wash our faces in the morning dew, the morning dew, so early in the morning," Annie started and Jean joined in.

"Will it make me beautiful, Mum?" Wee Jean asked.

"You're beautiful already," her Aunty Chiara told her as they gathered dew in their cupped hands to wash their faces.

The girls galloped around the ring of standing stones, shrieking in sheer exhilaration. The women went in different directions on private meanders.

I want that man out of my life, Joanne made the silent wish.

Crouching down, she wet her hands with soft grassy glittered in the rising sunlight dew, and with baptismal reverence she again washed her face and combed her hair.

Chiara too made her own ritual.

"A baby. A new life. For my Peter and my father," she half-prayed, half-wished, walking round and round the biggest standing stone.

Aunt Lita walked slowly, seemingly aimless, in and out of the prehistoric stone circle. Nothing was heard from her except a curious rising and falling toneless mumble. She was remembering other May Day rituals; the deep thread of ancient rites had not all been obliterated by the Church. She remembered family, and named them; friends and neighbors, and named them; the village, the hills, the countryside of her birth, she named them. Much had been destroyed. Orchards in ruins. Thousand-year-old olive groves up in smoke. Wineries devastated. Many buried without ceremony. Lita gave thanks, ritually listing her blessings. She did not ask for much. She hoped for another year of health and contentment. She would never tempt fate to ask for more. Survival was enough.

"Look at me," Annie cried. She stood on the top of the long, rounded burial mound, arms stretched out wide, silhouetted against the rising sun, framed in a halo of light. Instinctively, she knew this was the moment. Calling out in a laughing but solemn voice the young girl pronounced the blessing.

"Thank you for the sun and for this morning."

To her delight her mother repeated the refrain. "Thank you for the sun and this morning."

Her Aunty Chiara and Aunt Lita joined in and whooping and cheering and jumping and running, the five friends shouted in variations of the chant.

"Thank you, sun. Thank you, morning." Aunt Lita repeated the blessing in Italian. Eventually she brought them to heel with a "Who's for breakfast?"

They picnicked on a flat stone in a chilly but sunny corner of the woods. Breads and hams and cheeses and sweet pastries were all the more tasty for the early hour, the outdoor setting and the conspiracy of friends. Tired, content, satisfied, and about to face a day at school or at work or in the kitchen, they packed up and returned to the car, all five of them, knowing that this was a May Day to cherish.

✦　✦　✦

On the drive back to town, Chiara and Joanne agreed to have coffee before starting work. The girls could walk to school.

Driving across the bridge, Chiara slowed the car at the narrow passage between the sandstone pillars that anchored the suspension cables. Joanne was dozing and didn't notice the car until it had passed. She looked back.

"That was Mrs. Ord Mackenzie's car," Joanne said.

"Really?" Chiara had not been paying attention. Besides, she only knew of Mrs. Ord Mackenzie from Joanne's stories.

"Maybe not," Joanne yawned. "Those Rovers are common enough cars."

"Aye, if you can afford one," Chiara replied.

If you can afford one. . . . The reminder of the difference in status between Joanne and her oldest friend jolted her back to a memory that had her burning in shame—then and now.

"What's this?" A seven-year-old Patricia had shouted. "Morag Gillespie? That's not your name."

Joanne knew her parents bought her school uniform secondhand, she knew the name of the previous owner was written in indelible ink on the blazer label—and she had thought nothing of it.

"Can't your parents afford a new blazer?" Patricia had asked, astonished at the idea.

It was then Joanne discovered exactly what being a "scholarship girl" meant. It was then that Joanne knew, for the first time ever, that in spite of her father being a minister of the Church of Scotland, they were indeed poor.

What was worse, Patricia knew it too, and although she never teased her new friend, her sympathy for the "poor girl" made Joanne feel worse.

✦ ✦ ✦

Hector had it all wrong. That often happened to him, as he gleaned most of his misinformation by listening in on other people's conversations. Phone calls and even letters did not escape his curiosity. He was a person who had no life of his own. He had his photography. He had his granny and his little sister. That was it, his life. Now he had his job.

"Dancing in the May Day dew" was what he had overheard Joanne say. When was obvious. Where was the problem.

He asked Rob as discreetly as he could.

"Those strange folk at Boleskine House near Foyers will probably dance naked in the May Day dew," Rob told him.

Hector believed him, so he drove to Foyers, hoping for an early-morning rendezvous with white witches or druids or some such nutters, as he thought of them.

A May Day ceremony, naked, preferably, but robes and ritual would do, Hec thought.

He waited. And waited. By seven he gave up. Nothing stirred, except for the usual countryside busyness. He was not disappointed. Hector never had expectations. He never had disappointments. But a journey was a journey, and if he wanted petrol money from Mrs. Smart, he needed some pictures. He shot off a reel of film in the graveyard. He went down through the village to the edge of the Loch Ness to take more pictures. He waited—no monster about this morning. He started back to town, then decided to stop and photograph the lower part of the Falls of Foyers.

The burn was full, the water falling in a thick, heavy rush.

"Magic," he said, as he watched swirling, misty rainbows dance above the breaking water. *It'll be even better in the main fall.*

He was careful walking down the muddy track, sheltering his cameras under his coat. He stopped at the viewing point halfway down. It was nothing more than an outcrop of rock protruding out into the void. The spume from the main fall was fierce. Too wet for cameras, Hec decided, and continued down.

The path disappeared. There was a way down, but it was little more than a sheep track. Creeping on in a crablike motion, sometimes on all fours, clutching at rocks and ferns and overhanging tree trunks, Hec reached the bottom. The roar was loud, and louder the lower he went. It was worth it. The fall of water was spectacular. Hector wasn't sure, but he seemed to remember the drop was around a hundred and forty feet; it certainly looked it.

He found a spot, risked a few shots. He moved farther back, took a few more frames looking up the cliff to the path above. Worried that the fine spray from the falls would penetrate his cameras, he repacked them into his schoolbag and picked his way back up. He climbed mostly on all fours until he reached the better track above. Panting, he stopped; a few more shots into the gorge below, he decided.

He leaned against the stone cliff to steady himself, framing the shot. "Blast it!" Hec was not happy. "Thon rubbish in the pool spoils it."

With no thoughts of falling, he squeezed between a bush and a rock and the sheer drop. He took his time. One shot deep into the abyss, one shot, framed through fern and branches, up to the top of the falls. The rubbish was no longer visible so he took three more frames down into the falls.

With the sun beginning to penetrate the trees and the ferns, he knew he had at last captured the depth and the height and the menace of the Falls of Foyers.

Back at the car, he dried his cameras with a chammy leather, then stowed the camera bag on the floor of the backseat, where it joined wellie boots, a coat, a dog blanket, fish and chip wrappings, half a dozen copies of the first edition of the new *Gazette* featuring his first-ever published photograph if you didn't count school exhibitions, and a watering can.

Tootling along the road back to town, he was grinning, well pleased with his morning.

Once home he developed the films. As the images slowly emerged from the chemical elixir, he felt a pleasure he could not put a name to but a pleasure he recognized. They were not newspaper shots—there were no people in them—but these were good. Wee Hec grinned so wide his gums were showing.

Rob walked into the reporters' room. He had slept through the May Day dawn. Joanne was on the phone.

"Yes." She held her hand to her lips to silence Rob. "Yes, I know the picture you mean, with the person running away from the fire. Really? You do? Can you give me his name? Really? Can I have your name? Can't you tell me who he is? I'll say it was an anonymous tip-off. Hello, hello ..." She was left with the dial tone.

"Rob ..." She started. The phone went again. "*Gazette.*"

McAllister walked in the door and bellowed at Rob. "What's this about you joining the Aberdeen paper? I've had someone on the line asking for a reference."

"I haven't made a decision." Rob sat staring at his typewriter, trying to not look guilty.

"I can't believe you went behind my back." McAllister was waving his cigarette; Rob was ducking the flying ash.

"I was going to tell you when I'd made a decision." Rob was furious at the *Press & Journal* for contacting McAllister without warning him first.

"Maybe I'll have to decide for you." McAllister pointed a nicotine-stained forefinger at Rob. "I can't abide disloyalty."

"McAllister," Joanne interrupted, "someone phoned in a tip

about the person in the photo on the front page, but wouldn't give their name."

"Fine. Fine. Later." He flapped his hands as though he was shooing hens from the vegetable garden.

She shrugged a well-I-did-tell-you look, and turned her back on the both of them. This was not a discussion she wanted any part of.

"I couldn't talk to you about it." Rob was near shouting. "You would've gone mental, like you're doing now."

The phone rang again. Joanne picked it up, listened, and at first she couldn't make sense of her mother-in-law. "Pardon? Fraser Munro? Yes. What? Oh no! Poor Mrs. Munro! Yes. We'll talk later." She put down the phone. "McAllister."

"I thought you were keen to be part of the new *Gazette.*" McAllister was still loud, still furious, still smoking like a kipper factory.

Rob was saying nothing, staring at a blank sheet of copy paper. Joanne was wondering if they had finished; she wanted to speak to McAllister. The phone went again. It was Patricia.

"Finish your cadetship here," McAllister was saying to Rob, "*then* I'll help you in the next step in your career. If you don't keep going behind my back that is."

Joanne was half listening to the argument and half listening to Patricia.

"I didn't." Rob stood. "There's no use talking to you sometimes." McAllister did not intimidate him and he had had enough.

Patricia's voice was faint, but her tone was calm.

"Patricia. Say that again!" As Joanne listened, her forehead wrinkled between her brows. Something made Rob stop to watch, McAllister too. They waited and the office was quiet as though someone had said "*shoosh!*"

"Where are you? Right. Of course. Call me whenever you need me." Joanne put the phone down. She turned to look first at Rob, then at McAllister.

"If you two have finished with the argy-bargy, I have some news."

Rob grinned. McAllister grinned back at him, then at her. In that instant, she thought, *That McAllister's a lovely looking man.*

They waited. She looked at the ceiling as though heaven would help her arrange her thoughts.

"I've had a tip-off about the person who threw the petrol bomb. . . ." she started.

"Great!" McAllister was pleased.

"One of the farmhands on the Ord Mackenzie estate has died, maybe been killed. . . ."

"Really?" Rob asked. "Who?"

"And Patricia's husband, Sandy Skinner, fell into the Falls of Foyers. He's dead."

Wee Hec burst in the door, waving some prints. "Wait till you see the pictures I took the day. Magic."

Hec was completely ignored. But he was used to that.

SEVEN

❦

McAllister sensed not to say it to Joanne, but it was another stroke of luck that the news came in before deadline and another coup for the *Gazette*. He gave Rob and Joanne and himself half an hour to make phone calls and called a news meeting for twelve.

"Hec, go to the Market Bar and fetch Mr. McLeod."

"They won't let me in." Hec was sulking in a corner, still put out that no one was interested in his pictures.

"Hector!" McAllister shouted.

When Hec found Don, he had to put up with his annoyance too. Don had just ordered a pint and could only swallow half of it before Hec's bleating forced him to leave.

Joanne made phone calls to Achnafern farm—no reply, to her mother-in-law—Mrs. Ross knew only that Fraser Munro was dead.

Rob called the police station—no statement was forthcoming. He called the procurator fiscal's office—the same.

McAllister started the meeting.

"No one looked at my pictures." Hector was petulant.

"Shut up, Hec," Don said, absentmindedly doodling on his spiral-bound notebook, a small, lined one from Woolworth's that fit into his jacket pocket. He was drawing prison bars.

"Let's start with the major news—Sandy Skinner. Joanne?"

"Can I go over everything from the beginning? There is so much happening."

"Fine."

She looked around, surprised that everyone was listening, waiting, as though her information and opinion mattered. She paused, looked at her notes and, even though she was shaken by all the news, tried to be as professional as possible.

"First there was the anonymous call about the figure in the picture on last week's front page. The person calling said he knew who it was. 'Ask Sandy Skinner,' he said, 'he knows who threw the petrol bomb.'"

She paused, no one interrupted.

"Next, Mrs. Ross, my mother-in-law, called to tell me Fraser Munro, who is the son of the Ord Mackenzie's housekeeper and whose father, Mr. Alistair Munro, is the foreman on the estate, was found dead this morning. My mother-in-law got the impression the death may not have been an accident."

She looked around. Everyone was making notes, waiting.

"Lastly, Patricia Ord Mackenzie, sorry, Skinner." Joanne remembered her annoyance when she picked up the phone to yet another call from Patricia. "She said there had been a terrible tragedy and her husband, Sandy Skinner, was dead."

"You'll never believe this," Patricia had announced, "but Sandy fell over the Falls of Foyers. He's dead. It is a terrible tragedy, I know, but accidents happen."

What a cliché, had been Joanne's immediate thought, *Don would never let that through.*

"Poor soul," said Mrs. Smart quietly, bowing her head in respect for the dead. She was the only one in the room thinking of Patricia, not of a front-page story.

"A body in the pool would've made a great picture."

"Shut up, Hec," McAllister told him. "Joanne, anything else?"

"Patricia called Angus McLean, and said she was on her way to the McLean house."

"What for?" Don looked mildly surprised at this information.

"People like Patricia get their solicitor to do every little thing." Rob knew from years of phone calls and summonses to his father—after hours, during meals—some clients expected their solicitor to drop everything and obey orders.

"Aye, but why your father's house, why no I'm the police station?" Don answered his own question. "I suppose being an Ord Mackenzie gets you different treatment."

"With Sandy gone, the tip-off about the person in Hec's picture is dead in the water," Rob said.

"We'll make a subeditor of you yet lad," Don nodded approval.

"The death of Fraser Munro will have to be a plain story at this stage, facts only," McAllister decided. "The same with Sandy Skinner unless there is any more information before deadline."

"Never mind, two deaths, same day, same farm, and the day before deadline. Great." Don started scribbling, trying to work it all into one short, sharp headline.

Everyone at the *Gazette* was aware of that feeling that sometimes enveloped a newsroom, the air charged as before a thunderstorm. Events were in motion, and they were the hunters after the story.

Rob and Joanne left to search for more information, Hector hurried off to bring a selection of photos for the front page, McAllister and Don went to the editor's office.

"Good timing, these stories." Don lit a cigarette, McAllister likewise.

"Aye." McAllister let out the first draw of cigarette smoke. "As usual, it's either feast or famine for the *Gazette*."

"You're not your usual cantankerous but in charge self."

"I've things on my mind."

"Aye, and it's getting obvious you fancy the lassie. So do

something or forget it. But don't be like me and spend thirty years doing nothing."

"I take it you're attempting to give me advice on my personal life."

"If you have one, outside of books and jazz and the weird films you like."

"Don, it's none of your business." McAllister was annoyed, and when annoyed, his voice would develop a growl, his lips would compress. When Don saw the warning signs, he would sometimes drop the subject, sometimes not.

"You're right, it's not my business—except when it interferes with the good running of this newspaper."

"She's married."

That made Don laugh. McAllister had the good grace to smile at himself.

"You could always arrange an accident," Don suggested. "It seems to be the favorable way out."

"Patricia Ord Mackenzie?"

"Who knows? What we do have are two deaths—same day, same farm. Also an anonymous phone call. Joanne is on the inside in both cases."

"Aye, but can she do it? It's a big story, she has no experience." McAllister was leaning, elbows on the table, hands clasped, thinking through the conundrum. "I get the feeling Patricia Ord Mackenzie is using Joanne."

"It could be an opportunity for her to learn how to be a cold, hard-bitten member of the press corps."

"Like you and me."

"Aye," Don agreed, "and my Highland instinct tells me these stories will run for a whiley, so we'll all be needed to join the dots."

The tall skinny editor and the short round deputy editor, one a Highlander, one a Glaswegian, entirely different in age, shape, education, opinions, shared one thing—a lust for the adrenaline of a newspaper.

The predawn start to the day and the morning's frantic events left Joanne sleepy and hungry and with no energy to cycle home for lunch. She bought a sandwich—a real extravagance for her—then walked up to the castle. She usually found solace sitting on a bench, watching the clouds and the river float past. Not today. Sandy Skinner's accident, Patricia's demands, the fear in her mother-in-law's voice, and her own fear that her new job was beyond her, were all jostling for attention.

Funny that, she thought, *how this morning's two hours of happiness are so quickly wiped out by thirty minutes of anxiety.*

She yawned. She stood. She stretched her arms wide. She rolled her shoulders. She walked back to the office, walked up the stairs, hadn't time to take off her coat before the phone rang.

"*Gazette.*" There was a pause on the line. "Patricia, I've been worried about you. Are you all right? What's happening? Where are you?"

"At the McLeans' house." Patricia sounded far away, as though she were calling from another country.

"At my house," Rob said as he came in.

"Of course I wouldn't mind," Joanne reassured Patricia. "I'll do it later this afternoon. You look after yourself. Bye."

"She has no need to look after *herself,*" Rob told Joanne. "She has everyone else looking after her."

"Who does?" McAllister came in.

"Patricia, the grieving widow," Rob told him. "She wanted me to bring the farm Land Rover into town. She left it at the Dores Inn after the *accident.*"

There was something in the way Rob said *accident,* something in the way he waggled his head when he referred to Patricia that Joanne didn't like. "I told Madame Ord Mackenzie that I had work to do," he continued, "but I bet she's inveigled Joanne into doing it."

"I offered," Joanne fibbed, although she had no idea how she could get to Dores and back and still be in time for the girls coming home from school.

"Both of you go now," McAllister said. "Joanne, when you're there, see if you can interview the landlady. Rob, you talk to the men who found the body. Off with you, I need the stories by the end of the day."

Joanne enjoyed the ride to Dores on the back of Rob's bike. For a short while, the shadows of uncertainty were blown away.

The road to the south side of Loch Ness followed the river out of town for a mile. It was a leafy journey through bright-green new growth and fern and roadside wildflowers. The trip was only fifteen miles, and she enjoyed every twist and turn. *It won't be such a nice journey back*, she thought, *driving an unsprung Land Rover instead of being a passenger on a shiny, red Triumph.*

At the small whitewashed inn, Joanne found the landlady and asked her if she would talk to the *Gazette*. The woman agreed, but she was in such a state of nerves, nothing she said made sense.

"It was terrible. That poor woman. On their honeymoon. The police. Terrible." The landlady spoke in statements, not joined-up conversation, and very little of what she said constituted a usable quote.

"She had enough sense to make me pay for Patricia's phone calls though," Joanne told Rob when they were back in the office, writing up their notes. "Since Dores is out of town, it came to four trunk calls. I can't exactly ask Patricia for my money back."

At first, the landlady had wanted payment for three calls.

"I know it was an emergency, but I have a business to run," the woman told Joanne. Then she remembered that Patricia had made a longer trunk call before she and Sandy had set off on the road to Foyers.

"The woman paid for their tea, but no the calls, so I'll have to charge ten shillings altogether."

Joanne used the last of her week's housekeeping money.

Rob was equally frustrated. He went out to the edge of the loch to talk to the man who had retrieved the body from the falls. He could barely get a word out of the man.

"Aye" was all that the landlady's husband said to everything. Then he would step back, cast his rod, and continue staring out across Loch Ness.

"When did you hear about the accident?" Rob started.

The man shrugged.

"How did you retrieve the body?"

The man said nothing, staring at the water.

"He was dead when you got to him?"

"Aye." Another cast into the loch.

"So you brought him back here?"

"Aye."

"You didn't wait for the police to arrive before fishing out the body?"

That elicited a glare from the fisherman.

It was only later in the newsroom, when he and Joanne were exchanging stories, that Rob remembered.

"You know, the landlady's husband was no fisherman. Even I know it was the wrong type of rod for Loch Ness. I don't even know if there are fish in Loch Ness, the monster has probably eaten everything."

"He was probably trying to escape from his wife," she said. "She babbles on like a burn when the snow's melted, and makes as much sense."

"That would explain why the man only grunts and shrugs."

"Driving that rattletrap was really uncomfortable. You should have let me take the bike."

"Someone from the farm should have picked up the Land Rover. But I suppose it was too much for Patricia to think of that."

"Rob McLean." Joanne leaned over and cuffed him on the shoulder, "Patricia's husband had just died. . . . And Fraser Munro . . ."

They looked at each other.

"As Don pointed out, two men from Achnafern Estate on the Black Isle died on the same day." Rob started to bang out the words on his typewriter. "Maybe they will be buried on the same day too. It's a great story." He grinned at Joanne.

She had to agree. Great story.

Mid-afternoon, and Detective Inspector Dunne was about to begin the formal interview with Patricia at the police station.

He was not in awe of Patricia Ord Mackenzie. At least he didn't think he was. He had allowed the initial interview to be held at the house of Angus McLean, the solicitor, because Patricia was pregnant. It had nothing to do with her father's friendship with the chief constable.

"We will be as brief as we can, Mrs. Skinner, but I need to cover all the details so I can finish my report to the procurator fiscal."

Patricia had introduced herself as Ord Mackenzie. The inspector put that down to grief and addressed her as Mrs. Skinner.

"Of course. And I'd like the formalities over and done with so I can go home."

"You and your husband left home early."

She gave a watery smile, her nose red. But her eyes seemed untroubled. Or perhaps it was the light. "We went through this earlier."

"Please bear with me, you were distressed. The sooner I get the sequence of events clear, the sooner the procurator fiscal can make his recommendation to the fatal accident inquiry."

And I need answers before you retreat to the safety of your mother, father, solicitor, chief constable, and family name, he thought.

"Of course. Sorry." She brought her handkerchief up to her eyes.

WPC Ann McPherson was watching Patricia's every move, *as a good police officer should,* she told herself, and couldn't shake the feeling that this was all a performance.

"We left before dawn." Patricia spoke slowly, making it easy for Ann and DI Dunne to make notes. "We were taking a de-layed honeymoon. Being May Day, we stopped at the Clootie Well on the Black Isle. Sandy's idea."

"There were people there who saw you?"

"Yes. But no one I know." Patricia stopped. Sniffed. Started again. "We drove to town then, along the south side of the river towards Loch Ness. We stopped at the Dores Inn for tea, as I was feeling sick. After we left, we stopped near the Falls of Foyers because I was sick again. Sandy said since we were there anyway, he'd go and look at the Falls—he'd never seen them before."

He went to look at the Falls because we'd been fighting and he couldn't stand the sight and sound of my retching, Patricia remem-bered. But she was not going to mention that to anyone.

"I stayed in the car. I'm in a delicate condition, you know." She smiled at him.

Inspector Dunne was annoyed by the way she was trying to gain sympathy and ignored this.

"When he didn't return, what did you do?"

"I told you, I went down the path, but only a few yards—it was so slippery and dangerous. So I went back and waited nearly an hour. By then, I was really worried, so I drove to Dores."

"Why not get help in Foyers? Dores is a much longer drive."

"I wasn't thinking clearly." Patricia put a hand on her forehead. "I'm sorry. Could I have a glass of water, please?"

"Would you like some tea?" Ann McPherson offered.

"Oh, no," Patricia replied. "I don't want to put you to any trouble."

"You drove back to the Dores Inn, not to Foyers, which is nearer," Inspector Dunne continued.

"I panicked. I had no idea in which direction I was driving."

"What time did you arrive there?"

"I'm not sure. The people at the Inn will know. I told them I was worried, so the landlady's husband and another man went off to look for Sandy. When they came back, they told me Sandy was dead. He'd fallen into the falls, they said, and they found him in the pool at the bottom. He was caught up in a fallen tree."

Good job too, they had told her, otherwise he might have been swept into the loch and may not have been found for weeks, if ever.

"Thank you, Mrs. Skinner. I will let you know when we need to speak to you again." DI Dunne was polite and left no doubt as to who was in charge.

When they were alone the inspector asked, "Well, WPC McPherson, what do you think?"

She was startled. Never before, in five years as a policewoman, had any of her superiors asked her for her opinion.

"I . . ."

"How did she seem to you?"

"Calm, no, in charge."

"I expect that's her upbringing."

"Yes." Ann McPherson looked at her notes. "I'm not sure I got the time sequence right."

"No. I don't think Patricia Ord Mackenzie, as she prefers to be known, did either." DI Dunne waited, wanting to hear more.

The policewoman hesitated, not sure if she should venture the obvious question, then asked, "Why did she drive all the way back to Dores, probably twenty minutes away, when Foyers is less than a mile?"

"Yes. That is the question, isn't it?" His grey eyes looked thoughtful. "So far, there is only one witness—the widow. Unless anyone comes forward, there is only her version."

They were silent for a moment.

"Type up the notes. We'll talk again later."

As she left, Ann felt the thrill of being involved in a real case, not just sent out to comfort the bereaved, break up domestic disputes, and make tea for the lads.

"He's treating me like a real policeman."

Rob volunteered to babysit her girls so Joanne could visit Patricia. He did not say it, but he was pleased to get out of the house.

There was an air of jollity when Joanne came into the sitting room. Margaret McLean had been liberal with the gin and tonic, and Patricia was flushed, laughing at some remark of Margaret's.

"Look who's here," a more than slightly sloshed Patricia greeted her. "Perfect mother and now star reporter as well."

"Why thank you," Joanne laughed and curtsyed. The remark was said jokingly she knew, but it hurt. "How are you? Exhausted, I'm sure."

Patricia remembered her manners. "Yes, I am. The reality hasn't sunk in. And I've just been told the news about Fraser Munro. Poor Mrs. M." She turned to Margaret. "Thank you so much for offering me a bed for the night, I don't think I could manage the drive home."

"Absolutely no need to thank us," Margaret said. "Anyone would have done the same."

"Not that I've noticed," Patricia replied.

Margaret, who knew Janet Ord Mackenzie, did not contradict her.

Joanne was not surprised that Mrs. Ord Mackenzie had not come to comfort her daughter, but she was shocked that Patricia had been left to drive herself home.

I will never judge her harshly again, she vowed.

When they had been at boarding school, she and Joanne compared parents. It was almost a competition to see which of them had the coldest mother and the most distant father. They swapped stories of epic silences, of disdain and disapproval, and gothic tales of being left alone to sleep in unlit, unheated bedrooms, down dark hallways, far distant from their parents' rooms. All this for five-year-olds. No wonder they both enjoyed the escape to boarding school.

"Would you excuse me?" Patricia looked at Joanne. "It's been a dreadfully long day, I really need to lie down."

"Do you need anything?" Joanne asked as she rose to leave.

"Thanks, Joanne. You're a true friend. I'm exhausted. I shall sleep like the . . . God! How awful. I was going to say 'sleep like the dead.' This is still so unreal."

"Of course."

"I remind myself of the baby. He needs me. That will get me through. You know, the really terrible part of it all is that I wished Sandy dead—only for a moment or so when he was rowing with Mummy. And now he is." She stopped, sobbed a strange, dry, deep, half-sob, half-gasp.

Joanne came over and sat on the sofa next to Patricia, taking her hand, stroking it as she would if Wee Jean had fallen over or if Annie had had a bad dream. Margaret McLean saw it was time to leave the friends to themselves.

"It took only a few days to discover he was a liar, that he had only married me because he thought he could get his hands on my family's money. The marriage would have been a nightmare." Patricia spoke quietly, her voice flat-tired, emotion-drained. "For years I had been determined not to make the same mistakes as you. Then I found myself in exactly your situation."

Joanne couldn't see the connection, apart from them both being pregnant before the wedding.

Patricia rambled on. "When I found out you had to get married, I was amazed. You were always so in control. Always so certain of the path your life would take. School, university, you wanted to be a teacher, make a respectable marriage, maybe a wife of the Kirk like your sister. When I heard the news of you marrying beneath you, marrying a soldier, and with a baby on the way, I laughed. I was pleased that you had found a way out. Pleased that you had managed to spit in the eye of all those respectable Presbyterian expectations."

Patricia absently picked at a loose thread in the hem of her cardigan.

"It was a few years before I uncovered what had been happening to you. A bit of gossip here and there made me wonder. Your visits to the emergency ward were not unnoticed. After all, your mother-in-law is from the Black Isle, so there were bound to be whispers. Not that *you* would ever let on, and we were all too polite to mention it. I'm sorry," Patricia said, looking closely at her friend. "I should have done more. Been a better friend."

Joanne was silent, shocked at her friend's version of her life.

"Now my Sandy is dead," Patricia continued. "I didn't want that to happen. I really didn't." She looked up at Joanne. "I'm too tired even to cry," she joked. Then the tears came. "Help me through this, Joanne. Help me. Please."

Joanne stroked Patricia's hand, muttered all the soothing sounds she would use to her children, a mix of "there there" and "now now," and "it will be all be allright," and she was certain it would be allright, for Patricia.

EIGHT

Cycling home from the McLeans' bungalow under a night sky so thick with stars, she thought they resembled the holes in a kitchen colander. Joanne smiled at such a prosaic comparison.

Her legs ached, she was brightly awake with tiredness, all she could think about was bed.

When Joanne arrived home, Rob wheeled his motorbike down the street before starting it. He knew she did not want to alert the neighbors to her late night.

She was putting out the milk bottles on the step for the pre-dawn delivery when a dark figure standing in the shadow at the side of the doorstep stepped out into the light.

"Bill!" She jumped, almost dropping the bottles.

"What the hell have you been up to?"

She could smell him before she saw him. Her husband.

"You've been drinking," he snarled, as he stepped forward and she stepped back, grabbing the door for support. "Leaving my bairns with a stranger while you go off with your fancy man. You're nothing but a common hoor."

"Leave me alone." She slapped him, hard and loud, too outraged to fear the consequences. Breathing whisky and hatred, he grabbed her wrists, squeezing so tight she twisted in pain.

"You hit me, Bill, and I will go to the police. I told you before. I mean it." She tried to control her voice, not to show fear.

"You're my wife. I can do what I like."

And with that, he let go of her hands and punched her hard in the stomach. She doubled up, vomiting on the grass. He stood over her, kicking with a vicious malice, kicking her ribs, her back, her thighs. He couldn't stop. She couldn't find the breath to scream. A dog started to bark. The neighbors' porch light came on.

"Is everything all right, Joanne dear?" came the voice of the lady next door.

Joanne could barely reply. Only moan.

"Mind your own bloody business," Bill shouted.

"I'm calling the police," came the frightened reply.

Bill stopped. He bent down and whispered in Joanne's ear.

"If you say one word to the police, I'll go for a divorce. I'll stand up in court and tell everyone about you opening your legs for that bastard McAllister. Then we'll see who's on the front page. Everyone knows you were easy once, and they'll believe you're easy now." He gave her one final shove. Her head struck the concrete of the path. "And I'll get the girls off you." He shouted, "They'll no give bairns to a hoor."

Then he was gone.

When the call came in, the sergeant on the nightshift alerted WPC Ann McPherson, knowing they were friends. When Joanne left in the ambulance, the policewoman called Joanne's father- and mother-in-law and the girls were taken to their house in a police car. All Granddad Ross could think about was the children. His wife worried about the children too, but her main worry was the scandal.

At seven the next morning, Ann McPherson called McAllister.

"This is a totally off-the-record call from a friend. Joanne won't be in for work today. She's hurt." The policewoman told him Joanne was in the Infirmary, but would probably be released later that day.

"I'll be right over."

"I don't think it is a good idea for you to see her. . . ." But McAllister had already hung up the phone.

He was at the Infirmary car park in fifteen minutes. He found the ward, but Joanne was curtained off in a private cocoon.

"Three cracked ribs. She was lucky." The house doctor saw the look on McAllister's face. "Sorry, I should rephrase that."

"No. I know what you meant."

WPC Ann McPherson saw McAllister waiting outside in the corridor and walked up to him.

"Bill?" McAllister queried.

She took his arm. "Let's go out into the garden. I need to talk to you."

"And I need a cigarette."

They sat on a bench, huddled up in their overcoats. Snow had been forecast for hills above one thousand feet.

"McAllister, it's complicated."

"No, it's not. He beat her. Badly it seems."

"I know. He thinks he can get away with it because they are married." Her face was a picture of pity mixed with contempt.

"Will she press charges?"

"It's complicated."

"For God's sake," he was almost shouting, "what do we do? Wait until she is killed?"

"I know, but it is her choice." She put her hand on his arm as she said this, as much to control him as to comfort him. Ann was a tall woman, athletic. She could hold him back if she had to. She pointed to her uniform. "Don't let this get in the way—I'm talking as a friend."

"Aye," he muttered, and cupped his hands around the matches to light another cigarette.

"You must have attended enough Magistrate's Court hearings to know that in household violence, no one wants to prosecute. It's one person's word against another's," she continued. "Husband versus wife. For the woman, all sorts of allegations and innuendos will be made, and mud sticks. For example, Joanne sometimes goes to a public bar."

She held up her hands when he tried to protest. "I know, I know, with her colleagues, in the respectable saloon bar, but a bar nonetheless."

There was nothing he could say. He knew the truth in Ann's words.

"She works full-time, leaving her poor, defenseless children with their grandparents at least one night a week . . ." Ann McPherson was making a case from the procurator fiscal's point of view, "when her husband has made it clear she has no need to work. Also," the policewoman paused, unsure how McAllister would react, "Bill Ross is saying Joanne left her husband to take up with another man."

"What? I never knew that." His sudden look at her betrayed a stab of hurt.

"Well you should, because her husband is saying that man is you."

"That's nonsense."

"So what? Some people will always believe the worst. McAllister, if Joanne brings charges, he will sue for divorce, naming you as co-respondent. He'll ask for sole custody of the girls, out of spite. He has told her this. And I've a bad feeling he might win. Most people don't take kindly to women who have jobs and wear trousers. I've seen it happen before," Ann said.

"So have I" was all he could say. "So have I."

"So no visiting the patient, for her sake," Ann McPherson

advised. She also knew how deeply ashamed Joanne would be if McAllister saw her huddled, defeated form curled up in a hospital bed.

I'll never understand, Ann thought, *why battered women feel it is somehow their fault.*

John McAllister was a man given to thinking. Politics, philosophy, literature, the state of the natural and unnatural world, all fascinated him. He had an inquisitive, inquiring nature, well-suited to a journalist.

He used to joke, "I know a little about an awful lot, but not an awful lot about anything."

He leaned on the railing on the edge of the riverbank, watching the water flow, thinking. Joanne's situation pained him deeply. His feelings for her scared him. This senseless beating reminded him of all the intellectual discussions he had had over a beer or two with colleagues in Glasgow. Violence toward women was accepted, and even the worst stories never ran to more than a line or two—except when the woman died. All the journalists knew that. And the police.

A newspaper was a great place to be a bright young thing. Many of them became aging reactionary hacks in the end. Or drunks. But it was *the* place to be an idealistic young man. Or woman. Newspapers had a surprisingly large proportion of women working for them. In the Glasgow paper where he had trained, many a time he and his colleagues had laughed at the way a paternalistic Presbyterian rigid class-structured society treated women. But for the women, it was no joke.

Marriage failure was not an option, not when you had promised to love and of course obey, "till death do us part."

For a woman, the scandal of a divorce was so absolute that

few would choose that path. Many a divorced woman endured monetary disadvantage, being thrown out of the family home, and losing their children if they had dared to take another man.

For the husband, divorce left a question mark, and not much else.

Not everyone can be as lucky as Patricia Ord Mackenzie in their marital problems, he said to himself. *An accident. An easy way out. Knowing the folks I know in Glasgow, that option is certainly possible.* He laughed at the idea to hide the knowledge it was something he would contemplate.

This woman is so implanted in my mind I'm considering violence. The thought disturbed him.

He threw his cigarette into the river, and set off on the walk home, on the long but scenic route. He was a great believer in walking to clear the head.

On the Infirmary footbridge, he was buffeted by strong, icy gusts heading in from the North Sea. He strode along the footpath beside the river, passing the back gardens of the substantial houses lining this part of the riverbank. He headed up the steep steps that led to the upper part of the town. At the top of the escarpment, he stopped. There to the northeast, still in a mantle of snow, Ben Wyvis loomed big and squat over the Black Isle and the firths and the glens and the towns and the villages.

The lochs, trapped in the long, narrow glen by bleak and beautiful mountains, ended in an equally grand manner on the west coast. They could not be seen, but their presence, their geography, made the town what it is. And the people what they are.

What is it about this place, McAllister thought? *At first you believe it is a quiet, respectable, innocuous community. Yet underneath, the currents run as deep as Loch Ness itself.*

✦   ✦   ✦

It was noon and Rob had the office to himself. He was not pleased at the death of Sandy Skinner. It meant the death of his story. So much had surfaced on both east and west coasts about Sandy Skinner's affairs, and together they all had the makings of a good piece of investigative journalism.

Rob was also unhappy at the state of his relationship with McAllister. His anger, quite unjustified Rob thought, rankled. He had not even given him the chance to explain. A phone call from Aberdeen pressing him for a decision had come five minutes ago, triggering his discontent.

"Can I have two weeks?" Rob had asked.

"You're no that special," the voice on the end of the line had said. "But I like your cheek. I'll give you one week."

Rob looked up and jumped when he saw McAllister looming in the doorway. Expecting the editor to continue the argument about his career, Rob was taken aback at the sight of his face.

The Grim Reaper looks more cheerful, he thought, but for once he kept his flippant thoughts to himself.

"I need you to take over the news stories," McAllister said. "Joanne fell off her bike and cracked a rib. She won't be in for a couple of days." He was gone before Rob could ask any more.

Rob started to lift the telephone to call his mother. But his mother probably knew no more than he did.

Poor Joanne, he thought, *for her yesterday started at four-thirty in the morning, then there was all the excitement in the newsroom. . . .* He started to make a list of calls he should make to confirm some points on the Munro death.

She had a drink last night, but probably a small one knowing her. . . .

He next listed the calls to be made for an update on Sandy Skinner's death.

Then to fall off her bike.

He rolled a piece of copy paper into his machine, typed one half-sentence, then stopped.

But she was fine when I left her house.

Now he was seriously worried.

Fell off a bicycle, walked into a door, fell down the stairs—the oldest excuses in the book.

He leaned back in his chair and sighed.

Joanne, it's simple. Take him to court, have him locked away.

And to his twenty-one-year-old thinking, it *was* that simple.

NINE

Few on the Black Isle had telephones. Not everyone read newspapers. The radio broadcast little local content. Yet news of the two deaths would fly around the farms, the villages, the town, and the county as though borne in the wind.

That May Day morning had been bright in old-gold sunshine, but a raw, blustery wind swept over Achnafern Farm, over the fields, through the woods, along the beaches, into every crack and crevice of the solid-built stone farmhouses and cottages, and through the narrow streets and lanes of the villages of the isle that isn't an island. The Black Isle, a peninsula bound by two firths, was an island of the mind, the communities smaller islands, and the farms outcrops in a landscape that had a distinct geography of place and character.

On the land, below the ridge of dark, black-green pine forest, fields made a plaid of winter wheat, bright green, contrasting with the enclosures of dark, fallow earth where the previous year's crop, tatties, grew. On these bare fields a line of men made a slow, steady progress, gathering another seasonal crop, stones.

The men worked as they lived, the demarcation line between them unnoticed—Travelers to one side of the tractor, farm hands to the other.

"A great crop this year," one said.

"Aye," came the reply, an upward twist of the head signaled agreement, and the word was spoken on the indrawn breath.

Allie Munro, being the foreman, was not expected to join

them, and the men on the farm had given up expecting Fraser Munro. Walking, bending, steadily gathering the stones, throwing the new crop into the bogie, matching their pace to the Fordson Major tractor stuck in low, low gear, which hardly needed driving.

To a farming community, that mysterious crop—the stones—was accepted as part of the agricultural cycle. Children might fantasize about giant earthworms burrowing deep, throwing up the stones to clear their dens. The educated could speculate on the soil's deep layers on a stratum of rock from some distant, Precambrian period and the volcanic upheaval that created the Great Glen, or "fault line," to give it the correct geological name. To most, the stones were just an inevitable part of the farming cycle.

"When's Fraser due back to the regiment?" one of the farmhands asked.

The scare from the Suez Crisis was on everyone's mind.

"He's done a ten-year stint. Been in Malaya an' all. Maybe he's had enough." This was from Old Archie, being kind.

"A hero such as him'll be raring to go back," one of the Traveler lads taunted.

"The missus is happy to have her lad at home." This came from Allie Munro's neighbor as they were sitting in the lee of the tractor, eating their sandwiches, or "pieces," drinking hot sweet tea from a thermos flask. The Travelers—"tinkers" to all but themselves—took their break separately and had a fire going on the banks of the burn.

All the men had grown up on the same farm, as had their fathers and grandfathers for generations back. They were known collectively by their farm name, such as Mackenzie of Ardochter, McIntyre of Knockbain, Fraser of Kilmorack. The tilling of the fields, the clearing of the ditches, the naming of every nook and cranny, every woodland, every burn —that was their connection to the land.

The Traveling people of Scotland—the same families turning up at the same time of year, on the same farms every year—had their own, deep connection with the land. Their names were ancient: Stuart, McPhee, Williamson, Macdonald, Macmillan. Their campsites, horse fairs, the best stretches of the rivers for pearl gathering—that was their blood heritage. These places, always picturesque, where their ancestors had gathered and traded for centuries, were sacred to the Traveling people. Their ancient culture of stories and singing and piping, their nomadic way of life, marked them as different, yet they were as much a part of Scotland as the glens and lochs and mountains.

As for the lairds, most felt that their lineage made them more than just landowners; they were stewards of their inheritance.

"There she goes!" A cry went up from the tinkers. Zigzagging across the plowed earth, a hare, her grey-brown, earth-colored coat making her hard to see, darted off. But not far, the lure of the nest kept her close.

"Leave her be," shouted Old Archie, "she's got young."

This didn't deter the tinkers. Hunting for hare was their birthright. The three of them made a wide circle around the doe, one lining up his catapult for a shot at the frantic beast. He missed. The spectators cheered the hare, now running in dizzy circles, desperate to distract danger from her leverets.

Closer the men got, closing the gaps in the circle. With no young to distract her, the hare would have been long gone. Another slingshot went wide. The farm boys laughed. Thumping the soil, they set up a distraction. This time the slingshot hit, the stunned doe stumbled and tumbled. Like a lightning strike, a tinker lad was on her. The scream, like a seagull, like a child, made no difference. A quick chop to the neck and she was gone.

"Unsporting, that," said Auld Archie as he screwed the top back on his thermos flask. "But that's tinkers for you."

In the distance came the sound of a car driving too fast along the farm road. Archie shaded his eyes with one hand and squinted into the distance. "Thon's the doctor's car," he said, sounding worried. A doctor, driving fast, was not good. The men waited, but the car disappeared in the small wood between them and the farmhouse. They turned back to work. A vague anxiety hovered over them. *What was happening? Who might it be? A wife? A bairn?* Farm accidents were all too common.

A few minutes later, the local bobby's car came at an equally fast pace. Now everyone was really anxious, even the tinker boys.

"I'll away and see if there's anything up," Auld Archie decided. "But you boys get back to it, the stanes'll no clear themselves."

It was an hour before Archie returned with the news; Fraser Munro had breathed his last on the farm of his birth.

When the *Highland Gazette* came out that week, it sold out. Every word was read, reread, and dissected. The bare bones of the two deaths were there, but no details. Accidents? Or worse? No one knew, but plenty had opinions.

To the farming community, Sandy Skinner's death was a shock, but he was not one of them. Fishing and farming communities seldom mixed. But he was married to Patricia Ord Mackenzie, and she and her family were almost royalty in the community. And the manner of his death was as spectacular as the Falls of Foyers themselves.

Fraser Munro's death was equally fascinating. Many a conversation started with the phrase, "I know it doesn't do to speak ill o' the dead, but . . ."

The remark heard most often, in the post office, in the local shop, in the cottages and farm kitchens, and in the byres and pubs was "Two deaths on the same day, on the same farm—you'd hardly credit it, would you?"

Every move the police made—every stone they examined, the ditch they cleared, the burn they dragged, every interview they conducted—was discussed and dissected. There were those close to the events who said little, those distant from the events who professed a knowledge they did not have. There were those who found gratification discussing other people's sorrow, and those who felt nothing but sadness for Mr. and Mrs. Munro.

At Achnafern farmhouse, the curtains were drawn, the mirrors covered, and Mrs. Munro felt herself a guest in her own house. She sat, unable to rise from the chair in the seldom-used sitting room. Neighbors came in and out in waves, bringing food, making tea. Murmured condolences, whispered lamentations, made as much impact on her as the distant sound of the sea rising and falling on the pebble shore.

Allie Munro felt like a doorman. He would greet the callers, shake hands, usher them into the sitting room, sit around uncomfortably for ten minutes or so, accept the stilted phrases of condolence, then usher the visitors out. Often he would meet the next round on the doorstep.

Allie Munro had not yet told his wife of Sandy Skinner's death. By evening, he thought, *may as well tell her, she's numb. Another piece of bad news can't make it any worse than losing her firstborn.*

She greeted the news of Patricia's loss quietly.

"An accident. Poor Patricia," she said when her husband told her. An accident was in the great scheme of things, and could be accepted. Mrs. Munro spoke in slow, quiet bursts. It was taking every ounce of energy to find breath to ask, "Our Fraser . . . I was wondering . . . the police seemed to be thinking . . . surely they're mistaken . . . it's no possible . . . maybe . . . an accident . . . ?"

Allie Munro was not one for words. Nor gestures. He had no idea how to comfort his wife. When emotions surfaced, he dealt with them by chopping firewood. When his wife had given birth, both times, he had chopped enough firewood to see them through the winter.

The police had indicated there was something untowards about Fraser's death. They were asking questions of everyone on the farm and many in the village. It annoyed Allie that some of the local gossips had let his wife know about it.

"It's their job, lass. The police have to look at everything, then put in a report to the procurator fiscal. No use thinking about it. All we can do is wait."

Allie Munro was good at that. He knew how to wait out the snow, and the rain. He would wait for the exact day to mow the hay, or harvest the barley, or lift the tatties.

"It was good of the missus to come with Mr. Ord Mackenzie to offer their condolences. I didn't expect that," Mr. Munro said. He wanted to talk about anything other than the police.

"Always had good manners, the missus," his wife replied. "Good of Patricia to call over too—in spite of her own troubles."

Allie stood. "If you're fine on your own, I'll away out to check the fields."

"I'll be glad of some time to myself." Agnes Munro needed to wash up the visitors' cups, to clean the kitchen, to wash anything that did or didn't need washing.

It was too fresh for them to reminisce. Remembering him as a boy, remembering him before it had all gone sour—that would come. The slow erosion of the bad memories, to be replaced by the good ones—that would surely take place. But not yet.

Allie Munro walked the farm boundaries, checking a gate, looking over the cattle, pulling a stalk of barley to rub between his fingers. Thoughts came and went, welcome and otherwise.

He walked to the foot of a hill that gave him a view of the whole of Achnafern Estate created by the marriage of Miss Janet Ord and Mr. Iain Mackenzie.

Mostly this was an arrangement that worked; couples married and grew to like each other. Although he would never put it into words, Allie felt there was little affection in the Ord Mackenzie household.

Patricia could have suffered, but no, she's grown into a fine lass, he thought. He was proud of the girl he and his wife had raised until she was sent off to boarding school, and now, with his help, she was one of the best farmers hereabouts.

Not that I blame the missus was his next thought as he crossed the bridge over the burn. *Mrs. Ord Mackenzie was right sick after the twins were born,* he remembered, *then the wee boy dying, and her being in hospital all that time with her nerves. When she came home, well after Patricia's first birthday, the wee lass wouldn't go near her, crying for Agnes, calling her "Ma," refusing to go to her real mother. What a to-do that had been,* he remembered.

He moved on, following the burn, stopping to check the progress of the tatties. Golden Wonder potatoes were growing in this field—Allie's favorite. The crop was healthy, no sign of blight. It reminded him of his favorite hymn,

"We plow the fields and scatter,

The good seed on the land. . . ."

When Allie returned to the farmyard, he could see his wife in the kitchen window; the lights outlined her shape as she stood at the sink, staring into the distance, not moving. He grieved for her. It was then that he realized that in his walk around the estate, a whole hour nearly, he had not once grieved for his son who was now lying in the morgue.

The local policeman met the two detectives from Dingwall at the village hotel.

The landlord was the first to be interviewed. He gave his statement to the detective from the town reluctantly. In spite of being the landlord of a small hotel and bar, he did not like nor trust strangers.

"Aye," said the landlord, a man in his middle forties with about the same number of hairs on his head. "This is where Fraser drank." He was polishing glasses as he spoke. *What a stupid question,* he thought, *where else would Fraser drink?"*

"Was there any trouble the night Fraser died?" The detective asked, knowing there was no confirmation when Fraser had died. The early hours of the morning was the best guess.

"Not in here."

"That's not what I've been told."

"There was a few words, maybe."

"Who was arguing?"

"I never said arguing, a wee bit of a disagreement more like."

Detective Sergeant Wilkie too was middle-aged, and it showed in a face permanently set in a sour, disappointed frown. He had been posted here from Edinburgh, to what he thought of as the ends of the earth. His wife was from the Highlands and loved it. He hated it. He hated the people even more, and this was from a man who had been here eleven years.

"Answer the question or I'll have a word with the licensing board," he told the landlord.

The landlord shrugged, held up a glass, saw that it was shining-clear and started on another.

"The disagreement, the argument, whatever you want to call it . . ." the detective continued.

"I was busy, I didn't notice." *I'm not here to do your job for you,* the landlord was thinking, *and whatever happened to Fraser Munro, it's good riddance to bad rubbish.*

The landlord's wife was less discrete. It helped that her questioner was a local man, promoted to detective constable. She had known him as a boy and always said he had done well for himself.

"It's yourself young Davey. Or should I say *Detective* Grant? I'm always saying you've done well for yourself."

"Thank you, Mrs. Duncan. I need to ask you a few questions about the night Fraser died."

Knowing the woman well, the detective constable settled in for quite a session. The smell of stale beer and cigarettes made him long for one of each, but knew, with the detective sergeant there, his chances were nil.

"This is a respectable house, you know," Mrs. Duncan started. "We never have any problems. At least none we can't handle ourselves."

"The night Fraser died, what time did he come in?"

"The back o' six, maybe. I came in at half past and he was here at the bar."

"Did you hear him have words with anyone?"

"No more than usual." She saw by the constable's face and his fierce scribbling that she had said something important. "I mean, we did have a wee bit o' trouble wi' him an' his tongue. . . ."

"And his fighting?"

"Once or twice. But they were no really fights, drunken dancing with a few punches and kicks more like." She stopped, looked across at the closed shutters of the bar, worried that her husband might be there listening. He'd told her to hold her tongue with the police . . . but this was Davey, one of their own.

"Did you ever throw Fraser out of the bar?"

"Well, we did bar him, but it was only the once . . . no, twice. It's his father and his poor mother I feel sorry for. A right nice family they are. Allie Munro was born on that farm, and their Fraser was aye on about how he hated it, and hated the Ord Mackenzies." Mrs. Duncan leaned forward and dropped her voice to that hush usually used to describe a serious medical condition. "He wasn't the same since he came back from his regiment."

"So who was he having words with that night?"

"All the usual, the farm boys, the tinkers, anyone in earshot." She rattled off the names of two McPhee brothers and three of the lads from Achnafern Farm. "Aye, Fraser was going on about them all being mammy's boys, no real men, but no one took much notice." She shrugged, as though it was all nothing.

But DC Grant knew it was a nothing that could have led to Fraser's death.

"Was there any more than words?"

"It got a wee bit heated, so my husband threw them all out and after that I didn't see much. I heard a bit o' yelling from outside, but boys will be boys, nothing wrong in a wee bit o' fisty-cuffs—as long as it doesn't get out of hand." She realized what she had said and suddenly put her hands to her mouth in a half-prayer. "But it must have got out of hand, mustn't it?"

"Thank you, Mrs. Duncan." The policeman closed his notebook, satisfied. This was a good witness—respectable and indiscreet.

Next came the questioning of the lads from the farm. Faced with three men ages seventeen to twenty-three—three locals all born to families who had worked Achnafern Estate for generations, who collectively saw nothing, knew nothing, and supplied the minimum of information in grunts and "ayes" and "Aa canny mind"—DS Wilkie should have known better and handed over the questioning to the local policeman.

DC Grant had been at school with the oldest, knew the families of the other two, but no, the sergeant was in charge and he made sure everyone knew it. When it was time to head back to the police station, Grant was amazed to hear that the case had been solved.

"There was a fight outside the hotel, right?" DS Wilkie asked. His constable knew this was a rhetorical question and stood almost at attention, saying nothing.

"The tinker boys, Jimmy McPhee's brothers, had a fight with Fraser Munro. Right?" The sergeant spat out the name Jimmy McPhee.

Again the detective constable knew better than to speak.

"So there's the answer. One of the punches led to Munro's death, so it's manslaughter. Right?"

The smug look on the sergeant's face, the way he rubbed his hands congratulating himself on solving the case, made DC Davey Grant extremely uneasy, but he knew there was no questioning his boss once he had reached a decision. The investigation was closed.

Ten

◢

After two years in the local solicitor's office, Calum Sinclair had a deserved reputation as a bright young man—even a partnership was possible. One day. It would be a good opportunity, one of his tutors had advised when asked an opinion on the offer of a job in the small Highland town.

"Calum, you're one of my best students, but without family connections, you'd be lost in the city. Just another clerk in a law office," his professor had said.

From a small Caithness town, perched right on the northernmost coast of Scotland, to Edinburgh University to study law as a scholarship student, he was now a junior in a respectable solicitors' office.

Not a tall man, he gave the impression of reliability. Perhaps it was his strong jaw and his cheekbones, which looked as though they had been sculpted by the relentless wind of his home county.

For the first year in the Highlands, Calum Sinclair questioned his decision almost weekly. To say that he was bored would be understating the tedium of a small-town solicitor's life. Now there was the prospect of an intriguing case and even more intriguing clients.

The visit from Jimmy McPhee was causing interest in the office. Mr. Cameron, the senior partner in the firm, had no problem having a Traveler for a client.

"His money is as good as anyone else's," he replied when Calum had raised the matter.

This was not the opinion of some of the office staff.

"Whoever heard of a tinker getting a solicitor?" had been the reaction of the secretary.

The police, and all too often the law, treated Travelers differently. Prejudice against them was as deep as the prejudice against the Romany, and everyone now knew what had happened to them during the Second World War.

Calum Sinclair knew that if the McPhee brothers were charged with complicity in the death of Fraser Munro, he would have to allow for this in his defense strategy.

"So what charges could the polis bring?" Jimmy McPhee asked as soon as he was comfortable in the visitor's chair, only an arm's length across a narrow desk from Calum. The smallness of the room was made bearable by the view to the hills and mountain beyond.

"Mr. McPhee . . ."

"Call me Jimmy, everyone does." Jimmy's grin was so cheeky Calum couldn't help smiling back.

"You said on the phone that the police are looking for your brothers to question them in relation to Fraser Munro's death. Why do you think they will be charged?"

Jimmy's grin became a glower and Calum saw just why people were intimidated by him.

"We're tinkers. That's cause enough for some people."

Calum waited.

"And I have my sources."

"Mr. McPhee . . ." Calum Sinclair started.

"Jimmy."

"Fine—Jimmy—so if they are charged, and you want me to represent your brothers, I'll need some background on what happened."

Jimmy gave a brief account of the night Fraser Munro died.

Calum wrote quickly on a legal pad in his personal shorthand. "Your brothers were drinking in the hotel bar. Do they go there often?"

"No. They don't have enough money to drink more than once a week."

Calum noted that. "Was it usual to be out on a weeknight?"

"Not usual, but they'd had a hard day working at Achnafern and wanted a beer before going home, so they said. You know how it is on these long summer nights, no getting dark before ten, you feel like the day is never ending."

"And Fraser Munro?"

"He was a regular. Four or five nights a week."

"I'll confirm that." Calum looked up. "Next, the fight."

"A bit o' argy-bargy and some pushing and shoving. You couldn't call it a fight."

"Do you know why they were fighting?"

"It was all the usual stuff from Fraser—calling them names, trying to pick a fight, trying to prove he wis a big man." Jimmy had know Fraser for years and didn't think him much of a fighter—all show in his opinion.

"Did either of your brothers hit Fraser Munro?"

"They swore it was only a bit o' shoving, a kick or two, maybe a slap, but no real punching."

"Witnesses?"

"From what I heard, the landlord and his wife, some other o' the drinkers, and the lads from Achnafern Farm."

"Now," Calum reached for a map and unrolled it on the desk, "show me where all this took place."

"This is the hotel," Jimmy pointed, "this is the farm and the farm road." Jimmy pointed to a sharp bend on an unsealed road with woodland on either side. "It's no marked, but there's a bridge over a wee burn. It's called the Devil's Den. That's where Fraser Munro was found."

"Would your brothers walk home that way?"

"No. They'd take this road over the hill to where the boys stay with our cousins." Jimmy showed him. "The farm road would be well out of the way."

Unless they wanted a quieter place to finish the fight, Calum thought.

"Do you know if anyone might have seen your brothers on the road that night?"

"There were the other farm lads that left wi' Fraser Munro."

"Anyone else?"

"Naw." Jimmy paused to think. "Lambing is well over, there'd be no one out in the fields that late. One thing—the dogs at the schoolhouse on the road. The boys set them off barking just as a joke. They said they whistled and got a laugh when the old schoolteacher gadgie shouted at them to wheesht."

"That might come in useful . . . if they are charged."

Jimmy said nothing to that, but he knew that if Fraser Munro's death really was suspicious and if the police needed a culprit and if a McPhee was in the vicinity, then the McPhee would be charged.

"I know the polis will be coming for my brothers," Jimmy said. "If they're charged, I'll let you know." He stood to leave.

They shook hands, but before he opened the door to show Jimmy out, Calum knew he had to ask one further question.

"You're not hiding your brothers from the police are you?"

"Me? Would I do that?" Jimmy gave his signature, eyes-screwed-up-mouth-like-a-Halloween-lantern grin.

When he had gone, Calum answered for him. "Oh, yes you would, Jimmy McPhee—if it suited you."

He sat down to read his notes, thought through the visit and his impressions. It had been more than interesting—it had been entertaining. He had taken an immediate liking to the feared, hard man of the McPhee family. He almost wanted the brothers to be charged just so he could have a challenging case and the enjoyment of McPhees as clients.

It took two days for the police to call. Minutes after the results of the postmortem arrived, Detective Sergeant Wilkie took great pleasure in announcing the news to all in the station.

"We'll be needing extra men to go to thon tinker's camp and arrest the McPhee boys."

Jenny McPhee was matriarch of her branch of the Travelers of Scotland—"tinkers," "tinks," and "dirty tinks" to many of the locals and to the police. Now in her fifties, Jenny McPhee was witnessing the passing of her way of life and the loss of her language—the Travelers dialect of Gaelic.

She was still a handsome woman after seven children and a hard life on the road, living in horse-drawn wagons. Formidable some might say, scary was how others described her. Hard work at berry picking in early summer, lifting of the tatties in the autumn, selling lucky white heather and clothes-pegs door-to-door, often to insults and curses from the householder, had not left its mark on her. And amongst the Traveling people, her singing and her repertoire were legendary.

Her second son, Jimmy, might be a former boxing champion, and a hard man, but his mother could still put the fear of God in him.

Jimmy McPhee had brought the news of Fraser Munro's death. Jenny had immediately sent him to fetch the boys involved and spread the word amongst the clan that they needed information. Now three of her seven sons were in the room, and a family conference was taking place in the largest of five benders—large shelters constructed from bent saplings and covered with canvas and turf.

Erected on the banks of a swift river, in a pass between heather and birch-covered hills, the encampment was on a traditional resting spot for cattle-drovers and tinkers. There was a plentiful supply of young birch to construct the frames of the benders, river stones to make a fireplace, running water and narrow meadows for grazing the herd of horses and ponies—the campsite was as practical as it was beautiful.

The boys were not like their brother Jimmy. Their inheritance was that black-haired, blue-eyed, clear-skinned Celtic gene common throughout Scotland and Ireland. Fine specimens both.

Jimmy had twelve years on one brother and fourteen on the other. His wiry body was leaning over them as they sat sprawled in the velvet, brocade-covered sofa that sat plum in the middle of the bender. Jimmy's slicked-back dark hair and gleaming white false teeth added to the resemblance of a growling guard dog. That was what Jimmy was doing—guarding the family.

"You know the police'll be here soon. They'll no be wanting a cozy chat by the fireside."

"But we didney do anything," protested Geordie, the older of the two.

Jimmy looked at his wee brothers in amazement. "Do you no know the facts o' life yet? We're dirty tinkers to them. That's enough." He lit a cigarette, threw back another dram, not wanting to show his wee brothers his fears for them. "When they do come, and if they arrest you, you say nothing. Do you hear? Nothing at all." But Jimmy knew it was as impossible for them to keep their mouths shut as it would be for a cockerel not to crow at dawn.

Their mother was watching all this with a detached expression on her shrewd, dark face, leaving it all to Jimmy. She knew her boys were nervous, and it wasn't because of the police.

"Are you scared Jimmy might find out about the betting?"

"What's this?" Jimmy asked.

The boys wouldn't look at their mother. Jenny laughed. "There's not much escapes me."

Jimmy sighed. "Let's be having it. The whole story mind."

Geordie had the good sense to know they were caught. William too. They told the story, sentences bouncing back and forth between them. Both chimed in with the final statement in almost a shared breath.

"It was nothing to do with us. Fraser was fine when we left him."

The story was simple. The brothers had been running a small business for a year or so—betting on darts matches, the plowing competition, the winners at the Black Isle Show. It was no great empire. The farmhands were occasionally in debt to them, but only for shillings, maximum a pound. Except for the elder Munro son. He was into them for eleven pounds. Expecting his army payout, he seemed good for it. Then that night, when asked to pay, he told them to get lost. He was never going to pay dirty tinkers.

"We waited outside," Geordie told Jimmy. "We were going to give him a kicking, but Fraser left the hotel bar with the boys from the farm."

William continued the story. "There was shouting and swearing, a bit of pushing and shoving, a few kicks, but that's all. Honest."

"Aye," Geordie said, "somebody shouted they was going to call the police, so we left."

In their version, the scuffle broke up, they all went home.

Geordie and William left first. They could hear the others behind them, they said. They walked on, and were soon over the hill and saw and heard nothing more.

"That's it?" Jimmy asked.

"Aye," Geordie said. "Fraser Munro was well away, staggering and shouting and swearing, calling a' the others from the farms a bunch o' lassies, stay at home mammy's boys. Telling them he was a real man, he could fight, knew how to kill—but it was nothing new, he was aye going on like that."

"He was having a right go at the laird's daughter, Patricia," William remembered. "Right crude about her he was."

"So, let me get this straight," Jenny said, "you two fine wee laddies, you threatened Fraser Munro, you gave him a shove and a kick, all in front of witnesses?"

"Only after he said he would never pay us the money," William protested.

Jimmy ignored him.

"Then you walked over the hill, only a hundred yards or so separating you all until the turn-off to the farm, then on you two walked, on your own, into the night, and nobody saw you. Right?" Asked Jimmy, wanting the story clear.

"We saw each other."

Jimmy laughed with no hint of humor. Jenny looked worried.

"Have you heard any more, Ma?" he asked.

"Not much. The cousins are asking around. But no one can fathom how a kick or two at the hotel could kill Fraser."

"We didney kick him hard, we . . ." started up one of the boys.

"Enough," Jimmy bellowed. "Shut up the both of you and let me think. Go and see to thon two mares. I want them in perfect condition for the Black Isle Show. Get!" He stood, his five-foot-five body falling into a half-boxing stance, his fists in a half-clench, scaring the daylights out of his brothers. They were glad to escape to the comfort of the horses.

"I've a bad feeling about this," Jenny said when the boys were gone.

After watering the animals, the young men brushed and combed the two prize horses. The ponies watched on as the fairest of the mares were groomed, given a treat of molasses and generally fussed over. The Black Isle Show was eleven weeks away. This mare and maybe her companion had a good chance of winning their class.

A chill began to creep over the boys, and it was not from the gathering dark. Maybe it was not as simple as they had first thought. After all, they began to realize, what had the truth got to do with it, between a tinker and the law, between landowners and land dwellers, the landless Traveling people—the tinkers?

It was no more than a passing worry—with a mother like theirs and Jimmy as a brother, nothing could go wrong, nothing that couldn't be sorted.

When the police arrived in the early evening, DS Wilkie barged into the bender with neither a greeting nor an explanation. Jenny McPhee sat calmly in her chair and offered them a cup of tea.

"George McPhee, William McPhee, I'm here to arrest you on the charge of involuntary manslaughter." Wilkie was looking at Jimmy as he said this, furious it was not Jimmy he was arresting. And he was more furious that the procurator fiscal had refused to charge the McPhees with manslaughter, the lesser charge carrying a much lesser sentence.

An older policeman from Muir of Ord knew the McPhees well, had known Jenny since childhood, and had nothing against them. He gave Jenny a private nod of apology for the detective sergeant's manners and said, "Geordie, William, you need to come wi' me."

"Handcuff them." DS Wilkie ordered.

The older policeman shrugged. He knew it was unnecessary, but also knew better than to argue. He clicked the locks on the boys' wrists and for the first time, they were scared.

"I'll be down to the police station to see you the morrow," Jimmy told them. "And mind what I told you."

The boys left, a policeman apiece, and Jimmy poured himself and his mother a hefty dram.

"I hope to hell they remember to hold their tongues." But Jimmy and his mother knew they both suffered from verbal diarrhea. "I'll have the solicitor see them in the morning. Maybe a night in the cells will get it into their thick heads how serious this is."

"They think it's only an assault charge. Even that is no right. Thon sergeant would like a real go at a McPhee. So would many o' the rest o' them." Jenny knew the man as a vindictive, prejudiced outsider with no idea how the farms would suffer without the tinkers to help work the land. "Somebody gave the Munro lad a right good kicking, so I heard, and left him at the Devil's Den, bleeding, they say."

"Aye. And who better to blame than some tinker boys who'd already had a run in wi' him."

"We'll know more the morn. You have the solicitor lined up?"

"Aye. I has a talk wi' him," Jimmy replied. "When I gave him ma name, he knew who we are, and he doesn't seem to have prejudices about us. I liked him."

Jenny McPhee immediately felt better. This was high praise indeed from Jimmy and she knew his judgment was uncannily accurate.

If Jimmy likes this solicitor fellow, she thought, *he must be good.*

Eleven

Joanne knew she had to attend the funerals. No matter that her ribs hurt, it hurt to sit, the bump on her head throbbed, she had to be there to—in the Scottish parlance—"keep up appearances." After two days, the physical pain was easing. The shame less so.

She went to the Black Isle with her mother- and father-in-law. Children did not attend funerals, so the girls were with Chiara Kowalski.

"Are you all right?" Chiara had asked when Joanne brought Annie and Wee Jean to her house.

"I'm fine," Joanne replied. "I didn't sleep all that well last night, that's all."

Annie looked at her mother and Chiara would have said it was a look of contempt if it had come from an adult.

The day had two seasons, winter and spring. The Munro funeral took place in a subarctic squall of driving rain alternating with sleet. The Ord Mackenzie funeral, as everybody called it, was favored with crisp spring sunshine.

Patricia was sitting with the Munros as Joanne and her in-laws went into the gloom of the parish church. Granny Ross went to join her cousin, Mrs. Munro. She moved along the pew and the two women, sitting shoulder to shoulder, looked more like identical twins than cousins. Even their hats—dark, funereal felt bowls—matched.

The minister said the right things over the coffin of a boy he once knew, but a man who was a stranger. Mrs. Munro sobbed. Her husband stayed silent. Amongst the rest of the mourners, there was a restlessness, an absence of emotion other than pity for Mr. and Mrs. Munro.

The overriding feeling that day was curiosity and a barely suppressed thrill that an event as exciting as this had happened in their small community.

As they filed out of the church and walked to the grave, Mrs. Ross looked around counting the mourners. *At least a hundred*, she thought. She was pleased. It showed the Munros' standing in the community.

The funeral tea was well attended, and uncomfortable. In a land of the taciturn, the conversations were even more brief than usual. The visits to the farmhouse were perfunctory. Duty was done, but there were few takers for the ample supply of tea and whisky and ham sandwiches laid out in the front parlor.

Out the back, in the yard near the steadings, the male mourners discussed the arrest of the tinkers with little enthusiasm. Yes, the tinker boys had hit him, maybe it led to his death, but Fraser himself, hadn't he been the one to start the fight? It didn't seem right.

"Aye, weel, I always thought he had it coming to him," one of the bolder of the mourners said.

"Haud yer wheesht," Old Archie told him.

"I heard they've arrested two o' the McPhees," a neighbor said to Archie. "Always trouble that lot." The man's self-important nod made the old farmhand furious.

"We're here to bury the dead," he said in a voice audible to everyone. "No to gossip like auld fishwives."

The morning's harsh weather a distant memory, the Ord Mackenzie funeral was conducted in bright sunshine. There was an almost celebratory atmosphere as old friends met, onlookers stared, and Patricia was center stage, elegant in the role of grieving widow.

The pews of the church were packed, with all the major county families represented. Even the lord lieutenant was there. The mourners were attentive to the minister, but more attentive to the widow.

Curious glances at the deceased's few friends were discreet. None of his family had attended. The walk following the coffin to the Ord Mackenzie family plot was solemn but impatient. Most of the crowd couldn't wait to get back to the house for the funeral feast and a good gossip.

"Very grand for a fisherman's funeral," said one of the onlookers.

"Where are his family?" asked another.

Burial duly accomplished, the party returned to Achnafern Grange. No one would pass up the opportunity to drink the laird's whisky.

Joanne had just come from the kitchen, where at least she could have a cup of tea. The idea of drinking in daytime astonished her. *It shouldn't*, she thought, *this is Scotland after all.*

She was thinking how horrible both funerals were for the same reason—very few people seemed to care.

Patricia had been the perfect, dignified widow during the burial. Now, as Joanne watched her across the room, playing the gracious hostess, moving from person to person, pausing to thank them for attending, touching an arm, bending her head to accept condolences, Joanne was struck by the thought that an accident had solved Patricia's marriage problems, and why couldn't she be so lucky?

"How are you doing?"

Rob had come up from behind.

She jumped, spilling tea into the saucer. "I'm fine. I hate funerals, that's all." She couldn't look at him, scared he would read her thoughts. Rob had no time for her husband, Bill, and would probably have agreed with her.

"I see you've managed to find tea." He gestured to her cup and saucer. "Good idea."

"It's an exhausting business, death."

"For some." They both looked around at the throng.

"Lucky the funerals went ahead," Rob replied. "It was a bit touch and go. The police had to give permission for the bodies to be released. It seems Sandy Skinner's case is a straightforward accident."

Joanne glanced at him, and his face was as open as ever. *But he can hide his thoughts much better than me.*

"Fraser Munro's case is more complicated," he continued. "The procurator had to decide if the fight contributed to his death. The police think it did. That's why they've charged the two McPhee lads with involuntary manslaughter."

"Poor Jenny McPhee. Poor mothers. Losing a child is not natural."

"I know. It's a bad business all round." He paused. "Joanne, I want to say how sorry I am. If I'd known you were in danger the other night, I wouldn't have left. . . ."

"I don't know what you're talking about." Her body was statue-still, but her eyes were burning into his, willing him to look away. He did.

"Sorry," Rob muttered. "None of my business."

"We will be on the McPhee brothers story together."

Rob was glad she changed the subject. "I know. I hope there's no . . . how did McAllister put it, 'conflict of interest' for you."

"I'll have conflict with my mother-in-law if I upset the

Munro family. And I'm still in the bad books with Patricia over the *Gazette* headlines."

"Neither you nor Patricia had much luck in husbands."

"Thanks for pointing that out, Rob."

"Oh heck, I've done it again."

"Yes you have. I didn't need reminding, today of all days." Joanne walked to the kitchen, her back straight, her neck stiff, disguising the pain in her thigh and in her stomach, knowing he was right.

Rob sighed. Joanne was his friend. *You should be able to say anything to friends,* he thought. He looked at his watch. *Another fifteen minutes, that will look respectable, then I can skedaddle before I offend someone else.*

He wandered out to the front lawn, hoping to avoid anyone he knew. A rowdy discussion from a group of men who looked like a committee of the Black Isle Show Society, made Rob turn abruptly to his right. There he was confronted with another group, this time local lads from the estate. He tried to walk back into the house, hoping to find Beech.

The last Rob saw of him, Beech was standing with Mrs. Janet Ord Mackenzie, accepting on her behalf the murmurings of condolence that were bouncing back off the glacial wall she had erected around herself.

Mortimer Beauchamp Carlyle knew how much Achnafern Grange and the estate meant to Mrs. Ord Mackenzie. He knew that she saw herself as the chatelaine of all she surveyed. He suspected that she believed it her birthright as unequivocally as Henry VIII or any Louis of France believed in the divine right of kings. No wonder she hated Sandy Skinner.

Beech remembered her as plain Janet Ord. Her family was established in the northeast of Scotland for centuries. Even so, the double surname she took upon herself after the marriage, to preserve the family name she said, that was still seen as rather outré amongst the county set.

"Anything I can do to help? No? Jolly good," Mr. Ord Mackenzie broke into Beech's reverie.

He's become a caricature of himself, like a character out of a P. G. Wodehouse novel, Beech thought as he watched Patricia's father settle back down to his gathering of aging worthies and cronies from his former regiment. Beech wished his sister were here so he could share the observation. From the raised voices, Beech gathered that the new prime minister was the topic of conversation. One of their number either knew him or had been at school with him or had cousins with neighboring estates.

He saw Rob coming towards him and hoped he was coming to the rescue, but someone else got to Rob first.

"Rob McLean, right?"

A slightly rumpled, slightly drunk man, who looked like an aging student with his untrimmed beard, greeted Rob.

"Yes," Rob replied. "Sorry, I don't think we've met." *Just as I was about to escape,* he thought.

"No, but I read the *Gazette,* and I heard you work there." He held out a hand. "Neil Duff. Call me Neil. I'm the local vet and know the Ord Mackenzies through the farm."

They shook hands.

"Terrible, all this." Neil Duff gestured vaguely around. "Not that I ever met either of the deceased, but you know how it is, you hear things."

"Really?" *This is good,* Rob thought, *the local vet who goes to every farm in the district and he likes a dram and a gossip.*

"Poor Patricia. Not having much luck, is she?" Neil Duff continued. "Her husband of only a few weeks, and Fraser Munro, both gone. Mind you I heard Fraser never got on with Patricia, even as children. Jealous I'd say. Allie Munro is always singing her praises, telling everyone how well she runs the farm. Better than many a man, he says."

"I don't know anything about farms, but it all looks very prosperous," Rob said.

"Oh it is."

"The two deaths must be the talk of the community." Rob knew how to encourage a conversation.

"Talk of the Highlands." The vet looked at his empty whisky tumbler. "Pity I can't risk any more of the laird's best whisky, but I must be off."

"Could I ask you something in confidence," Rob said. "Not for publication, just as a friend of Patricia's. . . ."

"I'm not promising I'll answer. . . ."

"No, I understand," Rob said, "but I've known Patricia since childhood, and it really puzzles me how she got caught up with Sandy Skinner. I would have thought *they*"—he gestured to the group of farmers—"were more her type."

"There's many a man on the Black Isle would have married Patricia and are asking themselves the same question." Neil Duff spoke in the slow, careful voice of someone trying to convince himself he was sober enough to drive. "I have no idea why she would socialize with a local fisherman."

Very polite way of putting it, Rob thought.

"Maybe she just wanted to spite her mother," Neil Duff continued. He stopped, flustered. "Sorry, I shouldn't have said that." He held out a hand. "Good to meet you. Perhaps we'll bump into each other again."

"Well, well, well," Rob muttered as the vet left, "Patricia as femme fatale; who'd have thought it? Doesn't answer my question though."

Rob too had had enough of funerals. He fetched his bike,

wheeled it around the side of the house, hoping no one would notice his early escape.

From the top of the driveway to Achnafern Grange, the dip in the landscape where the small fishing village snuggled was distinct. Rob realized Patricia would be able to see Sandy Skinner's home if she looked out from the attics.

He paused, considering the idea, shrugged, and thought, *Might as well have a poke around while I'm here.*

Rob had the good sense to check in the village telephone box for a phone book and find the Skinner family's address.

No use phoning, he thought, *they will only hang up.*

Rob immediately recognized the man who opened the door at the Skinners'—the same narrow head, narrow eyes, in the weathered skin of a fisherman. Stating his business on the doorstep, which opened onto a street of similar cottages leading to the harbor, Rob felt an emissary of the Devil would have had a friendlier reception.

"We've nothing to say."

"Yes but . . ." the door was firmly shut in his face. Rob knocked once more, waited, then gave up. He had left his bike in the local inn's car park. As he walked back, he noted the fishing boats at anchor and admired their shipshape condition. Being twelve o'clock midday, the bar was open. There were few customers. No one would talk to him. He left.

Walking towards the village shop and post office, where he thought he might try his charms on some middle-aged female, he felt he was being followed. He turned. There was a black-and-white collie pulling a small man by a bit of string.

"A bad lot was Sandy Skinner," the man said to the dog.

Rob slowed down, waiting for the man to catch up, but the

dog kept his distance. Rob walked back to the harbor. They followed. He took shelter behind the seawall and waited. His pursuers walked past, stopped a few yards farther up, and continued their conversation.

"I don't blame them. I'd have done the same." The dog looked up at his companion. "Aye, you're right," the man agreed. "It was a shame. She was a right bonnie boat."

"Do you know who threw the bottle of petrol?" Rob asked, confident they were talking about the same thing.

"Now that would be telling." With a lopsided grin and a furtive look about him, the man whom Rob had taken for seventy was, on closer inspection, nearer forty.

"Do *you* know who did it?" Rob asked the dog.

"Families falling out, nothing sae vicious."

Rob gave a start. For a second he thought the reply came from the dog and, in this village, he wouldn't have been surprised if the dog *had* replied. But before he had time to ask more, the dog and his man scuttled round the corner. He went after them. They had vanished, leaving him with the strange sensation that he had imagined the whole encounter.

"Nothing would surprise me in this place," he muttered.

The smell from the large stone building made him notice it. The small windows were high set, a flagstone path led to double doors wide enough to allow a cart and horse or something industrial to pass through. Above the lintel, whitewashed lettering, well faded but clear, read, "A. Skinner & Sons."

"Sons," plural, Rob noticed. He checked the doors. A shiny new padlock joined a rusty chain strung twice between iron door handles. The smell of fish was strong but not unpleasant. Rob knew that the boats in the harbor were herring smacks and that the families made a good livelihood from fishing the famous Kessock herring.

Maybe this warehouse was the place where the herring girls—the "silver girls," Rob had heard them called—cured and packed the fish. Whatever it had once been, it was a substantial building.

So Sandy Skinner and his family were fishermen and a family of substance, Rob thought. Interesting. He turned to walk away, then stopped. *There is something wrong with this picture,* he thought. *It's Saturday, it's May, herring season, but this warehouse or fish processing shed is shut, padlocked, deserted. More than interesting,* Rob said to himself, *but what on earth does it mean?*

By the time Rob reached the shop it too was shut, Saturday being a half-closing day. It didn't discourage Rob, he knew in his bones he was on to a good story.

TWELVE

On Monday morning after the funerals, Patricia was feeling an after-party sense of letdown.

Mrs. Munro was not so much feeling loss—more lost. When she tasted the soup, she was shocked to discover she had left out the salt.

"Leave it," Patricia had told her. "Go home and rest."

"Thanks, lass, I will," Mrs. Munro said. "I'm that tired, I don't know what's wrong with me."

"Shoo." Patricia hugged her and sent her home.

It was mid-afternoon when the visitor arrived at the front door. Patricia was dozing on the sofa. She felt a flash of annoyance at being disturbed, but rousing herself, she went to answer the doorbell. She flinched when she met the eyes of the small, twisted bundle of venom glaring up at her.

"I'm Mrs. Skinner."

"Oh, I see. I'm Mrs. Skinner also," Patricia said. "You must be Sandy's mother, and my mother-in-law. Please come in."

Walking into the drawing room, momentarily blinded by the strong afternoon sun pouring through the westerly casement windows, Patricia turned and started at the strangeness of the visitor.

The tight, little figure was standing to attention before her. No movement was made to greet her daughter-in-law. Dressed in battleship grey, the coat that skimmed her ankles covered her like a carapace, giving the impression of an insect, a slater perhaps.

Wisps of wire-wool hair escaped the tight bun, pulled painfully from the scalp into a net of some sort.

A spare scrap from a fishing net. The silly thought lodged in Patricia's mind, and it was with a smile concealing a laugh that she stepped across the room and held out her hand.

"I am so pleased to meet you, Mrs. Skinner. I am sorry we did not get acquainted before now. It was a great shame you couldn't attend Sandy's funeral. You must be distraught over the loss. But let's hope for a brighter future. After all, I am expecting your first grandchild. Maybe a little Alexander."

All this was said with warmth. All the sentiments meant. So Patricia was unprepared for what followed.

"A child conceived out of wedlock is a bastard. No grandchild of mine. I don't make friends with sinners. Nor do they step into my house, nor sit at my table. The scriptures are clear."

Momentarily taken aback by the reply, Patricia replied meekly, "Surely Jesus taught us to forgive sinners?"

Silence.

"Well," Patricia sat down leaving her visitor standing. "Since you have made that quite clear, why are you here?"

"The police came a whiley ago. They took my youngest away."

"Sandy's brother? That must be why Sandy didn't want an investigation." Patricia noticed her visitor's lips compress even tighter at the mention of her first son's name.

"Oh, that was the least of it. Sandy, that fine laddie," she almost spat the name out, "had much to hide. No, he'd no be wanting a fuss."

"Is Sandy's brother charged with anything?"

"No, he's no. Helping with inquiries they say."

"Then if it is as you say, they will let him go."

"Aye. But it won't stop everyone poking their noses into what's private."

"My mother feels much the same."

The woman was completely unbending. A fierce moral code ruled her life. No transgressions allowed, no forgiveness allowed. Even for her firstborn son. Even in death.

So Sandy and I did have something in common after all, Patricia realized.

"I want you to fix it." Mrs. Skinner pointed her finger at Patricia. "Have a word with the police to drop the matter. My young lad has done nothing wrong."

"I can't influence the police," Patricia said.

"A person like you? In this big hoose wi' your money and your land and all your fine friends? You and your ilk can have anything you want." The woman was spitting her sentences, her rage coarsening her accent so Patricia could barely decipher the dialect.

"You corrupted my firstborn, brought the Lord's vengeance down on him, and on all his family. This is the least you owe us." She turned away as though the very sight of Patricia and her swollen belly was an insult to the Lord. "One thing more: I'll thank you no to go airing your dirty washing in a newspaper. I don't want my family's troubles in thon rag for all to gloat over."

Patricia smiled fiercely. "We agree on one thing. I don't like the newspaper stories either, but what can I do?"

"Use you hoity-toity friends to put a stop to it, that's what you can do."

"Shouldn't you be with your son at the police station?" Patricia had had enough of the woman. "Not wasting time with sinners like me?"

"Not that it is any of your business, but his uncle is with him."

"I still don't see what I can do. The police won't do or not do anything on my say-so."

"I knew it." Mrs. Skinner was happy to be proven right. "I

told my brother he's soft in the head suggesting the likes of you would ever help anyone." And with that, she scuttled down the hallway, not waiting to be shown out, reminding Patricia of a crab on the seashore hastening back to its lair.

Patricia sank back down onto the sofa. Then she laughed, partly in relief, partly at the awfulness of the woman.

"Poor Sandy. She is as bad as you said." Patricia considered the visit. *There is something she's not saying. That dreadful woman came for something more, but couldn't bring herself to ask. I wonder what it was?*

It was barely three minutes later when she heard a vehicle arrive.

"Good Lord, whatever next?" Patricia muttered before realizing the crunching of gravel was her mother's car. From childhood, she had always thought it a strangely expectant sound, never knowing what mood her mother would be in.

"Who was that walking down the driveway?" Mrs. Ord Mackenzie asked.

"Only my mother-in-law."

"I see."

The disdain Mrs. Ord Mackenzie could convey with those two words had haunted Patricia's childhood. She went to leave the room, pausing only to say, "If that woman visits again, make sure she uses the tradesmen's entrance."

Patricia gave a small laugh. "Don't worry, Mother, I'm certain she will never call again."

Across the farm, at the same hour, Mrs. Munro was as surprised as Patricia by her visitor.

Jenny McPhee had called at the back door as Mrs. Munro was dozing in her armchair. The knock made her jump. She was even more surprised by the sight of Jenny on her doorstep.

"Come away in," she told Jenny. "I'll just put the kettle on. You don't mind being in the kitchen?" She darted between sink and pantry and the Rayburn.

"Not at all, lass." Jenny settled into a chair and waited.

Tea was served in her best china cups. The women took their time, observing the formalities, asking after each other's families, commenting on the weather. They had known each other, not well, but had been acquaintances since childhood, their lives intertwined by the tides of the agricultural cycle.

Mrs. Munro was not completely at ease with Jenny McPhee, but her deeply embedded sense of Highland hospitality would never allow her to turn away any person, even the mother of the boys who may be responsible for her son's death.

Just as deeply embedded was a wariness of tinker women, fear of their disfavor, of their curses, fear that Jenny McPhee may have "powers." There were long-standing rumors that the tinker woman had the second sight.

When she judged the time was right, Jenny said, "I'm right sorry about your Fraser."

"Thank you," replied Mrs. Munro, reaching into her apron pocket for a hankie. Her eyes always welled up when her son's name was spoken.

"I remember him as a fine wee lad." Jenny didn't mention his later years, the years when he was known throughout the county and beyond as a troublemaker. "I know my lads are terribly sorry for what's happened an' all."

Mrs. Munro said nothing.

"I'm not saying my boys are blameless," Jenny started, "I know there was a bit o' push and shove outside the hotel. But that's all. My boys swear they went straight home after that and Jimmy has this solicitor fellow, Calum Sinclair, who thinks he can prove it wisney ma lads' fault."

Mrs. Munro didn't know what to think but she let the moment pass. They sipped their tea. The silence was not uncomfortable.

Again it was Jenny McPhee who broke the quiet.

"What I wanted to warn you is this. It might be that somebody else had a hand in it—the killing of your Fraser."

Mrs. Munro was shocked. "Surely no!"

"I just wanted to warn you," Jenny repeated.

"That can't be right." The teacup rattled in her hand.

"Calum Sinclair read the report on Fraser's injuries. He then asked another fellow, some expert on this kind o' thing, to look at the details o' Fraser's injuries. What this expert fellow said is, there was bruising on Fraser that happened hours after he left the hotel, and he says he thinks Fraser was alive until much later. Maybe as late as six o'clock."

Mrs. Munro stared at Jenny. Her eyes were small in her head, with dark shadows and lines that went deeper than those of age. Jenny McPhee felt for the woman.

"He's saying that if Fraser had been found earlier, he'd still be alive?" The thought horrified Mrs. Munro. "Are you sure about this?"

"It's what I've been told and I thought you should know." Jenny looked at her, deciding whether or not to say any more.

"So why did my boy die?"

"I don't know, lass. The bruises on Fraser, he didn't get all o' them from ma boys. That's what this man will say in court."

Mrs. Munro bent her head, looking down at her half-drunk tea. It was only the sound of the plop of a tear dripping into the teacup that made Jenny realize she was crying. She went over, took the cup and saucer from Mrs. Munro, put them on the draining board.

"I'm right sorry to bring the news. But better you hear it from me than it coming out and you no expecting it."

"Aye" was all Mrs. Munro could manage to say.

Jenny gathered her bag and her coat, and saw herself out.

After the visitor left, Mrs. Munro stayed sitting in her chair—the effort to move, to start preparing a meal, was beyond her.

She did not know what to think of the visit. And somehow, somewhere the niggle that had lodged itself in her head and wouldn't go away, this niggle that had been there since the day of the death, returned, more persistent than ever. There is more bad news to come, she felt it in her bones.

My Allie, he'll know what's what, she told herself. *No, maybe not. He'll just tell me to put it out o' ma mind. As if I could.* She blinked rapidly to stop a fresh well of tears.

Patricia was her next thought. *I'll talk to her. No, she has enough worries of her own. I know she's coping well with the death, but she was always a brave lass.*

My cousin, I could go over on the ferry and visit. No, she thought, *I don't want to make more of it than it is. Jenny McPhee could have it all wrong.*

The sound of the back door slamming frightened her. *I'm not up to more bad news,* she thought.

"Mrs. M. you'll never guess who came to visit," Patricia announced.

Mrs. Munro's first thought was, *How did Patricia know about her visitor?*

They exchanged stories. They talked away the rest of the afternoon. It was only when Patricia was walking back through the woods to Achnafern Grange that the thought struck her. *This is far from over.*

The fatal accident inquiry into Sandy's death—that would be held soon. Then Sandy's brother, what was his name? John. That would mean another police inquiry. Did he throw the petrol bomb? Did he destroy the family boat? But why?

Then she thought about the trial of the McPhee brothers. Did they kill Fraser? No. Surely it was an accident? He died hours after the fight. But they had been charged. There will be a trial. That will have everyone's attention—front page on the *Highland Gazette*. Mummy will be furious.

The thought made her smile.

Thirteen

McAllister liked to be there the evenings the *Highland Gazette* came off the press. He liked to lift a warm newspaper off the production line and glance through it. He liked the smell of newsprint, the crispness of the pages.

He liked knowing the delivery vans and their drivers were gathered in the lane below, waiting to take the bundles of papers to the trains and buses going northwest, due west, northeast, to the Black Isle, Daviot, Kingussie, Nairn, to the Carse of Moray, to all the small farming villages and crofting clachans.

McAllister was perched on a high stool with a mug of tea, keeping out of the way of the organized chaos around him, when the senior printer came over with a first edition of the *Gazette*.

"Happy with everything?" McAllister asked him.

"Aye, mostly."

"What's the problem?"

"Don McLeod. He's prejudiced. Never gives Clach a fair go."

"Hector Bain would agree with you there."

"Now thon's a good lad. His granny too. A fine woman."

Since McAllister had never heard anyone refer to Hector's grandmother except in terms of asking about her broomstick, this came as a surprise. The foreman noticed.

"She's of a fine, old family from Moidart. Speaks the Gaelic still. All that family do. Or did. There are not many of them left hereabouts. Shipped out to Canada, most of them. Still, she made sure Hector and his sister kept the tongue."

"Hector speaks Gaelic?" McAllister was surprised.

"Aye. His wee sister has the Gaelic too. You should hear her sing."

"The sister?"

"No, Mharie Bain, his granny. She does thon mouth music. A champion at the Mod. Right bonnie her voice."

McAllister remembered Graham Nicolson in Fort William telling him the *Gazette* could do more for the Gaeltacht and the diaspora of Gaelic readers.

"Is it possible to print Gaelic?" McAllister asked the head typesetter. "Do we have a font?"

"Aye, it could be done. Donny McLeod would have to proofread the copy."

"Aye" was all McAllister heard. A column in Gaelic, another coup for the *Gazette*—it didn't matter how many read it, it was filling the space that mattered.

The extra pages on the new *Gazette* scared McAllister—they may have some good stories now, but what happens when everything settles back into the boring routine of small-town life? Local content was what the readers looked for. The investigative stories excellently written—McAllister's major focus—had created a buzz around the newspaper. But the new columns—the crossword, the page for women, a small children's section—all contributed to what he wanted, a newspaper of quality.

He hoped the changes in the paper had upped circulation, but knew the stories in the last four editions were a more likely reason for good sales. The fire on the boat, two deaths linked to Achnafern Estate—these were real news, and he would milk them for all he could. He must also plan for the weeks of flat calm.

Rob would eventually leave. McAllister accepted that. But

right now, he was needed; to Rob, nothing was sacrosanct if it meant a good story. And he could write. McAllister also knew the *Gazette* needed Joanne; her freshness, her lack of cynicism, would remind him how the readers saw life. Above all, the new-style *Highland Gazette* had to work; his pride was at stake.

He bade the printers goodnight, walked home, put on a Charlie Parker record, poured a whisky, and sat down to plan.

Next morning, McAllister spoke to Rob first. "A word in my office," he said through the open door of the reporters' room.

Rob shrugged his shoulders at Joanne and walked out as nonchalantly as he could.

"Shut the door." McAllister lit a cigarette. "Aberdeen."

"I have to tell them soon but . . ." Rob started. "McAllister, I . . ."

"Let me speak. Then you can think about it. But let me know before you call them. Agreed?"

Rob nodded.

"As you may have gathered, we've still a long way to go before the *Gazette* becomes the newspaper it could be." McAllister looked straight at him. "Rob, there is no one here can do your job, no one with your abilities, it would be hard to replace you."

Rob shrugged an "it's nothing" shrug, uncomfortable at such praise, but also acknowledging the truth in the statement.

"You can write," the editor continued, "but more importantly, you have an instinct for a story even when it doesn't seem there is one. You're persistent. You get people to talk to you." He paused. "That said, you still have a lot to learn."

Rob nodded. "I know and . . ."

"I'm not done." McAllister held up the hand with the smoking cigarette, a typical McAllister gesture. "I may be the editor of a small paper in a small town, but I'm an experienced journalist. I know what's best for you, you just have to trust me."

"I do."

"On a paper like the Aberdeen one, you'd be a junior, on all the shite jobs—as well as making tea and fetching fags for the senior reporters. The training there is one job, one section at a time. You do all the work, a senior reporter takes all the credit. Five years of that, maybe only four if they make allowance for your time on the *Gazette*, it's a long haul."

"I know."

"At the *Gazette*, you cover every aspect of a journalist's job—sports, news, features...."

"I booked an advertisement last week...." Rob added.

"See what I mean? You have more freedom, more responsibility than you'll get on a big paper, and you'll learn a lot more."

McAllister leaned forward. "Here's what I propose. Stay here another two years, I'll make sure you learn everything you need to know, then I'll help you get a job on a national daily."

Quick as lightning Rob grinned, shook his head, and said, "Thanks McAllister, I'll stay. But forget the national daily, I fancy television journalism—it's the big thing of the future."

McAllister roared with laughter. "That's what I like about you, you're as direct as a heart attack. You'll do well, Robert McLean."

With a swagger and a grin, Rob walked back into the reporters' room and sat at his typewriter.

"Well?" Joanne asked.

"Well what?"

She took a swipe at him and missed.

"OK, I surrender." He held up his hands laughing, "I'm staying at the *Gazette*."

"Rob! That's wonderful." She hugged him.

"Joanne?" McAllister was standing in the doorway. With his eyebrows, he indicated his office.

"Sit down, please."

As he went to light another cigarette, he felt her nervousness, saw how she put her hands behind and smoothed down her skirt then sat with her legs together and slightly to the side, her back straight, her face set to pleasant and interested. He saw again how she was a daughter of the manse, and a credit to her very proper private schooling.

"You've been turning in good stories. Simple, factual," he started.

"Thank you." She waited, sure there was going to be a "but."

"So let's talk about you becoming a journalist."

"I need all the help I can get."

There was that earnest look again, McAllister thought. *I'm your equal,* he wanted to say to her, *not some demigod sitting in judgment.*

"Let's start with the direction the *Gazette* is going, see how we can help you with an abbreviated cadetship. Remember though, hard news is not for everyone. There are plenty of other areas in a newspaper where you can shine."

McAllister went through his thoughts and ideas.

"The new-look edition is into the fourth week," he reminded her. "Sales and advertising are good. Two more editions and the board of directors will make a decision whether to stick with the new format, or go back to the old-fashioned, been-there-for-centuries newspaper."

If that happened, McAllister would catch the first train back to Glasgow. He didn't tell Joanne that.

"I would have preferred ten editions before a decision was made," he told her. "Although my feeling is that as long as the revenue looks strong, I will be allowed to continue my way."

"Who are they, these mysterious directors?"

"An accountant," McAllister replied, "a solicitor, and a retired magistrate. They represent the owners of the company that owns the *Highland Gazette*, amongst their other assets."

He knew and would never tell, secrecy being part of his contract, that the Beauchamp Carlyle siblings ultimately owned a substantial holding in the parent company. Not that either Beech or his sister interfered. McAllister suspected Don knew. But nothing was ever said.

McAllister continued telling Joanne of the decisions and problems of revamping the *Gazette*. She was more than pleased to be treated as a confidante.

"One potential source of problems, the printers and typesetters, turned out to be allies. The change of leading, the space between the lines—they like it. Changing the font, making the leading deeper, combined with larger headings on all articles not just the main headlines, gives us a clean, modern look. 'It's much easier to read when you can't find yer glasses,' one of the hot-metal typesetters told me."

Joanne laughed at McAllister's rendition of the typesetter's accent.

"Don has no idea that my inspiration for the design of the *Gazette* comes from a Paris newspaper." McAllister grinned as he said this.

Joanne smiled. "He's not too keen on anything French."

"Or foreign. Or anything south of the Grampians come to that." He saw that she had lost that rabbit caught in the spotlight expression. "We need to produce a paper that increases our readership, is relevant to most of the Highlands and islands, is a serious rival to the Aberdeen paper, and is likely to keep Rob McLean happy for another two years."

"Has he said what his plans are?"

"Television."

"Really?" Joanne was surprised that Rob had not told her. Hurt too. "And my role?"

"You have good ideas and you think more like an editor than reporter. You never know, one day you could replace me. But I warn you, Mrs. Ross," he teased, "I'm not ready to leave just yet."

Joanne was astonished.

"Don't look so surprised—your articles of interest to women readers, your children's column, are good, solid ideas."

Joanne had found the solution to pay for the features page. The National Health Service provided a weekly competition to promote good health. It was better suited to children in the deprived areas of the cities than to those in a healthy Highland constituency, but the material was gratefully accepted. There was a comic strip featuring an egg for the main character. Another character was a pint of milk, and a bottle of cod liver oil and a jar of malt were members of the cartoon gang. Best of all, the government paid for the space.

She had also persuaded Beech to compose a crossword. Once a month, he said, too much work to make up one weekly. One of his cronies, a retired colonel living near Kiltarlity, had offered to make up a crossword on alternative fortnights. A fortnightly bridge column from a retired schoolteacher was another of Joanne's ideas. As well as the fiendishly clever bridge tips, the schoolteacher had agreed to select readers' short stories, poems, and reminiscences of bygone times, the prize being publication in the *Gazette*.

"Make sure the pieces are short," Joanne had warned. "Don McLeod is ruthless with his wee red pencil."

"The page is very popular, Joanne, your ideas and your choice of stories and correspondents make it work."

"Thank you. Being a reporter suits Rob more than it suits

me—he's too young to care what anyone thinks, and he's not afraid to come straight out with a question. Some of his jokes are in poor taste though."

"That could be said of the majority of journalists. Always remember, Rob has fine instincts and asks the right questions."

"I know. He's a good friend and I learn a lot from him."

"Joanne, please don't be offended, but I need to say this." He looked at her as she spoke, but she would not meet his eyes.

"I can see you want to make something of your life. But you don't seem to have a sense of who you are. You were born into one role, daughter of the manse, you married into another set of roles, wife and mother, now you are a separated woman—through no fault of yours. Here, you have a chance to change your life, to take charge; working at the *Gazette* can be more than a job, it can be a good career."

Joanne was listening intently to McAllister's every word, terrified he was going to talk about her stay in hospital.

"I hate the double standard where so-called respectability is what a woman is judged on. But times are changing. At the *Gazette*, you can become financially independent, and the job gives you the opportunity to use your brain. So tell yourself you can do it, and that you deserve it."

"Speech over." He stood. "So work with Rob, find out what's happening on the Black Isle, and write a story to keep our readers agog."

"I'll try." She smiled. "I'm curious about Fraser Munro's death. Curious about the charge too—involuntary manslaughter. I don't quite know what that means."

"Curiosity is what makes a good reporter, an unscrupulous sense of curiosity."

"I'll leave the unscrupulous part to you. And Don. Rob too. . . ." She hesitated, not sure how to ask.

"You talked before about conflict of interest."

He waited.

"I find it hard with Patricia. She's a friend. I feel sorry for her...."

"In law, the editor is responsible for the content of a newspaper, so blame me." McAllister sensed more hesitation. "You said your mother-in-law is related to Mrs. Munro. Will that be a problem?"

"I don't know!" Joanne was flustered at the thought of Mrs. Ross's reaction.

"It's the nature of the job," McAllister told her. "We are part of the town, but apart."

I already know that feeling, she thought.

"I'd like us to work together." She blushed when she said this. "What I mean is, I've a lot to learn."

McAllister, sitting there behind the editor's desk, was watching her every expression.

She found it impossible to say what she wanted to say: *I feel alive when I'm here, I feel I am worth something,* she wanted to say, *and I love it when you talk to me as though my opinions matter.* But all she managed was, "I'll do my best."

She stood and left so quickly it was only when she was gone he realized there was more. But what?

The room was empty when Joanne returned to her typewriter.

"Joanne, my dear. Just the person I want." Mrs. Smart came into the reporters' room like a lugger in full sail. "I have just signed up Arnotts for some advertising and they want a mention of their summer frocks."

"What do you want me to do?"

Mrs. Smart hesitated. Her promotion from secretary to business manager was a rise in status, but she wasn't sure how far her authority stretched. A story on summer frocks, while unusual in the *Gazette*, would be lovely in Mrs. Smart's opinion, and the advertiser promised a regular commitment if they were given a picture or a story each week.

"I wondered if you could speak to the lady in the fashion department to talk over ideas for an article."

"It's a lovely idea, Mrs. Smart, but perhaps we should mention it to McAllister first."

Rob came in, in a clutter of scarf and bike jacket and noisy boots and notebooks.

"What did McAllister want with you?" he asked Joanne.

"He said that as I am now a full-time reporter, you have to answer the phone, and I no longer have to make the tea."

"That's right." McAllister was leaning in the doorframe, making a diagonal slash with his long body. "I'll find the budget for a secretary to free you up for reporting duties. And she, or he, can make the tea."

Don came in, pushed McAllister out of his way, and spread the layout on the table.

"What are you all on for next edition? I need to fill these extra pages."

No one noticed Hector sitting in the corner, on the floor, next to the top hat, desperately trying to add up a column of figures. The total turned out different every time.

"Since everyone is here, let's nut out some ideas," McAllister said. He was still in his proselytizing mood.

He and Don immediately lit up—they were journalists, they could not possibly think without a cigarette or twenty.

Mrs. Smart sat erect on an extra stool, giving the appearance of a carved masthead on a ship's prow; Joanne and Rob were side by side at the large, black typewriters, looming out in the fug of cigarette smoke like monsters in the mist.

"I want to interview Jimmy McPhee," Rob said, "see what he has to say about the charges against his brothers."

Joanne mentioned their solicitor, Calum Sinclair. "Ask your father if he knows him."

McAllister turned to Joanne. "The Black Isle?"

"I thought I might talk to Mrs. Munro," she said.

"And Patricia? Why don't you see what's happening with the fatal accident inquiry."

Joanne did not think that was a good idea and dreaded the thought of asking Patricia for information for the *Gazette*. But she said nothing.

"What about *The Good Shepphard*?" Don asked. "Who's doing that? Graham Nicolson from the west coast called. He's tracked down the crewmen from the Skinner boat. He also mentioned there is an interesting story involving a west coast boat builder."

"I could take a trip over there," Rob offered.

"Phone first, see if it's worth your time." McAllister was grinning, pleased with the buzz of enthusiasm in the room. "Next up, I want to congratulate Mrs. Smart on the spectacular rise in advertising sales. We wouldn't have a new *Gazette* without her hard work."

Everyone clapped.

Clearing her throat, a trick she had learned from the Women's Guild public speaking event, Mrs. Smart began. "Thank you for your kind words, Mr. McAllister." She looked at her notebook. "I have an idea for a feature that would interest our lady readers. I mentioned it to Joanne. We thought we'd ask your opinion."

"Fill me in," McAllister asked.

"Arnotts have booked six, half-page advertisements. They will commit to a long-term contract if we write a regular feature on their fashion, new furnishings, and the like." She looked around, aware of the looks passing between the journalists. "I thought it would be nice. . . ." She finished off her sentence and softly deflated like a birthday balloon with a slow puncture. Rob looked uncomfortable. Joanne was puzzled. Hector was pleased.

"Can I take shots o' lassies in swimming costumes?"

"Shut up, Hector." Rob glared at him.

"Don?" McAllister's eyebrows signaled the question.

"It's like this," Don began, lighting up a Capstan full strength. "There's advertising and there's reporting . . ."

"And never the twain shall meet," Rob said.

"And this is the back door. . . ." Don continued.

"The thin end of the wedge," Rob added.

"Enough," Don told him. "Mrs. Smart . . ." He smiled at her. He thought she was a grand woman. "I'm as pleased as anyone with all you've done for the *Gazette*, but give those greedy so-'n-sos an inch and we'll be having endless requests for 'just a mention' from the fishmonger and the ironmonger. . . ."

"Butcher, baker, candlestick maker . . ."

"Rob!" Don paused. "He's right though, Mrs. Smart. There'd be no end to it."

"They said they might take a full page if we could give them a mention." Mrs. Smart was scoring thick lines through her notes, deleting all her ideas.

Don could see she was upset. "What you do is promise them a good position, front part of the book, right-hand page," he told her, "but only if they sign a contract."

"Thank you, Mr. McLeod."

Joanne was upset too. *I should have thought of that*, she told herself, *I should have known*.

"Next edition," McAllister brought everyone back to the point of the meeting. "Obviously we have to cover the other usual stuff. The problem is these news stories—there is too much happening."

He looked around the table. "Rob, Joanne, make up a tentative list of stories with dates due. The fatal accident inquiry into Sandy Skinner's death—find out when. Who threw the petrol bomb and why—we need an update. Yes, Rob?"

"Sandy Skinner's financial affairs seem shifty," Rob told everyone.

"He's dead," Joanne snapped him. "Have some respect." As soon as she said it, she wished her words back. *Impartial,* she told herself, *try to be impartial.*

"Sandy's financial situation may be the motivation for the fire," McAllister observed. He did not mean this as a rebuke, only as an idea to investigate. She felt it keenly all the same.

"Finally, the trial of the McPhee brothers is weeks away, but it does no harm to find out more. Joanne?"

"I'll get on to it."

"Thanks everyone." McAllister rose to go. "Let's turn out another humdinger of a paper."

Next day, Mrs. Smart told McAllister she had found an editorial secretary.

"Mrs. Buchanan is qualified, and it's good to promote someone who already works here, even if she was only taking the classifieds."

"It's your decision, Mrs. Smart."

"Find me a secretary" had been McAllister's instructions. Mrs. Smart's choice was a woman in her early thirties, a war widow. Although McAllister approved the appointment, he had slight reservations—the woman, Mrs. Betsy Buchanan, made him uncomfortable, and he had no idea why.

Blond hair that seemed to encase her head like a chrysanthemum, eyes as blue as a painted china doll's, she had an hourglass shape, which she showed off in a seemingly modest tweed skirt, twinset, and pearls—the standard dress of a respectable Scottish woman. That the skirt was a little too little, that the twinset was bought a size too small, that her walk—that well-shaped behind swaying independently of the rest of her—had taken a lot of practice to achieve, these were not things he could possibly know.

McAllister went to the reporters' room. *Soon we'll be needing more space—the room seems smaller, or we've all grown in a mysterious Alice way. Or maybe it is because we have that much more to do.*

"Mrs. Smart has found a secretary for the *Gazette*," he announced. "Mrs. Betsy Buchanan."

"Busty Betsy?" Rob asked.

"I remember her when she was just plain Betty and she bought her jumpers the right size," Joanne commented.

"I've been told her shorthand and typing are excellent," McAllister said. "And mind your tongue, young man. No names like that around here."

"You'd better get Don to tell the printers then," Rob told him.

Don looked up from the form guide. "I'm telling the printers nothing," he said. "Her name is Betsy. She has a big bust. They're men. What do you expect?"

Everyone went on with their Friday. Rob was on the phone, arranging a trip to the west coast for the next day.

Don made calls to his bookie for the weekend races.

Hector handed in his expenses. Mrs. Smart re-added his figures and came to a different total.

McAllister spent the morning researching the recent sighting of UFOs over Wigtownshire. He was planning some mischief for the next *Gazette* editorial.

Joanne wrote up a routine story about the hospital, but her thoughts kept straying to the talk with McAllister.

She had had little sleep that night. Time spent with him was always exhilarating. To talk properly with a man, to be respected, to be listened to—it was lovely.

There was something about the man that could give you the shivers, she thought, *but a man like him couldn't possibly be interested in me. Failed marriage, but still firmly married, two children, ignorant about the wide world out there. . . . But still*, she thought, *maybe it's possible. . . . Stop it. This isn't a true-romance story— this is the Highlands of Scotland. One thing McAllister had right—I need to be my own person. Someone's child, someone's wife, and a mother, I've never been independent.*

At lunchtime, Joanne took her favorite walk up to the forecourt and lawns in front of the castle, where the statue of Flora MacDonald stood plumb in the middle. The view up and down the river, across to the northern hills, east to Ben Wyvis, and west to the road to Loch Ness never failed to inspire her.

"Flora, there's no use looking westward," Joanne muttered as she passed the plinth. "He's long gone, like most of them. And he was never there when you needed him, like most of them."

The scudding clouds held a threat of rain. Capricious late-spring weather as always. She pulled her coat tight, remembering the old adage, "Ner'e cast a cloot till May is oot."

Joanne felt guilty whenever she thought of her girls. How could she work full-time, yet give them the attention they needed? Annie had retreated into her books. Wee Jean was clinging. They had to be forced to go to Sunday school. They were no longer happy to go with their grandparents on the Sunday walk.

"We want to stay at home," they said.

"We can play in the garden," they said.

"We don't want to go anywhere," they said.

"You'll miss your Sunday ice cream," Joanne told them.

Even that failed to change their minds.

"I have no idea what to do," she said to the passing seagulls. "They are not happy children."

Her words flew west on the wind and she turned her gaze back to the river. On the opposite bank, the new green of the trees and hedges shimmered with a color almost unnatural in its virulence. Beyond the town the gorse and broom, undistinguishable at this distance, made a strip of bright yellow delineating the canal banks. The asylum, crouching in the hills above the town, seemingly closer in the moisture-laden air, was as constant a reminder as the graveyard of Tomnahurich. A reminder of *what*, Joanne asked herself. *Of folly*, she concluded.

McAllister is right, Joanne told herself over and over. *The job will solve most of my problems, or at least give me an alternative to going back to my husband, my prison. But this newspaper game— I'm not sure I'll ever get the hang of it.*

Various bells went off for the three-quarter-hour mark, all a few seconds off from one another.

Joanne gave one last look at the river, took a deep lungful of oxygen to fortify her against the smoke in the reporters' room, and—hair flying, brain no clearer—she strode off down the hill to the challenge of being Joanne Ross, reporter, the *Highland Gazette*.

Fourteen

ᨊ

Rob left not long after dawn to drive the seventy miles down the Great Glen to meet Graham Nicolson at his shop in Fort William. McAllister had approved the trip, but told Rob he would have to ask Mrs. Smart to sign the expenses chit.

"I'm taking my motorbike, so it's the same cost as a trunk call," Rob told her. That did the trick.

Arriving at Graham Nicolson's newsagent's shop, Rob stretched his legs and studied the sky before going in. For once, it wasn't raining. As he went inside, the door gave off a *ping*, and a man bearing a close resemblance to a shaggy, Highland cow appeared.

"Mr. Nicolson? Rob McLean."

"Another great edition this week," Graham Nicolson said after they shook hands. "The new *Gazette* is getting a lot of attention hereabouts."

"Let's hope we can come up with another good story for next week."

"Aye," Mr. Nicolson agreed. "I told the fisher lads we'd meet at nine o'clock. Then we'll go straight to the boatyard in Mallaig. I think the journey will be worth your while."

The idea of taking the "Road to the Isles," as the journey to Mallaig was called, appealed to Rob. It passed by lochs and glens and the landing place of Bonnie Prince Charlie—places etched deep in the mind of every Scotsman.

"Great," Rob said when he saw the workmanlike café, "I need a big breakfast after the ride along the Great Glen."

Although it was not an Italian café, it was the type of café that Rob loved—one that served another of Scotland's national dishes, bacon rolls.

There were the usual chipped Formica tables, mismatched chairs, steamed-up windows, a pie display, and a tea urn. Nothing fresh whatsoever on the menu except eggs, and they were fried in lard to kill off any goodness.

"Two bacon rolls, with extra bacon and a mug of tea," Rob ordered.

Mr. Nicolson put three heaped teaspoons of sugar in his tea and looked around. He noted a pleasing number of the customers engrossed in the *Gazette*.

"There's almost too much to take in, in this week's paper," Mr. Nicolson said. "I saw from your article that no one's been charged with setting fire to the boat."

"Apart from the anonymous call Joanne received, no one is any the wiser—except Sandy Skinner."

"Well, he'll no be telling," Mr. Nicolson said. They laughed. "The boys from *The Good Shepphard* just want their money. Sandy Skinner commissioned a very expensive trawler. It is almost finished and payments are well overdue. The boatbuilder could go bankrupt. With all the job losses that would mean, it's a big story over here in the west."

Rob could see the headline—"Boatbuilder Goes Bust."

"I was wondering," Mr. Nicolson continued, "does his widow become liable? I wouldn't know the law on that."

"I could ask my father," Rob replied, "but he'll say, 'It all depends.' That's what he says when I ask him a legal question."

The brothers from *The Good Sheppard* came into the café, spotted Rob, and came over to join them.

Rob had a problem keeping a straight face. He was an avid reader of American pulp fiction, sci-fi books—a pilot at the Lossiemouth Air Base had given him about twelve or so magazines. His favorite plot was about babies cultured in test tubes, every child the same, hundred of children all *exactly* the same. *Maybe they do something similar on the west coast*, Rob was thinking, *and these boys are from the same batch.*

"Rob," Graham Nicolson nudged Rob with his elbow.

"Sorry. I was in a dwam." Rob came back to 1957, Highlands of Scotland, Planet Earth.

After their tea arrived, first one brother, then the next, contributed to the tale of the unpaid wages. Rob scribbled notes as they talked.

"The skipper said he was short on money," one said, "and asked could we wait until after the next trip. He told us it would be no problem, as after he was married, he'd be rolling in the money. We said yes 'cos we had no choice and it was to be the final trip anyhow."

"Sandy's wife can pay, she's rich," his brother added.

"I wouldn't bank on getting the money out of Sandy's widow," Rob told them. "What I don't understand is how did Sandy Skinner find you, and why did he hire you?"

"The boatbuilder put us in touch. He knows our father and knew we were between crews, so when Sandy was asking if there were anyone looking for a berth, the man told him about us."

"What happened to the original crew of *The Good Shep-phard*?"

"Sandy never said, but we heard the crew was his uncle and brother and he had a big falling out wi' his family."

"He was barred from tying up in his home port, barred from

landing his catch there an' all," the second brother—younger or older, Rob couldn't tell—told them. "Another thing is, we're no holy rollers like them, we don't mind fishing on a Sunday. That was one of the reasons for the fight wi' his family. None of them will fish on the Sabbath."

"I believe Sandy's family are Brethren and very strict," Graham Nicolson said.

"We did a few trips around the Minch," the boys continued, "but Sandy didney know the waters, so we fished the North Sea, his home grounds. . . ."

"Aye," the second brother said. "We got good catches, but we had to go through the canal locks and the lochs to get the fish to market. . . ."

"Then, on the last trip, the boat burned down. But you know that."

They both looked at Rob. "Aye, you went into the water same as the boat." The boys were grinning at the memory of Rob struggling in the canal.

He didn't need reminding, but he was a good sport and it *was* funny in hindsight. "Aye, you got the better of me," he grinned back. "It was the last trip you said?"

"Aye. We were to sell up the catch, then deliver the boat to the builder's yard."

"Do either of you know who threw the petrol bomb?" Rob asked.

"No, no idea." The first brother shook his head. "But I'm pretty sure the skipper knew."

The second brother nodded in agreement.

The fishermen waved as they left the café. Graham went to his shop to fetch the car saying, "Thanks all the same, Rob, but I'd no feel safe on the back o' a bike."

He gave Rob directions, and they agreed to meet at the boatbuilder's yard in Mallaig.

Rob followed the side of the sea loch to the turnoff to Mallaig, then sped off along Loch Eil and over the pass to Glenfinnan. Every mile of the forty-six miles of the "Road to the Isles" was spectacular.

"Over here," Rob waved as he saw Graham Nicolson's Morris Traveller pull in. Even with Rob's stop at the monument, he had been waiting a good half hour for his guide to catch up.

The boatyard was busy. *Saturdays are obviously a full working day hereabouts,* Rob thought.

"How are you, Mr. Nicolson?" A man wearing a carpenter's leather apron came out from behind a storage shed to greet them.

"This here's Rob McLean from the *Highland Gazette.*" Graham made the introductions.

"John Andrews. Pleased to meet you."

The man's hands were like sandpaper, Rob thought.

"I'm no one to go to a newspaper wi' my business affairs," Mr. Andrews told them, "but Heaven only knows how I'll get paid now Sandy Skinner is dead. I wouldn't mind you writing a wee bit hinting that a new owner could rescue the business. Save jobs."

"Is that the boat?" Rob looked up at an almost finished trawler resting in its—no, *her,* Rob corrected himself—cradle and, to his eye, she looked magnificent.

"Aye, it is. She was to be called *The Good Shepphard II.*"

"She's magnificent," Rob said. "A pity Hec's not here to take a picture."

"I brought my camera just in case," Graham Nicolson said. "The *Gazette* has published my photos before, so I'm sure they'll do the job."

When Rob asked, Mr. Andrews was reluctant to put an exact price on the deep-sea trawler.

"It'll cost what someone is prepared to pay," he said, "no use putting a price on her yet."

Graham Nicolson and Rob said their good-byes in Mallaig. Rob was keen to get home. It was a long hundred miles back.

"That's a very bonnie boat indeed," Mr. Nicolson pointed to her as they were leaving, "and she'll be a very bonnie price."

"Thanks for everything," and Rob took off.

"I'll send over the photos of the trawler first thing Monday," Mr. Nicolson shouted over the noise of the motorbike.

Rob tried whistling as he drove along Loch Lochy on the journey home. *This is a good story*, he was thinking. . . . *Then there is the Munro death and the tinkers in jail, another good story.*

He was nearing Fort Augustus.

The death of Sandy Skinner . . . maybe I should listen to my father, to Joanne, to the police—there is no evidence of anything other than a horrible accident. Convenient from the Ord Mackenzie point of view though.

Rob drove slowly down to the foreshore with Fort Augustus Abbey on his right, the waters of Loch Ness before him. He parked the bike and stood on the shore, stretched, shook his legs and arms and hands to rid himself of the cramp before picking up half a dozen likely stones and skimming them across the waters of the loch. It was a game he loved. Joanne told him it was one of her favorite games too.

Patricia Ord Mackenzie now Skinner, was she legally liable for her late husband's debts? Would she feel she had a moral obligation to pay the fishermen? Rob couldn't shake the thoughts of the story. When he was onto an idea, he became almost obsessed.

What really happened to Sandy Skinner? I suppose we'll have to wait for the fatal accident inquiry to decide.

In the meantime, no harm in having a poke around, he told himself.

Rob was unusual amongst his friends. He hadn't gone to university, doing a cadetship on the *Gazette* instead. Not that he had many friends in the town; the boys who were his companions from childhood and school days were nearly all gone, gone to university, to jobs in the big cities, to another life in other places—as had his girlfriend, Bianca.

It's been months since I saw her, he realized. *I wonder if she is still my girlfriend?*

Rob enjoyed spending time with older people like McAllister and Joanne and his mother. He enjoyed the company of eccentrics—even Hector was proving to be interesting. But Beech, a man in his seventies, intrigued him most.

"Mortimer Beauchamp Carlyle," Rob said the name out loud and laughed. "I like your style."

He walked back to the bike.

"Another year," he muttered to himself as he pulled on his gloves, did up his old Flying Corps leather hat, and wrapped his scarf around twice. "Two at the most. Then I'll be off south."

Rob had always known, from when he was eight and realized people were paid to write stories, that one day he was going to be *somebody*. He never put the thought into words, for fear of jinxing his chances.

He started up the bike, loving the sound and the feel of the engine, loving the idea of himself as this fancy-free young reporter with a future in the big, wide world outside of the Highlands.

At the end of Loch Ness, on the final miles into town, dusk was reaching up to dim the last of the light on the wooded hilltops. In town, streetlights were on. Rob was undecided where to go. He had nowhere he needed to be. No one he could think of to meet. He would love to pop round to Joanne's house and chat and laugh and play with the girls, then tell her, in exaggerated detail, about his trip to the west.

No, Rob thought, *not a good idea. The last time I went there, Joanne had ended up in hospital. He did not realize. She hid it well. She was keeping her distance because she was ashamed.*

Looking for an audience, Rob made for the Market Bar. It was a racing certainty that Don would be there this time in the evening. Don McLeod loved stories about boats and he would love the description of the trawler. *One thing is sure*, Rob thought, *I can make facetious comments about death and coincidences without fear of falling out with Don.* But Don wasn't there.

As Rob came into the driveway, he smiled to himself; Saturday night at home with his mother—this did not at all fit his self-portrait of an up-and-coming journalist with a future.

"Jimmy McPhee called," his mother told him. "He said he'd call back."

And he did, not five minutes later.

"I hear you wanted a word," Jimmy said.

They agreed to meet at twelve the next day, "But no on the Black Isle," Jimmy told Rob. "We're no very popular there the now."

Jimmy was already in the Beauly Hotel when Rob walked in.

Beauly was a large village or a very small town—depending on whether you came from there or not. The square was bordered by the main road north on one side and solid, respectable buildings, constructed in equally respectable grey stone on the other. An occasional turret broke up the no-frills façades.

The hotel bar reflected the town: solid wooden furnishings, from circa 1880, heavy, gilt-framed mirrors, and a clientele almost all dressed in tweed—tweed jackets, tweed knickerbockers, and tweed to-and-fro caps with a tuft of pheasant feather or perhaps an elaborate fishing lure stuck in the hatband.

It was not a bar for a tinker, but no one dared ask Jimmy McPhee to leave.

Rob saw him and waved and mimed a drink. Jimmy held up a whisky glass. As Rob waited, he realized he was glad to be in the company of Jimmy McPhee. Jimmy was not an eccentric, but there was something irrepressible about the man.

Rob McLean was the well-educated only son of a respected solicitor. Jimmy McPhee was the second son, born into the aristocracy of Travelers, who had only sporadic schooling while traveling the roads of Scotland, in the army, and in prison.

The oldest McPhee brother, Keith, had abdicated in favor of a life of study. He had finished school, and was accepted by Glasgow University—to the great glee of his brother. Not because Jimmy wanted to inherit the mantle of unofficial chieftain of the clan, but more because he could gloat that a tinker could make it to university.

Sitting himself down at Jimmy's table, Rob felt the ripple of murmurs. The son of Angus McLean at the same table as the son of Jenny McPhee would be the talk of the community. That they should meet, talk, joke, was another reason Rob loved working on the *Highland Gazette*.

"*Slainthe mhath*," Rob held up his shandy. "Thanks for agreeing to meet."

"I'll help if I can. I owe your editor. As I said, I canny talk about the details of ma brothers' trial . . . unless you have any information to help them."

"I'm looking for information on the Skinner family."

"I know little about they fishermen," Jimmy shrugged. "A tight, closed bunch they are. Look after their own."

"Like your lot then," Rob remarked.

"Aye. You're right, and you'll never catch a tinker at sea. River fishermen and pearlers, we are. Poachers an' all."

"I know it's not relevant, but I'm really curious as to how Patricia Ord Mackenzie met Sandy Skinner and why on earth did she marry him?" Rob asked.

Jimmy gave his full beam Jimmy grin, making him look like a naughty boy, not a legendary hard man.

"The *why* is obvious by now," he laughed. "I heard that she was havin' a bit o' hochmagandy wi' Sandy for many a year. How they met? I'm no sure, but Sandy Skinner used to pal around wi' Fraser Munro. After all, they were in the same class at school, from five-year-olds to leaving. Right troublemakers they were."

"Really?"

"Ask the schoolmaster. He was always reaching for his belt wi' those two." Jimmy paused, "I'm no sure, I'll check wi' Ma, but I seem to remember Sandy coming to Achnafern a time or two to work at the tatties. It wasn't unusual for a fisherman's lad to work the harvest, there's good money at tattie picking. Great company too—farm workers, tinkers, loads o' young folk, from the town even—we all work thegether, have a bit o' a laugh at day's end. Making a fire, roasting tatties in the embers, a song or two. Patricia loved it. Always managed to wangle a holiday from thon posh school o' hers at tattie harvest. And she worked as hard as anyone."

"I did the same a few times," Rob remembered. "I worked with one or other of your cousins."

"That'll be right," Jimmy said, "the Black Isle is hooching wi' McPhees. Anyhow, why do you want to know about the Skinners?"

"I'm mystified as to who set fire to the boat."

"You're the only one who doesn't know then," Jimmy laughed.

"What?"

"It'll cost you." Jimmy held up an empty glass. "Make it a double this time."

Rob did as he was told, but shuddered at the thought of how on earth he could wangle the expenses past Mrs. Smart.

"*Slainthe*," Jimmy toasted. "Lovely drop, this." He smacked his lips, enjoying making Rob wait. "John Skinner," he announced, "was questioned by the polis. Now he has been charged."

Rob grinned. He had a story. Then he thought about it. "That makes no sense."

"Does it have to? The boy could have done it to spite his brother, simple as that."

"Aye, possibly." Rob sipped his shandy, thinking. He didn't notice it was flat and oversweet. "I'm certain there's more. I went to their village. The Skinner warehouse was locked, and this is in the middle of the herring season."

"No, it's no," Jimmy told him. "It was open a couple o' days ago. I saw it maself when I was asking around about Fraser Munro."

"Did you find out anything useful?"

"That would be telling." Jimmy enjoyed the look on Rob's face, enjoyed teasing him. "All right. Seeing how you bought me a drop of the good stuff, I'll tell you. Thon big shed, where the lassies box the herring, was sold to another family in the village. John Jack bought it and at a good price, so I heard."

"Really?" Rob couldn't take it in. "I've no idea what that means."

"Means Skinners needed the money. Why else would they sell?"

"Right." Rob needed time to think about this. "How about your brothers? Is it hopeful?"

"We're tinkers, we need more than hopeful."

"You have Calum Sinclair. My father says he's good."

"Aye. He seems right smart. I have a bad feeling that we'll need him." Jimmy paused. "You're likely to find out soon enough, being the nosy fellow that you are. . . ."

"What's that?"

"Fraser Munro didn't die until early morning, dawn or a wee whiley after."

"Does that help?"

"Maybe someone else attacked him—later on that night, or early morning."

"Do you have any idea who?"

"Aye, that's the question, isn't it? No writing this in the *Gazette*," Jimmy warned.

"Never," Rob assured him. Jimmy looked at Rob, looked straight into his eyes. Rob had to look away. What Rob saw, he didn't want to see again. He took a sip of shandy to recover, but the glass was empty. "If I hear anything, I'll let you know, Mr. McPhee."

Rob knew that Jimmy had said all he was going to say. It was time to leave before any more glares scared the life out of him.

"Thank you very much, Mr. McPhee." Rob stood. "Thanks for everything. I'll let you know if I hear anything." Rob knew he was gabbling. Jimmy did too.

When he heard Rob's motorbike roar down the road, Jimmy thought, *Haven't lost ma touch, one look is all it takes to scare the daylights out o' them*. He finished his drink, made his way across the room, giving the stare. A vacuum of silence followed him. *Aye*, he thought with great satisfaction, *works every time*.

◆　◆　◆

When Rob reached home, he ran to his room, took the cover off his portable Olivetti, a secondhand red one that he loved and cherished and wished he could use at work. He sat down to write up his notes.

After an hour and a half of feverish typing, he thought, *I wish it wasn't Sunday, I can't wait to get to the office.*

Once again the ace reporter scores a scoop, he congratulated himself as he rolled the sheets and the carbon paper out of the typewriter. *No*, he realized, *it's scoops, plural.*

FIFTEEN

Patricia read about the charges against John Skinner in the *Highland Gazette*. Her first thought was, *my ex-mother-in-law will be livid*. Her next thought surprised her. *I must help him.*

It was the report from the boatyard that really set Patricia thinking. She had not considered her late husband's financial affairs because she knew little about them—only that he was desperate for money and had even suggested they sell one of Achnafern's fields to raise cash.

The new boat was partly paid for; that was what the *Gazette* article stated. So was she, as Sandy's widow, part-owner of a boat or owner of half a boat? And the wages owed to the crew of the boat that was destroyed? The *Gazette* had quoted them as saying they were hoping *she* would pay them. Was she obligated? Was she liable for Sandy's debts?

One problem at a time, Patricia told herself. First the fatal accident inquiry into Sandy's death—let's get that out of the way, then I can find out my legal position.

That the death of Sandy Skinner would be declared an accident, she had no doubt.

Next morning Patricia met Allie Munro earlier than usual, seven o'clock instead of eight. The court hearing was scheduled for ten.

Five weeks had passed since Allie Munro lost his son and Sandy Skinner had his accident. Time passing hadn't made it easier for Allie. It was the sense of a deep, abiding sadness that

Patricia noticed. She felt it emanating from his voice, his face, the way he moved, the way his finger was less precise when pointing at the map of the farm as they discussed farm business; she was in the presence of a man who had aged ten years in five weeks.

Farm business dealt with, Patricia went to the kitchen to fetch the car keys. When she had asked her mother for the car, she had had to put up with the usual rigmarole. "No Mummy, I do not want a lift. No, I will not take the bus into town. No, I am not driving the Land Rover, not in my condition." Her final point—think how it would look if anyone in town saw her, especially on the day of the hearing into her husband's death—won the argument.

Mrs. Munro was scrubbing vegetables when Patricia came in, "I've time for a quick cup of tea before I leave," she said, putting the kettle on the hob. "How are you, Mrs. M?"

"As well as can be expected, lass."

Patricia went over and gave her a hug. She was surprised by the way the older woman clung to her. She stepped back, looked at the crumpled face, the pink eyes, the hair without its usual immaculate side parting showing a pink line of scalp. "You look all in."

"I canny sleep."

"I can understand that." Patricia, by contrast, looked bonnie and blooming in her grief.

"You look well, lass."

"Thanks to this little fellow." She laughed, patting her stomach.

Patricia insisted on making, then pouring the tea. They sat at the table as they always did, side by side, close.

"Mr. M seems a bit out of sorts."

"Aye, it's hit him hard, all this." Mrs. Munro shook her head.

Her eyes filled with tears. One slowly rolled from the faded blue of her right eye, dropping audibly into her tea.

"Salt and sugar together. I hope the tea tastes all right," Patricia joked.

"You always do me good, lass. Everyone, the neighbors, the wifie in the shop, or her in the post office, they don't know how to treat me. It's like I have a disease."

"I know. Me too. And as for the bump, people don't know where to look. They generally fix their eyes on a point halfway to Tain."

They smiled, a brief and healing respite from grief.

"I'll start a bit o' knitting. I could do with something to take my mind off things. A shawl, I think."

"I'd love that. I'll get some wool for myself and a simple pattern. You know me, a plain purl girl."

"You were always too busy outdoors to knit," Mrs. Munro fondly remembered. "Get white Shetland two-ply for me, ten ounces."

When Mrs. Munro heard the car pull away, she went back to Patricia's remark. There *was* something worrying Allie. She felt him sigh in the night, she heard him get up and go out into the dark to smoke a pipe, she saw his face line and crinkle a little more each day. No longer could she tell herself this was only to be expected—it was more than grief that was troubling him.

She went to the pantry to fetch the meat for a shepherd's pie. As she worked, her mind wandered.

What were those funny wee brass monkeys Patricia had had since she was a child? Hear no evil, see no evil, speak no evil?

I'm just like them. If there is something bad going on, I don't want to see nor hear. Her eyes filled with tears. She hated this need to cry, she'd never been a crying sort before now. *Given time, it will be all fine,* she told herself, not really believing it. *Talk to Allie, ask him what's wrong.* "A trouble shared was a trouble halved," her granny used to say. *Aye, and there's plenty of troubles on this farm.*

On the ferry crossing to town, Patricia leaned on the railing. There was a chilly edge to the wind. She watched the white horses race across the water, towards the mouth of the Beauly River in the far distance. She watched three fishing boats working the firth, May and June being the herring season. She looked up at the forested crag of Craig Phadric and below she saw the whitewashed lock keeper's cottage, with the stumpy white lighthouse jutting out into the water, marking the beginning of the Caledonian Canal.

This is where it all came to grief, Patricia thought, *the sinking of the boat. No, not true—married life with Sandy Skinner would have come to grief sooner or later.*

Patricia parked beneath the castle rampart. She checked her lipstick in the rearview mirror, she patted her hair into place. She got out, locked the car, put on her camel-hair coat and headscarf, hooked her handbag over her arm. *I look as good as Queen Elizabeth on a trip to the shops in Balmoral,* Patricia thought. *We're the same age, but I'm sure she didn't have such problems with her husband—or her mother.*

She climbed the steps to Castle Wynd. Five minutes to spare, before she was needed as the star witness in the inquiry into the death of Alexander Skinner.

A stranger watching her or a friend looking at her—even Mrs. Munro—could never see how sick she felt. The death of her husband was an escape from certain disaster, but he was the father of her child, a man she had once been passionate about.

The inquiry took an hour and a half, not the whole morning

as Joanne had expected. She was covering the hearing for the *Gazette*. Not her idea, but McAllister had told her to go, and she was aware Rob was contributing much more column space than her. *The boatyard story, John Skinner's arrest—Rob discovers stories—he is a real journalist. I cover events already in progress.*

With her confidence suitably low, Joanne took her seat on the bench in the Sheriff's Court.

The proceedings opened. WPC Ann McPherson gave the account for the police. The medical report was read out. The sheriff noted that the blood-alcohol level was unusually high for so early in the morning.

"Mrs. Patricia Skinner."

When her name was announced, Patricia felt a flash of annoyance. She hated being a Skinner and would change that as soon as respectable.

"Please excuse me if I feel faint," Patricia smiled around the court. "It is all very distressing, and I am in a delicate condition."

How does she do that? Joanne thought, *make all these men melt like that?*

"Of course. We will be as brief as possible," the procurator fiscal told her. Then he led her through that morning's events.

"We left home early, before dawn. It was the first day of May, so we went to the Clootie Well. Silly I know, but I love the old traditions." Again that sweet smile. "We intended to drive to Fort Augustus the long way round.

"After we left the town, I had a bout of horrid morning sickness, so we stopped at the Dores Inn." Patricia told the story well. There were no interruptions, no questions. "After a cup of tea I felt better, so we drove on, but we had to stop again as I was sick."

"Sandy came from a village a mere thirty miles or so from some of the most beautiful places in Scotland and had never visited them," she told the court, as though this was a fault, an idiosyncrasy, forgetting that most people did not have a car, could not travel on a whim to see scenery.

"We stopped near the track to the Falls of Foyers. I said I'd sit in the car until I felt better. Sandy said he'd go down to see the Lower Falls." She took a sip of water from a glass the clerk of the court handed to her. "I waited nearly an hour, then I began to worry."

She didn't mention his last words to her, "You stupid cow." He had yelled when she leaned out to be sick. She would never tell anyone she was crying.

"I went down the track to find him, but it was so slippery, and there is a drop on one side of the track. I was scared, so I turned back. I called out many times, but the noise of the water was really loud."

Patricia paused, looking down at her hands. The procurator paused, waited.

"Would you like a break?" he asked.

"No, thank you. I'd like to finish."

"So you went for help?"

"Yes. I drove back to the inn. The landlady and her husband were most helpful. They said they would try to find Sandy. I waited, I fell asleep for a while, then . . . I'm sorry."

"Hankie time," Joanne muttered. Sure enough, both Patricia and a lady on the visitors' bench pulled out handkerchiefs.

There was only one point that Patricia faced any pressure over.

"The Falls are immediately outside of the village of Foyers. Why did you drive all the way back to Dores, almost twenty miles away, to report your husband missing?"

Patricia looked directly at the sheriff as she answered.

"I ask myself that constantly. I have no idea why. Perhaps

it was because I was feeling so wretched. Perhaps I wanted the comfort of a place I knew, where I could take a room."

There is a hotel in Foyers, Joanne remembered. But no one commented.

"Perhaps it was because Sandy was cross. . . ."

"You'd quarreled?" the fiscal asked.

"Not at all. It was the smell of sick that Sandy hated."

There goes the hankie again, Joanne thought.

"I have no explanation. I deeply regret my panic. I should have gone straight into Foyers . . . perhaps he could have been saved." Patricia looked into her lap. This time she tried no theatrics with the hankie, letting the tears run silently.

The sheriff had three daughters; he could never cope with tears—not a good quality for a man in his position. He looked over to the fiscal, who said he had no more questions, and proceeded to sum up the case.

The sheriff listened to the recommendations. He concurred. The finding was accidental death by drowning. Recommendations—the construction of a guardrail at the viewing point above the falls.

The hearing into the death of Alexander Skinner was over.

Joanne met Patricia on the steps outside the Sheriff's Court.

"How are you?" she asked.

"I couldn't bear thinking about that day," Patricia answered. "It was horrible."

"Patricia, I'm sorry, I have to ask, can I have a comment for the *Gazette?*"

"You must know how I'm feeling." Patricia looked at Joanne with an expression too hard to read.

I don't, Joanne thought, *and I seldom know what you are thinking. That is the problem.*

"Just say I am still in shock, but relieved the hearing is over."

Patricia had another of her sudden switches of mood. "Let's meet in Arnotts for lunch, twelve-thirty? I'll have recovered by then. My treat. Bye-bye."

She was off down the wynd, picking her way carefully over the cobblestones, certain the reply to the invitation was "yes."

Joanne was left feeling like a fish—hooked, landed, and floundering on dry land. She didn't know what to think—or write. *The facts,* Don always advised, *the bare, simple facts. But a life was gone. The sheriff's recommendation that a guardrail be erected didn't seem much of a memorial for a life. No,* she corrected herself, *he will be remembered. Sandy Skinner left behind a baby, a boat, and a story, which, given time, will become part of local folklore.*

"Sit down. Let me get tea. Or would you prefer coffee?" Angus McLean asked.

"Coffee?" Patricia was surprised at her solicitor's modern tastes.

"I send out for it from the café where Rob spends half his life." He smiled at her. He had known her since childhood and was one of the few not intimidated by her mother. Patricia always appreciated that.

"Thank you, I'd better not. This is a brief visit, as I have rather a lot to do today."

Angus waited.

"The verdict was accidental death."

"I see."

"Thank you for offering to be there. But as I said, there was no need." She gave him her full regal one hundred watt ingratiating smile.

Again he waited.

"I also wanted to apologize for being difficult over the

Gazette; I had no right to take out my hurt and frustration on you. All this business of Sandy, Fraser Munro, and everything else, has been a great strain. I now see they were only doing what a local newspaper is supposed to do, report the news."

"Think nothing of it. Forgotten already." He found the apologies rather fulsome and suspected a tinge of insincerity.

"I'm here to ask about my legal position now Sandy is . . . gone."

Looking at her, knowing she had come straight from the Sheriff's Court, Angus McLean noted how businesslike she appeared.

"Your late husband left no will as far as you know?" Angus said.

"No, there was no will. My concern is his debts. According to the *Gazette*, the amount owing to the boatbuilder is substantial. Am I responsible? Could the boat be sold? Can I recover part of the original payment?"

"I will look into it for you."

Patricia had a final question. "That solicitor in Dingwall . . . thank you for the recommendation."

"Calum Sinclair."

"Yes. He has agreed to represent Sandy's brother over the fire on the boat."

"I have heard only good reports about him."

"After all this mess with Sandy is cleared up, would you mind if I took my personal business to Calum Sinclair? I'd like to separate my legal affairs from the estate's business and from Mother and Father."

Another dazzling smile was switched on.

"I quite understand and am not offended in the least. Tell Sinclair to give me a call and we will sort out the formalities."

Angus McLean was a solid man, solid in weight and

reputation. He had been a solicitor for thirty years. He knew a schemer when he saw one. *What is she up to now?* he wondered after Patricia had left, certain there was another reason behind the decision. Whatever the reason, he meant what he said, it did not bother him in the least to lose her as a client.

"Arnotts, twelve thirty, my treat." It had almost been a command, Joanne thought as they waited for their first course.

"I'm sorry I've been snappy these past few weeks," Patricia apologized. "I've been under a great strain. I had to apologize to Angus McLean too. My tactlessness has been worse lately, and as I never had much tact to start with . . ."

"I won't comment on that." Joanne laughed.

"This is for you." Patricia handed over a small gift-wrapped parcel. "Open it, I'd like to see if the color is right."

"Pure silk. You shouldn't have." Joanne felt a rush of embarrassment. *I've been so uncharitable to her lately—it's this job, we see the worst in everything.*

Patricia leaned over and draped the scarf around Joanne's shoulders. "You deserve it. Besides, who else is going to treat you if not your best friend?"

As with so many remarks from her friend, Joanne immediately felt defensive. *Patricia doesn't mean to hurt,* she told herself.

"Have you recovered from this morning's ordeal?" she asked.

"Thank you. You are one of the few to recognize what an ordeal it was." All the cheerful, "I can cope, I'm doing fine" façade slipped, and Patricia's sudden change in spirits went a long way in mollifying Joanne.

They ate their lunch, both in a subdued mood, and when Joanne said she had to get back to work, they were both relieved—though neither showed it.

"Heavens, I must dash too. Lovely to catch up with you. Must do this again soon. I'll call. Love to the girls. Bye. Bye-eee."

A rustle of bags, a hug for Joanne, a waving off of the change brought by the waitress, Patricia negotiated her way through the tables in the dining room, like a sturdy tugboat sailing against the tide. Joanne sat in the wake of her friend's departure, amused, perplexed, and vaguely wondering what Patricia wanted.

Not one word had been spoken about the inquiry. Nothing had been said about Sandy Skinner, his life, the marriage, his death.

Maybe it is life on a farm that makes her seem callous, Joanne thought, *you learn not to become attached to the sweet little lambs that you bottle-fed, knowing you will have to send them to market, knowing they will end up on your plate for Sunday dinner.*

The bank was a typical, heroic, Scottish stone building—tall, grand, with a Grecian façade, complete with columns, decorative urns, and an imposing frieze atop—a perfect monument to the power of money.

Patricia had not made an appointment, but when she asked for the bank manager, it was in the firm expectation that the name Ord Mackenzie would change anyone's schedule.

The bank manager, who always saw his title in capital letters, led Patricia to his office, which was equally grand. A sleek, seal of a man, he carefully adjusted his suit jacket and trousers before sitting at a desk constructed in the same grandiose scale as the bank. *Look,* the building shouted. *See,* the fabric and furniture said. *This is the power of money.*

They waited for an underling to fetch the file. He asked after her father and her mother. He murmured all the correct sentiments when she told him the sheriff's verdict. She handed over the death certificate, she took out a small leather-bound dairy, and they got down to business.

"It is all straightforward. As you quite rightly stated, this is an account that allowed you to operate either individually or jointly."

"Sandy was insistent on that, and it turned out to be a wise decision." Patrica spoke quietly. It would be bad form to speak in anything other than hushed tones in a temple of money. "Your letter said the funds from the bank cheque have cleared."

"Yes. I am sorry we were unable to forward your late husband an advance against this payment. It was a substantial sum of money he requested. I had to be cautious, as a promissory note is only a piece of paper until the funds are deposited."

Patricia thought for a moment, then asked, "Do I need to do anything? Legally I mean."

"Not as far as the bank is concerned. The funds in the account are legally yours." He cleared his throat in a clichéd signal of a question—for he was a cliché of a bank manager.

Patricia saw the man was nervous. "Is there anything else?"

"The transfer of the funds from the Achnafern Estate account to your joint account is still waiting on your mother's co-signature."

"I don't think we need bother with that anymore." She smiled.

"Quite." He smiled back.

"Should I close this account and open one in my name only?"

"That is what I was going to suggest."

They finished the paperwork. Patricia was given a statement. She glanced again at the amount written clearly on the bottom of the page, making sure she had not mistaken the number of zeros.

"One final question. If I were to purchase a motorcar, what is the best way to pay?"

"Request a bank cheque be drawn up for the amount."

As she left the bank, Patricia glanced at her watch, calculating how much time she had. *I could look,* she thought, *Macrae & Dick is not far. They should have a car suitable for me.*

Patricia crossed Union Street to the sporting outfitters and fishing-gear emporium. She chose a shooting stick to replace the one her father had lost.

"Please wrap it," she said. "It is a present for Daddy."

"Of course, Miss Ord Mackenzie," the shop owner was almost bowing with respect.

Next the market arcade for Mrs. Munro's wool.

She then crossed the street to the garage and car showroom and stared in the window at the various models on display.

Not too large, she thought, *but room for a carry-cot in the back. Not too bright, definitely not red or maroon, black maybe. That one looks nice, that sleek one, just the thing for an Ord Mackenzie.*

She went in, she sat in the car, she asked the price, she said she would arrange payment, she agreed on a delivery date. When she left, the salesman stared after her in disbelief.

"I've never know a woman make up her mind so fast," he said to his assistant.

"I can't wait to see Mummy's face when the car is delivered," Patricia said to herself.

Sixteen

Joanne was attempting to write up her notes on the morning's court proceedings. Three drafts so far, and each ended in the top-hat-cum-bin, a crumple of rejected words.

"I'll never get this blooming thing to behave himself." She banged the return carriage, taking her frustration out on the typewriter.

"A male typewriter?" Don walked in.

"Of course. Stubborn, awkward, unreliable, and needs oil at least once a week."

"That's your opinion of men?"

"Of course—present company excepted." She flashed Don a smile and went back to her typing.

"What's the problem?" Don asked when it became clear Joanne wasn't volunteering information.

"I'm not going to ask you, because I know the answer: 'Write the facts, just the facts.'"

"The fatal accident inquiry, I take it."

"Yes. I can't manage to put any color into it. Not the way Rob does in his stories."

"This is different. It is a factual report. No more. If you did put fancy bits into it, I'd cut them." Don wiggled his wee red pencil at her, grinning like an evil troll. "So, start at the beginning, get to the end, then we'll look at it."

She glanced at her notes again, rolled her shoulders, then with a spurt of confidence, and her fingers and wrists and elbows,

Joanne banged out the report. Finished, she unwound the copy from the typewriter.

Don read it. He deleted a word or two, did a quick word count, then pronounced "Exactly what's wanted."

"Really?"

"You should do that more often," Don told her. "You look like a beam o' sunshine bursting out from behind the Cuillins when you smile."

He glanced at the report again.

"'Mrs. Skinner explained that in her panic, she drove to Dores rather than to nearby Foyers to report her husband missing,'" Don read aloud. "Believe her, do you?"

"Of course. She was sick, she was worried. . . . Patricia may be difficult, but she would never . . ."

"Patricia would never do what?" Rob came in.

"Push her husband into the Falls of Foyers," Don answered.

"Only if she knew she could get away with it." Rob laughed.

"I don't believe you two." Joanne stood. "How can you say that? You have no idea what Patricia has gone through lately." She started to yell, "Plus, she is pregnant."

"Would that work as a defense?" Rob asked Don.

"What a dreadful thing to say." Joanne brushed past Rob, grabbed her coat, and ran down the stairs.

When she reached the bridge, she realized she was shaking, but she didn't know why.

It was not the conversation in the newsroom—Don and Rob frequently speculated on worst-possible scenarios. It was not her beating—the bruises had almost healed, only her ribs still hurt.

I'm tired. I'm scared I'm not up to this job. I don't want to let McAllister down. Joanne was leaning on the side of the bridge, looking down through the rush of whisky-colored water to the stones of the ancient ford below. *I am lonely.* The observation startled her.

A woman laden with shopping bags brushed past Joanne, knocking against her with what felt like potatoes, startling her out of her reverie. The woman apologized. Joanne apologized, and turned in the direction of the office, then changed her mind.

Chiara will be in the café. Coffee and good company, just what I need.

Joanne should have known something was up the minute she walked into the café. Gino Corelli's grin was so wide his eyes disappeared, making him look like an Asiatic nomad.

"Tell Annie it was dancing at dawn round that standing stone that did it." Chiara laughed when she told Joanne the news.

"Phallic object, my friend Beech calls it."

"What's that?" Chiara asked.

"It's a . . . Chiara, stop teasing."

"I don't care what it is, all I know is I am well and truly pregnant."

"Chiara, I am so thrilled for you both!" Joanne was laughing as she bent down to hug her tiny friend.

They ordered coffee, and they chatted and caught up with each other's news. When Joanne said she had to get back to work, Chiara asked the question only she, as Joanne's closest friend, dare ask.

"Have you heard from Bill again?"

"No." Joanne looked down at the last of the froth in her coffee cup. "I made the right decision to leave, but sometimes . . . I don't know. . . ."

"You mean it would be better to stay with a man who beats you?"

Joanne flinched at her friend's frankness.

"No. It's just that . . ." The whole story came out: the girls' behavior, the disapproval of her parents-in-law, the difficulties of working and being a mother, the impossibility of divorce. It was the same conversation they had had again and again for the last year. The happiness and laughter of a moment ago vanished.

"Now listen to me, Joanne," Chiara was fierce when aroused. "You've fought hard for what you have—a home of your own, a great job—so no giving in now. I understand absolutely that divorce is not possible, why do you think it took me so long to find a husband? It drove Papa and Aunty crazy that I waited until twenty-seven to find the right man. So stay strong."

"I'll try. But, just before Bill hit me, I saw his face in the streetlight, and Chiara, he was *crying*."

In Joanne's experience, men would rather throw themselves off a bridge into a river in spate than cry.

"Can you count the times he promised to change? Is ten years long enough to give him a second chance? Do you want your girls growing up thinking this is how marriage is?" Chiara was relentless.

Joanne examined the red-and-white pattern of the table.

"Another thing. We hardly see you. Papa, Aunty Lita, my Peter, we are your family—all refugees together in this Highland land...."

"I'm sorry."

"Don't be sorry, just promise that once a week, we all have dinner together. You, the girls, we make it a Friday-night tradition, *si*? You come, Aunty Lita cooks, Peter plays with the girls, you and me gossip. *Si*?"

"*Si*." Joanne laughed. "Do I have a choice?"

"Never. I want the godmother for this little person happy."

"I'd love that." Joanne was thrilled.

"Good." Chiara got up, went round to Joanne and hugged her. "Now go back to work and make cow's eyes...."

"Sheep's eyes."

"I know, but cows have lovely eyes—sheep don't. Go back, and you flirt with that McAllister. There is a real man."

"Chiara! Stop teasing! The last thing I need is another man. Once was enough." Chiara's bright, shining happiness was infectious. She touched her lightly on the arm. "Thanks, Chiara." Then she remembered.

"On May Day morning, do you remember I said something about seeing Mrs. Ord Mackenzie's car?"

"Vaguely. You thought it was her car, but weren't sure."

After she had left, Chiara considered Joanne's situation—her loneliness, her optimism, her fears, her severance from her parents, the impossibility of remarrying, of finding happiness with a man who truly loved her. And Chiara concluded, not for the first time, that a society where women were the possessions of men was not a society she would allow her daughter to inhabit. Even if it were only a society of three—herself and Peter and the baby—that was how it would be.

When Joanne got back to the office, only Don was there.

"I saw Chiara Kowalski," Joanne told him. "She's pregnant."

"I bet the baby will be a wee stunner, just like its mother."

"The dad's pretty handsome too, so I'm sure he or she will be gorgeous."

Five minutes passed. No one interrupted them.

"So are you going to do anything about the hiding Bill gave you?"

"What hiding?" She didn't look up.

"I know. It's none of my business."

"You're right. It *is* none of your business," she snapped.

Her eyes filled with tears. She hated it when that happened.

Don saw. He hated it too. It made him furious and helpless and ready to belt the living daylights out of her husband. But he wouldn't do that. He was more a wait and exact vengeance when you'd never be found out type of man.

"Sorry, I know you are trying to help." Joanne looked across the table and smiled.

Don hated that weary, apologetic smile of hers, the way her shoulders hunched as she shrank into herself whenever her husband's name was mentioned. It's as if she's trying to make herself the smallest target possible, he thought.

"There is no way out of an unsuitable marriage."

"A visit in the night from some of my unsavory pals? A carefully arranged accident?" He was about to joke, "like your friend Patricia," but knew that wouldn't go down well.

He looked at her. He took in her bravery, her spirit, and her kindness. He admired the way she tried to make the best of her lot.

"I've a great idea. One of my best ideas yet. Here's what we do." He lit a cigarette. Joanne sat back to enjoy another of Don's preposterous stories.

"You and me, we book into thon motel that's just opened along the loch. As Mr. and Mrs. Smith, of course."

"Of course."

"We have Hector burst into the room and take photos. You get a divorce with me named as your fancy man. Then, you marry me."

"Don, that is the nicest proposal anyone has ever put to me." Joanne was laughing.

"Of course," Don continued, "for it to stand up in court, Hec will come bursting in after the deed."

"After the deed?"

"Naturally." He winked and it made his heart glad to watch her laughter.

Mrs. Betsy Buchanan came in carrying some papers. Today she was in powder blue. Powder blue skirt—tight, powder blue jumper—tight, and a string of bright-blue beads the size of marbles. Joanne secretly thought the tones of blue made Betsy resemble her neighbor's pet budgie.

"Hello, can I join in the joke?" Betsy asked.

"Sorry. It's private," Don told her.

"That's a shame. I love a good joke." She waited. Silence. Joanne turned back to the typewriter. Don searched for his pencil and found it behind his ear.

"There were some calls for you when you were out, Joanne—here are the numbers."

"Thank you, Mrs. Buchanan." Joanne took the notes.

"Anything else, Don?" Betsy asked in her bright bird at dawn twitter.

"Aye," he replied. "It's Mr. McLeod in the office, thanking you. And Mrs. Ross. And Mr. McAllister. But Hec is Hec."

Betsy fled.

Joanne looked down, smiling.

"Don't forget my offer, Mrs. Ross." Don picked up his racing guide to leave. "I'm available anytime." He waggled his head, his eyes wide, his grin wider.

That evening, Joanne discovered the plot. A harsh word, "plot." A word with resonance for every Scot brought up on a history of plots—successful plots, rare; failed plots, common; plots by the English; plots by the clan chieftains; plot upon plot. Now plotting had come to the Ross family.

Granddad Ross? How could he? Joanne felt the betrayal

keenly. She loved her father-in-law. Then she dismissed the idea. No, he probably has no idea. And if he did know, he wasn't party to the plotting.

Annie and Wee Jean always spent Wednesday nights, press night, with their grandparents. Other days, the girls walked home from school, let themselves in, and were alone for an hour before their mother came home. Joanne didn't like it, but it wasn't unusual for children to do this, and they were safe.

They would listen to *Children's Hour* on the radio, Joanne would prepare supper, Annie would do her homework, then it was time for a game or crafts before bed.

This evening, Wee Jean was at the table, immersed in making a picture of a Highland cow from scraps of wool and fabric. Lots of paste was involved. Annie was cutting out paper planets to color in. The tip of the child's tongue was sticking out the left of her mouth as she concentrated on making every planet perfect. She wanted to beat Sheila Murchison, who, Annie was certain, got her mother to do her projects for her.

"Jean, I told you before. Rest the brush on the saucer. I don't want paste all over the table."

"Sorreeeey Mum," Jean replied for about the third time.

"These rings on Saturn are so difficult," Annie wailed. "I've cut them too thin."

"Stick them in the book first, wait for them to dry. Then color them in."

"But I haven't time to wait. I need it for tomorrow."

"There's an hour and a half to bedtime. They'll dry soon." Joanne spoke calmly, used to Annie's dramatics.

"Granny won't let us use paste. When we live with her, we'll never get to make a mess," Jean reminded her big sister.

Annie glared across the table and whispered, "You promised."

"Promised what?" Joanne asked.

"Nothing." Annie kept cutting, but her scissors were trembling.

"Tell me," Joanne asked, trying to control her voice, "I'm your Mum. We don't have secrets."

Annie took two seconds before making the decision. She too had promised to keep it secret, but she was unhappy with the whole idea.

"Granny says Dad says we can't live with you anymore, but we won't have to live with him. We'll live with Granny and Granddad instead."

"But we'll see you nearly every day," Jean assured her mother. "And Granny says I can bring Snowball with me even though she doesn't like cats."

"We'll have a room each at Granny and Granddad's house," Annie told her mother. This was the only point that appealed to her. "We won't have to share anymore."

Joanne knew from long habit that to stop her voice quavering—in hurt, in anger, in pain—speaking loudly and brightly helped. "You are not going anywhere. Now, who'd like cocoa?"

"Me please," the girls chorused.

Joanne went to the kitchen, stood at the sink, gripping the edges of the stone, the cold tap running unnoticed, splashes wetting her dress. She breathed deeply to quell the nausea in her stomach, she shut her eyes tight to hold back the tears.

It was more than outrage—it was the betrayal that hurt her most.

Surely not, her mind was racing, *not Granddad Ross . . . he wouldn't . . . Granny Ross, maybe . . . no, she wouldn't, but Bill can twist her round . . . but surely not Granddad.*

Joanne poured out the milk. She spooned the cocoa into the pan, then the sugar. She whisked the mixture furiously. Every movement she made, every action, was instinctive—making cocoa was a nightly routine. She was in the sitting room, mugs in hand, before she knew how to continue the conversation.

"I like the Highland cow," Joanne started. "Annie, your planets look great."

"Thanks, Mum," Annie yawned. This set Wee Jean off yawning.

"It was really nice of Granny to say you could stay with her," Joanne forced the words out. "She knows how upset you both get when Dad is angry and says he will take you away."

"Can you come too, Mum? Then you'd be safe an' all." Jean was as oblivious as a newborn. The sweet voice, the innocence of her, was almost the undoing of Joanne.

"No." It was Annie who answered her little sister. "I like this house. I want to stay."

Against all her principles on not questioning her children about the Ross family, Joanne had to know.

"What does Granddad say to all this?"

"It's a secret. Granny says we'll surprise Granddad later."

Annie wasn't fooled. Her ear, finely tuned to the nuances of life with warring parents, caught Joanne's anguish. She had no faith in her mother's ability to stand up to her father. They didn't live with their dad anymore, granted, but after years of arguments and fighting and her mother hiding the bruises, Annie seldom believed the word of an adult.

She thought her mother beautiful and funny and clever. She thought their life in their little house was lovely. But Annie kept waiting for it all to end—her mother would give in to their dad as she had so many times before. Mum will say, "We have to pack up and go back, Dad promised this time it will be different." Annie could hear the conversation in her head.

It will never be different, she thought. That was why part of her agreed with her grandmother's plan. *Dad will never do anything with Granny and Granddad around,* she reasoned. *But Mum will be on her own,* was her next thought, *and maybe next time he'll hit so hard she will be really hurt, maybe even . . .*

Annie had been coloring the planet Mars a deep red. Her pencil caught in the paper, and looking down she saw she had pressed so hard with the pencil there was a hole in the paper. Afraid she would cry, she left the table and went to the bathroom, locked the door, and ran a bath. *When I'm grown-up, I'll get him,* she thought. *I'll be a policewoman like Mum's friend WPC Ann. I'll put him in prison. He'll be locked up and stay there for a long, long time, even if he says he's sorry, and he'll never hurt Mum again.*

Twenty past four in the morning, Joanne tiptoed into the kitchen for a glass of water. She knew she must have slept some of the time, although it didn't feel like it.

The water tasted bitter. She emptied out the glass, rinsed it, and ran fresh. It too tasted bitter. *It's me,* she realized, *my mouth tastes foul.* She made tea instead.

She tried to read, then shut her book when she realized she had read the same paragraph over and over with no comprehension.

Joanne knew she was weary to the point of exhaustion. The first faint twitter of the dawn chorus started. As the predawn light spread over the garden, she kept thinking, *I can't go on like this. I am allowing Bill to win.*

It was as though by merely thinking this, she reached the tipping point. *I will no longer let him win.*

Feeling lighter than she had in years, she smiled to herself, curled like a cat, and fell asleep with her head on her arm. She didn't see the slight crack in the girls' bedroom door. She didn't see Annie.

The child stood, feet chilled blue on the bare linoleum, watching over her mother, only relaxing her guard when at last her mother fell into a proper sleep. Then sensing a change, a lightness and rhythm to her mother's breathing, she went back to bed and she too went to sleep.

Next morning, Joanne woke exhausted, but with a sense of clarity like the light on the sea after a storm. For Bill to attack her was one thing, to use their children another. She was yet to recognize it, but the metamorphosis had begun.

Saturday was usually a half-day at the *Gazette*. Being the end of the football season, Joanne knew Hector and Rob and even Don would be working most of the day and celebrating or consoling themselves in the pub afterwards.

The girls were with their granddad. First it would be the matinee at the Palace cinema, then the library.

Public libraries throughout Scotland allowed the borrower four books. The rules were a work of nonfiction for each work of fiction. Luckily, Annie and Granddad Ross had the same taste: travel books, history books, geography books—any book on foreign lands.

"Thon book on the Canadian Mounties was smashing," Granddad said to Annie. "There's lots of pictures. Right bonnie, Canada looks."

"I read about Canada in *Anne of Green Gables*," Annie told him. "I liked this book on China. The women have bandages on their feet, so they can't walk."

"Surely no?"

"Aye, that's what it says."

"Let's borrow a book we can read thegether."

Annie was thrilled. There was nothing better than having someone to talk about books with. These days, her mum was always working or too tired, her friends weren't interested in "grown-up's books." Only Granddad understood. He'd been abroad too, she remembered, in Belgium and France, but he wouldn't talk about it.

It's nice being with Granddad, she thought, *but I want to live Mum. Why can't Dad be dead like Auntie Patricia's husband?*

The child felt no guilt thinking this. It was a logical solution to her fear of her father. At almost ten years old, she knew the thought was wicked, and she was wise enough to keep the idea to herself.

The *Gazette* office was one minute's walk from the library, but Joanne had left already, leaving a message that she could be contacted at the McLean house. She needed Margaret McLean's advice.

When Joanne finished telling her friend her dilemma, Margaret surprised her. She clapped her hands at Joanne's story and laughed.

"How wonderful. It is as good as any story from *The People's Friend.* Family dramas are always so, so . . . ?"

"Nasty?" Joanne asked.

"Gothic, I was thinking."

"Margaret!" Joanne was outraged and laughing and embarrassed, and this was why she had come to visit.

"I know a thing or two about mother-in-laws and wicked stepmothers too," Margaret continued. "This doesn't strike me as either. It seems more like a sounding out of possibilities."

"Maybe." Joanne was not so sure.

"Mrs. Ross is besotted with her only son. As am I with mine. She will do anything to help him—within reason. From what you have told me, she would never harm those girls." Margaret was firm. "If Mr. Ross doesn't know, and I cannot believe he does—such a nice gentleman Mr. Ross—then I have a strategy which always works."

"You do? Yes, of course you do."

Margaret McLean made Joanne feel she could say anything. And she was the only person really interested in Joanne's career at the *Gazette*. She never mentioned Joanne's marriage unless invited, never mentioned Joanne's past, but would discuss it if Joanne wanted.

Margaret entertained Joanne with tales of dancing in Paris and London and Edinburgh and in drafty castles or baronial keeps in the Highlands and islands and Lowlands of Scotland. They talked about books and music and legends and Margaret's deep, abiding passion for couture clothes and shoes. "You could ask Angus for advice. If it comes to your husband attempting to divorce you, with you as the guilty party, he would help," Margaret offered. This was only said to give Joanne hope. Margaret knew her husband's opinion and his horror of divorce cases.

It was not that Angus McLean was prejudiced against women suing for divorce, it was more his experience that divorce was a scandal that marked a woman for life. And the children by association.

"Thank you," Joanne said. *When could I afford a solicitor?* She thought. "There is nothing that will satisfy Bill Ross other than me giving up my job and crawling back to him."

"If it were me . . ."

Not likely, Joanne thought.

". . . I'd do nothing," Margaret continued. "Keep smiling, always be cheerful, greet your enemies with overwhelming niceness. That really rattles them. And makes them feel guilty."

Joanne thought that a very odd approach, but appreciated the logic.

198 • A. D. Scott

"Margaret, you're a wonder. I shall do exactly that. It won't work with Bill, but I'll try it on his mother. Doesn't take much to make a Scottish woman feel guilty about something. My mother-in-law is not such a bad soul. She just thinks her son is . . ."

"Her sun," Margaret supplied.

The joke was lost in the saying, but whatever way Joanne looked at it, Margaret's advice was good advice.

As she was wheeling her bike out of the gate, Margaret called out, "Remember, dazzle the enemy. Smile like a car's headlights on high beam."

In the days and weeks to come, Joanne did just that.

SEVENTEEN

꧁

Jimmy McPhee's visit, he had enjoyed. Calum Sinclair was now finding the case against the McPhee brothers intriguing.

At lunchtime, he went to the Station Hotel bar. He limited himself to a half-pint. The landlady prepared the thick ham sandwiches for him alone. Food was seldom served in a Scottish bar.

From here, in the company of men likely to be summoned for jury duty, he knew he could gauge the atmosphere in the community. Here, he could anticipate the thinking of a jury and be prepared for the trial ahead.

He settled in with *The Scotsman*'s crossword for camouflage, but really, he was imaging the proceeding against the McPhee boys. In his mind's eye, he was watching the performance, as it would be played out before a judge and jury. First the prosecution, then the defense, the witnesses in the case for and against his clients—he could hear the voices in his imaginings. Finally came the summing up. At this point, he could only offer a fair, impartial summing up, and with a judge, this did not always happen.

The evidence was circumstantial. But, Calum conceded, it was possible a stray kick or slap or punch *had* caused a brain injury. There was no evidence though. A fair summing up would warn the jury against this, and against prejudice. Calum supposed it would be just as hard for a Campbell to find justice in Glencoe.

"Can I interrupt?"

The sound of a female voice in the public bar of a public house gave him a start.

"Patricia Ord Mackenzie." She smiled down at him.

He stood, clumsily knocking the table and almost upsetting the beer over his papers.

"Yes, I know."

"Really?"

"I recognize your voice from the phone conversation. Plus, there are not many women who will enter a public house."

"There is no law against it, although some men would like there to be." She smiled. "I know it's scandalous and I don't care."

"Can I get you a drink?"

"A lemonade would be lovely."

While waiting for the drinks, Calum watched Patricia in the bar mirror. She was looking around, and she nodded to a couple of men at a table across the room and smiled at the man who turned to glare at her for daring to be in a man's domain.

"Do you want to move to the snug?" Calum asked when he returned.

"Perhaps we'd better."

The cramped room behind the bar smelled of damp and disuse—*all the better to discourage women from drinking,* Patricia thought.

"I'd better warn you. I asked one of the secretaries in your office where to find you, so expect more gossip."

Calum laughed. "I'm sure it will enhance my reputation being seen with you."

"Thank you, kind sir." She dipped her head, extended her elbows, in a mock half-curtsy. "I ought to be able to move in a man's world, as I am as good as any farmer hereabouts. But no, the success of Achnafern Estate is credited to my father. Never mind that he rarely stirs from his study. His obsession with Napoleon makes life at the turn of the nineteenth century more real than the present for Daddy. It's a shame I wasn't born a boy, is, I believe, the general opinion of the community."

Calum was examining her as she spoke—her body, her face were animated. She smiled a lot. With white, even teeth, clear skin, shining reddish-gold hair, she had the glow of a Russian propaganda poster showing a classic countrywoman harvesting the wheat.

"I shouldn't complain, but the attitude annoys me. Just last month, I overheard the remark that I was a good judge of livestock, 'for a lassie.'" She laughed.

Calum smiled back.

"So, it's good to meet you in person. And as I said on the telephone, I'm pleased you agreed to help the Skinner boy, my brother-in-law I should perhaps call him."

"Not at all, I'll do what I can."

"There is no need to involve me in this business. In fact," Patricia looked at Calum, "the Skinner family want nothing to do with me. Other than pay the bill of course. So it might be best if you don't mention my name."

"I see," Calum said. He didn't, but it was obviously not a matter Patricia wanted to discuss. "Won't you want to know the outcome of the Skinner boy's case?"

"I shall probably read about it in the *Gazette*." She smiled. "But yes, I'd like to know how he gets on." Patricia glanced at her watch. "Heavens—I must go. I have to meet my housekeeper, Mrs. Munro. She'll have a fit if I keep her waiting—she's terrified I'll be burnt to a crisp by a biblical bolt of lightning. Although I did ask exactly where in the Bible God commanded 'thou shalt not visit a public bar if thy name be woman.'"

"I must get back to work too." But he didn't make a move.

"Thank you." Patricia stood and held out her hand.

"Not at all." He stood and took the hand. It was warm and slightly rough. *A farmer's hand*, he thought, and liked her all the more for that.

As she made her way towards the swing doors, Patricia waved her fingers at the overawed barman. When she left, a buzz ran through the room like a swarm of bees in June. She enjoyed that.

Calum smiled as he gathered his papers to leave. He had enjoyed every moment of their meeting.

On his walk back to the office, he suddenly remembered the fatal accident inquiry. "Dam and blast it! I forgot to ask how it went."

He would read about it in the newspaper, *but I should have asked her in person.* All he knew about the death of Sandy Skinner he had learned from the *Gazette.* Remarks overheard in the office from the junior staff filled him in on the community's reaction. The chief comment was how Mrs. Janet Ord Mackenzie must be relieved her unsuitable son-in-law had met a most unusual end. "The kind o' thing you see in a film," one had said.

It had been two weeks since the inquiry into Sandy's death, two weeks since Joanne's account of it was published. Since then, she had heard nothing from Patricia.

No word from Bill either, nothing about the girls' future, nothing about a divorce. *All this quiet is unnerving,* she thought.

"The hearing with John Skinner is at eleven, do you want to come?" Rob asked Joanne.

"I'm up to my eyes in this report from the local council. It seems it will be doomsday before we get a new bridge. Anyhow, I've had enough of the Skinners."

"You should have more confidence in your work," Rob told her with all the experience of a twenty-one-year-old. "One of the best ways to learn is to look at what you've written, then look at it in print after Don has slashed your copy to shreds—always cutting out the best bits, naturally."

"McAllister said the same." Joanne smiled, "but I really have to do this. We can't always be having dramatic headlines, so council stuff it is."

"Can I come and take a picture?" Hector asked Rob.

"Fine, but it's probably a terrible idea. Remember the last time you took a picture of a Skinner?" Rob and Hector simultaneously had a vision of Rob splashing about in the waters of the canal. "This time, be discrete—if that's possible."

"I'll sneak behind something and take a picture as they leave the court. You'll never notice I'm there."

When they reached the Magistrate's Court, Rob left Hector to wait.

Hector was good at waiting—lurking in corners, behind trees, round the back of dustbins, was his specialty. Time meant nothing to him if he thought there was a good picture in it. He removed his lime-green bobble hat, convinced he was now invisible, forgetting that his beacon of hair was equally lurid.

When Rob entered the court he was surprised to see Calum Sinclair with John Skinner. He was also curious as to how the Skinners had linked up with the solicitor—it did not seem their style. Patricia, was his guess. Then again, he didn't think the Skinners and Patricia Ord Mackenzie were on speaking terms. Curiouser and curiouser.

He took his usual seat in the courtroom. A few seats down, he saw a figure he recognized. It was the man who had closed Mrs. Skinner's door on him when he was asking questions in the fishing village—John Skinner's uncle. Seated next to him was a woman Rob took to be Sandy's mother. *She looks as friendly as barbed wire*, he thought.

The hearing had barely started before it ended. Rob was furious. *Another nothing story*, he thought.

Calum Sinclair had obviously been given his instructions at the last minute, as there was a sheaf of papers on his table. Folders too. He had prepared well to argue a not-guilty plea and looked no more happy than Rob.

"I understand you wish to plead guilty to the offense," the magistrate said.

John Skinner looked down and said, "Yes" in a faint voice.

"I have here the report from the procurator fiscal about the incident. I hope you understand the seriousness of the charges," the magistrate continued.

"Yes."

"This is one of the worst cases of vandalism I have come across." There was a pause while the magistrate consulted his papers. "However, because of your age, because you have pled guilty, and you have never been in trouble before, the procurator fiscal has recommended a fine. But the sentence could well have been Approved School. Do you understand?"

"Yes." John Skinner looked down, unable to meet the magistrate's eye.

"I also have to remind you that a conviction means you will have a police record for the rest of your life."

For the first time, the boy reacted. He glanced at Calum, who nodded an "I told you." He glanced at his mother—who did not move—then, turning his back on both of them, he said, "Aye. I mean, yes, I understand."

Rob had to suppress a smile—it must have been a challenge for the boy to say "yes" instead of "aye" to the questions.

"I'm sorry," John Skinner muttered.

"Speak up, boy." The magistrate had heard, but wanted the boy's contrition stated loudly and clearly. Humiliation was good, in his opinion.

In that moment, Rob remembered John Skinner was fifteen. He watched as the boy again looked at his mother. The woman did not, in any movement of body or lips or expression, acknowledge her son.

In a loud, clear voice, barely controlling his anger, John said, "I am very sorry *The Good Shepphard* burned down."

"Fined fifty pounds," the magistrate announced.

The next case was called.

Rob hurried out the court ahead of the Skinners and waited on the steps. It took him a moment to spot Hector, who wasn't hiding, only loitering.

The Skinner trio walked from the courthouse so fast Calum Sinclair had to hurry to keep up.

"John . . ." Calum asked, "why did you change your plea?"

John Skinner looked at his mother and said nothing.

Politeness demanded a pause, a thank-you and a handshake between Calum Sinclair and the uncle. Mrs. Skinner made a "tssk" sound of impatience. John Skinner studied the pavement and didn't once take his hands out of his pockets.

Rob stood in front of them and said, "*Highland Gazette*. Can I have a minute of your time? John, isn't it? Why did you burn down your own boat?" They tried to push past him. Rob didn't move. Only John hesitated before his mother yapped, "John. Wi' me." The Skinners parted and moved around Rob.

"John, what will you do now you no longer have *The Good Shepphard*?" Rob called after them. "Will you be joining another fishing boat? John?" he shouted when they were a good fifty yards away.

All the while, unnoticed, Hector was firing off shots, not game to confront a Skinner again, even if it was a woman.

Calum Sinclair stood by, enjoying the theatrics—it was a modicum of revenge for the way Mrs. Skinner had dismissed him and his hard work in preparing a defense, which, he believed, would have returned a not-guilty verdict.

"Have *you* any comments, Mr. Sinclair?" Rob asked when the Skinners had vanished.

"No, no comment. But I like your style." Calum laughed.

"Ta," Rob grinned. "No comment on the guilty plea?"

"It would not be worth the bother to comment on Skinner business."

All through the brief encounters, Hector had been as good as he had promised—taking the photos discretely and unnoticed.

That was not the bigger surprise for Rob. "Get any good shots?" he asked as they walked back to the office.

"Aye," Hec said.

"Great. We got some good editions out of *The Good Shepphard*—fire, bombs, intrigue, great stories, great pictures. Pity the hearing was a fizzler."

"How so?" Hec asked.

"Because John Skinner, Sandy Skinner's wee brother, pled guilty to throwing the petrol bomb that burned down the boat, so the hearing was really boring," Rob explained. "John stood up, admitted he was guilty, said he was sorry. He was fined. End of story."

"John Skinner. Was he the lad I took the photo of outside the court?" Hec asked.

"Aye. Did you get a good shot of him?"

"I did."

They were nearing the office. "Come on, Hec, I'll buy you a coffee."

"Fine."

Rob noticed Hector did not do his usual jig when he was asked out for coffee.

They took the long, steep steps down to Castle Street, and had gone about twenty yards before Rob noticed Hector was no longer with him. He turned. Hec was plodding along, camera around his neck, head down, hands in his pockets.

"Get a move on," Rob called.

Hec caught up.

"What's your problem?"

"I canny tell you. I'm scared of what Mr. McAllister will say."

"Tell me, maybe I can help." Rob was used to Hec. A problem could be anything from filling out an expense sheet that would pass Mrs. Smart's eagle eye to discovering a Second World War spy living in a Dalneigh council house disguised as a coalman.

"Fine." Hec stopped in the middle of the pavement. The pedestrians parted around the pair as water round a rock. "You said it was Sandy Skinner's wee brother, the lad that was in court that threw the milk bottle that burned down the boat."

"Yes. . . . And?"

"It wisney him that threw the bottle."

"What? Are you sure?" Rob tried to remain calm, but his instinct was to run across the road, up the wynd, and rush into McAllister's office shouting "scoop" or something equally childish.

"I think I'm sure it wasn't him." Hector's bottom lip was sticking out. Rob knew not to ask again. Hec could be stubborn when his judgment was questioned.

"It's something about him," Hec explained with his hands. "He's no the right shape, his head is no right." Hec's hands moved as though describing a ball. "But I'll need to develop the film to be *sure* sure."

"There's a bus—run. We'll make it." He grabbed Hec's hand.

They made it and went upstairs to the front seat. "Two to Dochfour Drive please," Rob asked the conductor.

When they had recovered their breath, Rob told Hector, "We are going to your wee shed, you are going to develop this film, I am going to wait, then you are going to explain to me, no, *show* me, what on earth you are talking about, Hector Bain."

"Promise you'll no tell Sergeant Patience?" Hec was jiggling his legs as though he needed to pee.

"Promise."

I won't tell the sergeant, thought Rob, *but if Hec is right, McAllister will have to tell the inspector, and I will have another great front page.*

There was no hurrying Hector. Rob did not wait patiently, but at least there was a good collection of *Broons* annuals to while away the time.

Prints and negatives ready, Rob asked Hec to bring his magnifying glass and they left for the *Gazette* offices.

Rob was a long time with McAllister. Hector was with them some of the time. Don spent a half hour with Rob and McAllister, then Hector was sent home to blow up two particularly interesting shots. When Hec came back, there was another long and argumentative meeting.

"Joanne, come and join us," McAllister asked.

"May as well have the meeting there," Don pointed out, "more room on the reporters' table."

"Aye, but shut the door." McAllister did not trust Mrs. Betsy Buchanan. Seemed too nosy, was his opinion.

"Right," McAllister started, "look at these."

At the head of the table, he laid out one shot of a person, standing, watching as the deck caught alight. Then below this, he fanned out a selection of shots of the person running or hurrying away from *The Good Shepphard*.

"Quick answers, no thinking," McAllister commanded. "This one," he pointed to the top shot, "male of female?"

"Don't know," Rob.

"Could be either," Don.

"No idea," Joanne.

"I canny tell in this picture," Hector.

"Next." McAllister chose three pictures of the moving figure.

"Don't know," Rob and Don spoke at once.

"There's something about this one. . . ." Joanne hesitated.

"It's the walk." Hector was sure of himself. He grew up when talking about photographs. "It's the way this person kind o' scuttles. See, here, the steps is too short, and the arms are held out like this. . . ." He stood, held his arms out from his sides slightly, his hands at forty-five degrees. "Looks like a woman to me."

Joanne smiled at Hector's imitation of a woman; it was funny but also impressive—he knew what he was talking about.

"This is the most important shot, though," Hector took over the meeting from McAllister. McAllister did not mind one bit.

"See, the hood from the jacket has fallen down." Hec pointed to it with a pencil. The shot was taken at such a distance that the blow-up was blurry. "Never mind the face," he continued, "look at the head. See, small, 'cos the hair is flat, and see this," he tapped a dark blur at the back of the head, "I'm thinking this could be a woman wi' her hair in a bun."

The others stared. Hec reached for another print of the same image and passed it to Joanne.

"I see what you mean," she agreed.

"Now look at these." Hector pulled out the pictures taken that morning outside the courtroom. There were two shots of

the Skinner family as they descended the steps and one as Calum
Sinclair shook the uncle's hand.

Hec then produced blow-ups of the heads of John Skinner
and his mother, taken at different angles. Mrs. Skinner's hat
obscured the top of her head, but a small, round skull, with the
hair in a tight bun at the back, was clear.

What was really interesting were the shots of John Skinner
and his uncle. Like the late Sandy Skinner, their skulls were long
and narrow.

Weasel-like, had been Joanne's mental image of Sandy
Skinner at that terrible Easter Monday picnic on the Black Isle.
The photos in front of them confirmed that impression—there
was indeed something feral about the Skinner features.

"Well?" McAllister held his hands up and out like the ring-
master in a circus. "Are we sure?"

"It's her." Rob was certain because he wanted it to be so. "She
was the one who started the fire."

"It certainly looks as though it could be her," Joanne said.

"I agree, it's her," said Don, "but remember what happened
the last time. The police will no be happy when they see this." He
tapped the picture of Mrs. Skinner running away from the fire.

"The police?" Hector wailed like a banshee. "I'm no going to
the police! Rob, you promised."

Don stuck his fingers in his ears. Joanne put an arm round
Hec. Rob looked away. McAllister rolled his eyes, "Hector, shut
up. We have to report this."

"I'll run away," Hector moaned.

"Hector, listen to me." Rob was terrified Hec might cry.
"I made you a promise and I meant it. Listen, this is what I'll
do . . ." For once, he was stuck for an idea.

McAllister took over. "What *I'll* do is tell DI Dunne how
Hector Bain has done their job for them. I will point out that

it took the photographer from the *Highland Gazette* to discover what no policeman noticed, and how Hector has solved the crime for them."

"You'll be a hero, Hector," Rob said.

"Really?" Then Hec thought of something more, "But if Sergeant Patience thinks I've showed him up, he'll hate me even more."

"Leave that to me," Don told him. "If the Sergeant says one word, I'll tell him it will be front page of the *Gazette* that our photographer showed him how to do his job."

"Jings." Hector's mouth dropped open, and even after years of a diet of Irn-Bru, boiled sweeties, and sherbet dabs, Joanne could see he had not one filling in his back teeth.

It took a day before McAllister received the call telling him of the arrest of Mrs. Skinner. The uncle had also been questioned, but there was no evidence he had been involved, especially as John Skinner refused to implicate him.

"Thanks for the tip-off," DI Dunne said when he called McAllister.

"Not at all," said McAllister. "We want to keep on the right side of the police."

"And have a front-page scoop."

"Absolutely," the editor agreed. "Will you need Hector as a witness for the trial?" McAllister asked.

"Not if I can help it," DI Dunne said.

The tone in his voice made McAllister laugh.

"No," the policeman continued, "we have no problems with the case. Mrs. Skinner gave a full confession. She admitted throwing the petrol bomb. The idea of blaming John Skinner was all hers—she believed he would get off lightly because of his age and no previous record."

"I suppose that is why she persuaded him to plead guilty, to avoid scrutiny."

"Yes, that's what she said."

"Did she say why she burned down the boat?" This was the aspect of the whole affair that intrigued McAllister and everyone else at the *Gazette*.

"Only that Sandy Skinner was no son of hers, and she'd rather the boat was destroyed than him have it. Family feuds," Dunne continued, "they never make much sense."

"One final piece of information . . ."

"Yes?" McAllister said.

"You didn't hear this from me, but the fiscal is furious at the waste of police time over this whole business. He will be asking the magistrate to give Mrs. Skinner a custodial sentence."

"Sure he's not furious because it took the *Gazette* to discover the truth?"

"Now, now, no need to rub it in," Dunne said, although privately he knew this was true. "But it's true. If it hadn't been for Hector Bain, we'd all be none the wiser."

"I don't suppose you could let him know that?" McAllister asked.

"Don't worry, I have it all in hand. Sergeant Patience will be writing to you and to Hector on behalf of the constabulary, thanking you both for helping bring the real culprit to justice."

DI Dunne had to hold the receiver away from his ear as McAllister roared in laughter.

Two days after his hearing, John Skinner turned up at Achnafern farmhouse. He was too scared to come to the big house, so Allie Munro phoned Patricia, explained, and asked if she would come over to the farm.

"Of course," she replied.

John Skinner was sitting at Mrs. Munro's kitchen table when Patricia appeared. *The poor boy*, she thought when she saw him.

"Hello John, it's lovely to meet you at last. I am very sorry about all that has happened and I hope we can be friends."

John doubted that, but he had come to say his piece and he wanted it over with.

"I'm sorry too," he started. "I came over to say I'm sorry for what Ma—I mean, my mother—did because the boat was rightfully yours and the baby's, since Sandy died and you're his widow."

"I beg your pardon?" Patricia stared, unsure she had heard right.

The lad continued speaking in a rush, as though in pausing for breath he might lose his courage.

"I want you to know it wisney me burnt the boat and the police came this mornin' and they took Ma away."

"What?" Patricia's eyes widened, flashing in surprise with hints of glee and amusement. "Sandy's mother? Your mother?"

Mrs. Munro was so surprised all she could say was, "Well I never!"

John Skinner was bright pink from the effort of speaking to Patricia—she dazzled him. "I came to say good-bye, I won't be back for a long time . . . if ever."

"Ever is a long time." Patricia said the cliché automatically, busy trying to understand the revelation.

"John, I'm quite lost," Mrs. Munro spoke to him as though he were a wee boy. "What's this about your mother?"

Her voice worked as well as a Celtic spell to calm the soul.

"It was our mother," he started, looking down, his eyes not yet ready to meet Mrs. Munro's. "She threw the milk bottle, but she didney mean for the boat to be burnt down."

Not that John knew this—it was more that he would never understand his mother's reasoning.

"Whyever would she burn down your own boat?" To Mrs. Munro it was an incredible act, especially for a woman and a mother. *Someone might have been hurt,* she was thinking.

"She was angry at him fishing on a Sunday. And she was angry him leaving the faith. She didn't like . . ." he glanced at Patricia, "his friends. She was always angry."

He stopped. There was no way he could tell them of her rages. As a child, he had thought a ball of fire was burning inside of her. How could he explain that she was always angry at Sandy. He himself avoided provoking her. He was the good boy. Not so Sandy. The fights had been continuous and fierce. Periods of calm came to the household when Sandy was old enough to join the crew of *The Good Shepphard.* But his mother's rage returned the minute Sandy came ashore.

His father was hardly ever at home. He was at sea, or he was down at the harbor mending nets, or keeping the boat spruce and seaworthy. He seldom spoke and never intervened. John loved him. Then he was swept off the deck by a freak wave. Sandy took the boat, took everything. There was nothing his mother could do to stop him. Then she burned down the boat.

"You'll take some tea?" Mrs. Munro interrupted his silence. He hadn't noticed her make it, but said "thank you, two sugars."

"I had no idea." Patricia was thinking of Sandy. "No wonder he found it hard to really care for anyone." She looked at John and saw a quiet, almost scholarly young man, who was obviously miserable. "What will you do now?" she asked quietly.

"When things are cleared up, I want to go to sea, but no as a fisherman. I've always wanted to get into the institute in Stornaway and join the merchant navy as a navigator. But Ma . . ." He was going to say, "Ma won't let me," before realizing that did not matter anymore.

"An excellent idea." *Get away from that poisonous mother*, Patricia thought. She gave him a brief pat on the hand.

John didn't move, but it felt strange to feel a woman's touch.

"I know I'm not popular in your family," she continued, "but if I can ever do anything to help, come and see me here at the farm." Bending down to reach into her bag, she came up with a white envelope. "When I heard you were here, I brought this to pay your fine. Now it can help you start a new life."

She would never say how, before knowing about Mrs. Skinner's arrest, she was planning to give John Skinner the money in the hope that he would desert his family.

John took it, too surprised to refuse. He held it, staring as though it was a magic trick that would transform into a white rabbit.

"Put it in the bank," Patricia advised. "Perhaps use it to study at sea school. And John, good luck."

"Aye," John said, standing, "thank you." He knew he was dismissed. "Good luck to you too." He made for the kitchen door, said one more thank-you, and was gone.

"That was right good of you," Mrs. Munro said.

"I've accepted an offer for my share in *The Good Shepphard II*." She didn't tell Mrs. Munro that the offer made for the new boat was enough to clear the debt to the boatbuilder and put another substantial sum into her bank account. "And John Skinner deserves some help."

"All the same . . ."

"One hundred pounds will give him a good start and I think he will use it wisely."

To Patricia, the payment closed the whole episode of the

Skinners. In time, she would come to believe her baby had been conceived if not by divine intervention, then by power of her own longing.

"One hundred pounds." This was more extraordinary information for Mrs. Munro to digest. The amount was enough to buy a wee but and ben or a coble fishing boat or . . . "That was right generous of you," was all she could manage to say.

"I have more good news, Mrs. M. My new car is to be delivered next week. Won't that be wonderful?"

"A car of your own? That *is* good news. I'm pleased for you, lass."

No more begging the missus to use hers, was what she meant.

Patricia gave Mrs. Munro a hug good-bye and as she was walking back to the big house, she thought about the money from her share of the sale of the boat, plus the money in the bank, and knew that one hundred pounds to John Skinner, although substantial to a young man, made only a small dint in the total.

She went to the study-cum-farm-office, making sure her mother was not around. She dialed the number.

"Patricia Ord Mackenzie here. Mr. Sinclair, please." She waited. "Hello, you will have heard the news, I take it?"

"No?" She smiled. She was enjoying herself. "John Skinner came to the farm to tell me his mother has been arrested for throwing the Molotov cocktail." She laughed. "Yes, I was as surprised as you are."

She listened again. "I will have to come to your office to settle the account, so perhaps we could talk then. Yes, tomorrow morning is fine. I look forward to it." As she put down the phone, she realized she was indeed looking forward to seeing Calum Sinclair.

Eighteen

He's a perfect witness." Calum Sinclair was as pleased as he would be if Ross County ever scored a goal.

"How so?" Jimmy McPhee asked. "I grant you, Duggie the Dummy is a good laugh. Problem is, he's dumb."

"No, he's no," his mother intervened. "He just canny speak."

"Mr. McPhee, Jimmy, the witness's name is Mr. Douglas Donald." Calum was determined to have the name right. "If you're sure he will appear in court as a witness, we can request an interpreter."

"Yon schoolteacher from Culbokie can follow his hands and his sounds," Jenny McPhee smiled. "I know Duggie will agree to testify. I told him it meant a trip to the town. He's never been there in all his fifty-two years."

"Aye, I knew some like that in Sutherland," Calum nodded. "Never been to the town, even though it was only fifteen miles away."

"The Black Isle to town is a matter of a few miles," Jimmy observed.

"The point is that Mr. Douglas, no Donald . . ." Calum was confused.

"Better call him Duggie like everyone else." Jimmy laughed.

"The point is, he was in the woods that night." Calum was sure this would help their case. "He saw and heard your brothers on their way home."

"How does that help?" Jimmy was still to be persuaded.

"Your brothers were on the road to Culbokie. About ten minutes later, the farm lads came along with Fraser following on behind. Duggie can testify to that."

"So, Duggie will say that Fraser Munro was alive and well about half an hour after the fight?" Jenny asked.

"Please use the word 'scuffle.' Fight sounds serious."

Jenny McPhee saw the sense in this and nodded.

"It might be argued that your sons doubled back to get at Fraser when he was alone." Calum would have tried that argument if he were prosecuting. "But Duggie was there most of the night and is certain the lads were not around. There are slight problems with him as a witness—it was estate land, and I've been told Allie Munro warned him off the estate for poaching."

"That's more a joke than anything," Jenny McPhee told Calum. "Everyone catches a few rabbits. Allie Munro warns everyone so as to keep thon auld bat Mrs. Ord Mackenzie happy."

"I have also been told that Fraser Munro was known to tease Duggie about his disability."

"Aye," Jenny said. "I remember. It was more than teasing. When we were working at the tatties, all the lads would play-fight with the rotten tatties, but Fraser threw stones, pretending they were tatties. He was always picking on Duggie, laughing at the noises the poor man made. Mind you, Allie Munro gave Fraser a good clip round the earhole when he caught him at it."

"That's what I mean. It could be said there is animosity between Duggie and the Munro family." Calum wanted to cover all possibilities. "So I hope Mr. Donald won't back down."

"He won't when I've had a word with him," Jimmy said.

"I didn't hear that, Mr. McPhee."

"Jimmy! Haud your tongue, you'll no say nothing." Jenny glared at her son. "Now, Mr. Sinclair, you were saying . . ."

"It's important to emphasize the time of death and question the cause of death. Fraser didn't die directly from the kicking, but the procurator fiscal is saying the earlier injuries contributed to his death, hence the lesser charge of involuntary manslaughter. If we can prove he knocked his head against the bridge, or when he fell into the ditch, or even establish that possibility . . ."

Jimmy folded his arms, sat back in his chair saying, "This is nonsense. Fraser Munro was completely pished. He fell over, hit his head, then he died. My brothers are on trial because we're tinkers. Simple as that."

"Perhaps," Calum agreed.

Jenny looked closely at the young solicitor when he said that. She was pleased and surprised. That one word did it—"perhaps." Here he was, an educated man, but a man of the north, born and bred, and he wasn't disagreeing with the idea that a tinker could be charged just because he was a tinker.

Calum caught the look from Jenny McPhee.

"Do you have a question, Mrs. McPhee?"

"I hope you won't be offended, Mr. Sinclair, but can I ask if you have any Traveler blood in you?"

He laughed. "I'm not in the least offended, Mrs. McPhee. As far as I know, I am not related to any Travelers. Nor have I any prejudices against your clan. My father brought me up on Robert Burns and his favorite is 'A Man's a Man for Aa' That.' I'm sure Rabbie included Travelers in his sentiments."

"Why is no one questioning the farm boys?" Jimmy wasn't interested in this conversation. Books and poets were for his older brother, not him. "They could just as easily have turned on Fraser. I heard he was giving them a right hard time that night—calling them big lassies and worse."

"Their story is that they left him not far from the village. They say he was fine then. Not too drunk to see himself home."

"Aye, they would say that, but didn't the dummy write that he heard them together?"

"Mr. McPhee. The witness's name is Mr. Douglas Donald." Calum sighed. *Thank goodness Jimmy is not needed as a witness,* he thought, *or his brothers would find themselves locked up for a long time.*

"Mr. Sinclair," Jenny intervened. "I'm trying to get this right in ma head. Can we go over it once more, then we'll leave you to get on?"

Calum was liking this woman more and more. He smiled at her, then summarized the case.

"Your sons had an altercation with Fraser Munro outside the hotel. They left straight after that and walked home.

"Next, the men from the farm accompanied Fraser part of the way home, but he became abusive and they left him behind. Then they too went straight home."

"So they say," Jimmy interrupted.

"I agree it is possible they pushed him or hit him, but three men with the same story? Hard to dispute," Calum pointed out.

"Next," the solicitor continued, "Mr. Donald saw and heard your brothers a good mile from where the victim was found. In order to have attacked him, they would have had to turn back and walk a mile or so along the private estate road. From studying the map, there are no shortcuts except through thick woodland.

"Fraser Munro was found in the ditch a short distance from the bridge. There was blood on the stonework, so he probably fell there first. Also, someone—probably Fraser Munro—had been sick.

"Finally, the medical report. There was bruising, but no broken skin on Fraser's legs and thighs. That ties in with your sons' version of events. There was bruising to Fraser Munro's upper arms, as though he had been defending himself. There was also bruising on the back of his neck, just below the skull.

"The prosecution will say that the earlier scuffle with your sons left Fraser weak and injured, causing him to fall against the bridge, and as a result he died. They might also say they came back and hit him sometime later, but that we can disprove. The most important point is the time Fraser died. Duggie will put his death much nearer dawn than midnight. He may not know the time by the clock, but he can tell who was where when the moon set."

"So Duggie's testimony is important. He may no be able to speak, but he can hear a mouse a hundred yards away." Jenny saw the sense in all of Calum's points, but not how they improved her sons' prospects.

"That reminds me," Calum said. "Patricia Ord Mackenzie has volunteered to be a character witness for your boys if needed."

Jenny looked at him, surprised, then suspicious. "Has she now?"

"If they are found guilty, it would help a lot to have someone of her standing speak up for them before they're sentenced."

"I hope it doesn't come to that, Mr. Sinclair." Jenny stood, pushing an obviously heavy handbag up her arm. Calum was surprised yet again at how short she was. Her presence made her seem a much larger woman.

She thanked Calum for his time. He shook hands with Jimmy and ushered them out, ignoring the stares of the secretary and her assistant.

Jimmy and his mother were halfway down the street before Jenny voiced what they had both been thinking.

"That was nice of Patricia."

"I wonder what she's up to?" Jimmy did not catch the irony in his mother's voice.

"We'll never know what the likes o' an Ord Mackenzie thinks. Speak o' the Devil . . ." She nudged her son.

They watched Patricia maneuver into a tiny parking space. It took an effort—the turning circle of a Land Rover was reputed to be half a mile. Mrs. Munro climbed out the passenger door, collected her basket, had a brief word with Patricia, then walked off in the direction of the Co-op. Patricia crossed the road and went into the solicitors' office.

"We have the same solicitors as the Ord Mackenzies," Jimmy laughed. "We must be coming up in the world."

Allie Munro and his younger son Alistair always had tea on the stroke of five o'clock. But not today. When Mrs. Munro came back from town, she found policemen in the farm office, using it to reinterview everyone on the farm. She found the change in routine more upsetting than their presence.

"But why?" Mrs. Munro asked Allie. "They've already spoken to everyone."

"I don't know, lass. But the trial is only three weeks away and they wanted to go over the statements again. Just being careful, I suppose. It was either here or at the police station in Fortrose. I said here to get it over with."

The words of Jenny McPhee kept swarming around Mrs. Munro's brain like wasps after the jam. ". . . *Even more trouble,*" Jenny had said. *So if the McPhee brothers weren't responsible, then who?*

Her grief intermingled with worry, making a tight knot in her chest as impossible to untangle as a pack of fighting dogs.

Something about the morning of Fraser's death was bothering Allie. *What was it?* She remembered she had been asleep, but awakened when Allie rose half an hour before usual, as they were going to start on an early cut of hay.

Allie had gone to wake Fraser. There had been harsh words the day before, when Allie told his son he had to work. He told his son they were shorthanded and Fraser couldn't keep turning up to work only when he felt like it.

Nothing out of the ordinary had happened until later.

It was May Day. Some of the women in the district who still believed in the old ways had been out and about even earlier—washing their faces in the morning dew, hanging rags at the Clootie Well. *A right bonnie morning it was,* Agnes Munro remembered.

So what was it that was worrying Allie? Why was he was kicking and turning in his sleep? Why was he exhausted before putting in a day's work? Worse still—he wouldn't tell her.

"No lass, I'm fine," he had said.

"I'm just a wee bitty tired," he had answered.

"Don't you be worrying about me," he had reassured her.

But the more she considered it, the more she felt the shadow of trouble hanging over them.

There had been a schoolteacher in her young life, a lovely woman, from Falkirk, she remembered, and this teacher was always saying these wee sentences, ones that stuck in your head, ones that the teacher said were good to remember, to help you through life. "A trouble shared is a trouble halved" was one of them.

She went to the phone. She picked up the receiver and dialed.

"Dochfour 251," her cousin Mrs. Ross replied.

"Elsie, it's me, Agnes, I wis thinking of coming over for a visit."

That night, when Alistair had gone to bed and Allie was sitting in his chair picking at the newspaper, not taking in a word,

Mrs. Munro said, "Father, I'd like to go to town and visit ma cousin."

"Grand idea, lass."

"I was thinking I might stay the night."

"Why not? See Joanne and those bairns an' all. It'll do you good."

"I could leave some pies in the larder and a pot of soup. There's a cake in the tin." She suddenly remembered. "I'll have to ask the missus, I hope it will be all right with her. . . ."

"You leave the missus to me. Just go, lass. Me and the young lad, we'll no starve. Tell me when you're ready and I'll drive you to the ferry."

It was the thought of not having to ask the missus for a day off that did it. She would go. "Come on Saturday," her cousin had said, "stay for Sunday. Catch an afternoon ferry back, that'll give us time for a good blether."

When they arrived at church, the girls went into the church hall to Sunday school and Joanne walked down the aisle to her usual seat beneath the pulpit. Mrs. Munro, Aunty Agnes to everyone in the family, was there with Granny and Granddad Ross.

In this very new church, built to serve the spreading housing estates, there were chairs rather than pews. The pulpit, plain and simple, was in wood and the altar the same, with a lush midsummer floral display on either side. The heavy cross that dominated the plain, whitewashed walls was also in unadorned wood.

Duncan Macdonald, minister, father, brother-in-law, and friend, believed in plain speaking as much as a plain church. His Christ was "fishers of men," the carpenter, the obedient son. His was the Christ of love and forgiveness. Exactly the Christ for Agnes Munro in her pain and confusion. She listened to the sermon, not once bored. She followed the thoughts. She understood, and was comforted by, the message.

The singing of the Twenty-third Psalm almost undid her. It's message of hope, comfort, and abiding goodness, brought comfort to the grieving mother, and Mrs. Munro left the church feeling lighter than in a long time.

After the service, the Reverend Macdonald stood on the steps of the church for the ritual handshakes. When it came to Mrs. Munro's turn, he leaned forward, they spoke quietly, and Joanne could see her nod in agreement.

She collected the children from Sunday school. They all walked slowly back to the Ross house, Agnes Munro with her cousin, Joanne with Granddad Ross, pausing to greet neighbors and friends as they went—another ritual.

Sunday dinner was always the same: soup, roast beef, bottled fruit, and custard. The girls ate every last bit of the custard. After a cheerful argument with Mrs. Munro that she was a guest and wasn't allowed to help, Joanne and Mrs. Ross cleared up, washed and dried the dishes in good time for Granny Ross to check the results of the football pools.

Mrs. Munro was told to put her feet up on the sofa and rest. She couldn't rest. She was fretting, afraid the bus would be late, afraid she would miss the ferry, afraid that Allie and her youngest couldn't manage without her.

"Come away into the garden, Agnes, see my rockery," Mrs. Ross said, knowing there would be no peace with her cousin "up to high doh" as she always put it.

Agnes Munro told her what was bothering her.

"It's the minister," she said, "he's coming round in his car at three o'clock. I feel I'm imposing, but he wouldn't take no for an answer."

"He's a good man." Mrs. Ross was glad the minister was going to talk to Agnes. She felt unable to truly comfort her cousin, for she had never liked Fraser. She had thought him a bad lot, especially this last time he came home, and felt hypocritical when she had to mourn his loss. But she felt deeply for Agnes's pain.

"I insist on running you to the ferry," Reverend Macdonald had told Mrs. Munro. "No arguments."

Mrs. Munro didn't like to argue, but wasn't Sunday his busy day? He had the evening service, and he probably had to pray and do whatever it was ministers did to talk to God so he could tell them what to preach from the pulpit.

"The bus is fine," she said, "I can't impose."

But no, he insisted he would take her there.

He collected her from the Ross semi-detached. He said he could not come in, but stopped to admire the new rockery. The drive to the ferry did not take long. Parking his car near the ramp, Duncan suggested they wait by the sea wall.

"No need for you to wait, Reverend Macdonald."

"If you don't mind, I'd like to wait. I love watching the ferry. A grand sight, the old *Eilann Dubh*."

As they waited in the shelter of the sea wall, Mrs. Munro spoke without any forethought. The question popped up from somewhere deep inside a troubled conscience. Afterwards she was amazed at her daring.

"I think my husband is hiding something about how our Fraser died. I don't know for sure. I ask, but he'll no talk. He keeps saying 'everything's fine.' But he willney look at me when he says it. He thinks I don't know our Fraser was kicked out the army, he thinks I don't know what Fraser got up to; I'm his mother, I'm no blind to Fraser's faults. Besides, you can't help but hear every bit o' gossip on the Black Isle. That's no all, something else is bothering my man, I just know there is."

This was the longest speech of Mrs. Munro's life. All her fears came tumbling out, each sentence a pebble dropped into a pond of despair, making ripples that would reach into their lives for a long, long while.

"What can I do to help?" Duncan asked. He towered over the small, plump figure. Without his robes, she could see how skinny he was. *Needs proper feeding*, she thought.

"Oh no. I mean . . . thank you for the offer Reverend, but you've already helped," she replied. "You did a right fine reading o' the Twenty-third Psalm." She smiled, remembering. "My father was a shepherd, you know. When I was a wee girl, I used to help him with the newborn lambs, feeding the ones who couldn't suckle. We kept them in a dog basket in the kitchen."

"The Lord is my shepherd. I shall not want," Duncan Macdonald quoted.

"Aye. Just like that." Again Mrs. Munro felt the comfort of the words. "My favorite bit is, 'In pastures green, he leadeth me. The quiet waters by . . .' It's like the back burn at our place. Lovely it is, with the quiet pools and the waterfalls. A comforting place to walk."

They stood in quiet contemplation of the ancient words. It was Mrs. Munro who broke the silence.

"I didn't remember the morning my Fraser was taken, not at first. It was walking along the burn, listening to the quiet that reminded me. . . . It was quiet that morning . . . it was different only in that we had to be up early for the hay. . . . I never noticed anything, not really. . . .

"Sorry, Reverend, I'm thinking out loud, trying to make sense o' it all."

"Talk all you want, it often helps." His voice was smooth and calming, yet distant, not intruding into the unconscious stream of thoughts.

"Goodness and mercy . . ." she again quoted. "Mercy can mean forgiveness, can't it?"

"To forgive and to receive forgiveness. That is our Lord's message."

They stood quietly. It was as though the thought was a reminder that life was not only of the body, but of the soul.

"Thank you, Reverend Macdonald. You've been a great help, and a comfort." She looked up at him, gave him a shy, wee smile. She was still overawed by the minister, but that is as it should be, she felt. He was a man of God.

His immediate thought came from a favorite Burns poem.

"Wee sleekit, cow'rin', tim'rous beastie,
Oh what a panic's in thy breastie!"

And like the fieldmouse, he knew her panic was not for herself, but for her family.

The ferry drew up, ropes were secured, then the ramps lowered with a clatter that echoed across the firth to the Black Isle shore. Across the fast-flowing tidal race, Mrs. Munro could see the distant shape of the farm Land Rover waiting for her.

"God bless you and keep you, Mrs. Munro. Remember, I am always ready to listen if you need someone."

There was nothing more she needed to say so she simply said, "Thank you."

As the ferry left, she saw the minister standing beside the sea wall, watching the boat leave. She gave a little wave. He doffed his hat and used it to wave back.

Watching his wife as she walked up the jetty, Allie Munro was glad she was back.

"How are you, lass?" he greeted her.

"I've been thinking about what happened to our Fraser," she came straight out with the sentence, none of her usual hesitations.

"Best not," he replied quickly. "We'll never know for sure so best not to dwell on it."

It was said. And they did not speak of it again until there was no alternative.

Nineteen

After another impressive edition of the *Gazette*, with the arrest of Mrs. Skinner taking up most of the front page as well as a detailed account of the saga on page three, McAllister sat in his office, alone, looking out the window at nothing much—clouds, a passing seagull, two pigeons preening their oil-on-water plumage on the window ledge.

He was in that letdown-after-major-triumphs state of ennui.

"You're busy. Maybe I should come back later." Rob stood with his hand on the doorknob trying to suppress a smirk.

"One day, someone will thump you," McAllister told him, but he did not take his feet off the desk.

"The McPhee brothers' trial is three weeks away. I'm thinking of going to the scene of the crime with Hec for some background shots in case we need them."

"A good idea."

It was only when Rob shut the door and sat down that McAllister moved his legs. "So, what do you really want?"

"Sandy Skinner."

"The verdict was accidental death." McAllister lit a cigarette. He had no opinion one way or another on Sandy Skinner's death, but he was open to an argument.

"It's nothing much," Rob started. But McAllister saw from the way he leaned forward, from the way his eyes lit up, that it was much more than nothing.

"First," Rob counted, "the time between Sandy walking down

to the falls and Patricia waiting in the Land Rover—for over an hour according to her. But no one saw her there."

"Did anyone look for verification?"

"Not that I know. Second, why Dores? It doesn't make sense."

McAllister leaned back in his chair, interested in Rob's thinking. "Joanne said it was because she was distraught. And sick."

"Mmmm." Rob rolled his eyes.

"Spit it out," McAllister told him.

"I'm sorry Joanne covered the hearing, not me." He saw the editor frown and quickly added, "It's not that I don't think Joanne is up to the job, but she doesn't have a clear head when it comes to Patricia. I should have gone to see how Patricia played her audience."

"A bit harsh." But McAllister nodded when Rob said this.

"I've watched Patricia Ord Mackenzie in action before."

McAllister knew what a coup it would be for the *Gazette* if there *were* something suspicious about Sandy's death.

"Any nosying around must be discrete. Don't tell anyone what you're up to. Talk only to me if you find out anything. Above all, do not alert Patricia. Mr. Ord Mackenzie is a friend of the chief constable, the lord lieutenant, and probably the Almighty himself."

"Don't worry. I can be discrete when I need to be." Rob gave a mock salute and left McAllister to think about his proposal.

There might be consequences in poking into a case that was firmly closed, but the editor trusted Rob's instinct.

On Saturday morning, Joanne and Rob were going over to the Black Isle with Hector. He was to give them a lift back to the ferry when they had finished, before continuing on to photograph the Ross County football match.

"Remember, I want shots of the goals—not the supporters and not the goalkeeper's dog," Don had warned Hector.

The problem with the arrangements became apparent on the first part of the journey, the short drive from the office to the ferry. Hector may have been blessed with a marvelous eye for a photograph, but had no eye for the road and was constantly distracted by passing scenes, mentally framing them in a camera lens.

"Hector, keep your eyes on the road!" Rob shouted as they passed over the Black Bridge.

"What? Oh, aye."

He swerved back onto his side of the road, avoiding an oncoming lorry.

"Hector!" Joanne shouted from the backseat. She shrank down low, away from the doors, trying to present as small a target as possible to each oncoming vehicle, parked car, or inconvenient tree. "I'm keeping my eyes shut till we get to the ferry."

Another half mile and Rob couldn't look either. "Stop, Hector, pull over. I'll drive."

"No you'll no. It's my car and I'm driving."

"Pull over then. I'm getting in the back with Joanne, and we'll both keep our eyes shut." He climbed in the back, and he and Joanne held hands and tried not to look on the final mile to the ferry ramp.

The little black car stopped at the top of the jetty. They tumbled out of the backseat.

"I feel sick," Joanne said.

"Me too." Rob's face was white with a distinct green tinge. "I've never been so scared."

Hector was shouting and waving his tourie. One of the crew walked up, took the keys, drove up the metal ramp onto the boat, and parked the car. Joanne and Rob looked at each other.

"That's not usual," Joanne said.

"Neither is he," Rob pointed to Hector in his lime tourie with oversized pom-pom, his Clachnacuddin football scarf, and his leather schoolbag.

After the intrepid trio had crossed the firth and driven the final eight miles, "no faster than twenty-five miles an hour," Joanne had told Hec, they reached the village hotel.

"That was the longest eight miles of my life," Rob told Joanne.

"Never, ever again—I have children." She opened the door, glad to be standing on firm ground.

After a tour of the car park, and a discussion of what photos might be needed, Joanne said she'd walk to Achnafern farmhouse.

"It's only two miles," she told Hector, who was insisting on giving her a lift. "You have work to do, I'll enjoy the walk."

As she strode up the hill through the village, Hector was torn between taking photographs, running after her, or listening to Rob, who was calling him into the hotel. He compromised by taking a shot of Joanne striding past the village cemetery. He knew it was where Fraser Munro and Sandy Skinner were buried and wanted pictures . . . *just in case*, he thought.

The reception from the occupants of the hotel bar was cold to the point of arctic.

"We might as well have landed from Mars for all we have in common with the people over here," Rob said, as they sat with a half of shandy apiece. Hector was used to this treatment, so he hadn't noticed. No one even took up the offer of a free drink. So they talked to each other, which surprised Rob—he hadn't had a conversation with Hector since primary school.

"The best way to figure it out is to look at the map," Hector suggested. "I've got one in the car."

Rob was trying to ignore being ignored when the landlady

brought over an unasked-for beer. She put the glass down, then leaned over to pick up the empties. "If you want to know anything, ask at the post office."

"Oh. Right. Thanks."

Hector returned with an Ordinance Survey map showing the countryside at half an inch to the mile. All the farms were named, cottages marked, even standing stones were noted.

Rob's finger traced the road to Culbokie. The turn-off to the private farm road was clear.

"Fraser Munro was found at the Devil's Den—here. The McPhees would have had to go well out of their way to follow him."

Hec pointed to the large expanse of forest marked on the map. "I bet it's scary in the dark with all them trees."

"Not to mention the risk of meeting a bogyman. Or the Devil." Rob made horns above his head like a bairn at Halloween.

"He met the Devil at the Devil's Den."

"Hey! That's good, Hector. I'll use that."

Rob folded the map. "No use hanging around here, no one is going to talk to us."

He paid, and leaving Hector to take shots of the hotel, the car park, the road, the church, anything that caught his magpie eye. Rob walked across the road to the post office, a small wooden shed that could only accommodate two customers at a time. He did a double take when he saw the postmistress.

"Aren't you the landlady, or are you her twin?"

"No, it's me. I help my husband out in the bar when I'm not in here." She came out from behind the counter and turned the sign in the door to Closed. "Now I don't want you saying you got this from me but . . ."

"I promise."

"There's a lot more to Fraser Munro's death than anyone's

willing to say. Maybe you should ask about the fight farther up the road with the other boys on the farm."

"Fight?"

"Maybe no a fight as such. But definitely a falling out. No one's going to say anything because they all grew up together, work together, live right next to each other. I not overfond o' tinks, but it's no right they're getting all the blame. There's times I might have hit Fraser maself, but he was the kind o' man who'd hit even a woman back."

"So who *will* talk to me?"

"Aye, that's your problem, isn't it? The way people round here see it, charging the McPhee boys is better than charging them on the farm."

"Maybe I'll ask Beech," Rob said, more to himself than to the landlady.

"Is that Mr. Beauchamp Carlyle?"

"It is."

"That's fine company you keep." The landlady-cum-post-office-mistress looked impressed.

Rob realized he had gone up a minimum of five notches in the woman's estimation. He made a mental note to add her to his Black Isle contact list—so far a list of two, the others being the vet and of course Beech.

Next, Hector drove them to the scene, stopping at the turnoff to Achnafern Farm to take pictures. On one side was the forest, on the other the fertile agricultural land that gave the Black Isle its prosperity.

Worth marrying Patricia to become laird of all this, Rob thought. *Nah, nothing would make it worth marrying Patricia.*

Half a mile farther on, the farm road made a sharp left turn. The road dropped steeply, made a right turn to a set of two stone bridges with a narrow island between, then rose from the gloom of the fern and forest to the brightness of skylarks and open farmland above.

Hec stopped the car between the two bridges.

"This is why it's called the Devil's Den," Rob informed Wee Hec. "The island is between two streams, where the Devil can't get to you, as he doesn't cross water."

"Like 'Tam O' Shanter.'" Hector loved that poem.

Taking his cameras from the car, Hec scrambled around the banks of the twin streams, looking for angles to maximize the shafts of light dappled by reflections from the water. The burns were swift and noisy, the water divided by a large rock at the top of the small valley, funneled into narrow channels under each of the small bridges. The keystone of the larger one, covered in rust-colored moss, would photograph beautifully.

The sun disappeared. The now-heavy light, the thick forest, the ferns, dark green and moist from the tumbling burn, made Rob shiver. It was indeed a place of the dead, and perhaps the Devil.

Hector jumped onto the parapet of the bridge. "I'm a troll, fol-de-roll. I'm a troll."

Rob watched Hector giggling like a thing demented, and was grateful for the diversion.

"Aye, I can see the resemblance, but you're not scary enough."

The funny thing was, Hector did look like a troll with his bobble hat and his wee, short legs.

"Hurry up, Hec, I'm cold."

"Me too."

Rob walked a few yards up the road. "That isn't where Fraser was found, you know, it was farther up, in the ditch."

"Aye, but a ditch is ditch, and this here looks great. Very spooky." Hector was putting the lens cap back on. "Besides, Devil's Den reads much better than roadside ditch."

Rob stared at Hector. "I never knew you could read."

Watching Hector chortle at the insult, Rob started laughing too.

"Let's get the heck out of here, Hector," Rob said in his best John Wayne voice. "Come on . . . Hector. . . . It's not that funny."

Still chortling, they got into the car.

"Right," Rob decided, "let's collect Joanne from Achnafern Farm."

It took a long ten minutes to drive the car out of the Devil's Den—Hector had never mastered the skill of hill starts.

Joanne had walked up the garden path to the farmhouse noticing that the daffodils were finished, the narcissus too. But there was a fine display of violets, lilies of the valley, and the azaleas were in fine bloom.

She noted how prosperous Achnafern Farm was: the neat cottages, the well-kept byres and steadings, the very shiny new-looking tractors, and, in the distance, the cows fat and gleaming. A lot of them too, she thought.

Joanne had knocked on the front door and waited. She had knocked again after a minute or so. It was not unusual. People seldom used their front doors—they were reserved for formal guests, visitors of importance, so she walked round the back.

The door to the porch was open, the door to the kitchen ajar. Voices could be heard, not clearly, drowned out by the sound of clattering pots and pans and running water.

"Mrs. M, I hate seeing you upset, but we can't interfere . . . Joanne. Hello."

"Hello," Joanne's voice was loud, embarrassed she had walked in on an argument. "I knocked, but you mustn't have heard."

"Goodness, I lost track o' the time. Come in, come in." Mrs. Munro was upset that a visitor was seeing her in a state.

"Patricia, how are you?"

"Couldn't be better. It's Mrs. Munro who is rather out of sorts."

"That's no' fair, Patricia. I can't stand by and let the McPhees take all the blame. . . . This shouldn't be happening."

Joanne had no idea what Mrs. Munro was talking about, but she had clearly taken offense at Patricia's dismissal of her unease. The phrase "high dudgeon" came to mind. Joanne loved the word "dudgeon," but had never quite known what it meant—until now.

"I'll make the tea." Mrs. Munro went to the sink, her shoulders still carrying her anxiety.

Patricia and Joanne discussed Patricia's health, the weather, the best place to shop for wool. The conversation was running down. Mrs. Munro rescued them with tea and Dundee cake.

"Oh for heaven's sake," Patricia shook her head like a pony tossing away bothersome flies, "we may as well tell Joanne. She will find out sooner or later."

"I don't want you putting this in the newspaper," Mrs. Munro warned. The unexpectedly fierce voice surprised Joanne.

"Joanne, this is completely confidential. It will come out at the trial, but . . ." Patricia turned to Mrs. Munro, "it is better Joanne writes it nicely than some horrid reporter in another rag."

"I know," Mrs. Munro sighed. She knew there was no avoiding more newspaper headlines.

"Calum Sinclair, the solicitor, informed Mr. and Mrs. Munro that he asked for another opinion on the postmortem report. It seems Fraser was injured a second time, and some time after he left the hotel." She spoke in one long stream, in a factual, head-prefect-giving-a-speech voice. "It is possible Fraser died as late as six o'clock that morning."

Joanne didn't know what to think. "How will this affect the case against the McPhee brothers?" she asked.

"This is only one expert's opinion. It doesn't change anything. Not yet anyway," Patricia said.

"Our Fraser was always one for fighting. . . ."

"Best not tell anyone that, Mrs. M." Patricia said it lightly, but her glance was towards Joanne.

"More so since the army." Mrs. Munro was off on a tangent of her own. "It was an accident, I'm thinking—too much to drink, he fell, he hit his head, then he . . . Forgiveness . . . that is what the Lord teaches us."

Joanne and Patricia looked at each other. Patricia gave a slight shrug, but said nothing.

"It's terrible no one found our Fraser earlier. Maybe then he'd be alive . . . but only us uses the farm road . . . and no one went looking for him until morning." Mrs. Munro had said the same to Allie, and to her cousin Mrs. Ross. It was a thought that she couldn't leave alone.

"He was a grown man, Mrs. M., and a soldier. You couldn't look after him all the time." Patricia leaned over and covered the older woman's hand with hers.

Joanne watched the tenderness between them. She envied that touch. She could not remember when last someone had touched her with love.

The sound of Hector's car meant the end of the conversation. All three women, all for different reasons, were relieved it was over.

"Bye, thanks for the lift." Joanne waved at Hector from the ferry.

"I hope nobody sees me on the bus," Rob grumbled when the ferry was halfway across. "Not good for my image."

"You could have gone to the football with Hec."

"Never!" Rob shuddered at the thought of another mile with Hector Bain at the wheel. "So, a worthwhile trip?"

"Yes, but with more questions than answers. You?"

"The same."

"Patricia was there," Joanne said casually.

"How is she?"

"Getting big. She said it's a sure sign it's a boy."

"Really?" Rob said carefully, not wanting to put his foot in it again. "If she does have a son, it will be the first time in many generations for that family. Maybe that's why Patricia went for Sandy—to stir up the gene pool."

"Oh Rob!" Joanne elbowed him, laughed, then ran ahead towards the gangplank. "Race you to the bus stop."

They arrived at the office. Everyone had gone except Mrs. Smart. Joanne fetched her bike, Rob wheeled out his motorbike.

"Fancy a cup of tea, swap notes?" he asked.

"Love to, but I have to get home. Granddad Ross will be dropping off the girls."

"Tonight?"

"A Saturday night? Haven't you got better things to do than sit with a middle-aged married woman and drink tea?"

"I could steal some of my mother's gin."

After the girls had gone to sleep, and that took much longer than usual because they loved seeing their uncle Rob, he and Joanne settled down to talk. Rob had tried tuning in to Radio Luxembourg to hear the latest music, but there was so much static he gave up.

They settled down with a pot of tea. Rob enjoyed Joanne's small bungalow, with the mismatched furniture and the pots of lush ferns and trailing plants and shelving full of books and annuals and magazines and knitting patterns and boxes overflowing with felt and fabric and rolls of butcher paper. Children's paintings, posters, postcards, and drawings filled one wall.

Opposite hung a variety of mirrors in round, oval, square, or long and narrow frames in gilt or plain or wood or rococo, reflecting the light and the artwork and the greenery, making the room seem twice the size and twice as interesting. The very untidiness felt artistic.

"Next time I'm at Hector's washhouse-cum-studio, I'll ask him for a picture for you," Rob said. "Some of his work is really interesting."

"Did you tell him that?"

"Never." Rob laughed. "Which reminds me . . ." He described Hector's troll dance and was glad to see Joanne laughing.

"Where Fraser died is gloomy, well-hidden, and yet only a short distance as the crow flies from the farmhouse. An ideal place to commit a crime."

He smiled, but he had been spooked by the Devil's Den and glad of Hector's clowning. "Your turn," he finished.

"Well," she started, "I walked in to a discussion between Mrs. Munro and Patricia. When they saw me they immediately went quiet."

She told him most of what she had found out.

"Remember, not one word to anyone about the uncertainty over the time of death." Joanne shook her finger at him.

"Scout's honor." He gave the three-fingered salute. "Interesting that Fraser was alive until early morning."

"That's still a matter of opinion. But what does it mean exactly?"

"No idea. Could have been the other lads on the farm did for him, could have been anyone, even the tinkers. It's interesting and frustrating—yet another piece of information we can't publish."

"I think Mrs. Munro is hiding something. She also has this deep vein of forgiveness, and doesn't think the McPhee brothers should be on trial."

"Great headline that, 'Mother of Victim Forgives Accused.'"

For once Joanne didn't chide Rob for being flippant—she was getting the hang of the newspaper culture.

He stretched his arms and legs and yawned. "I must be off, all that country air . . . Joanne, I'm glad you decided to stick at the job. You're a good reporter."

"Early days yet," she smiled at him, pleased with his praise. "I have no idea what I'm doing a lot of the time. McAllister said he'd teach me."

"Better watch out. He fancies you."

"Rob!" She looked away to cover the hot prickly rush of blood to her face.

As he was leaving he asked, "Do you want me to sneak out the back garden? I've left my bike well up the street."

"I . . ."

"Consider it done."

As she was locking the doors, something she had never done before the problems with Bill, Joanne felt a sudden sadness.

Yes Rob, she thought, *I really do want to be a reporter. And I want to be happy. But it's hard when I have to sneak friends out the back door, and I jump at every noise in case it's my husband come to threaten me, or worse.*

Cycling to work on Monday morning, Joanne knew she should have spoken to Granny Ross before now, but she'd never found the right moment. The trial was starting soon—that had been her excuse. So today was the day she would preempt her mother-in-law. The thought gave her and her bicycle the wobbles.

A double-decker bus pulled into a stop in front of her. She waited, not wanting to cycle past it only to have the bus overtake her on the narrow bridge. *This is the exact spot I thought I saw Mrs. Ord Mackenzie's car.*

As she reached the *Gazette* building, the smell of acid and ink and newsprint and damp stone walls hit her—as it did every morning. *If I had known when I started what I know now, would I still want this job,* she asked herself as she climbed the stairs. *Yes, I need this job if I am to be me.*

The reporters' room was empty except for the smell of stale cigarettes and men and the fountain of crumpled copy paper issuing from the top hat. It took Joanne a moment to realize what was missing—the constant ringing of the telephone. Betsy Buchanan was now in charge of the downstairs switchboard.

Joanne was yet to decide which was worse—continually answering the phone or the sound of Betsy's "Hold please, I have a phone call for you, Joanne, oops, sorry, Mrs. Ross."

Joanne also suspected that not all calls for editorial were getting through, with Betsy making her own decisions as to who was important enough to speak to a journalist, and who was to be dropped into a disconnected netherworld.

She picked up the receiver.

"Good morning, Joanne," Betsy Buchanan chirped.

"It's Mrs. Ross at work, please." *Heavens I sound childish,* Joanne thought, "Could I have an outside line, please?"

"Give me the number and I'll connect you."

"An outside line, thank you, Mrs. Buchanan."

Joanne was feeling cross by the time she got through to her mother-in-law for the first skirmish in Margaret's battle strategy of "dazzle them till it hurts."

"Dochfour 251."

"Hello, it's Joanne." Her voice sounded unnaturally bright. *Calm down, calm down,* she told herself.

"Is anything wrong?" Mrs. Ross sounded anxious.

"Not at all," Joanne reassured her. "I'm phoning to say that as Mrs. Munro is staying with you the Wednesday of the trial, the girls will be going to my friend Chiara's."

There, I've said it. Joanne was finding it hard to breath. She was phoning her mother-in-law, scared that if she were alone with her, she would say something she would regret. Every time she thought of Bill and his mother scheming to take the children from her, she trembled at the betrayal.

"I see . . ." Mrs. Ross was suspicious, waiting to hear the catch.

"Only for that week, though. The girls love staying over, and they'll really miss their night with you and Granddad."

"It's no trouble having them," Mrs. Ross replied, again sounding as though she was waiting for a punchline.

"I'm pleased to hear it." *This is it, tell her. Now.* "In fact, just the other night, Wee Jean was saying how you told them they could always live with you and Granddad if anything should happen to me." Joanne ignored the stifled noise at the end of the line. "It's *so* good of you to think of that. Very reassuring for me . . . and for the girls . . . to know you and Granddad are there."

Joanne managed a laugh, which she was certain sounded completely false. "I'd better watch myself crossing the bridge on my bike. Don't want anything to happen that might put me in hospital again. Mind you, young girls can be quite a handful, even for fit and healthy grandparents like yourselves."

"Aye, it would be hard but . . ."

"Anyhow, I must get on with my work. Thanks for the thought about taking care of the girls. We'll talk later about the trial, maybe go together to show cousin Agnes our support." *Stop blethering Joanne,* she told herself. "Cheerio Mum. See you soon. Thanks again."

Joanne barely heard the "cheerio" returned.

As she was about to put down the phone there was a click on the line, but Joanne was so relieved the call was over to give it much attention.

Next, Joanne thought, *I will have to tell her that I've arranged for the girls to go to Chiara's house on weekdays after school. But that will mean one less accusation of neglect Bill can throw at me. And the girls will love it.*

TWENTY

꧁

Jimmy McPhee was sitting in a bar, thinking deeply, drinking moderately—for him.

"Can anyone join the party or are you waiting to be turned into a pumpkin. Or, in your case, a turnip?" Rob had been standing unnoticed at the end of the table.

"You do come up with a load of shite sometimes."

He and Jimmy grinned at each other. Rob took a seat.

The corner was dim. The early summer sun attempted to penetrate a window opaque grey with grime. The bar was part of an old inn on the north road, part of the town's history. Frequented now by railway men and bus drivers, in its day it was a resting place for coachmen, and drovers in for the cattle auctions. It was said to be haunted—perhaps by a clansman fleeing Culloden—if he had had the time to stop for a drink. More likely the ghost was a customer unhappy with the beer, coming back to haunt the landlord.

"Since I'm staying on the *Gazette*, leaving my break for the south another couple of years, I want this to be a good story," Rob told Jimmy.

"Wise move, staying for a whiley more."

"You think so?" He was pleased to have Jimmy's opinion. He was also one of the few who understood that beneath the rough, menacing exterior there lay a very rough, menacing interior. But intelligence with it.

"Aye. You know what they say about big fishes and small lochs. I suppose you're wanting information?"

"I want an idea of this trial before it begins."

"In that case mine's a double Glenfarclas."

I'll never get this past Mrs. Smart, Rob thought, *this time McAllister will have to sign the expenses chit.*

The drinks arrived. They settled down to talk. It was not so much an interview, more a think-aloud session.

"Remember, for your ears only."

"I'm too scared of you to break my word," Rob told him.

"As it should be."

"If Fraser didn't die until dawn, he must have lain by the roadside all night," Rob started the discussion.

"Maybe. He should have sobered up by the early hours, though. Lying on that road by the Devil's Den all night doesn't seem right. Maybe he had a carry-out."

Rob looked at him, waiting. Jimmy was picturing the geography of the farm.

"If you cut over the field a wee bit farther on, there's a great big shed where the tractors, the combine harvester, the Land Rover, all the farm equipment is kept. There's also plenty o' straw bales to make a good bed. So I was thinking, he might go there to sleep it off."

Rob made a note. "Has anyone checked it?"

"Aye, the polis searched the farm buildings and found no sign o' him."

"So?" Rob couldn't follow Jimmy's thinking.

"If he could have, he'd've gone there, I hear he'd done that before. So maybe something else happened to stop him."

"Do you think he got into a fight with the farm lads?"

"Maybe. Fraser had a right nasty way o' getting under yer

skin. He was always calling them a bunch o' big lassies who'd never traveled far from the farm and never would. Maybe no a fight, maybe a wee set-to, same as my brothers had."

Jimmy paused to take a sip of the excellent whisky.

"Another thing," he continued after smacking his lips in loud appreciation, "Fraser's wee brother. No one has said one word about him in all this. But he was around that night. He hated his big brother for the way Fraser disrespected their da.

"Then there wis the dogs—they barely barked when the farm lads returned, just a wee welcome yelp or two. But I heard that just before dawn, something spooked them. They was barking enough to set the dogs in the big hoose off as well."

"How do you know all this?" Rob was fascinated. Jimmy McPhee was very well informed.

"It's been common knowledge this past year that Fraser had gone too far wi' that tongue o' his. His fists too. Don't forget, we Traveling folk work on most o' the farms hereabouts. More and more o' our cousins have left life on the road and settled. You canny have a pish in the burn without us knowing."

Rob knew this to be true. The old way of life of the Traveling people was coming to an end, sometimes forcibly. He thought it a pity, but not many would agree with him.

"Anything else? Anything more solid?" Rob was fascinated by the speculation, but he couldn't see how any of it would help Jimmy's brothers.

"Sinclair has this idea that there was some injuries that didn't come from a kicking from lads wearing wellies," Jimmy told him.

"He can prove this?"

"Maybe, but no for sure. Whoever kicked him or hit him must have been in a right rage."

"The trouble is," Rob pointed out, "the procurator fiscal doesn't have to prove your brothers killed him, or that they had any intension of killing him. For involuntary manslaughter, all that needs to be proven is that the injuries received outside the hotel led to his death."

"I know. And the eejits have admitted the fight . . . no, no a *fight*, a *scuffle*, wi' Fraser."

Jimmy was not happy with the brothers. "If the worst happens and the boys are found guilty, Calum Sinclair says that since the boys have never been in trouble afore, that will help. He's also lined up the minister from Culbokie as a character reference, and Patricia Ord Mackenzie—she'll say they are good workers, no trouble ever."

But as Jimmy said this, Rob could hear the doubt in his voice. Once a tinker, always a tinker would be the feeling in the court.

Rob had a sudden thought. "Could a woman have done it? Hit Fraser? Women kick out when they're furious. Isn't a man more likely to punch?"

"Aye. If they square up to their opponent, a man will punch. A woman is more likely to kick and pull hair and . . ." He stood abruptly, spilling some of Rob's untouched shandy. "Thanks for the drink, lad. I have to be off."

"To see a man about a horse, I suppose."

"That as well. Say hello to yer mother. And mind, this conversation is between us." Jimmy was gone before Rob could put in any witticisms about his mother and her bookie.

Rob took a sip of his drink. He thought through the discussion and decided there were far too many permutations of possibilities in this case. He closed his notebook, pleased at the prospect of the next episode in the family drama. That was how he saw it, family—the Ord Mackenzies, the Munros, the farm workers, the tinkers, all with their allotted place in Achnafern Estate, all part of the tight-knit community of the Black Isle, and therefore family.

I hope this isn't another story where I can't write up the juicy bits, he thought. But cheerfulness was in his bones. *The trial will be a cracker of a story one way or another.*

In another bar in another town, Calum Sinclair was having similar thoughts. He was still smarting from the John Skinner fiasco. Apart from being lied to and made to look an idiot, Calum felt he had been cheated of a chance to show his abilities.

He was hoping that the trial of the McPhee brothers would compensate, and establish his reputation.

He sighed. This was a messy case—too much information, too much speculation, with a large dollop of innuendo. Added to this, there were many possible contributing factors in the death of Fraser Munro. And no alternative suspects.

But as the police said, Calum reminded himself, *it is possible the kicking did lead, however indirectly, to Fraser Munro's death.*

He put down his pen and reached for his beer. He enjoyed his pint, enjoyed being solitary in the company of drinkers, had no wish to return early to his lonely lodging house. There was another reason; from here in the Station Hotel bar, he could gauge the atmosphere of the community. Here he could anticipate the thinking of a jury. And be prepared.

He had heard the mutterings in the town.

"Stands to reason, they hit him, he died, so they done it," one farmer had started, before spotting Calum across the bar.

"One of my friends at school was a tinker. . . ." the barroom barrister would begin.

"My auld dad always gave them work," the son of a two-acre croft would contribute. "When they could be bothered to work, that is."

"He's done well for himself. For a tinker." This came from

a punter who had placed a bet with Jimmy McPhee on the two o'clock at Ayr and won a substantial amount.

Calum was not without his fanciful side. A highly rational man, he had an endearing but valuable asset for a solicitor—a sense of the drama of a trial, a sense of the unsaid. Trials had undercurrents. This trial would have more than most.

He set his pint on the table alongside his camouflage documents, donned a warning frown of concentration, and put himself into the role of the foreman of the jury.

The court usher made the usual declamation. The sheriff settled in. The match began.

Calum imagined the procurator fiscal presenting his case. He listened to himself for the defense. He heard witnesses for the case against his clients. He heard the testimony from their side. He could clearly picture them all, could hear the voices. He imagined the sheriff, saw the robes and the wig, but not the face. He tried to listen to the summing up, then snapped back into the here and now. His fervent imagination could only offer what *he* considered a fair, impartial summing up. Who knows what the sheriff would say?

Being the son of an ardent, active socialist of the Keir Hardy variety, Calum was brought up to be aware of prejudice and its rotting corrosive effects. The cause of wars even. He remembered the gypsies, the Continental equivalent of tinkers. Another race had suffered the larger evil, but the fate of the Romany should never be forgotten.

The charge was clever. It wasn't necessary to prove the McPhee brothers directly responsible, only that their actions set off a chain of events leading to Fraser Munro's death. However lesser the charge, it could still mean time in prison.

A fair summing up would make the case difficult to

prove—the evidence was circumstantial. The sheriff could warn against taking into account who the young men are, who their clan was. He could warn the jury not to give undue weight to testimony from those from the farm, as they were almost family to the deceased. He could point out that postmortem findings were not an exact science . . . he could . . . he should . . . Calum knew enough to know never to speculate on the foibles of the Sheriff's Court.

Yes, he thought, *this case will be quite the challenge.* And he acknowleged the thrill of the challenge.

A murder trial was rare in the Highlands. That the charges were manslaughter didn't count; that it was murder was the general consensus of opinion.

The trial was rushed. Everyone wanted it over before the summer recess, especially the two lads waiting in the gaol. It was not the adventure they thought it would be.

The McPhee brothers, like all of their family, had seldom lived without the constant of sky, the blue or the grey or the black, star-pierced, ever-changing canopy of sky.

The raspberries would be over. This year, for the first time since they were small boys, they would not pick the berries where, in the rigid rows of canes, in the company of friends, there was good money to be made. They talked about missing the short season of the sweet wild deep-purple-red rasps, and the dirty-gold yellow variety. In roadside hedges, on the fringe of woodland, along the banks of burns, in patches of bramble, in beds of nettles, the wild raspberries grew. Then it was quick quick, pick them, eat them, before the grubs got them, yes, there was no harm in swallowing the wee white wriggly creatures, maybe even made the berries that bit sweeter.

The hay making too, that they had already missed. The smell of fresh-cut meadows, the itchy arms and legs, the aching backs from tossing, bending, tossing, working the pitchfork as an extended limb with hardly ever a spill, tossing the hay up above to the bogie and riding home at the end of the day, lying on the fragrant pile of work, tired, happy, the day never seeming like work.

And after the long day in the still bright late evening light, they would miss the jumping into the pool under the short falls of the Goose Burn. And the fire, and the charcoal-flavored tea, and the tatties roasted in the embers, and whatever their ma had cooked in the cauldron that hung on a tripod over the fire, so old it could have been used by *Macbeth*'s witches.

They remembered the laughing and pushing, wrestling games with a brother or cousin, teasing each other over a girl or the Stewart sisters from Muir of Ord, and being struck dumb if ever a girl spoke to them. The many falls-off-a-horse stories, or a story so long-standing it had grown with each telling, grown so not much of the truth remained except the beginning, which was, "Mind when . . ."

And when it hurt to remember, they took turns in saying, "Jimmy'll sort it out."

Rob was to cover the trial. Joanne would attend and add her thoughts to the reporting. Journalists from the *Press and Journal* and the *Ross-shire Journal* would be there. Rob was hoping he would have a short write-up accepted by a prestigious Scottish daily. If the coup of national publication came off, Rob would make sure the stringer from the Aberdeen paper knew. Modesty was not one of his virtues.

Others from the *Gazette* would attend—deadline allowing. Mr. Beauchamp Carlyle would put in an appearance for the pomp and pageantry and as a resident of the Black Isle. McAllister wanted to watch Calum Sinclair in action to see if he was indeed a young man going places. Don would show his face occasionally to give support to Jimmy McPhee.

Margaret McLean thought she might attend. Patricia Ord Mackenzie would be there to support Mr. and Mrs. Munro, as would Granny and Granddad Ross. That Patricia was a possible character reference for the defendants had not been mentioned.

The Black Isle contingent—Mrs. Munro, Allie Munro, three farmhands, a neighbor, the landlady from the hotel, and the local postman, who witnessed the scuffle in the car park—all came over on the ferry for the trial, all in various degrees of anxiety and excitement. Such an event in their uneventful lives would become the stuff of barroom and sitting-room and out-in-the-fields and indoors-in-the-barn conversations for years to come.

The jury of eleven men and four women was as neutral as could be hoped for. A railway clerk, a pharmacist, two schoolteachers, an architect, a senior civil servant who worked in the county buildings, an unknown but virtuous minister's wife, a butcher, a nurse, a hill farmer, and five others Calum didn't know. All fifteen jury members seemed safe enough—if you discounted the restless plumber who wanted it over quickly, as he had a big job on and didn't trust his new apprentice.

From Calum's inquiries, it seemed the sheriff was impartial, at least no one said otherwise. Edinburgh establishment was the word on him, not a farming background as Calum had feared. Farmers and tinkers had a symbiotic relationship, which even the landed gentry acknowledged. The loss of so many Highlanders in the war meant the seasonal hiring of Traveling people was even more vital. But the collective memory of Hogmanay losses of various fowl, especially geese, kept the prejudices alive and fresh.

So, Calum thought, *no more than the usual prejudices against tinkers—and that is substantial enough.*

He shared his opinion of jury and sheriff with Jimmy and Jenny McPhee, "The jury is about as good as we could hope for."

"No one from Muir of Ord, that's good," said Jimmy.

Quite what Jimmy had against the denizens of Muir of Ord, Calum didn't know—or didn't want to know.

"But thon farmer, I don't like the sound o' him," Jimmy added.

"From his address," Calum told him, "it seems he's a hill farmer from the back of Daviot. They don't employ Travelers on their land."

"Maybe so," Jimmy was not reassured, "but they have prejudices a' the same."

"So do you," his mother reminded him. "I've heard you make many a joke that wouldn't bear repeating about sheep farmers."

"The butcher from Kiltarlity should be on our side. If he wants his Christmas geese, that is."

Calum made a choking sound. "I didn't hear that, Jimmy."

Calum left them. He wanted to, not that he needed to, review his papers before the start of the case against George and William McPhee.

The *Highland Gazette* office was quiet—Joanne had gone home, Don disappeared. As McAllister was leaving, he noticed Rob alone in the reporters' room.

"How did it go in court today?" McAllister asked.

"Interesting. I'm just finishing up my notes. Tomorrow should be better, though." Rob was looking forward to it.

"Fancy coming to my place for a drink?" McAllister asked. "I can't be bothered with the public and the barroom journalists telling me how to do my job."

"Why not?"

They walked downstairs.

"Do you want a lift on my bike?" Rob asked.

The look on McAllister's face said it all. "I'll walk, thanks. See you at my house in fifteen minutes."

Rob was waiting on the front doorstep when McAllister arrived.

As he walked into the sitting room, the slight smell of damp offended McAllister. It might be summer, but high ceilings and Highland temperatures still warranted a fire. Plus he hated his books smelling fusty.

He put a match to an already-set fire—back copies of the *Gazette* started a fine blaze. He found a bottle of wine. He poured himself and Rob a glass, and the color and the scent and the taste made him all the more glad of the warmth from the fire.

My blood has thinned after all those years in Spain and in France, McAllister thought.

"*Slainthe,*" Rob toasted.

"*Santé,*" McAllister replied. "So," he asked after a good swallow of a lovely Burgundy, "before you tell me about today's trial, have you come up with any new information on Sandy Skinner's accident at the Falls of Foyers?"

"Ac-ci-dent?" Rob pronounced each syllable slowly, separately.

"That was the verdict."

"It was. And no, I know nothing more. It probably *was* an accident, it's just . . . well, you're always telling me to trust my instinct, and . . . and nothing really. It's all too pat. . . . Sorry, that sounds like a Don pun."

His grin made McAllister feel his age. *This is the new generation,* he thought.

"I keep coming back to the same question," Rob continued. "Panic. It's a plausible explanation for driving all the way to Dores to report him missing, but panic is not Patricia."

"Hang on to your instincts, keep an open mind, and all the usual clichés that Don would delete."

McAllister knew, as Rob now knew also, that without Don, and subeditors the world over, there would be no decent newspapers.

"So, today's trial. What happened?"

"It was a roll call of the witnesses to the fight outside the pub. In spite of all the fiscal's efforts, it was clear it was nothing more than a drunken kerfuffle. The McPhee boys were sober; they only had a pint apiece, taken in halves—all they could afford. It was also agreed that Fraser Munro was completely pished."

Rob thought about the witnesses who had taken the stand.

"The postie was straightforward, he described the incident, and nothing could shake him. The landlady was next. She enjoyed the drama and described the evening with much sighing and 'it was terrible.' So, so far so straightforward."

"How was the atmosphere in court?" McAllister was interested in the subtleties that could sway a jury into making mysterious decisions.

"The real surprise of the day was Calum Sinclair. It was like he was starring in a film."

Jimmy had told Rob that the solicitor was good. Rob's father had said Calum Sinclair was an up-and-coming man. The word around Ross and Cromarty was that he was one to watch. Today he had shown his abilities.

Rob described how the fiscal tried to keep the hotel landlady to a straightforward account of the evening's events—no simple task. Calum, however, went for the embroidered version.

"Mrs. Forbes," Calum had asked, "did you ever bar Fraser Munro from your inn?"

"It was terrible, he was shouting and swearing . . ."

"So you had no choice but to bar him?"

258 ◆ A.D. Scott

"Aye. We couldney have that. We're a respectable . . ."

"I agree. I've visited your hostelry. So, tell me, how many times did you have to bar Fraser?"

"Two times already this year . . . and it was only April. It was terrible. His poor mother . . ."

"Did you have to ask him to leave at other times?"

"Aye, before Christmas and at Hogmanay. He was also barred when he was home on leave a few years ago."

"Thank you. Would you say he was drunk when he left that evening?" Calum continued.

"Aye, well away. And he bought a carry-out—a half-bottle of whisky."

"He had a half-bottle of whisky for the road home?"

The procurator tried in a halfhearted way to object that no one knew if Fraser had consumed the drink, although he knew an empty half-bottle had been found near the body.

"What Calum Sinclair did," Rob told McAllister, "was he made it all seem real. He had the witnesses telling it in their own way, in their own voices. Calum showed the court that beyond doubt Fraser was as drunk as a stoat when he left the bar that night. Calum also made it clear Fraser Munro would make a saint lose their temper."

"Anything else?" McAllister asked.

"No. Although I did end up feeling sorry for the prosecution. Try as he might, the fiscal couldn't get anyone to say the McPhee boys hit Fraser Munro particularly hard, or with malice. The main impression was that the dead man deserved what was coming to him."

"That could also work against the defense."

"You mean the McPhee boys had good reason to double back and hit him again?" Rob thought it over. "Perhaps," he conceded.

"Tomorrow?"

"Tomorrow will probably be about the finding of the body. The police, Mr. Munro, Mrs. Munro maybe, the medical reports . . . I hear Calum Sinclair is to make a thing of the initial medical opinion."

"When will the McPhee boys be on the stand?"

"Never—if Sinclair has any sense," Rob laughed. "They were a complete liability. Smiling, waving, behaving as though their release was a foregone conclusion."

"The jury won't like that. Nor the sheriff."

"To be fair, it was probably a huge relief for them to be out of that prison and into some fresh air," Rob conceded, "but they were way too cocky."

"When do you see the trial finishing?"

"Maybe Wednesday if the medical stuff becomes complicated."

"Deadline day then," McAllister said.

"Don't I know it!" Rob groaned.

"From what you've told me," McAllister said through a haze of cigarette smoke, "it looks like there is a story here for my friend on the Glasgow paper. So, write it up for the *Gazette* first, then another news story for down south, then a few days later a more thoughtful article for the Sundays. Write that the charges are flimsy, bringing up the subject of prejudice against tinkers. Mention a small, farming community shaken by double deaths on the same day. . . ."

"I can mention Sandy Skinner's death?" Rob asked to be sure.

"The facts—two deaths on the same day, of men from the same farm . . . quite a coincidence." McAllister caught Rob's doubtful expression. "OK, Sandy only recently married into the estate, but we are in the newspaper business. Find a way to make the story fit the facts, or . . ."

"Or, never let the truth get in the way of a good story."

"You've been listening to Don McLeod." McAllister laughed.

They finished the evening with McAllister's famous cock-a-leekie soup—to which he added an un-Scottish dash of wine, and bacon rolls.

When Rob had left, McAllister finished the bottle by himself with a well-worn copy of *Travels with a Donkey* for company. It was a story he had read many times, and just as many times he had promised himself to travel in Stevenson's footsteps. He would never admit this, but he found Modestine to have much in common with some women of his acquaintance—past and present.

At the end of the first day, Calum Sinclair was also reviewing the trial. He now knew the problem was not going to be just prejudice against tinkers, it would also be prejudice against the accused. And it was all of their own making.

They were sublimely unconcerned by the day's proceedings. They smiled at everyone. They waved at their mother. They called out, "John, how are you doing?" to one of the witnesses, a farmhand their own age, whom they had known since they were children.

They smiled at the jury. They nodded agreement with the hypotheses put by the prosecution, interjecting an occasional, "aye," or "no we didney." The boys agreed with all he, Calum, asked in his cross-examination of witnesses. They said, "Thank you, Mr. Shand," to the postman when he spoke up for them. By mid-afternoon, the sheriff gave them one final warning to be quiet or they would have to leave the courtroom.

"The eejits," Calum muttered, having caught the expression from Jimmy.

The problem was, he had had no idea how to shut them up.

He could see how frisky they were and felt for them. It was like a Highland terrier bitch he'd had as a child, who, when in heat, had been shut in the washhouse for a week. When she was released, she had gone crazy for a fortnight.

"The daft galloots," Jenny said when Calum had discussed it with her. "They're sure that big brother Jimmy has fixed everything, that no harm can come to them when he's around."

"That's not all of it," Calum told her. "They believe that with their mother, the famous Jenny McPhee there in court, it is even less likely anything can go wrong."

Jenny knew in some parts of the Highlands, she was not so much famous as infamous.

"I feel like giving them a good shaking," she said.

Jimmy agreed. "It'll be more than a shaking if I get hold of them."

"Can I quote you?" Calum asked Jimmy.

"Mr. Sinclair, make it clear to them that if they don't stop their carrying on, I will personally wipe the grins off their faces."

"That should do it," Calum laughed. "I'll let them know."

TWENTY-ONE

❦

Morning, Joanne."

"Goodness! You made me jump. I don't expect to see you in so early."

She looked up at McAllister to see if there was a problem, a reason for him to be in the office at twenty to nine in the morning.

McAllister grinned. "And I of course expect you to be in a good half hour before anyone else," he teased before perching himself on the edge of the reporters' table. "No, I'm in early because of the trial. Don and I want to prepare two front pages for this week, in case we don't get a verdict before deadline."

"I hope it finishes quickly too."

"Now you're sounding like a newspaperman, sorry, woman."

She didn't tell him she hadn't given the *Gazette* deadline a thought; she was hoping the trial would end early for the sake of Mr. and Mrs. Munro.

"I might pop in today if I can find the time. My mother-in-law would appreciate me supporting her cousin Agnes Munro." *And I want to keep on the right side of Granny Ross*, Joanne didn't tell him.

"Of course. Pass on any typing to Betsy. Tell her I said so."

He's noticed, Joanne thought, *he knows Betsy will do nothing to help editorial if it's me that's asking.*

"I was going to go myself," McAllister continued. "Rob filled me in on the first day. It sounds like it might hot up. Second days of trials are often like that."

"Do you want me to write about it too?"

"You don't have to," McAllister said, "but a contribution from you is always welcome. I like your style. It makes a good contrast to Rob's writing."

Joanne fiddled with her pencil. She was childishly pleased at the compliment. "We'll see what happens," was all she could say.

"Talk later then."

When McAllister left, Joanne went back to finishing a write-up on plans to renovate Bridge Street. She was trying to work out how to imply that "renovate," in this case, meant "demolish." She couldn't concentrate. *Blast that man*, she was thinking, *he always manages to make me feel sixteen and never been kissed.*

A noisy clatter echoed up the stairwell. Rob arrived.

"How come your new bike boots make such a noise?" Joanne stared at them.

"I put tacks on the heels so I could slide them along when I'm driving. You get great sparks."

Joanne waved a pointed forefinger at him and, in her best Edinburgh schoolmarm accent, said, "So tell me, Robert, *how* old are you?"

Rob was saved by the phone.

"Hello. Oh. I see. Yes Betsy, I'll tell her." He turned to Joanne, "Betsy said your mother-in-law called, checking whether you'd be in court today and Betty told her yes, you would, because she has to do your typing."

"How dare that woman answer my calls for me!" Joanne ripped the sheet of copy paper from the typewriter, scrunched it up, threw it at the top hat, and missed. "She's a cheeky bissom . . . I'll get her back one day."

"So tell me, Joanne," Rob was laughing and backing out the door as he said it, "*how* old are you?"

He was down the stairs and on his way to the court and she still couldn't think of a reply.

"Budge up." Joanne pushed into the bench beside Rob.

Onlookers were jammed together, the trial being something of a spectator sport. Joanne saw her mother-in-law behind them and gave her a little wave and huge smile. Jimmy and Jenny McPhee were sitting on the opposite side of the aisle. Calum had instructed them to keep out of sight of the boys.

Joanne looked around. The procurator fiscal she did not recognize. Calum Sinclair she did not know either, but was impressed by her first sighting of him. He looked solid, trustworthy, a mother's favorite son—he would go down well with a jury. She noted the McPhee brothers looking suitably subdued, the jury suitably expectant.

They were all commanded to rise by the clerk of the court. The sheriff entered, all in the court rose, the second day of the trial commenced.

The first witness to be called was Detective Sergeant Wilkie, who gave his evidence in a stilted stylized bullying an inferior voice.

They must train to be this boring, Rob thought, *train to speak in that special courtroom voice*. He had a theory that the police believed if the jury was sufficiently bored, they wouldn't remember the evidence and find the defendant guilty by default.

After the policeman, who only established what had been covered in the previous day's session, came the doctor who had certified the death.

His evidence was brief. All he established was that when he arrived, Fraser Munro was dead.

Next, the findings of the postmortem were tabled. Fraser Munro had died as a result of a cerebral hemorrhage.

It didn't take long for the prosecution to make clear in the minds of the jury that a knock on the head from a fall due to a push or a shove could induce a brain hemorrhage.

"Bleeding on the brain," the fiscal decided to call the condition.

Good move, Calum thought, *makes a nice clear image for the jury, most of whom would hardly recognize the word "hemorrhage" never mind spell it.*

The procurator fiscal asked the local pathologist to list the injuries. Unfortunately, the man described every tiny cut, graze, bruise, wound, without indicating if they were fresh or otherwise. There was a bruising to the thighs and ribs, a bruise on the neck, and gravel rash on the side of Fraser Munro's head consistent, he told the jury, with a fall.

"So," the fiscal summarized, "Fraser died from bleeding on the brain, caused by a blow to the head. This blow could have been inflicted hours earlier. Fraser Munro collapsed, perhaps hours later, and Fraser died."

"Yes." The pathologist sat waiting for Calum Sinclair's questions.

Calum took his time. He had noted his opponent's frequent use of the victim's name—"Fraser this", "Fraser that." *Another good move,* Calum thought, *makes the jury feel like Fraser was someone they knew.*

And, Calum thought, *I'm willing to bet he calls the boys,* "McPhee this" and "McPhee that." The McPhee name had not many positive connotations in the Highlands of Scotland.

He looked at the pathologist. Before him sat a man who worked exclusively with the dead. His suit and tie had first seen life perhaps thirty years earlier. And, almost to the point of cliché, the man had a voice that had the life sucked out of it.

"Do you have any questions?" the sheriff asked Calum, becoming impatient with what he saw as delaying tactics.

"Sorry," Calum said, "I was thinking over what has just been said and I'd like to repeat it—to be clear."

Then Calum spoke, only looking for "yes" and "no" answers from the doctor.

"Mr. Fraser Munro died from bleeding in the brain?"

"Yes."

"The blow *was perhaps* inflicted hours earlier?"

"Yes."

"Mr. Munro collapsed *perhaps* hours later?"

"Yes."

"Mr. Munro could *possibly* have been hit again?"

"Yes."

"*Perhaps* hours later?"

"Yes."

"Thank you, that is all."

Rob nudged Joanne in the ribs and hissed a triumphant, "Yes," seconds after the last "yes" was heard clearly throughout the court.

The minor victory for Calum Sinclair was mitigated by the next witness—Allie Munro.

Not a big man, he looked solid. Not a handsome man, he looked dependable. Most of all, to the jury he looked like one of them. From years of working closely with the Ord Mackenzie family, Allie could moderate his Black Isle dialect and glottal stops, giving the impression of a man of substance. His suit—navy blue, bought off the rack from a high-street chain of tailor shops—was the same suit worn by three members of the jury.

When he had finished his description of finding his son dead on the roadside, one of the female jurors hid tears, one man had to clear his throat, and all of them, men and women, were moved by his account. He was indeed one of them.

"You went out when?" the procurator fiscal asked.

"Half past six."

"That is when you usually start work?"

"No, seven, but seeing it was May we were doing an early cut to make silage, and I wanted to go by the milking shed to talk to the man who's in charge of the . . . the cows." He stumbled over the word, he would naturally have said "coos," but this was the Sheriff's Court.

"Then what did you do?"

"I took the tractor out. I always have a wee look around the farm first thing."

"What happened then?"

"I was driving along, and being high up, I could see into the ditch. I saw a jacket, and . . . and it was ma son."

"Just before the Devil's Den?"

"Aye. I thought he was drunk, then I thought he was hurt . . . so I got off the tractor and I . . . I touched him and . . ."

The fiscal waited, no questions, allowing Allie to tell the story in his own time and words.

"I kneeled down beside him," Allie Munro continued, "and I touched his head and I held his hand and there was no much of anything I could do because he was dead.

"But I pulled him up a wee bit 'cause it wisney right him lying in a ditch, and I laid him on the grass. There were lots o' them wee orchid flowers there," *the kind Agnes likes*, he remembered but didn't say, "and I put ma jacket over him."

Allie paused for a moment, thinking through the sequence. *What next? Oh. Right. Our Alistair came up the road, but he didny touch his bother, nor come near him, he somehow just knew, and he turned and ran away. But no need to mention any of that, Allie decided.*

"Then I ran to the big house to use the office phone," he continued. "I didny want Mother to know what had happened to Fraser, not just yet. All I could think was to call the doctor. He said he'd be right out, and told me to call the police. So I did. Then I ran back and waited wi' ma son Fraser. . . .

"Then they arrived, the doctor first, the police after, and a wee whiley later I took the tractor back an I went across the yard an told Auld Archie, who'd come looking for me, and he said he'd get everyone working, and then . . . then I talked wi' Agnes. . . ." This was a part he never wanted to remember.

It was the noise she made. It was a roar, a sound coming from deep inside of her, it coursed through her lungs and her heart and her bone marrow, dislodging some piece of her that would never be replaced.

Standing in their kitchen, helpless, holding her, he had heard the echo of another roar. Not the same sound, but of the same source, a positive to this negative, a light to this blackness. That other roar he had heard ringing across the farmyard, twenty-nine years earlier. He was forking hay into the loft and his Agnes was giving birth to their firstborn. A roar, a cry, a mewling sound, and his sister Effie shouting across the morning, "It's a boy!"

He wouldn't let Agnes see Fraser. "Not yet," he had said. But she saw him later . . . when he was tidied up, much better than seeing his face and the blood and the sick all over him. Allie shook his head the way you would when you were working and fiercesome midges were biting and nothing could make them go away.

The procurator fiscal looked at him, then at the jury, then back to Allie. "Thank you, Mr. Munro. No more questions."

An excellent move, Mr. Fiscal, thought Calum, *leaving everyone in court, reliving that morning with Allie Munro.*

Calum stood. "Mr. Munro, I am sorry you lost your son."

He paused, ostensibly to allow the witness to recover. Calum had been watching Allie Munro throughout his testimony. He had been waiting for some bend in the flow of the story, but he felt not a ripple.

"Tell us about the night Fraser went out and didn't return. Did you hear anything unusual that night?" Although Calum's voice was soft, it had the knack of carrying to every corner of the room.

"Not a thing."

"Are you a heavy sleeper?"

"I am that. It's hard work on a farm."

"Did you hear the other farmhands return?"

"No, I never did."

"Dogs, did you hear dogs in the night?"

"Nothing."

"Early that morning, was there anything different?"

"No."

As Calum questioned the witness he sensed, no *felt,* something was bothering Mr. Alistair Munro—he was answering the questions with too much certainty. It could be the courtroom, it could be the sight of the men who had attacked his son, it could be he was telling everything he knew. Calum did not believe for one moment the man was lying, but *there is something unsaid,* he thought.

What? Calum asked himself. *I have no idea,* he concluded. So he said, "I have no more questions."

Allie Munro's face remained its clear, trustworthy self. But deep in his brain, as brief as lightning, visible only if you were looking into the hazelnut brown of his eyes, there was a flash of relief. And Calum was looking. It was a trick one of his professors had taught him. *Watch them when they think it is all over,* he had told Calum.

Calum watched. Now he knew. He looked at Allie, holding his eye for a fraction of a second, then nodded, letting him know he knew. Then Calum sat down.

Allie Munro waited. All in the room waited quietly, recovering from the testimony. The hush had an intensity to it; to lose one's child was a fate no one should have to bear.

"Thank you, Mr. Munro." The sheriff looked at the clock. "Court will reconvene at two o'clock."

The shuffling and rustling of people and of papers was all that could be heard as the court dismantled until the next session.

Joanne and Rob left together and stood outside on the pavement, waiting for Mrs. Ross.

"I thought Calum Sinclair would have had more questions, didn't you?" Joanne asked.

"My father says you have to be part-actor, part-lawyer when it comes to appearing in court," Rob replied, "and that last round was all about timing. See, the jury was so overwhelmed by Allie Munro's story, it was the wrong time to ask too much."

"What a thing to have happen, to find your child like that...."

"Joanne," said a woman's voice.

Joanne turned. "Hello, Mum." She stepped forward and took her mother-in-law's arm. "Are you all right? You're not looking too good."

"Hello, Mrs. Ross," Rob said. "Why don't you wait here with Joanne for a minute. I'll borrow a car and give you a lift home."

"That's right good of you," Mrs. Ross said. "I'm fine. Really. It was just hearing all that about finding Fraser."

"I know," Joanne said. "Tell you what, I'm coming home with you, and I am making the tea. Won't be as good as yours, but you're letting someone look after *you* for once."

The poor soul, Joanne thought. *She really must be feeling unwell, I've never known her to take up an offer of kindness on first asking.*

Rob thought the afternoon session was another triumph for the procurator fiscal's side.

The fiscal, although a cautious man, felt that once he had a McPhee on the stand—it didn't matter which brother—he could conclude his case confident the accused would do his job for him.

Next to them, on an easel, standing close to the jury where all the court could see, was a large, simplified map of the area.

Geordie McPhee was called.

Good choice, thought Calum, *he's the most glaikit of the two.*

"Mr. McPhee, let's go through this with the aid of the map," the fiscal started.

The accused looked around to see who Mr. McPhee was before he realized it was himself.

"You and your brother had a fight with Fraser Munro here." The fiscal was using a teacher's pointer to touch the spot on the map where the hotel was clearly marked.

"No a fight really, more like pushing n' that," Geordie replied.

"When you and your brother left the car park, where was Fraser Munro?"

"In the middle, lying on the ground."

Calum tried his best not to groan.

"Then, Mr. McPhee, when you walked home, on this road,"

again he used the pointer, "you were not too far ahead of Fraser Munro and his friends."

"Aye, we could hear them behind us."

Calum scribed a note to himself that Fraser couldn't be that badly injured if he set off home immediately after the fight. Remembering his own warning, he put a line through the word "fight," and scribbled "scuffle."

"After the turnoff here," the fiscal said, "you walked past the schoolhouse here," again the gesture with the pointer, "and you set the dogs off."

"Aye, we did that." Geordie smiled as he remembered him and his brother shouting and singing to annoy the schoolmaster, who had given them many a belting with the extra heavy tause when they were boys.

"Now, Mr. McPhee, the Devil's Den, where Fraser Munro was found, is here. Diagonally across this woodland."

Calum realized that the fiscal was now into a rhythm. With his map and his pointer and his "Mr. McPhee" this and "Mr. McPhee" that, he was making an impression on the listeners.

The fiscal was not a man that anyone would notice in real life. He was the person whom witnesses would say was "ordinary." Ordinary height, ordinary brown hair—even his wife would have to pause and think if asked his eye color. But a gown and wig transformed him into a creature of stature and authority, and his wits sharpened when he donned the costume of office.

"Aye." Again Geordie agreed. "That's the Devil's Den right enough."

"So you *could* have," the fiscal said, with the emphasis clearly on the "could," "quite easily cut through the woods here to the Devil's Den?"

Calum shot up with an objection, but not before the fatal reply.

"No easy, but aye, we *could* have. . . ."

The final bit of Geordie's sentence was lost in the objections and the sheriff overruling the objections, so no one heard the faint, "But we didney."

Calum looked down at his papers—he daren't look at the jury after that answer.

"Let's go back to the hotel car park."

Once again Calum recognized a clever move and knew this would be the last question. Returning to the fight would leave the scene vivid in the minds of the jury.

"You said there was some pushing and shoving. Did you kick Fraser?"

"Only on his legs."

"Did your brother kick him too?" the fiscal asked.

"He wanted to get stuck into him, but thon farm boys stopped the fun."

"Did you kick him again? When he was on the ground?"

"Only the once when his friends wisney looking," the accused replied cheerfully.

The procurator fiscal looked around in a careful, exaggerated turn of the head, his eyes sweeping the jury and said, "No more questions."

It was no surprise to Calum Sinclair, but some of the spectators and most of the jury thought it abrupt when the procurator fiscal turned to the sheriff and announced that he had no more witnesses to call.

His case was simple and straightforward and hard to refute. The McPhee brothers hit Fraser Munro. Fraser Munro died.

Better the fiscal leaves it at that, Calum thought, *than to allow the time gap to be examined too closely.*

And better to leave when the appearance of Allie Munro was

fresh, and the disaster named Geordie McPhee was imprinted on the minds of every juror.

No, Calum thought, *me neither, no more questions, get Geordie off the witness stand as fast as possible.*

"I have no questions at this point," Calum said.

"In that case, we will have a fifteen-minute break," the sheriff announced. "Then Mr. Sinclair, you will present your case."

Twenty-two

❧

The girls were delighted with the idea of spending deadline night with their Aunty Chiara.

"It's good practice for me," Chiara said when she offered to look after the children. "Tell you what, let them come over for the Tuesday night of the trial as well. You can have the night off to go gallivanting."

"Gallivanting on a Tuesday in the Highlands," Joanne laughed. "What possibilities that conjures up!" But she loved the novelty of solitude and accepted the offer.

Annie even agreed to Aunt Chiara meeting them in the afternoon, at the school gates. Chiara was beautiful, foreign, exotic; to Annie she was a heroine from a book, a star from a film, she was someone whom Annie could boast about in the school playground. Best of all, she let Annie try on her dresses and jewelry.

Wee Jean was happy because Chiara always gave them ice cream.

"How was school today?" Chiara asked as they walked home.

"Fine," Annie replied, thinking *why do grown-ups always ask that? School is school.*

They reached the river. Directly opposite, the castle filled the southern skyline.

"That's where they have the court for bad people," Annie pointed to the reddish sandstone not particularly attractive Victorian construction. "Mum will be there for her job on the newspaper."

"Yes, she will," Chiara agreed

"Will they lock the bad men away?" Jean asked.

"That depends," Chiara answered. "First of all they have to be sure that they are the men who did it."

"Granny said they killt Aunty Agnes's boy," Wee Jean spoke, in an exact, unconscious imitation of her granny's voice.

"We don't know that for sure," Chiara told them. "That's why there is a trial, to find out what happened."

"Of course they did it," Annie said. "Why else would they be in gaol?"

Chiara thought, *this conversation is tough. I wonder if this is what it is like being a parent?* "Not everyone who is locked up is guilty."

"What's 'guilty'?" Wee Jean asked.

"It means they did it," her sister said with an air of "I know everything," "and they will go to gaol."

And around the town and in the county and in the Highlands, the same conversation with the same attitudes had the accused guilty before being tried. After all, they wouldn't be there if they hadn't done something, went the reasoning. "And I heard . . ." went many a comment. "My cousin, uncle, friend, the farmer up the road, was telling me . . ." went many a conversation.

Chiara was distressed at the thought of anyone being locked up in that nineteenth-century horror of a gaol. She had visited there once when her husband had been detained, only for two days and one night, and she had been shaken to the bone.

"Annie, you are old enough to know that everything is not always as it seems."

Annie looked confused, but the sentence stayed with her. It was a sentence, uttered lightly, but a sentence she knew was important. She was a child who would think about it, consider the idea of it, just as she would ponder a difficult sentence in a book her granny thought was too old for her. Then she would store it away for a future she was certain would not be in this town of her birth.

"Now, let me see." Chiara stopped. She put on a little show for the girls. Pretending to look puzzled, she put her forefinger to her check, cocked her head, and said, "I don't think we have anything for pudding. Should we go to the café for ice cream?" She laughed at the shrieks of agreement. "But you have to eat all your dinner . . . including the vegetables."

High above town, the court had resumed sitting.

Joanne finished her article on plans for a golf course, then ran down the stairs to the administrative office and dumped a sheaf of typing on Betsy Buchanan's desk.

"Mr. McAllister said to give you the typing. I have to be in court."

She was out the door before Betsy could complete the protest that began, "But I . . ." Joanne was smiling as she hurried up the wynd.

When Joanne arrived the afternoon session was about to resume and McAllister had joined Rob on the courtroom benches. She pushed her way in and sat next to Rob, faintly disappointed it was not McAllister she was squashed up against.

When the witness was called for the defense, it took a moment or two for Rob to realize what was happening. "This is unusual," he whispered.

Joanne raised her eyebrows in question. Rob sat closer and they bent their heads together, touching. It could have seemed intimate to an outsider, but to Joanne, Rob was her pesky wee brother.

"Calum is calling his own expert to question the postmortem findings," he explained.

Joanne nodded. Although she had no idea what this signified, in the company of McAllister she wanted to appear worldly.

Calum was reading out a long list of qualifications of the consultant pathologist, one Dr. Mitchell of Edinburgh, whom Calum Sinclair had asked to appear for the defense.

Aside from being eminent in his profession, Dr. Mitchell was a prickly man. Small, immaculate, intolerant to having his authority questioned, he had a brusque manner that intimidated juries. But his certainty in his opinions was well founded—he knew the secrets of death.

The train journey from Edinburgh had not improved his demeanor; there had been no kippers on the dining car breakfast menu. He was also determined to make the evening train home—to him the Highlands were as barbaric now as they had been in the time of Dr. Johnson's celebrated journey.

The preliminaries over, Calum Sinclair began the case for the defense.

"You have read the finding of the postmortem conducted by . . ."

"Of course, that is why I am here."

Not a good start Calum thought, *but kept calm.*

"And you came to the Highlands to conduct your own examination of the deceased."

"I did."

"Dr. Mitchell, I would like to ask about the time of death."

"I agree with my colleague's opinion, it was between three and six in the morning."

"About the cause of death . . . ?" Calum asked.

"I agree with my colleague. Cerebral hemorrhage."

Calum paused. Dr. Mitchell looked at him. Dr. Mitchell saw the cogs in Calum's brain freewheel. In normal circumstances, he would sit in the witness box and watch the council for either party stew and sweat, and he would relish the spectacle. But there was a train to catch.

"Yes," Dr. Mitchell elaborated, "cerebral hemorrhage caused by a blow to the head." He paused. Always create a nice piece of drama was another of Dr. Mitchell's maxims. "It is *probable* that the fatal blow was struck within an hour of the victim's death."

"What?" Calum was stunned.

The murmur that rattled the courtroom indicated that he was not the only one.

"Could you repeat that, please?" the sheriff asked.

"The bruising was along the hairline and it is probable that the fatal blow was struck approximately one hour before death." The consultant pathologist was enjoying the commotion. "The bruising was along the hairline, so it was easy to miss. But it was this blow which caused a massive and rapid buildup of blood in the cavities of the skull, which in turn put pressure on the brain and caused death."

"You are sure?" the sheriff asked.

"Of course I'm sure." Dr. Mitchell was cross. He had an hour to get to the station otherwise it meant staying the night in this outpost of civilization. "I came all the way up here from Edinburgh, I examined the body, I know what I saw."

So why didn't you tell me, Calum was thinking, *why only let me know now?*

"If you weren't looking for it," Dr. Mitchell continued, "it was not obvious. The blow was at the base of the skull with little bruising, caused by the proverbial blunt instrument. And yes, it could have been caused by a kick. As I have already stated the blow was certainly administered in the early hours of the morning, between four and five-thirty, and if I were asked an opinion . . ." this last part was said to Calum, who was standing staring at the pathologist, "I'd say the blow was struck nearer five-thirty than four. It is there in my report."

"Ah yes," Calum said, "the addendum to the first report. The one I received from you *this lunchtime*."

"I had to be certain," Dr. Mitchell said, and glared at Calum. Calum glared back.

Dr. Mitchell was not one to give credit to others, particularly the local doctor, a lowly general practitioner, but he broke his own rule—two of his own rules; he gave evidence without being asked.

"If you look at the detailed notes the local doctor made at the scene of the crime, you can see that he had the foresight to take the deceased's temperature. The body was warm, the temperature had hardly dropped, hence my conclusion as to the time of death."

Not now, Calum told himself, *don't let the pompous old fart get to you. But why on earth didn't he tell me this before? Why wasn't it included in his report?*

The procurator fiscal was also furious. DS Wilkie had not provided him with a copy of the local doctor's medical report, only his statement.

"I see no mention of this in the post mortem report. Why is that?" Calum asked.

"Because the man is a GP, not a qualified pathologist."

Leave it at that, Calum told himself. *The man's medical bombshell is more than we could have hoped for—even if he is an arrogant so-and-so.*

"Thank you, Dr. Mitchel." Calum said and sat back down at his table.

The procurator fiscal rose.

"Dr. Mitchell," he said, "is it not possible that the original blows, which the victim suffered the previous evening, caused the bleeding to the brain?"

"Yes," the doctor said, "it is certainly possible. But not *probable*."

There it is. Calum almost shouted his pleasure on hearing the statement—the sacred tenant of Scots law was "the balance of probabilities."

And in uttering the qualifying adverbial phrase beloved by all Scots, "certainly possible," Dr. Mitchell had stated his opinion loudly and clearly. In any other version of English, "certainly" meant the man was certain, sure, without a doubt. In Scots English, "certainly possible" equals not very likely. That a blow from eight hours earlier had caused the death was "not probable" in Dr. Mitchell's opinion—an opinion that could never be doubted, so the man himself believed.

"Thank you, Dr. Mitchell. No further questions." The fiscal said. He knew when he was on difficult ground.

As soon as he uttered the words, the man was gone. Only his statement lingered—". . . certainly possible. But not *probable*."

It took Calum a moment to regather his thoughts. Not that that mattered, the procurator fiscal and the sheriff and the jury were also busy considering the import of the pathologist's testimony.

Douglas Donald was next for the defense. Calum prayed the McPhee boys wouldn't wave at him, or call him Duggie the Dummy. He had put the fear of Jimmy into them, and so far, it was working.

Initially, Calum had not expected much from Duggie, seeing him as at best a distraction. *Now however* . . . Calum thought.

"Douglas Donald," came the announcement.

At the battle of Messina, a piece of shrapnel had removed Duggie Donald's tongue. The scars on one side of his face and mouth had ruined not just his face, but also his chances of marriage and family. But his hearing sharpened. He hated daylight and the looks from strangers and children, so he lived for the night. Owls were his favorites, and foxes—he admired foxes.

What brains Duggie had been born with remained intact, but had been modified by the constant company of the creatures of the forests and woods and hedgerows and ditches of the Black Isle.

After Duggie swore the oath, which took a good four minutes, Calum began. Having an interpreter signing Duggie's answers slowed the proceedings.

"Where were you on the night Fraser Munro died?" was Calum's first question.

A flurry of hand gestures, and the reply was spoken by a young, fair girl who looked sixteen, but was twenty-seven and a teacher of sign language.

"The Black Isle, the road across Mount Eagle to Culbokie."

The sheriff suspected the woman had shortened the reply and was grateful.

"Did you see or hear anyone on that road that night?"

The teacher watched Duggie closely. "The McPhee brothers," she interpreted.

"How did you know it was them?"

"I heard them talking."

"Did you see or hear anyone else?" Calum continued, keeping his questions short.

"I didn't see, but I heard Fraser Munro and three others. I don't know their names, but they live on Achnafern Farm."

"Where was this?"

"On the farm road." The sweet voice of the interpreter gave

the answers innocence that did the McPhee brothers' case no harm.

"How do you know it was Fraser Munro?"

"He was shouting and swearing and walking on his own. The others were up ahead of him."

Now we get to it, and I hope to God those boys were telling the truth, Calum thought.

"May I?" he turned to the procurator fiscal and borrowed the pointer.

"Here is the road to Culbokie and here is the schoolhouse. Here are the woods where you were . . ." *Leave that out,* Calum thought, *we don't want to know he was probably poaching.* "Here is the farm road and this is the bridge and the Devil's Den, where Fraser was found."

Duggie was nodding throughout this.

"Now, on that night, did you see or hear the McPhee brothers on the farm road?"

"No," replied the interpreter. She needn't have said a word—the violent shaking of Duggie's head was enough.

"Did anyone else go through the woodland that night?"

This time the interpreter saw she needed say nothing. Duggie shook not just his head, but his shoulders and the whole upper body.

"Were you in the woodland *all* night?" Calum asked.

"No, I left just before first light." Back to the sweet voice.

"In that time, did you see or hear anyone apart from Mr. Fraser Munro and the farmhands at the Devil's Den?"

"No." A pause. "Fraser was there all night," Duggie signed.

"How do you know that?"

"I could hear his snoring," the interpreter told them.

"One final question. Did you see or hear Mr. Alistair Munro arrive next morning?"

"No. I was back in my bothy before first light."

The fiscal had no questions. He was yet to recover from the testimony of Dr. Mitchell, consultant pathologist.

"The court will reconvene tomorrow morning," the sheriff announced, and the day was over.

It was almost five o'clock when Rob and Joanne and McAllister returned to the *Gazette*. Tomorrow—deadline day—would be more than busy, so they continued working.

Rob was typing up his notes from the trial, McAllister was working on his editorial, Don was subbing copy, Joanne was staring at a blank piece of paper perched between the rollers of her machine.

"McAllister, rein in Mrs. Smart or we'll have an advertising ratio that'll make us look ridiculous," Don said as he took another look at the blank spaces in the dummy.

"I agree," Joanne said. "I have to write five hundred words for what you so kindly call the 'Madame Defarge column,' and I'm stuck for an idea."

"What, no death-by-knitting story?"

"Ha ha." Joanne made a face at Don.

"When I was a cub reporter, I lifted ideas from the local school magazines," McAllister told her.

"I'll call in to the academy first thing tomorrow. Thanks McAllister, you're a genius."

"I know," he said.

Rob was in a dilemma as to how much he should write given that the trial was still in progress.

"The facts. Only the facts," Don reminded him.

"Yes, but if I write up today's events and something more interesting happens tomorrow, you'll massacre my copy with your wee red pencil."

"Such is the lot of a reporter," Don said. "Tell me, how did this afternoon go?"

Rob filled Don in on the testimony of the pathologist. The testimony of Duggie Donald, he described with hand gestures, voices, and much waggling of the head. "So at the end of day two, the verdict is looking good for the defense, but . . ." Rob finished, "you never know."

"You're right," McAllister told him when he had finished his performance, "you're lost on a newspaper—you'd definitely be God's gift on television."

Across town, in the small hotel where he was staying for the duration of the trial, Calum Sinclair was discussing the day with Jenny and Jimmy McPhee. Listening to what Jenny had to say, he did not like all he was hearing.

"I couldn't for the life 'o me think what I was forgetting about that morning, but it's so obvious I'm kicking maself for no thinking o' it earlier," Jenny started.

She was a woman who never missed much and whose opinion and intuition Calum had come to respect. He watched her coal black eyes, and her sun-dark skin and the way she sat—completely relaxed, as though the room in the small hotel were open to the sky and all the stars were shining in their glory.

"Sandy Skinner," Jenny continued, "died the same day as Fraser Munro. We all know that. Didn't Patricia say him and her left on their wee jaunt in the early morning?"

"Yes, she did," Calum agreed. "They left before dawn."

"Fraser Munro died around that time. So maybe she noticed something?" Jenny McPhee looked at Calum, and he could not hold her gaze. *She knows,* he thought, *she knows I have messed up. I should have thought of that. I should have checked. I have read*

Patricia's statement, but I should have asked Patricia again, not relied on the police report.

"I have the copy of Miss Ord Mackenzie's statement here," Calum said. "I'll recheck it."

"Aye, you do that," Jenny told him. "And as far as I know, Patricia is still Mrs. Skinner." She looked at him as she said this, her eyes seeming to see into his soul. Calum had to look away.

"Another thing," Jenny continued, "Allie Munro is hiding something."

"I felt that too," Calum was now certain Jenny had the sixth sight, "but he is a difficult man to question."

"Aye, you'd no get much out o' him if he doesney want you to. His missus though, she'd be a different matter." Jenny looked at Calum again. "If you could harden yer heart to the poor soul, I think you could find out what her and her man are not saying."

Jimmy had been watching from a corner of the room and knew that, after this exchange with his mother, whatever needed to be done, Calum would be on to it.

"That was magic this afternoon," Jimmy was smiling, "worth every penny of his fee thon manny from Edinburgh was. Creepy sort o' a fellow though—I suppose it must be all them dead bodies he cuts up."

Calum was grateful for Jimmy's intervention. "Yes, his evidence will make it hard for the fiscal to prove his case."

"But we're not there yet," Jenny reminded them.

"No," Calum agreed. "We are not."

They said their goodnights. Jenny and Jimmy McPhee disappeared into the gloaming of a perfect summer night, and Calum was left with the thought of the task to be done.

He turned the thought over and under and sideways until his brain felt as thick as silage. The thought stank like silage too.

It was true, Patricia and Sandy Skinner had left very early that day. Calum knew that Patricia had said they had driven down the drive from Achnafern Grange to the main road. They had no reason to drive past the farmhouse and along the back road, past the Devil's Den. It was not a shortcut—it was a road used on farm business.

He checked the copy of her statement for the third time. Patricia's interview was short and succinct; she and her late husband had left before dawn, taking the driveway—not the farm road—from Achnafern Grange to the main road. They saw nothing. Witnesses? None.

Telephone her, he told himself, *ask her outright. If you don't, it will always be there, an unasked question like a splinter in the thumb.*

He smiled, remembering his mother telling him not to be such a baby as she came at him with the iodine and her sewing needle to remove the splinter deep in his hand after he and his dad had been stacking firewood for the winter. How scared he had been. And in the end it hadn't hurt at all, and his mother had told him, "See—making yourself scared aforehand is worse than the doing of it."

He checked the time. Twenty past nine. He dialed the number.

"Ord Mackenzie household."

"Calum Sinclair here, I know it's very late to call . . ."

"Not in the least," Patricia said. "Do you need me as a character witness tomorrow?"

"I don't know yet." He paused. "Please forgive me for asking, but I've been rechecking statements. . . . Did you notice anything or see anyone the morning of Fraser Munro's death? Anyone hanging around the farm perhaps?"

"I don't mind you asking," she said, "you are only being thorough. As I said to the police, we took the road from our house, not the farm road. Sandy was driving. I was half-asleep, and it was barely light, and no, I didn't see anyone."

"Thank you." Calum was hugely relieved that Patricia had not been offended by the question. "I would appreciate it if you were available tomorrow—just in case."

"Of course. I will be in court anyway to support Mrs. Munro."

They said their goodnights. Calum poured himself a dram. Now he could sleep.

TWENTY-THREE

Highland Gazette."

"Early bird. I knew I'd catch you."

"Patricia," Joanne said. "You're right, but I like being in first, gives me time to get the annoying jobs out the road. How are you? I was expecting to see you at the trial."

"I haven't been needed," she said, "but Mrs. M. will be appearing today, so I'm here to support her. Also, I am on standby in case Calum needs me as a character witness."

Joanne noted the "Calum," not "Mr. Sinclair," not "Calum Sinclair," just plain "Calum." *Another man Patricia has managed to twist round her little finger,* she thought.

"I see." Joanne's voice was flat, noncommittal, waiting to find out what Patricia wanted.

"Can you pop out for a coffee?" Patricia asked.

She sounds very bright, Joanne thought. "It's not easy to leave on deadline day, and today we're having to make two front pages in case the trial doesn't finish so . . ."

"Joanne, surely you can spare time for your oldest friend?"

"All right, I can manage a quick coffee in fifteen minutes—if we meet in the Castle Brae café. Then I am going to the trial."

"Me too," Patricia said. "We can go together."

Joanne put down the phone. "Drat that woman, she always gets the better of me."

"That was Patricia, I take it." Rob came in.

"However did you guess?"

"I've the second sight. Talking of Patricia, I noticed it hasn't come up so far," Rob began, "but she and her late, not-so-lamented husband were up and about early on the morning Fraser Munro was lying in the ditch."

"What are you suggesting?" Joanne was fed up of Rob continually having a go at Patricia. Patricia could be a nuisance always wanting a favor, but she was kind, she was generous, and she had to live with *that* mother. Joanne was certain she would never do anyone any real harm.

"Hold your horses. I'm not suggesting anything—just cynical about coincidences, that's all."

Eight thirty—the half hour rang out from the steeples across town.

"Is that the time? I have to go. See you in court." Rob ran down the stairs. Knowing there was an hour before the final day of the trial began, he took the chance to grab a quick coffee. He liked the idea that he was one of the tiny coffee-drinking set in the town, if not the whole of Scotland. Coffee bars were seen as louche, not quite respectable; tea was the national drink, second only to whisky.

He walked through the back alleyways. He liked the cobbled lanes, the back doors chained and padlocked, the high walls concealing who knows what, and the sense of history hidden behind the High Street and hurrying housewives shopping with that grim sense of purpose.

Coincidence. Rob's thoughts kept returning like a criminal to the scene of the crime. *Two deaths, two funerals, same farm, same day—why,* he thought, *was I the only one interested in the coincidence?*

Because, he thought, *Miss Patricia Ord Mackenzie said she, they, had left before Fraser had been discovered and she saw nothing. And she, Patricia, said Sandy Skinner fell into a waterfall all by himself. And no one questions the word of Patricia Ord Mac-kenzie.*

He turned down a lane with no idea where he was going.

Who could contradict her? Certainly not her husband. Was there any evidence? Any facts, as Don always said, to prove Patricia's version of events? *Nothing,* Rob thought, *not one eency-weency smidgen of a suggestion that Patricia was being anything other than truthful. So why do I not believe her?*

Rob found himself at the end of the Victorian covered arcade. He saw the station clock. He had half an hour before the trial would restart. He changed his mind about the coffee and went into the splendidly plain, unadorned—except for a wrinkled calendar featuring Castle Urquhart at sunset, tearoom in the covered market. He took a stool at the high bench in the window. He ordered a tea—perfect with bacon roll. He sat staring at the traffic, feeling vacant. When Patricia appeared, center stage, on the steps from the Station Hotel, he registered her companion.

Well, well, he thought, *I have to hand it to you Patricia, you've managed to entice Calum Sinclair into your web.*

He watched her stumble. *Deliberately,* Rob thought. He saw Calum hold out his arm for support. He saw them cross the station car park. He saw Calum hold the car door open—*nice car,* Rob noticed—and he watched, and Calum too watched, as Patricia drove away.

Rob grinned to himself. Poor man, he will never know what's hit him. Rob would love to share the incident with Joanne, but thought she would disapprove of his cynicism.

"Don, I'm taking a fifteen-minute break, that OK?" Joanne asked.

"You're a big girl now, you don't need teacher's permission." He didn't look up from the copy he was marking.

Joanne took the flight of steps down to the Castle Street car park. The café where she was meeting Patricia was across the road. Halfway down the stairs, she noticed Patricia climbing out of a sleek, black car.

"Hello," Joanne called out and waved. *She's noticeably pregnant now*, she thought.

Patricia turned, saw Joanne, waved back, and waited.

"What do you think?" Patricia asked. "My new car."

"Goodness, it's very smart," Joanne said. *Very expensive too*, she thought. "So your mother relented at last."

"Oh no. This car is all mine, bought with my own money." Patricia linked arms with Joanne and, steering her across the road, said no more on the subject of the car.

They took a table in the window. A waitress, in an old-fashioned black dress and white frilly apron, appeared.

"Tea for me," Patricia said. "Coffee makes this little fellow kick."

"Coffee for me," Joanne ordered. "I need it on deadline day. So, how are you keeping?"

"I'm so healthy it's ridiculous," Patricia grinned. "Also running around like crazy. I am doing most of the work on the farm, as poor Mr. and Mrs. M. have to be here."

"How are they coping?"

"They are coping—just. It's hard on both of them, but it's Mr. M. that I worry about. He seems so withdrawn."

"Everything will be back to normal soon." *What tripe you talk*, Joanne said to herself, *it will never be normal for Mr. and Mrs. Munro.*

"I hope so," Patricia put her cup down and tried to look casual, but all she managed to do was make Joanne more alert.

"I met Calum earlier this morning. He called me last night to check if Sandy and I saw anyone the morning Fraser was killed. He had read my statement, but felt he had to ask again."

"He is only doing his job, Patricia."

"Exactly what I said. He's rather dishy don't you think?"

"Patricia!"

"I know. I've been a widow two months, I am five months pregnant, but I can *fancy* Calum, can't I? Like you with John McAllister?"

"Patricia!" Joanne was dismayed at the remark. *Were people talking? Had her mother-in-law heard some gossip? Was that why Bill accused her? But,* she would only ever admit this to herself, *there was something fascinating about McAllister.*

Patricia grinned and sat back in the chair. "There is no harm in a private fancy."

"You are incorrigible." They laughed.

"Thank you, Joanne. I knew I could count on you." She touched Joanne's hand. "That's the first good laugh I've had in a long time."

"Me too," Joanne smiled back.

"So, as I was saying," Patricia was all business again, "when Calum phoned to check my statement about the morning Fraser was found, I said no, I didn't notice anything unusual. But in the wee hours—I have to constantly get up to the lavatory in the night now, I remembered. I hadn't thought of it before, it was so familiar, you don't notice.

"As we came down the driveway, I heard the rattling and at the turn into the main road, the man and his boy were there, loading the churns onto the lorry that collects the milk from the end of the farm road. I'm sure the driver will remember seeing us."

"Patricia, you know no one would doubt your word."

"I know. But . . ." she smiled, "I don't want Calum to have any doubts about me."

Goodness, she is serious about him, Joanne thought. "I'm sure he has none." She hoped her qualms weren't obvious.

"That's what he assured me." Patricia sighed, a deep slow soul shaking sigh. Her voice, when she spoke, was deeper, sadder, a reminder to Joanne of why they were friends.

"What a mistake I made. I should have had the courage to have a baby out of wedlock. If Sandy had lived—God, that would have been a nightmare!"

"Why did you, you know . . ." Joanne didn't know how to ask.

"'Lie with him' as the Bible says?" Patricia giggled. "Because he asked . . . he was the first man to show me real attention. And it was fun at first . . . sneaking out . . . defying my mother . . ." She was watching out the window as passersby labored up the hill, leaning forward against the steepness of the climb. "I may not show it, but I'm really sorry Sandy died." Her face had a faraway look. "He didn't deserve that."

For the first time, Sandy Skinner was acknowledged in a genuine eulogy. They were quiet for a moment.

"Joanne, you remember the bedrooms in our house?"

"I remember the one I stayed in."

"The rooms in that wing are all the same. We had them modernized three years ago."

Joanne was wondering where this was leading.

"The plumbing was hugely expensive. We had a bathroom put in at the end of the hall, and washhandbasins in the bedrooms." Patricia leaned across the table. "That was how I knew I could never stay married to him." She dropped her voice. "Sandy, when he needed to go, couldn't be bothered walking twenty yards to the bathroom. He would wee-wee in the basin."

Joanne stared, half-disgusted, half-transfixed at the information.

"I now understand why, in spite of the scandal, you left your husband," Patricia continued. "It's all very well taking a fancy to a good-looking man, but when they are not in your social class, it can be quite confronting, can't it?"

Patricia noticed Joanne's face and realized she might have gone too far. "Joanne, no one blames you. We all know your marriage was unavoidable. You couldn't help it that your husband turned out to be a bad lot." She glanced at her watch. "Heavens, court will be starting in fifteen minutes. We'll have to hurry." She stood. "We'll catch up properly when the trial is over." She dropped half a crown on to the table. "Are you coming?"

"I must call into the office first" Joanne said, making the only excuse she could think of.

"I'll see you later then. Bye-ee." Patricia was gone in a rush of bags and coat and matronly headscarf, her bump preceding her.

It was only when the waitress asked, "Can I clear the table," that Joanne came to. As ever, an encounter with Patricia had left her completely mystified. *What did Patricia want? Why had she made her feelings for Calum obvious? Why had she told her about Sandy Skinner's distasteful personal habits? Why were they friends?*

She had no answers to all except the last question—they were friends because they had gone through ten years of schooling together. They had snuggled up together in the dormitory, two lonely little girls. As they grew older, they were drawn together when the other girls talked of missing their mothers. It was a given that one loved one's mother, but Patricia and Joanne had shared their suspicion that their mothers did not love them.

We share a loveless childhood, Joanne concluded, *we share a history, a history longer than my marriage, that's why we're friends.*

And as she climbed the steps to the *Gazette*, Joanne had trouble erasing the image of Sandy using the washhandbasin as a lavatory. Surely it was not enough to kill someone over?

She found Rob's suspicion that Patricia might be responsible for Sandy's death ridiculous. She *knew* Patricia. She was certain that Patricia was clever enough to have found a sound, legal way out of the marriage, without a stain on her reputation.

When Joanne walked in, McAllister was sitting at a typewriter in the reporters' room, the desk covered with what looked like extra large confetti.

"I'm trying to think what to lead with if the trial doesn't finish on time." He pulled a sheet of copy paper from the typewriter and tore it in half, throwing it up in the air to fall and settle with the other discarded thoughts. "Any ideas?"

"Sorry?"

"You look away with the faeries."

"I've been with Patricia Ord Mackenzie." Joanne sat at her typewriter. "I know I'm being unfair, but I felt she was using me. Goodness knows why."

"Do you feel the same when you're with your friend Chiara Corelli?"

"Kowalski now," Joanne reminded him. "No, I don't. I always feel great after being with Chiara. She's a ray of light. We have fun. With Patricia I always feel . . ." she searched for the word, "defensive." She looked at him. The room was too small, the spaces between the high chairs and typewriters too narrow, and he was too close.

"McAllister, I know you know I don't have a lot of self-confidence, but why do I have even less when I'm with Patricia?"

"Perhaps she's the same. Perhaps that's why she's so bossy."

"Really?" The thought took Joanne by surprise.

"Don't ask me. I know very little about women." He grinned. "I know newspapers though, and as we are on deadline, here's what we'll do: you spend the rest of the day in court. It should be over by this afternoon, then you and Rob can both turn in a story. I need to fill these holes here . . ." he tapped the front page, "and here." He tapped a large space on page three of the dummy. "Rob will do the factual stuff. So, go and get me a humdinger of a story with pathos, even bathos."

"Sir." She clicked her heels to attention, saluted, and left.

McAllister rolled another sheet of copy paper into the monster and started to retype his editorial, grinning all the while.

Joanne spotted her mother-in-law. She had to squeeze past two stout women in slightly different shades of green. Both were in tweed skirts, twinsets, and hats with lethal hatpins—so beloved by early detective novelists—anchoring the felt creations to their skulls. Rob, in the row below, turned, grinned, and gave a wave.

"How are you, Mum?" Joanne asked.

"I'm fine. But poor Agnes is worn to a frazzle. She didney get much sleep last night."

"It will be over soon." Joanne patted Mrs. Ross's arm. She hated seeing Mrs. Ross shrink in the presence of the panoply of the court.

The court was told to rise, the sheriff entered, the trial recommenced.

Calum Sinclair began by calling Mrs. Munro to the stand.

"Mrs. Agnes Munro," announced the clerk of the court. Joanne remembered him. He was the man Rob had bought his motorbike from.

Mrs. Munro took the oath then took her seat. Joanne noticed how much the woman had shrunk in body and spirit. Even sitting up straight, she was tiny in the chair.

Mrs. Ross was leaning forward on the bench, as if to catch every word and whisper and sigh. Joanne noticed that Patricia, slightly to her left and two benches down, did the same.

Calum Sinclair gave Mrs. Munro a slight smile and a nod, trying to reassure her. He hated what he was about to do.

"Now, Mrs. Munro, I want you to recall the night your son didn't return from the village." He was trying to keep his vocabulary as inoffensive as possible.

"Yes."

"That evening, when did Fraser go out?"

"The back o' six."

"Did he tell you where he was going?"

"No."

"Did he tell you who he was going with?"

"No."

"Did you see or hear anything more of your son that night?"

"No."

"You said you didn't see or hear anything of *Fraser* that night, but did you see or hear anyone else?"

"I heard the lads across the farmyard come home."

"How do you know it was them?"

"Their dogs didn't bark, but mine gave a yelp or two. That's what woke me."

"Anything else?"

"One of them, I don't know who, called out, 'see you in the morn.'"

"Did you hear *anything* more that night?"

She hesitated, and thought. It had taken her a long time to get back to sleep, she remembered. Every whisper of wind, every move of her husband she heard, every chime of the clock in the hallway, but no sound of Fraser returning. The dogs in the big house had barked in the early hours, but they were always a bit flighty those ones—pets, not real working dogs like the farm dogs.

"No. No, I never heard anything more that night."

"When did you first notice that Fraser had not come home?"

"I didn't. My Allie told me."

"Your husband?"

"Aye."

"And what time was that?"

"Nearly eight o'clock. See, I don't go and wake our Fraser like I used to. . . ." She paused, recalling how, one time, he had yelled at her when she had taken him a cup of tea at half past six, expecting him to be up, ready to join his father and his brother in the fields. The language had horrified her, so once was enough.

"Sorry?" She hadn't heard the next question.

"When your husband informed you that Fraser wasn't home, what did he say?"

"He said, there's been a terrible accident, and he had phoned for the doctor. Then ma husband said that the doctor wouldn't be any help because our Fraser . . . he died."

Her husband hadn't told her that the doctor insisted on calling the police; that piece of information she had overheard when the doctor came to the farmhouse to wash. After climbing into the ditch, his hands and his shoes and his trousers were muddy.

A nice man, our doctor, she thought.

A tear trickled out, but she wasn't crying. It was something that happened regularly since she lost her son, and she didn't notice anymore.

Calum Sinclair paused. "I'm sorry I have to ask you these questions. I realize how hard this is, so I'll try to be as brief as possible."

She nodded. "Thank you."

Joanne felt Mrs. Ross tense. Jenny McPhee shifted in her seat—it may have been her sons on trial, but she felt for Agnes Munro.

"Mrs. Munro, you said that that night, you heard the others from the farm return."

"Aye, that's right."

"You said you heard nothing more that night."

"Aye."

"That morning, the morning Fraser was found, did you hear anything *unusual?*"

There was a long pause.

"No, I heard nothing unusual."

Calum went to his table, ostensibly to pick up another sheet of paper, but thinking rapidly how to put the next question. *What had Jenny McPhee said? "She's no telling everything"? What had Mrs. Munro just said? "I heard nothing unusual."* He had it.

"Mrs. Munro, earlier that morning, you heard nothing unusual." He looked at her. "Did you hear or *see* anything, an everyday event perhaps, something so normal that you forgot?" He spoke slowly, carefully pausing between the commas in his questions.

"I don't know what you mean." But Agnes Munro was incapable of lying. She sat with her arms tight into her sides, her hands clutching onto the life raft that was her handbag.

Joanne, along with everyone else in the courtroom, was watching Mrs. Munro and what she saw was a woman in her late fifties looking like Wee Jean caught out in a lie.

"Before you heard the news about Fraser, what did you hear or *see* that was *not* unusual? That was completely ordinary?"

The only sound was of Mrs. Munro, repeating in a voice punctuated by sniffs, "I'm sorry, I'm so sorry."

She opened her handbag. She rummaged in the depths. She

found a clean hankie. It didn't help. She couldn't stifle the sobs or stop the tears.

"We'll will take a fifteen-minute break," the sheriff announced.

The sigh from everyone in the courtroom was as soft and loud as a gust of wind through a pine forest.

Calum Sinclair sat in his chair, not happy about the break.

So close, he thought, *so near. When I question her again, I will seem like a monster . . . but it has to be done, she knows something.*

Thinking exactly the same as Calum, Rob joined Joanne as she was leaving the court saying, "Drat, just as it was starting to get interesting . . ."

"Rob." Joanne gestured to her mother-in-law just ahead of them.

"Ooops, sorry, I hope she didn't hear me," he whispered. "Joanne, what did you make of all that?"

"I can't talk now, my mother-in-law is really upset."

"Later then." Rob watched Joanne as she went to comfort Mrs. Ross. *Whatever it is that Agnes Munro is hiding, Mrs. Ross knows too*, he realized. *But will Joanne have the nerve to ask her?*

Rob returned to the courtroom, taking his place on the bench.

"Mum, is there anything I can do?" Joanne was surprised how tightly her mother-in-law clutched her arm. She looked down at her and noticed how all this had aged her.

You poor soul, Joanne thought, *family means everything to you.*

Mrs. Ross looked up at Joanne, "I need to see how Agnes is doing."

"I don't think they'll let you into the chambers. Why don't we find a bench and wait."

Sitting close, ignored by the steady stream of passersby

chatting in whispered excitement, Joanne instinctively took her mother-in-law's hand, and Mrs. Ross squeezed back.

"You're a good lass." Mrs. Ross's words were murmured down into her lap. And Joanne was all the more overwhelmed as she knew the words were truly meant.

They continued to wait, nothing more was said, nothing more needed to be said.

I know I should ask her what's going on, Joanne thought, *but some things are more important than a job.*

Five minutes later Joanne returned and told Rob, "The sheriff has allowed the doctor to see to Mrs. Munro. I'm not sure if the poor woman is ready to answer questions yet."

"Joanne, she has no choice."

"I know."

They were silent while all around, the murmur ebbed and flowed like the tide on a shingle beach. Thirty minutes passed and nothing changed. Forty-five minutes passed and the clerk of the court appeared. The defendants returned. The procurator fiscal and Calum Sinclair came in together. The sheriff was announced. The court rose. The sheriff sat. The court sat. The sheriff nodded to the fiscal. The fiscal rose.

"Your Honor, ladies and gentlemen of the jury, additional testimony has been given, and therefore the prosecution wishes to withdraw the charges against George Williamson McPhee and William Stewart McPhee."

The fiscal sat.

A babble of voices filled the courtroom, echoing off the high ceilings, disturbing the pigeons sitting on the stone window ledges—a babble that could be heard throughout the administrative offices in the castle and down the hill to the police station.

It took the threat of clearing the courtroom before the sheriff could continue. He thanked the jury, told them they were dismissed, thanked the two opposing councils, stood, and left.

The noise level soared again. Then a lone voice cut through the confused murmur.

"Ma, can we come hame noo?"

"Aye boys," Jenny McPhee used her singer's voice. It echoed through the courtroom. "You can come hame."

"What the hell was all that?" Rob asked no one in particular.

"That was the sound of ma brothers being let out o' gaol," a voice came from behind.

Rob turned. "Jimmy, what's going on?"

"No idea," Jimmy McPhee said. "But I'm happy."

"Joanne?" Rob asked.

"Search me," she replied.

"Come on," Rob said, grabbing her arm "we have a front page."

"Well?" McAllister asked when Joanne and Rob rushed in.

"We have a front page," Rob told them. "Trouble is we have only part of the story."

"Something more is about to happen," Joanne said. "I feel it in my bones."

"When? I need this story now." Don was standing with what few pages he had ready for the typesetters.

"The fiscal dropped the charges against the McPhee brothers," Rob announced.

"He what?" McAllister stared.

"I wasn't expecting *that*." Don was equally surprised. "What happened?"

Rob had their attention. "I don't really know. Maybe Joanne can explain."

She did.

"Let me get this straight," McAllister said when she had finished, "Mrs. Munro was asked what she saw or heard that was absolutely ordinary and she wouldn't answer the question?"

"Couldn't," Joanne said. "She started sobbing and couldn't stop. A doctor was called."

"So what happens now?" Rob asked.

"You go straight round to the fiscal's office and get a statement," McAllister told him. "And don't come back until you have the full story."

Rob left.

"Joanne," McAllister continued, "you write up this morning's events. You have two hours." She had a flash of panic, followed by a flash of pride. She took out her notebook, glanced at it, and started to type. *Don't think about it*, she told herself, *just picture it, and write it.*

McAllister turned to Don. "You have Rob's copy for the first two days of the trial?"

"Aye," Don told him, "subbed and set."

"Fine. What else needs doing?"

"A bottle or two will sweeten the printers if we have to run late," Don informed him.

"Aye, but it would need much more than a bottle to delay the trains and the buses and the ferries so we can get the *Gazette* out to the Highlands and islands."

"True," Don said. "The only other solution is to fall down on yer knees and pray we have the full story in the next three hours."

"We will," McAllister said firmly, more to reassure himself than from certainty.

"You want to bet? Five shilling for each hour past five o'clock."

"A pound if we have the full story before five o'clock?"

Don considered the odds. "Done," he said. They shook on it.

No one from the office of the procurator fiscal would speak to Rob, nor to any of the other reporters.

"We will be issuing a statement tomorrow at midday," the clerk announced.

"That's your deadline gone," the skinny fellow from the Aberdeen daily reminded Rob.

Sergeant Patience was on desk duty at the police station when Rob arrived. He had been told that no information was to be given out regarding the case, especially to the gentlemen of the press.

When Sergeant Patience looked at Rob, he remembered writing *that* letter. He had not and never would recover from having to apologize to Hector Bain. Then there was the lecture from DI Dunne.

How did the inspector put it? "We must maintain good relations with the Highland Gazette"? *So, I've been told, "no reporters," but on the other hand . . .*

The policeman looked around. No one was near. He beckoned Rob closer. Rob smelled engine oil on the sergeant and was momentarily distracted.

"Hang around outside," the policeman muttered. "I'll see what I can do." He turned back to his paperwork.

"Great," Rob grinned. He spotted the ingrained oil in the cuticles around the nails of the sergeant's big hams of hands. "I can see you're a mechanic."

"What? Oh right." The sergeant was flustered. He spent hours scrubbing the oil off, but no use, some always remained. "I'm restoring a bike."

"A motorbike?"

"A BSA. One o' the first ones ever made."

"Really? Can I come and see it? I love bikes." Rob was genuinely interested.

"Aye, I've seen you and your Triumph around the place." The sergeant thought it over. "I could show it to you on Sunday."

Rob walked out to the Castle Wynd to wait. *One more triumph for me, he thought, Police Sergeant Patience is my new best friend.*

Rob waited an hour and a half. He didn't mind. Sergeant Patience appeared on the steps. He beckoned. WPC Ann McPherson was at the reception desk.

"Hiya, Ann. What's happening?" Rob was pleased to see her. He had gone out with her a few times, but she was too much the policewoman for it to work.

"Detective Inspector Dunne will speak to you now." She had gone formal on Rob.

"Aren't there any other journalists with you?" the chief inspector asked when Rob walked into his office. Then he smiled. "Don't worry, Rob, you're the local press, you're the first to be told, as I know you have a deadline. The others can get the information from the procurator fiscal's office tomorrow."

He switched to his professional persona.

"Mr. Alistair Munro of Achnafern Estate, the Black Isle, Ross & Cromarty, has confessed to hitting his son Fraser Munro. Fraser Munro subsequently died. Alistair Munro pushed the body into the ditch, where he pretended to discover it an hour later."

Rob stared at the policeman and the policewoman. "Are you sure?"

"That is Mr. Munro's statement."

"Has he been charged?"

"Not yet. The fiscal's office is finalizing the charges. Mr. Alistair Munro is in custody. He is being represented by Calum Sinclair. That's all I can tell you."

"Will Mr. Munro be allowed bail?" Rob asked.

Inspector Dunne was a decent person. He felt nothing but pity for Mr. and Mrs. Munro.

"I hope so," he replied. "Patricia Ord Mackenzie is going assurance for him. I hope it can all be sorted before the day's end."

Rob ran the short distance to the office. He charged into the reporter's room.

"Allie Munro has confessed to hitting Fraser and putting him in the ditch."

"Never!" Joanne was shocked. Mr. Munro was the last person she suspected. But it made a kind of sense. "Poor Mrs. Munro."

McAllister looked at the clock. It was seven minutes to five.

"You owe me a quid," he told Don.

"Don't I know it," Don replied. "Right, boys and girls, let's get going. Joanne, where's your copy? Rob, get on wi' it. McAllister, you finish the last o' the sports pages, I haven't the time."

Another deadline, another issue of the *Highland Gazette*, and another scoop—but there was no rejoicing.

By early evening all that remained was to finalize the "wee fiddly bits," Don's immortal phrase.

McAllister was at the reporters' table, leaning back in his chair, smoking—a pose that would become part of the McAllister legend.

Joanne was making small stacks of copy she couldn't be bothered filing. Not tonight.

Rob was completing a list of records he wanted to buy.

Don came into the silence and laid the proof of the front page on the table. He lit up, then started.

"We had this auld dog," he took an audible draw on the cigarette. "Nearly fifteen she was and had arthritis something terrible, couldney walk, so it was time to put her down. Ma father went for his gun, and we took her out to the back o' the byre. I was thirteen and I'd know Bess all my life. Dad said to leave, so I looked at her one last time. I've never forgotten her eyes. She knew."

He took his pencil from behind his ear, and after a nod from McAllister, he signed off on the front page.

"Aye," Don said. "I'd rather think about ma auld dog than this."

He tapped the headline.

"Father Confesses to Killing Son."

TWENTY-FOUR

The McPhee trial had been over for three weeks, and Joanne was back to juggling work and two schoolchildren. It was even more difficult now the long summer school holiday had started.

The girls occasionally stayed with Chiara, but mostly they stayed with their granny. They were the only children that Annie knew whose mother worked, but instead of feeling the stigma, Annie enjoyed the freedom it gave her.

At first she thought it was because she was almost ten that her granny let her wander on her own for the first time. She went to the swimming pool by herself, to the library on her own, and was allowed to take her bike to the islands unsupervised. In spite of the natural self-absorption of a child, she began to notice that Granny Ross was different. And Granddad Ross was being extra nice.

Granny's not angry, Annie thought. *She's not sick.* Unable to diagnose a case of disillusionment, she left it as one of those imponderables that affected adults.

Joanne walked into the kitchen in the late afternoon to collect the girls. Late July, summer was full-blown, not yet tipped into the excess of August. The nights were still bright, the days still warm—mostly. But the heather was not yet in bloom.

"Hello, Mum, I hope they were good."

"Course we were," Wee Jean answered on her granny's behalf.

"Don't be cheeky," Joanne laughed. "Run and tell Annie I'm here and get your bags."

"Tea?"

"I'd love a quick cup." Joanne was still on her mission to be extra nice to her mother-in-law and wasn't finding it at all an effort.

Mrs. Ross warmed the pot, spooned in the tea, poured in the boiling water, and set the cozy on the pot.

Joanne asked, "Mum, what are your plans for the Black Isle Show? Patricia has invited us to spend the night at Achnafern Grange."

"Has she now?" Mrs. Ross said with all the enthusiasm of a cat contemplating the rain.

"I know you always meet Mrs. Munro and . . . Mum, is anything the matter?"

"It's not for me to say."

"Mum, please." Joanne caught the brightness in her eyes, the tremble in her hand. "Sit down, I'll pour. Tell me what's the matter."

"It's not my business." Mrs. Ross folded her arms across her pinny.

Seeing that gesture—the arms defensive across the bosom—Joanne knew no explanation would be forthcoming.

"We'll all go to the show together," Joanne suggested. "Afterwards Patricia can take us back to Achnafern. She has her own car now so we won't have to wait around for Mrs. Ord Mackenzie."

"Bill usually comes to the show wi' us all," Granny Ross said, waiting while Joanne struggled for an answer.

"I don't see why he can't come with us," Joanne offered, but she would be amazed if Bill agreed to come with them—she knew he would much rather be with his drinking cronies.

"You don't mind?" Mrs. Ross asked.

"Mum, he *is* the girls' father. I have made it clear to him he should spend time with the girls. I have no problem if he wants to come with you and Granddad and the girls." *And I will make myself scarce,* she thought.

Going with Bill to the Black Isle Show had been an annual ordeal almost as bad as Hogmanay; he was usually so drunk by mid-afternoon that Joanne and the girls would pretend he weren't with them.

"We'll see," Granny Ross said. "I'm helping in the Women's Institute tea tent as usual, but I'm not sure Agnes will be there this year. Her man certainly won't."

So that is what's upsetting her, Joanne thought as she walked home—it's unknown for someone from the farms to miss the Black Isle Show and it's probably the first time since they were children that Allie and Agnes Munro would not be attending.

Joanne knew Mr. Munro was waiting for his hearing before the sheriff, but was not in custody. Patricia told her that Mrs. Munro was keeping very quiet.

"She's even avoiding me," Patricia had said over the telephone.

The next morning, Joanne was writing an item on the forthcoming show, reminding *Gazette* readers of the attractions, the judging classes, and giving advance notice of new events. The press release from the Black Isle Agricultural Society was informative but dull.

"This press release is as boring as my social life," Joanne complained.

"McAllister will take you out on the town."

"Don!" Joanne protested.

"McAllister!" Don shouted towards the open door of the editor's office, "Joanne needs a person to take her on a date."

312 ◆ A. D. Scott

"Don!" she protested for the second time.

McAllister came in. "Where would you like to go? Dinner? The pictures? A drive to Nairn or Strathpeffer, somewhere out of town to preserve your reputation?"

"Good idea," Rob said.

"Hold on you lot," Joanne said as she looked across the table at Don and McAllister and at Rob, who was sitting beside her. "Do I get to make a decision in all this?"

"He's free." Don pointed at McAllister. "He's paying. . . ."

McAllister nodded in agreement.

"You've chucked your husband out. . . ."

"Don!" she was laughing and blushing.

"So what's your problem?" Don finished.

"A babysitter."

"I'll volunteer," Rob said.

"Fine. I'll do it. I don't see why I can't go out with a friend." Joanne grinned, but couldn't help thinking, *If someone sees us it will be all over town.*

"Thank you, Don," she said. "As you so kindly pointed out I'm a free agent so, McAllister, how about the film at the La Scala? The one with Grace Kelly."

"Agreed," McAllister said. "You get to watch Grace and Frank and Bing and I get to hear Louis Armstrong. But I do believe you've seen it before, Mrs. Ross."

"Three times, Mr. McAllister. And I still love it." She laughed. "One condition, though. I am not going to sit in the back row with all those necking teenagers. I want to see the film."

"We shall have a very chaste date at the cinema. I might even treat you to some chocolates."

"It takes more than a box of chocolates to get round me, John McAllister."

◆　◆　◆

McAllister arrived at Joanne's pre-fab five minutes after Rob. Annie answered the door.

"Hello, Mr. McAllister," she said, "Mum is ready to go out with you."

Annie approved of Mr. McAllister. He treated her the same as he treated everyone and never once bent his long, lanky frame to talk to a girl half his height.

"Stay out as late as you want," Rob told them. He turned back to the girls, "Now, where were we?"

"I'm the princess, you're the baddie," Wee Jean said. "Can we start now?"

"Give us time," Rob laughed. "Annie and I still have to write the play."

It was late when the girls finally went to bed. The play had been a great success. Even Rob had enjoyed it. At the end, the baddie turned into a prince, he was allowed to kiss the princess, and they all lived happily ever after.

"I stole the idea from Prince Rainier," he told Annie. "A film star and a prince . . . not the most original script we'll ever write."

But Annie didn't care. Rob had listened to her suggestions, and they had written their very own play.

"I'm going to be on television one day," Rob had told her, and Annie was absolutely sure he would be.

McAllister left the car in the station car park. In full view of the bar, and on the busiest street in town, Joanne thought, not exactly discrete.

Outside the cinema there was a long queue for tickets. The weather had turned dreich in the space of an hour. Intermittent rain fell on the waiting queue, and gusts of wind swirled around their legs. McAllister looked questioningly at Joanne. She found a solution.

"Rhona."

An embarrassed teenager saw Joanne and blushed. She was with a boy her parents detested.

"Hello, Mrs. Ross."

"Would you get us some tickets?" Joanne asked the girl. "We're going across the road for a coffee before the film starts." McAllister produced a ten-shilling note.

"Oh aye. Of course."

"And don't look so worried," Joanne reassured her. "I know you're babysitting at my place."

Sitting in the steamy window seat of the café, looking across to the slowly moving line, the commissionaire at the heavy swing doors, and the crowded, brightly-lit foyer, they waited.

"I'd never have dreamt this town could be so busy," McAllister observed.

"It's Friday night and it's the only warm place to do your courting. Even you should remember that. Or hadn't they invented the cinema when you went courting?"

"In my day, they hadn't invented electric."

"I knew they were backward in Glasgow."

They sipped their coffee, with Joanne creening over the back of the mock-leather banquettes from time to time to check the progress of the queue. She suddenly slithered down the seat.

"I don't believe it!"

McAllister turned to see what had caught her attention.

"Don't look." Joanne grabbed his arm. Rhona came rushing in.

"Here's your tickets, Mrs. Ross," she said, dropping them on the table. "I have to run."

McAllister took them. "We should go now if we want decent seats."

Joanne was shaking and peeking over the booth, staring

down the street towards the couples still lined along the pavement. It took him a moment to realize she was fighting to control her mirth.

"Will you please tell me what's going on?" he asked. "I hate missing the beginning of a film."

"We're not going."

"Why not?"

"Look. Just before the ticket booth. See?"

He peered through the darkening evening. It took him a moment to register the scene. There, caught in the bright lights of the foyer, was the unmistakable outline of Betsy Buchanan. Her male companion turned to her and offered her what looked like a box of chocolates. He was rewarded with a hug. Then the two of them went arm in arm over the red carpet towards the usher, who took their tickets, then opened the heavy door into the cinema.

"I bet he bought tickets for a private box." Joanne could now sit up.

"Maybe, but so what? Betsy is entitled to a night out. She's a widow after all."

"Aye. But he's definitely not a widower. He's my husband."

McAllister did an involuntary impersonation of the ventriloquist's dummy before he too started to laugh.

"Busty Betsy. Well I never."

"And where is Hec when you need him? This is one occasion where I would definitely like a photo."

"So. Where to now? I can't even get a refund—the show's started."

"And I've washed my hair so I have to do something."

"Yes, but what? This is the north of Scotland, you know. Not Paris or New York or . . ."

"Glasgow."

316 ◆ A. D. Scott

"You might be pushed for entertainment even in Glasgow."

"That leaves only one option."

"Are you suggesting what I think you are suggesting, Mrs. Ross?"

"Absolutely, Mr. McAllister. A nice cup of tea by your fireside. After all, Busty Betsy got her chocolates. Now I want mine."

"How about a glass of wine?"

"Even better."

On the drive to McAllister's house a thought struck Joanne. *Is that why my mother-in-law is being so strange? Does she know, or suspect her son is seeing another woman?*

At the front door, both were aware that in the soft bright late summer's night they were visible to the neighbors, passersby, the curious, and the gossips of the town. And Joanne didn't care.

McAllister fumbled with the key in the lock. He opened the door.

"You put a match to the fire in the sitting room, I'll get the drinks. There is not much to eat, but I can rustle up some cheese and oatcakes and a rather superior Beaujolais. Will that do?"

"*Mais oui, monsieur.*"

They sat. They talked. They sipped the wine. They listened to music—jazz. They played cribbage. They talked. Joanne asked him his opinion on various political issues. She knew he was passionately opposed to a war or even a skirmish over the Suez Canal. She knew he hoped for salvation for Hungary and had said hope was as fragile as a newborn. She knew he had not much respect for the "Auld buggers" who made the decision to send men off to conflicts when the country was still recovering from two world wars.

She asked about his reading. Then asked to borrow one of his translations of the French philosophers he admired. He suggested a book, and it came with the admonition that she should probably start to wear black and maybe a beret, "to get in the mood."

But not once did they mention what they had witnessed outside the cinema. It was not that they had forgotten, not that it wasn't on their minds, rather it was a built-in reticence to discuss anything personal. They belonged to a country where analyzing feelings was unheard of.

McAllister fetched another bottle.

They talked on, speculating on what brought the "Onion-Jonnies" to town every autumn, wondering why the east coast Highlanders had lost their Gaelic, discussing the book on the Loch Ness monster by Compton Mackenzie. "Cabbages and kings" could describe the conversation. It was almost midnight before Joanne had to put her hand across her mouth to hide a yawn.

The clock in the hall chimed. She knew she should leave, but was reluctant to move from the fire. She had never had a friendship like this—stimulating conversation, new and fascinating music, frequent laughter with a man who found her interesting, valued her opinion.

"It's not important, but can I ask for your perspective on something?"

"Of course." Her hesitant tone told him it was not unimportant.

"You know my friend Patricia," she started, "she's my oldest friend, but, if you asked me, I could never say what she would or would not do in a situation, nor what she is capable of. I can never guess what her thoughts are. I'm not even sure she has any thoughts—not ones that really matter." Joanne stopped. "That's an awful thing to say, but, well, you know what I mean."

He listened between the lines, heard her trying to express her instincts, the mental whispers. He did know what she meant and attempted to put his observations about Patricia and people like Patricia into words that made sense.

"There *are* people who don't think," he started. "Not in the conventional sense of course. They are concerned with everyday matters, concerned about family, neighbors, their jobs, their way of life. But the whys and the wherefores, the big questions, don't bother them. The spiritual dimension of their lives is for Sunday church only."

Joanne said, "I kind of know what you're saying. There are people who think the word 'spiritual' means using a Ouija board or being a member of a congregation where shaking and rolling around and foaming at the mouth is how they pray." She smiled at him. "Sometimes I envy people like that. Life would be much simpler if I *didn't* think so much."

"This is spiritual." McAllister went over to the gramophone and put on a new recording of Charlie Parker. "So is that." He gestured to a well-worn copy of *The Works of Robert Burns* on the mantelpiece. "And I know what you mean—it would be simpler to take life as it comes, do what needs to be done, and don't think too much. But that would be anathema to me, and to you." He examined the embers of the fire through the red of the wine before looking up and grinning. "Boring too."

"Rob floats through problems, whereas I take it all too seriously. And unlike him, I doubt I'll ever make a reporter—I believe everything people tell me."

"Don't worry, between Don and myself we will have you a cynic in no time."

They laughed, and no more was said until the last poignant notes of the music faded.

Joanne looked at the clock. "I have to go. It's well past midnight."

"Now a *true* cynic wouldn't be saying that."

"Oh really?"

"Not taking revenge against an erring husband? Shows you are a true daughter of the manse."

She laughed. "I know. I can't help being what I am."

"So what will you do about your husband?"

There had been enough red wine between them for McAllister to ask, and for Joanne to answer. "I don't know."

He offered her another glass, she refused, so he poured himself the last of the bottle.

Joanne spoke carefully, feeling the red wine and the need to explain as exactly as she could. "These last few months, I've been wrapped up in my job, and although it's been difficult at times, it has also been fascinating. I've felt useful, tired, stimulated, frustrated, and . . . *alive*.

"Seeing my husband with Betsy Buchanan was a shock, but only for a second. . . . What I really felt was relief."

"So what will you do?" he asked again.

"Nothing." Joanne was quite firm about this. "I shall do absolutely nothing. I will stay strong and wait and a solution will come. Bill Ross is not a man who can survive without a woman running after him.

"Children don't matter—no, that's not true—*girls* don't matter to him. He needs a son. Maybe Betsy can provide him with one. I know she can do the 'yes Bill,' 'no Bill,' 'three bags full Bill,' stuff very well—something I could never manage, so good luck to them.

"As for the future . . ." she stretched her arms above her head. Her jumper rose, revealing a tiny strip of skin, and McAllister

thought for one brief moment that he might reach out, touch
that tiny exposed line of flesh, caress it. . . .

"I need to be on my own. Do you realize it will be for the first
time ever?" She smiled at the thought. "As you yourself reminded
me, I was someone's daughter, then someone's wife—now I want
to be me. Then we shall see." The clock struck the three quarter
notes.

"This time I really must be going." She stood.

"I'll drive you."

"Thank you, but I want to walk. It will only take half an hour.
Besides, I want to dream about my lovely future as a free and
independent woman."

*And I can't bear sitting in a car with a man who has had a
drink,* she was thinking.

He saw her to the door. They said goodnight.

"Thanks, McAllister, I've had a lovely time."

"You're welcome."

He didn't know if he should touch her. *Better not,* he thought,
I'm not sure I can trust myself.

He shut the door and went to clear up. He was rinsing the
glasses carefully, rubbing the rim of Joanne's wineglass, rubbing at
the faint trace of lipstick. He stepped back, unable to finish, and
sat at the table. The sense of desolation was palpable—a pain he
had not felt since his lover in Spain had abandoned him for an
American photographer who, unlike McAllister, had offered her
the safety of marriage and a passport out of war.

But he had been young then and the heart recovers.

You are an old fool, he told himself, *imagining there might be a
future for you in her plans. Joanne is a friend, and an employee, and
that will have to suffice.*

✦ ✦ ✦

Joanne walked through town, pausing on the Infirmary Bridge to watch the clouds race past a gibbous moon.

"The moon was a ghostly galleon tossed upon stormy seas," she recited to herself.

She smiled, remembering Patricia and herself at school enacting the poem. Patricia, bossy as ever, insisted on being the highwayman, relegating Joanne to the role of the cowering victim.

"The road was a ribbon of moonlight over the purple moor,
And the highwayman came riding—
Riding—riding—
The highwayman came riding, up to the old inn-door."

"But we're not in school anymore, Patricia."

Joanne spoke out loud. She remembered Dorothy finding herself in Oz, when the film changed to color and the adventure began. The image made her hug herself in delight. With one last look at the moon, she walked along the river, then up past the bowling green to her home, and her children, and her very own adventure.

TWENTY-FIVE

⚜

The McPhee brothers had been acquitted, Allie Munro had confessed to killing his son, and five weeks had passed. The Munros knew that every part of the tragedy was being discussed, gossiped about, and speculated upon.

They knew that at this year's Black Isle Show, they, their family, their story, would be as important a matter to the rural community as who won the medals in the livestock competition, who bought the biggest tractor, and who had the bloodiest fight and with whom in the beer tent at the end of the show. Mr. and Mrs. Munro accepted this. It was unspoken between them, but they knew they could not face the certain glances and stares and nudges that would greet them.

The annual agricultural show had grown hugely since the end of the war. It now attracted people from the towns and villages outside the agricultural community. To the children the attractions were the animals, to the teenagers "the Shows," as they were called in the north—carnival rides elsewhere.

The Women's Institute had a large tent. Prizes for the best Victoria sponge cake or the best shortbread or jams were as sought after as an Olympic medal.

The prizes in the livestock categories were equally competitive. Hens, pigs, sheep, horses, cattle—in various age and breed categories—were solemnly judged, and the winner rosettes displayed on the pen or on the animal's halter.

The most spectacular were the Aberdeen Angus bulls. Murmurs went through the crowd as they were paraded round the ring. The onlookers couldn't help be impressed by the sheer size and weight and power of the gleaming beasts. On one side of the ring, a shrill of giggles rose and fell—a group of young women were pretending not to hear the comments on the bulls' prowess from the nearby bunch of lads. As the ribald comments were called out, the boys were also picking out their own prizewinners, examining the girls as closely as the judges examined the animals.

The display of the latest big bright shiny tractors and combine harvesters also had its admirers, not least boys between ages three and one hundred and three. The machines would never be this gleaming again.

Joanne loved the carthorses best. The huge beasts, in matching fours, pulling a distillery dray or marching in pairs, were impressive. The carefully combed fringe of hair and the polished hooves accentuated the size of their huge feet. The manes and tails were plaited and beribboned. The harnesses gleamed and the silver medallions glinted and jingled with every step.

Joanne loved any horse, from the milkman's carthorse to the neighbor's tiny bad-tempered Shetland pony she rode as a child. She would speak to horses, and knew they understood.

It was hot and humid for this year's Black Isle Show. The distant thunder rumbled around Ben Wyvis, but stayed on the mountaintop. It was one of those August days when everything—the trees, the flowers, the crops, the sun, and the air—was overbearing.

Patricia had arranged to meet Joanne at the tea tent, but the queue was too long, the sun too stifling. Mrs. Munro was there, looking miserable.

"I nearly didn't come," Patricia said. "Now I wish I hadn't—the looks I'm getting, you'd think I should be *inside* the judging ring along with the prize milk cows." She turned and smiled at Agnes Munro. "I had an impossible time persuading Mrs. M. to come with me, but I'm glad we made the effort. We can't not be here to represent Achnafern Estate."

Mrs. M. doesn't agree, Joanne thought as she watched the woman staring at her feet, as though in lifting her eyes she might accidentally meet the stare from a curious passerby—or worse, the sympathy of a well-wisher.

The three women made for the straw bales stacked at the side of the riding ring. The shade from a canopy helped them escape the bronze glare of afternoon sun, the straw, though prickly, made good seats. They settled down.

Joanne kept smiling, forcing a cheerfulness she did not feel.

Mrs. Munro just sat, every ounce of her wishing she were at home in the cool and quiet of her kitchen with only the chiming of the clock to mark the hours.

Patricia felt large. Her body was grumpy from heat and pregnancy. She too wanted to go home, but she had promised to hand out the prizes in the pony-jumping events.

Announcements over the Tannoy kept blaring out the results of various competitions. The sound was pitched at just the right level to agitate even the mildest of souls.

Patricia looked towards the ring. "Mummy is judging this event. I hope she's more generous with her marks than when I was in the Pony Club."

Later, when Joanne thought back over the conversation, she remembered seeing the heat roll over them like waves on hot tarmac when driving a car on a long straight stretch of road. She remembered watching the trickle of fine moisture on Patricia's forehead, the pink on the back of her neck, and the deeper flush in the deep cleft between her swollen breasts. It was disconcerting to witness a softer Patricia.

"So how is the new car?" Joanne asked, not particularly interested, but thinking it a safe topic.

"It is lovely, so comfortable after the Land Rover, but I haven't even run the engine in yet. Thank goodness petrol rationing is finished." Patricia looked at Mrs. Munro, who was leaning against a bale, her eyes closed. "We haven't been out much, have we Mrs. M.?"

"I've no been feeling up to it," Mrs. Munro replied. What she meant was, *I don't want to see anyone*, but she would never say this to Patricia.

"It's funny," Joanne said, "one morning in town, early, I thought I saw you in your mother's car, but it couldn't have been, because a man was driving."

"When was that?" Patricia asked.

"No, I was wrong, it couldn't have been you. I mean I didn't see properly. It was just an impression. Something you see out the corner of your eye and . . . no, I must be wrong, a man driving . . ."

"Joanne, stop blethering."

"It was May Day morning and we had been out to the Standing Stones . . ."

Mrs. Munro suddenly looked up at her.

"Oh no! I'm so sorry." Joanne put her hands to her mouth as though that would take the words back, "I'm an insensitive idiot to bring up that day. . . . I forgot it was the day . . ."

"Don't be silly, Joanne. I can talk about *that* day now. . . ."

But perhaps Mrs. Munro can't, Joanne was about to say before Patricia continued.

"That day was partly why I spent such a lot of money on a new car for myself. I was sick of my mother playing her games—I had to ask to borrow her car to pop out even for a newspaper. I was sick of Sandy mocking me for asking. That is why I agreed to take her car that morning without asking permission.

"I had morning sickness, I was trapped between Sandy Skinner and my mother, I was desperate to get away, I took Mummy's car. So yes, it probably *was* us you saw."

"The morning our Fraser died—you were driving your mother's car?" There was a lull in the continuous announcements from the Tannoy and Mrs. Munro's voice, her faint timorous voice, was clear.

"I know Mrs. M., it was a disastrous decision on what turned out to be a disastrous day. Goodness," Patricia leaned towards Mrs. Munro, "are you all right, you're looking terrible."

"I'm no good in the heat."

"I'm sorry, Mrs. Munro," Joanne said. "I should never have mentioned that day. Granny Ross will be here soon with the girls. Perhaps we should leave then?"

"Absolutely," Patricia agreed. "I've had enough of the heat myself." She leaned back into the straw and, completely oblivious to Mrs. Munro's distress, Patricia continued, "It's a wonder Sandy didn't scrape Mummy's car on the pillars of the town bridge. When you saw us, Joanne, I was about to pull on the handbrake and get out and walk. Sandy's driving was terrifying! We almost collided with the milk lorry at the bottom of the driveway. . . . I told you about that, didn't I?" Patricia asked Joanne. "I know I told Calum, as it gave me an alibi for . . . sorry, Mrs. M., I'm being my usual insensitive self again."

Patricia let out a squawk like the laugh of a jackdaw that has stolen a gold ring.

"Sandy and I were up before dawn to go to the Clootie Well, a silly idea, but fun. When I was little, before I was sent away to school, Mrs. M. would take me to the Clootie Well in the old pony trap. Remember?"

Mrs. Munro was so pale Joanne feared she would faint.

"Can I get you a drink or something?" Joanne asked her.

"That's kind o' you dear, I'm fine," Mrs. Munro said. "Tired, that's all." But she looked as though she might faint.

"I made a wish," Patricia chattered on. *It came true*, she thought, but she didn't tell Joanne how quickly her wish had been granted. "Then Sandy and I continued on through town. We were driving to an estate above Fort Augustus. Friends had lent us a cottage for a few days, though goodness knows what Sandy would have made of all that moorland."

"Well that's that mystery solved," Joanne said. "Mrs. Munro, are you sure you're all right?"

"I need to get home." Mrs. Munro was now trembling and a dangerous shade of pale. "I need to get home," she repeated, and now the trembles became shakes.

"Oh Lord, what on earth is the matter?" Patricia moved over to sit beside Mrs. Munro. She put her arm around her and asked Joanne, "Will you fetch a first-aid volunteer?"

"No," Mrs. Munro said. "No. Take me home. Please, Patricia. Take me home."

"I'll go and get your cousin, shall I?" Joanne asked. "I left Granny Ross by the coconut shy, I'm sure I can find her."

"I just want to go home."

The tear trickling down the older woman's face scared Patricia.

They stood. "Here, Mrs. M., lean on me." Mrs. Munro had to reach up to link arms with Patricia. "Let's get you back. A cup of tea will revive you." They slowly walked towards the field of cars parked in rows as though waiting their turn for the judges and their rosettes. "Come on, it's not far."

Patricia was smiling and murmuring and holding on to Mrs. Munro as though she was the mother and the older woman the child.

"You can manage. It's only a hundred yards. Another twenty minutes and we'll be home and you can put your feet up. Come on. One step, two steps. Remember how you used to say that to me when I didn't want to leave your kitchen to go back to the big house? Only a few more yards. Mr. M. will be ready for his tea. Mustn't keep him waiting . . ."

Joanne had been following behind, making up a slow procession of three, carrying Patricia's handbag, her own handbag, a hamper, Mrs. Munro's basket, and a picnic blanket. She put them in the boot of the car while Patricia settled Mrs. Munro into the front seat. She watched them drive off before it occurred to her that she and the girls were supposed to be going with Patricia to spend the night at Achnafern Grange.

Mrs. Ross and Annie and Jean were waiting by the straw bales when Joanne returned.

"Hello you two, you're looking tired. Mum, you must be exhausted."

"It's that hot," Mrs. Ross replied. "Where's Agnes? I thought we were meeting here."

"She was feeling faint. The heat. She . . ."

A flash of lightning and a not-too-distant clap of thunder broke the heavy air. Mrs. Ord Mackenzie came hurrying up.

"Where is Patricia? This thunder will spook the ponies. I need her to help me calm them and those foolish girls."

"Mrs. Munro was feeling unwell, so Patricia has taken her home," Joanne explained.

Mrs. Ord Mackenzie was not pleased. "How inconsiderate! Patricia promised to help me. Now I will have to deal with everything myself." She glared at Joanne as though it was *her* fault. "They could have waited. There are plenty of first-aid people around."

"No, Mrs. Ord Mackenzie, they couldn't wait. Patricia's first concern was to Mrs. Munro."

Mrs. Ord Mackenzie didn't bother to say good-bye; she strode off to take out her frustration on the juniors of the Pony Club.

Joanne saw the look of satisfaction on her mother-in-law's face—a "that's telling her" look. She winked at Mrs. Ross, who smiled in return. *I'm learning more than journalism from Don McLeod*, Joanne thought, *I can now wink with the best of them.*

Their big day out ended in shambles. It took Joanne a good while to reassure Mrs. Ross that Agnes Munro was not ill, only overcome by the heat and the day.

And it took sixpence each, payable immediately, and the promise of a weekend in a caravan in Nairn for their summer holiday to placate Annie and Jean. Not that they were too upset at not spending the night at Achnafern Grange, the sight of Mrs. Ord Mackenzie having reminded them of the disadvantages.

Joanne and her family stayed under the canopy, sitting on the dry bales, watching the spectacle. The gaps between lightning flashes grew shorter, the thunder grew nearer, the rain started, a few drops then a downpour. The sounds of lowing and bleating and the cry of a terrified pony could be heard through the drumming of rain on canvas.

A particularly loud thunderclap boomed overhead. The sounds of distressed cattle and men shouting came from the enclosure where the prizewinning bulls were.

Everywhere people were running towards cars and vans and buses, yet the fairground loudspeakers kept churning out songs and the hurdy-gurdy noise of the merry-go-round did not cease.

Joanne turned to her mother-in-law. "What should we do?"

"We'll wait," Mrs. Ross replied. "It might clear. Then maybe we can get a lift with Granddad Ross and his friends on the British Legion bus." But she didn't sound hopeful. It would take more than thunder and lightning to shift the old soldiers from the beer tent.

Twenty minutes passed, the rain let up a little. Joanne and Mrs. Ross were despairing of a lift back to town when McAllister appeared behind them.

"Afternoon, ladies." He lifted his hat. "You look like camp followers after the battle of Borodin."

"McAllister, you really talk nonsense sometimes," Joanne told him. Ignoring the look from her mother-in-law, she added, "If you have your car here, you can take us home before we get completely droochit."

"I'm hungry," Annie grinned. "All I've eaten all day is candy-floss and ice cream."

"Me too. An' I feel sick," Wee Jean said. She looked shyly through her thick fringe of hair and, with pink-rimmed-candy-floss lips, she smiled and asked McAllister, "Are you my Mum's fancy man?"

Joanne stared at her mother-in-law, who had the grace to look away. Annie sniggered. McAllister didn't bat an eyelid.

"I work with your mother," he told her, "and she is my friend."

"Can I be your friend too?" the child asked.

"You can that," he replied, but his smile was for Joanne. "Follow me, ladies, my car is over there. I will give you a lift home," he said, bending towards Wee Jean, "but promise to tell me if you are going to be sick so we can stop."

"Promise," the little girl said and took his hand to walk to the field of cars.

On the bends on the stretch of the road along the firth, the little girl went a pale shade of green and Joanne worried that the child might break her promise. But they made it back home safely.

Friends, Joanne thought as they neared the town, *I like that.*

Friends, McAllister was thinking all along the drive back, *I suppose I will have to settle for that.*

Mrs. Munro did not say a word on the way home from the Black Isle Show. Patricia helped her into the farmhouse kitchen, where Allie Munro was dozing in his chair, the wireless on, unheard.

"Mother, are you all right?" he jumped up when they came in.

"It's the heat, Mr. M.," Patricia explained, "thank goodness the rain is here."

Mrs. Munro wouldn't sit down. Not till she had told her husband. She grabbed his sleeve. "Patricia wasn't in the Land Rover, she was in her mother's car." Her voice was rasping as though her throat hurt. "It wisney her."

Mr. Munro was staring at his wife as though she was speaking in tongues, so she said it again.

"Patricia wasn't driving the Land Rover on May Day morn when our Fraser . . ."

"I'll make the tea." Patricia fussed around with kettle and water and teapot. "Do you need an aspirin, Mrs. M.?" she asked as she reached for the teacups.

"I canny take it in." Mr. Munro stood staring at his wife, who had sunk down into her armchair, her eyes so large and shining she looked consumptive.

"Patricia says Ronnie wi' the milk lorry saw them," Mrs. Munro said. "I knew it couldney be her." This time Mrs. Munro really did cry—big sobbing shuddering tears.

Patricia sensed the electricity between Mr. and Mrs. Munro and was sacred and nearly to tears herself. She took Mrs. Munro's hand and asked, "What's wrong? I don't understand."

To Patricia, Allie Munro always seemed a slow man. Slow to move and slow to anger. But she knew that was a mistaken impression. "Unhurried" was a better word to describe him.

"Pour that tea, lass," he told Patricia. "We have some talking to do."

They gathered round the kitchen table to talk. They took their time. Mrs. Munro cried. Patricia cried. Allie Munro sat with his big hands clasped on the table listening, talking when he needed to, watching his women slowly unwind as comprehension dawned. Then it was his turn to make tea, a tea so strong that Mrs. Munro hardly noticed the whisky in it.

"I heard the Land Rover, early," Allie started. "I was along the road a wee bit, opposite the woods, above the Devil's Den. I heard shouting. And swearing. I ran. The Land Rover had taken off down the road by the time I reached Fraser. He was in the ditch. He died." He did not tell them it had taken some minutes for him to die. "I found your father's shooting stick. It had blood on it. I took it and I hid it. Then I went for the doctor, but I knew it was too late."

"My mother." Patricia was too shocked to speak in more than a whisper.

"We don't know that. Maybe . . ." Mrs. Munro's voice faded when she found Allie and Patricia looking at her.

"You thought it was *me* driving the Land Rover," Patricia spoke rapidly. "You thought I'd . . ." She stopped, stared, unable to take in the revelation. There was absolute silence between the three of them until she put her hands to her face to hide her despair.

"Lass, I'm right sorry." Allie Munro was more than sorry. He was ashamed. But he did not have the words to say this, not yet.

"That is why you confessed? Because you thought I had . . ."

He nodded. "Not that I blamed you . . . never. Fraser was . . ." He did not have the words to continue but they all knew what Fraser was.

"We took Mummy's car without asking," Patricia started her

side of the story. She needed to speak, to try to make sense of the tragedy. "Goodness knows how Sandy talked me into it, but at that point I was more afraid of his temper than I was of my mother. He didn't know it, but I left her a note saying we would be away for a few days and I had borrowed the car."

Mrs. Munro was listening and rocking lightly, one hand clasped around the other as though in prayer.

"We went to the Clootie Well like I told you." Patricia was calm when describing the predawn escape, trying not to remember how helpless she felt with Sandy harassing her on one side and the thought of her mother's fury on the other. "We drove along the firth—it was too early for the ferry, then through town, and took the road to Dores. I was feeling horrible. We had to stop twice for me to be sick and stop again in Dores. When we reached the bridge over the burn that becomes the Falls of Foyers, I told Sandy I couldn't continue another minute. He was furious. He went to look at the falls . . ."

"You don't have to explain dear," Mrs. Munro said. "We know."

"Yes," Patricia said, "but what you don't know is, when Sandy didn't return, I called Mummy from a phone box in Foyers."

Mr. Munro sat helpless, hoping Patricia wasn't going to cry again—he never knew what to do with a crying woman.

Mrs. Munro interrupted, "We're all exhausted. Tell us in the morning."

"No, Mrs. M., I want to tell you now." She took a deep breath, let it out loudly and long, then continued.

"Mummy must have driven like a fury. She reached me in an hour and a bit—lucky with the ferry I suppose. I had called her because . . . I couldn't think what else to do. I know how strong she is. How good she is with officials and . . . I thought she would help organize a search, the police, the rescue people . . ."

Patricia shuddered. Mrs. Munro waited. Allie Munro looked away, not able to bear what was to come—for he knew, or guessed, or at least had an idea what Mrs. Ord Mackenzie didn't do.

"She was so angry, I have never seen her so angry. She screamed at me for taking her car. I told her about Sandy, how he had disappeared, how I couldn't find him. I told her I went down the path a little, I said he wasn't there. I said, 'I can't find him anywhere. It's been over an hour and a half,' I said, 'and he's not back.' I said, 'maybe he's had an accident.' I wanted to get the police, I asked her to do something. I asked her to look for him. I was upset, I was crying, I couldn't even be sick properly, I was retching and my mouth tasted horrible, I had these terrible hiccups, I needed to change my dress because I had been sick down the front, and all she said was, when I told her I couldn't find Sandy, all she said was, 'Good riddance.'"

And Patricia continued, the words spewing out of her like the bitter bile of morning sickness—no stopping them even if she tried.

"Mummy asked me for the car keys. I couldn't find them. I remembered they were in the car, in the ignition. She threw the Land Rover keys at me. She drove off, leaving me. I was alone. I . . ."

Patricia let loose decades of tears. Not tears for her late husband, not tears for Fraser, nor the Munros—they were tears of frustration and anger at herself. At almost thirty years of age, Patricia had hoped that for once, seeing her daughter's anguish, her mother would help her only child face an appalling situation.

"I should have known my mother would never help me." She said this more to herself than to Agnes and Allie Munro.

But Allie Munro heard her. Heard her despair. He took the words and he stored them for later consideration. He would let the words simmer and act on them or not, but he would never forget the pain in that simple phrase. . . . "I should have known. . . ."

"Sleep," Allie Munro declared. "We all need sleep." He stood. "Patricia, you stay here tonight. Mother, you see to Patricia." He had spoken and the women obeyed. "In the morning we'll know what to do."

When alone in the kitchen he reached for the bottle, poured a dram potent enough to calm his deep white anger.

"That woman . . ." he toasted, "damn her to Hell."

Patricia was calmed by being told what to do, decisions being beyond her for now. Mrs. Munro clucked around, checking the bed was aired, the linen fresh. She insisted Patricia have a hot-water bottle, "Just to cuddle," she said, and she tucked Patricia in, just as she had tucked her in when she was a child.

"Nightie-night," Mrs. M. said as she leaned over and smoothed Patricia's hair.

"Nightie-night."

Then they both went, "Nightie-night, sleep tight, don't let the bugs bite, mind you cover up your nose, and don't leg the midgies get at your toes."

And they both went to bed and to sleep, both with a sense of hope, a sense that, although there were more storms to come, the air was clearing as surely as the air had cleared after the thunderstorm.

On waking, Joanne had that sense of Sunday that had been with her her entire life. How, she could never explain, but the second she awoke her inner radar always sensed Sunday mornings as different. "Hallowed" her father would have said. It wasn't the absence of the milk cart, the coal man, or any other of the horse-drawn drays that clopped the streets in the early hours; she had no need of church bells—it was as though the hand of God rear-ranged the molecules in the air so no one could ignore the imperative of church or kirk or chapel or meetinghouse.

This particular Sunday was also one of the annual hangover Sundays—the day after the Black Isle Show.

Joanne's first thought was, *What is the weather up to?* Her second was McAllister. *A friend. Good friends? Maybe. A special friend? In time perhaps.* She smiled to herself, the smile of someone with a secret, and went to put the kettle on for tea. It was only then she remembered Mrs. Munro and Patricia Ord Mackenzie.

What had happened yesterday at the show?

We were all tired, she decided. *Nothing more. I'll phone from the Ross house before we go to church.*

Tea brewed, she poured herself a mug and went back to bed for those precious five minutes or so that she had to herself before one or both of her girls woke and climbed in beside her and were loving, lovely children for ten, perhaps fifteen minutes before the bickering started. The ritual of another Scottish Sabbath in the household of Joanne Ross had begun, and it surprised her to know she was happy.

"Hello Mum, hello Dad, ready for church?"

"You're bright and early," Granddad Ross replied.

"May I use your phone to call Patricia? I want to be sure she and Mrs. Munro got home safely."

"No need," her mother-in-law said, "I phoned Agnes half an hour ago and they're fine."

"Good." Joanne looked at her mother-in-law, took in the set expression that meant "no more will be said for now" and knew there was no point in asking, she might as well save her breath to cool her porridge.

The Ross family, minus Bill Ross, walked in procession along

St. Valerie Avenue towards the church. The bell, a new-fangled electric chime that Granddad Ross hated, had not yet begun to toll—they were early and they walked slowly. The girls ran ahead, skipped back, stopped to argue about nothing, ran on again, covering twice the distance of the mile or so to their destination.

They were halfway there, Granddad was lagging behind, talking to a neighbor, when Joanne sensed the change in her mother-in-law. It may have been her steps, more purposeful than of late, it may have been the way she held her head, but she was different.

Joanne was only making passing conversation, but as soon as she spoke, she knew. "I'm glad Mrs. Munro is feeling better. She looked terrible yesterday."

"Aye, but she's fine now. Patricia too." Mrs. Ross didn't look at Joanne and didn't alter her walk, but she seemed softer.

"You know something, don't you?" Joanne said quietly, "Whatever happened with Mr. Munro, you know."

"Aye, I do. But it's not my place to tell you." Mrs. Ross would never betray a confidence. "Don't worry dear, it'll all be fine in the end." She reached up and patted Joanne on the arm and in that gesture Joanne knew her mother-in-law was right.

"I know," she agreed. "It *will* all be fine in the end."

Patricia had woken early. The dawn chorus was in full song, but it was more her bladder than the birds that accounted for the early rise. She didn't go back to bed, too thirsty. *All those tears,* she thought.

She looked at her face in the small, dappled mirror of the dressing table that sat beneath the small window in the small room in the eaves of the farmhouse that had been her nursery as a child. Calm, clear eyes stared out of a swollen, blotchy face, but she felt safe. Empty, but safe, and it felt good.

"Good morning, Mr. M.," Patricia said as she came into the kitchen and caught Allie Munro fussing with the teapot. "Here, let me do it. I couldn't cope with the tar you call tea this early in the morning."

She stood beside him and he leaned close, letting their shoulders touch—an instinctive gesture, as close and as caring as a huge carthorse with a foal. Patricia had to fight back the tears she knew he hated.

"I need to go home," she said when they were settled at the table with their tea.

"Mother and me want you to stay with us awhile," he answered.

"You know, I'd really like that."

"Mother is right tired," Allie said after a minute of quiet, comfortable silence broken only by the frantic chirping and fluttering from a family of sparrows fighting for scraps put out on the kitchen window ledge. "I'll let her sleep in some more."

"It was all that whisky you slipped into her tea," Patricia giggled.

"It's right good to see you smile, lass." Allie looked at her. "Do you want me to come to the big house wi' you?"

Patricia thought about it.

"Yes, I would. I'll pack some clothes. I don't want to speak to my mother . . . but if she is there, I may not be able to avoid her. And no church for me today, I couldn't face it."

Allie drove Patricia in her car the short half-mile to Achnafern Grange.

"I'll wait outside, if that's all right."

"I won't be long."

Patricia was hoping her parents were still in bed. It was nearly eight o'clock, but Sundays usually started late.

"Where on earth did you get to yesterday afternoon?" Mrs. Ord Mackenzie was in the kitchen. Even at this hour, her hair was immaculate, her lambswool twinset matched the tweed skirt exactly, her pearls were just right, but she had not yet applied lipstick or powder. "You let the Pony Club down, Patricia. You broke your promise to hand out the prizes."

"Mrs. Munro was sick."

"Mrs. Munro would have been fine. You had more important responsibilities."

"How do you know she would have been fine?" Patricia looked calm, a little pale, and she was terrified. "And Mrs. Munro is more important to me."

Mrs. Ord Mackenzie sensed a confrontation and sensed that for once her daughter might not back down. "You embarrassed me in front of the parents and the committee of Pony Club. Please have the manners to write to them apologizing."

She turned to walk away, to leave the kitchen to Patricia and the dogs when Patricia said, "I know you killed Fraser Munro."

"What utter nonsense." She was standing in the doorway, and did not turn round.

"I know you hit Fraser Munro and pushed him into the ditch. You were seen."

"By whom? Allie Munro?" She spun round as fast as a viper about to strike. "He has confessed to killing that appalling son of his. Now he is having second thoughts and trying to blame someone else."

"I will not stand by and allow you do destroy Mr. and Mrs. Munro."

"Don't be so melodramatic."

It was always thus—every word Patricia uttered rebounded off her mother, making Patricia feel *she* was the guilty one. She gripped the kitchen table for support. One of the dogs in the basket reached out and licked her bare ankle. The warm sweet rasping tongue sent a rush of comfort coursing through her.

"On May Day morning, you drove the Land Rover . . . ." Patricia faced her mother. He mother faced her back. They were like gladiators throwing out challenges before a fight to the death.

"I would never have given you and that creature my car."

"You took the Land Rover. You drove along the farm road. . . ."

"I was trying to catch you at the ferry to retrieve my car. . . ."

"Something made you stop. You hit Fraser Munro with Daddy's shooting stick. . . ."

"How on earth do you know that?"

"Mr. Munro found it in the ditch."

"So that's what happened to it."

"Mummy, please . . . this is destroying Mrs. M. You have to tell the police what really happened."

"Did Mr. Munro say he was going to go to the police?"

"No, he . . ." Patricia stopped. It was beyond her comprehension why Allie Munro refused absolutely to talk to the police. He had told Patricia that if she called them, he would deny everything.

"It's for the best," he had said.

Janet Ord Mackenzie took a step towards her daughter, but was stopped by a low, grumbling growl from the older of the dogs—the mother.

"All this is *your* fault, Patricia." She pointed her forefinger at her daughter and, for the first time ever, Patricia did not flinch. "None of this would have happened if it weren't for you and that—father of your child. You brought disgrace to the Ord Mackenzie name with your ridiculous marriage."

The baby chose that moment to give its mother some gentle fluttering kicks. Patricia clasped her hands over her tummy, protecting the unborn child from her mother's venom.

"You have never understood that Mr. Munro and all who work here are part of this estate," Mrs. Ord Mackenzie drawled in her regal, mistress of Achnafern Estate voice. "The workers owe the Ord Mackenzie family their loyalty. We in turn give them a home and a livelihood . . . we look after them even when they are old. . . ."

Patricia half-chanted, half-sang.

"The rich man in his castle,

The poor man at his gate,

God made them, high and lowly . . ."

"What on earth are you on about?" her mother snapped. "Honestly Patricia, you have no sense."

"It *is* Sunday. I am remembering the hymn."

Mrs. Ord Mackenzie turned to leave, but stopped when Patricia called out, "I want you to telephone the police and tell them what really happened to Fraser Munro."

"I will do nothing of the sort."

"There is one thing I will never forgive you for." It took Patricia ever ounce of self-control to speak in a calm, ordinary voice, as though they were discussing the expected price of the barley crop. "When you heard Mr. Munro had confessed, you must have worked out that they thought it was me who killed Fraser."

"Whomever they thought they were protecting, they were showing nothing more than the loyalty expected of someone in their position."

"You let them believe I killed their son."

"Don't be so histrionic, Patricia. It doesn't suit you."

When my mother purses her lips like that, thought Patricia, *makes that "O," makes her mouth like a prune, I used to hide under the table, in the basket with the dogs. Not this time.*

"I blame myself for your relationship with the Munros," Janet Ord Mackenzie continued. "We should have brought in a proper nanny. It took years to get rid of that appalling local accent you acquired, and as for the way you kept running to Mrs. Munro and calling her 'Ma' . . ." she shook her head and shuddered. "We packed you off to school as soon as possible, but the damage had been done."

"Fraser Munro," Patricia reminded her.

"Fraser Munro jumped out in front of the Land Rover, waving his arms around, staggering all over the place. He refused to get off the road and let me drive on."

"So you hit him with Daddy's shooting stick."

"He deserved it. He called me vile names, cursing and swearing. . . . How dare he speak to his betters like that! The Munros forget their place sometimes."

"You killed him."

"I don't suppose you confessed to your dear friends the Munros that you pushed that ridiculous husband of yours over the falls?"

"Sandy's death was an accident."

"Don't be silly, you must have pushed him. When I met you, you were distraught, your shoes and clothes were muddy."

"I went to look for him. I couldn't find him. Of course I was distraught and muddy." Patricia stared at her mother. "Just because that is what you would have done, doesn't make me a murderer . . . unlike you."

"Do what you will Patricia, I can't stop you. But remember this, if you accuse me, I will make sure everyone knows you killed your husband."

"I didn't."

"Will that matter? It is what people think that matters."

Patricia had had enough. She knew she couldn't win with her mother.

"You are right," she agreed, "you will never be sure what happened at the Falls of Foyers. I am my mother's daughter, after all. As for the death of Fraser Munro, people would believe Allie Munro if it is your word against his."

Mrs. Ord Mackenzie's grievance with her only surviving child was deep and dark, and had festered from never having been cleansed in the light of logical examination.

"You were a cuckoo in my womb." As the poison poured out, a small foam of spittle formed at the corners of her mouth. "My son died because of you."

"I . . ." Patricia gave up. There was no point. She sat down and the dogs came out of the basket and she ruffled their necks and they rested their heads, one on each knee, their soft brown eyes staring at her, comforting her, and whatever her mother had to say, it no longer mattered.

"When your brother died and you survived, I was persuaded by your father that no matter how much I hated you, I could not disown you without a scandal."

Janet Ord Mackenzie had said it. She had uttered the words Patricia had always known—her mother hated her. Her mother's words no longer contaminated the sun-filled room, as Patricia no longer cared.

"Allie Munro knows his place." Janet Ord Mackenzie had not finished. "The Munros owe everything to Achnafern Estate. If he opens his mouth, he will be out of the farmhouse, out of a job, without references, and I will make sure no one in the county will employ him. Who would believe the word of a farmhand against mine?"

"I would."

The dogs ran across the kitchen. The younger one couldn't stop himself from half jumping against Mr. Ord Mackenzie's pajama-clad legs and, no matter how dramatic the moment, he couldn't stop himself from reaching down and scratching the dog's chest.

Patricia looked at her father, standing there in his dressing gown, pajamas, and slippers. She smiled. He smiled back.

He looks old, she thought. *He is old*, she remembered.

"I think we have some talking to do," he said. "I will get dressed. And Patricia, I noticed Allie Munro outside with that splendid new car of yours, why don't you invite him in, then we can talk this over together."

TWENTY-SIX

The Monday morning meeting had been in progress for almost an hour when Betsy Buchanan breezed into the room with the official photographs from the Black Isle Show Society.

"These have just arrived," she said.

Hector snatched the envelopes and spilled the prints onto the table.

"I like your hair," Joanne remarked in her best sweet voice. "The Kim Novak look, isn't it?"

"Why, thank you, Joanne." Betsy, oblivious to sarcasm, patted her hair, stiff with enough lacquer to withstand a force-ten gale from the Faeroes, then swayed out the door in her tight skirt and stiletto heels.

"What was that all about?" Rob asked. "I thought you couldn't stand her."

"It's the way she refuses to do anything I ask," Joanne protested. "But when McAllister asks it's 'yes, Mr. McAllister,' 'no, Mr. McAllister,' 'anything you say, Mr. McAllister.' She's a fluffy imitation of a woman. If Flopsy Rabbit had big breasts, she'd look exactly like Betsy."

"Meow!" Rob grinned at her.

McAllister grinned through his usual morning cloud of cigarette smoke and said, "Children, please. Can we get on with the paper? We've nothing much for a front page, so, ideas?"

"We canny use these photos," Hector declared. "A heap o' shite, that's what they are."

"Language," Don told him.

"Sorry, Mrs. Smart, Joanne," Hector blushed. "But look—they're rubbish."

The photographs consisted of shots of prizewinners being presented with cups and rosettes. Lined up in a row, staring straight into the camera, everyone looking as though they were being photographed for a police mug shot.

"We will have to use them," Mrs. Smart said.

She was right, McAllister and Don knew, the politics of not using the official photographs was too fraught, the Black Isle Show Society being a powerful gathering of local worthies.

Hec was not happy. "Where are my photos going to go?" he complained. "What about the front page?" he had asked at least three times already.

Rob held up a particularly striking shot of the prizewinning Aberdeen Angus bull.

"This picture is great, Hec. The bull's dangly bits are spectacular." Rob waved the photo around for all to admire. Joanne was trying to suppress a giggle at Rob's polite description of the bull. She laughed outright at Don's reply.

"Aye," Don said, "Joanne could use this on her wimmin's page along wi' a recipe for sweetbreads."

"*Gazette.*" Joanne was still laughing as she answered the phone.

"Front page! Ideas please," McAllister shouted. The team continued their discussion. Joanne continued her phone call.

"Hello." The voice was faint. Joanne stuck a finger in her other ear and turned away to hear better.

"Patricia. How are you? Did you get back from the show all right? I have been worried about you. . . ."

"Joanne, please listen."

Three minutes later, Joanne put down the phone. Sitting

absolutely still, staring at the yellowing wall, not seeing the inky print of Don's thumb, nor the streaks of mud off someone's coat, nor—just below the windowsill—what could have been a faint smudge of blood from who knew where, she was staring, tying to take in the news.

"All you okay?" Rob asked.

"Was that your friend Patricia?" McAllister was watching her across the table.

"Yes," she replied, her voice quiet, distant. She shuddered. "Sorry." She looked at her colleagues who were waiting, watching the shock shadowing her eyes. "That was Patricia," she told them. Then she paused. It was as though she could not quite believe what she had heard. "Mrs. Janet Ord Mackenzie has been arrested and charged with the manslaughter of Fraser Munro."

"What?" McAllister.

"Goodness me!" Mrs. Smart.

"Great!" Hector.

"Front page!" Don.

It took a good minute to regain order. Everyone was firing questions at Joanne, who answered "I don't know" to most of them before McAllister intervened.

"Settle down everyone," he commanded. "Rob, you contact the Ross & Cromarty police. Hector, do you have a photo to go with this story?"

"Aye, I've a great one o' the big house. Really spooky."

"Joanne, can you talk to Patricia Ord Mackenzie again?" McAllister looked at her carefully, knowing what he was asking.

"I'll try." Joanne felt, once again, she was in that tricky space between friendship and professionalism. "Later, when we know more, I'll call her."

"Don?" McAllister indicated the layout of the *Gazette*.

"I'll block out a front page, then page three for a longer piece, then . . ."

He was interrupted by Betsy arriving with a sheaf of typed copy and a huge grin.

"How exciting," she trilled. "Mrs. Ord Mackenzie arrested! Who ever would have thought it?"

It took Joanne a fraction of a second to register what Betsy had just said.

"How do you know that?" she asked. "Have you been listening in to my phone calls?" She stood. "How dare you!" She stepped towards Betsy, standing so close it seemed to Hector their bosoms might collide. She raised a finger and waved it in Betsy's face. "You *have* been listening in to my personal calls. . . ." She had Betsy backed up against the wall. "If I ever catch you doing that again, I'll . . ."

"I'll fire you," Mrs. Smart spoke without raising her voice but her resolve was as clear any general issuing an order on the battlefield.

Betsy fled. Joanne turned to thank Mrs. Smart, who was sitting at her place at the top of the table, notebook open, pen in hand, neither moving nor changing her expression of calm efficiency until Joanne said, "Thank you, Mrs. Smart." Then Mrs. Smart nodded back, acknowledging the thanks with a dismissive wave in the manner of Queen Elizabeth The Queen Mother, and said, "Now, where were we?"

The men, and Hector, who had sat through the episode in various degrees of astonishment, were staring at Joanne. Unable to help herself, she licked her forefinger and drew an imaginary mark in the air. "Joanne—one. Betsy—nil."

She joined in the laughter and, pink with embarrassment, it hit her—this was her place, this was her future.

"So, where were we?" McAllister looked around, desperate to continue the news meeting. It amazed him how much effort it took to appear nonchalant. When he was watching Joanne sit back at her typewriter after dealing with Mrs. Betsy Buchanan, watching her flushed face, seeing how she pushed a stray strand of hair behind her ear and let out a deep sigh of satisfaction, he felt his knees tremble in panic. He lit a cigarette, knowing he could no longer deny to himself that he was in love with her.

"Janet Ord Mackenzie," Rob smiled. "I never thought I'd be thanking that woman, but the Ord Mackenzie clan have supplied us with another great front page."

The adrenaline buzz ran around the table and they settled down to chase the story and compose another edition of the *Highland Gazette*.

It was not an easy phone call to make. Joanne waited until late afternoon, when the reporters' room was empty, before she dialed the number.

"I knew it wouldn't take you long to call back," Patricia said.

"I'm calling because I'm concerned about you." Joanne hated the way Patricia made her feel guilty.

"Are you sure you're not calling for the inside story so you can impress your precious editor?"

"Patricia, if it's a bad time, I'll call back."

"Of course it's a bad time. In a few days it will be worse as the news spreads around the community. But at least I won't ever again have to share a house with my mother. She is having difficulty finding a solicitor to represent her, so she is being kept in custody overnight. With any luck, she won't be given bail."

"I see." Joanne didn't know what to say. "No, sorry, I don't see, but it is none of my business."

"Oh Joanne," Patricia laughed, "you're hopeless. If you're going to do that job of yours, you must *make* it your business."

Joanne didn't know how to reply.

"Tell you what," Patricia said, "I will be at the hospital in town tomorrow for a checkup, let's meet. I will tell you all I can. I'd rather you tell the story than have some other newspaper make it up. Agreed?"

"Thank you."

Joanne walked across the landing to McAllister's office. The door was half-open and she knocked.

"Enter."

He had his back to her and was reading some reports typed on yellowing bits of paper that looked old enough to be papyrus sheets from the time of Moses.

"I've spoken to Patricia Ord Mackenzie. We're meeting tomorrow."

"Good," he said, indicating she take a chair, "and I've been reading a report from forty years ago on the marriage and settlement of marriage between Janet Ord and her Mackenzie husband. It seems she brought a substantial amount of land and Achnafern Grange to the marriage. He contributed a largish and prosperous farm to form the estate, but she kept her share in her name only." He handed the papers to Joanne. "This *was* all about the land and estate, wasn't it?"

"No, I don't think so," Joanne said. "I think it was all about preserving their name and reputation. Plus Janet Ord Mackenzie seems to believe in the divine right of the landed gentry to own her workers in much the same way as she owns the livestock."

"Not an uncommon attitude."

"No," Joanne replied, "but as you have often pointed out, we are in the middle of the twentieth century, and no longer a feudal society."

"It's highly unlikely we can publish the feudal complexities of this story, but talk to Patricia, write a news story, then take your time and write it up with the background nuances explained. Then I will see if I can place it in a national newspaper."

"No! Really? I couldn't. No. I mean—yes, I'll try. But I'm not a writer." Joanne stared at him, marveling at the very idea of it.

"Never know till you try."

She had the distinct impression he wanted to say something more, but he didn't, so she left saying, "Thanks, McAllister. I'll do my best."

Patricia and Joanne met in Arnotts tearoom. They took a table in the window and watched the Tuesday morning traffic along Union Street, mostly pedestrian, mostly coming and going from the covered Victorian market. Joanne was glad of the view—it gave her somewhere to look when Patricia's story became too embarrassing.

"I didn't think one way or another about the Land Rover," Joanne said when Patricia finished explaining about the car.

"Neither did I," said Patricia, "but that was where the whole debacle started: Mr. M., seeing the Land Rover disappear round the corner, believed I was driving and covered up for me; Mrs. M. eventually found out, thought I could have . . . Oh God, it is horrible! How could my mother do that to me?" Patricia shuddered as though a ghost had passed by.

"But Mr. and Mrs. Munro now know the truth," Joanne reminded her, "and Mr. Munro must care for you very much to cover up for you."

She looked up and Joanne saw the dark smudges under her eyes. "It helps to know that, especially after your own mother has declared how much she hates you."

"Your father cares."

"I know. It was Daddy who told the police."

"Really?"

Patricia's lips narrowed imperceptibly. Joanne remembered the expression well. She remembered it as the face that was about to deliver some cruelty or cutting remark.

"Isn't this the moment you whisk out your little notebook and write down everything I say? Or haven't you mastered shorthand yet?"

Joanne blushed.

"Sorry, sorry, it has been an exhausting few days." Patricia reached for the pot and poured a second cup of tea, her sandwiches, on the silver tray in the middle of the small table, still uneaten and beginning to curl at the edges.

"I wish I smoked," Patricia began. "Right, yesterday. After the confrontation on Sunday, I went back to the farmhouse and stayed there. Early on Monday morning, Daddy arrived. He told me that he and Mr. Munro had an appointment with Calum Sinclair. Daddy said I needn't come with them, but I wanted to. So we went in my car."

The journey to Dingwall was as though they were off to the cattle market or any other everyday farm business. Her father had chatted about the Alvis, admiring it, telling her what good judgment she had in cars, as in everything else, and she remembered that all she could think of was the road, concentrating on a road she knew so well she never had to think of the turns and twists and blind corners.

"Calum Sinclair listened to Allie Munro," Patricia told Joanne. "Mr. M. had trouble at first, he kept hesitating. Daddy urged him on, told him to tell Calum every little detail, everything he had seen and heard. I told Calum—and Daddy confirmed it—how controlling my mother was over her car. How it would be easy for Mr. M. to believe I was the driver.

"Then Calum called the police, and a sergeant came over to take our statements. By then it was late morning and when they said they were going to Achnafern to arrest my mother, we all stayed in Dingwall until the police telephoned Calum and said my mother was in custody. For some odd reason, I called you. I needed to tell someone. It was only after I put down the receiver that I regretted the call. But it was done. You would have found out anyway, as Mrs. Munro told your mother-in-law."

"Do you mind if I write this up for the *Gazette?*"

"Honestly, Joanne? I am so tired I am beyond caring. All I ask is that you protect the Munros as much as possible."

"I will do what I can."

"And please get word to Mrs. Jenny McPhee, will you? I'm not up to that either. I want to keep on the right side of the tinkers. It would be hard to harvest the tatties without them."

The change of subject threw Joanne and she agreed.

"I'll ask Rob to find Jimmy and let him know."

"I knew that the whole idea of going on a honeymoon with Sandy was ridiculous," Patricia began. "That morning, before it was even light, we had a dreadful fight. And on the drive from the Black Isle, and on the drive to Dores, he kept on and on about money. He refused to believe we don't have limitless amounts of cash. He'd never heard of money being locked up in investments. He thought you wrote out a cheque and that was that. When he realized I was telling the truth, he said we could sell off a field or some woodland, we'd never notice he said, as the estate is so big. Also his driving was scaring me senseless, and he blew up when I asked him to stop and swap places."

"Patricia, I am so sorry you've had to endure all these terrible events, especially in your condition."

Patricia looked at Joanne. "The difference between us is that when you found out what your husband was really like, you put up with him for what, ten years?"

"Bill is not a bad person—he's too fond of the bottle, that's all."

"For heaven's sake, Joanne, you don't have to pretend with me."

They were both quiet for a moment.

"Go on, ask me." Patricia was angry in a quiet simmering anger. "You been dying to ask, haven't you?"

"I have no idea what you are talking about."

"Here we go again, Miss Goody Two Shoes, or should I say Mrs. Perfect, hiding all your troubles, putting on a brave face. You, who were off to university, destined to marry a minister of the church . . . having to marry a common soldier . . . a man completely beneath you in class and education . . . disgracing your family, running away to the Highlands so you wouldn't have to face the shame of a baby after six-months of marriage. You are so self-righteous."

"Patricia!" Joanne was appalled at such a bald, but factual summary of her life.

"You think I killed Sandy, don't you?"

"No matter what anyone else has implied, I have always defended you."

"Joanne. Don't you see? *That* is what is so unbearable about you. You are always so *nice*! And by defending me, you're implying I *need* defending. Joanne, please, I don't need your condescension."

"Mr. and Mrs. Munro defended you even when they thought you had killed their son."

Patricia waved dismissively. "They had good reason to think I was guilty. They thought it was me driving the Land Rover."

"I have never thought you had anything to do with Sandy's death." Joanne was reeling after Patricia's accusation and could not manage any conviction in her voice. The words came over as lame—even to her.

"Really? Well, whatever happed to Sandy Skinner was an accident and I really don't care if you believe me or not." Patricia reached into her purse and took out her share of the bill with nothing allowed for a tip.

Joanne would never forget Patricia's parting words.

"Joanne, stop being such a martyr, I'm sure I'm not the only one who can't stand it." She rose to leave. "I know my family's story is all over the front page of the *Gazette*, but don't expect me to read it."

They didn't know it, but this was the last time Joanne would meet with Patricia, apart from the usual Christmas cards and the occasional phone call. This was their last real conversation. Friends since they were seven and alone and abandoned at their boarding school, this was the last time they would ever really talk.

As Joanne walked back to the *Gazette*, taking the shortcut through the lanes, although Patricia's words would never leave her, she realized she was not upset at the passing of the friendship—she was relieved.

The freshly printed copies of that day's *Highland Gazette* lay scattered on the reporters' table. Joanne was looking at Hector's photograph of Achnafern House. He made it look like a Black Isle version of the House of Usher. And seeing the Ord Mackenzie name on the front page, seeing the story as others would see it, Joanne knew that the scandal would pass down through the generations, or as long as the Ord Mackenzie name was remembered—exactly what Janet Ord Mackenzie had been fighting to avoid.

Rob was cutting out his writing to paste into the portfolio of work he was accumulating, ready to show future employers when he made his break for the big time.

Hector was sorting through various envelopes, some small, which he used for negatives; some medium, which he used for proof sheets; and one large one, which he kept for prints to be filed in the *Gazette* photo library.

"Here," Rob reached into his drawer and took out a manila envelope. "You might as well have this back." He pushed the envelope towards Hector. "It's the photo of the Falls of Foyers I was going to have framed for Joanne."

"Don't you like it?" Hector asked.

"I haven't looked at it," Rob told them. "I thought Joanne might not appreciate having a framed photo of the scene of a crime hanging on her wall."

"For the last time, Rob, it is *not* the scene of a crime. Sandy's death was an accident." Joanne said this with more conviction than she felt. "But thank you both for the idea, I'd love one of your pictures, Hector."

"The bull with his dangly bits?"

"Rob!" she laughed.

"Come over to ma studio," Hec said, "choose a photo for yourself."

"I will." She added her finished copy to the tray in the center of the table then rolled her shoulders asking, "Anyone fancy going out for a coffee?"

"Me." Rob stood.

"I'll see you there," Hec said. "I want to finish filing this lot."

With a pencil, he was marking the file number on the back of the prints, filling in the corresponding numbers and a brief description in the photo ledger. He worked quickly; in this and only this, he was neat, tidy, accurate.

He picked up the envelope Rob had given back and took

out the print from his May Day jaunt to the Falls of Foyers. He looked at it carefully, trying to decide whether to file it or not.

No, he thought, *I'll keep it—if it were printed in a newspaper, those two wee figures standing next to each other on the edge of the falls would look like dirty smudges. Pity,* he thought, *they give perspective to the photo, show the height and the depth and the magnificence of the falls.*

You really can't make out the figures clearly, he thought. *I never even saw them when I took the shot. That person is standing far too close to the edge, makes it look really scary.* But no, Hector decided the focus isn't good enough. A pity.

He put the photograph back into the envelope, and hesitated. *Was it a three? Maybe a two? No—a three for third rate,* he decided and wrote the date on the envelope.

He put the envelope into his satchel, to file later in his private collection of over five thousand prints, and like most of the photographs in the file marked "three," it would be forgotten about.

Even after Hector was famous, and his work sought after, it would not be archived along with his more famous portraits— like the one of the Aberdeen Angus bull in all his glory.

Epilogue

Highland Gazette
October 27, 1957

    Mrs. Janet Ord Mackenzie of Achnafern Grange, the Black Isle, Ross & Cromary plead guilty to the manslaughter of Fraser Munro of Achnafern Estate on April of this year.

Mrs. Ord Mackenzie was sentenced to six years imprisonment.

Highland Gazette
November 16, 1957

    Births

Mr. Iain Ord Mackenzie of Achnafern Grange is pleased to announce the birth of his first grandchild. A daughter, Morag Agnes, was born to Patricia Skinner née Ord Mackenzie at Raigmore Hospital on the 3rd November. Mother and baby are well.

Highland Gazette
December 18, 1957

    Engagements

Mr. Iain Ord Mackenzie of Achnafern Estate is pleased to announce the engagement of his only daughter, Patricia, to Mr. Calum Sinclair of Thurso, Caithness. The marriage will take place in March of next year.

Acknowledgments

To my friends in Cat Cat View Hotel, Sa Pa, Vietnam, for looking after me as I write. To Pete Wilkes for his love, his wise words, and for always dropping everything to go on a bike ride. To Dilh Khac Tiep, a true artist and inspiration. To Glenn McVeigh, dear friend and "handbag," thanks for the encouragement, the wine and cups of tea, and for listening. To Tran Duc, chef extraordinaire at Mango Mango, Hoi An, and to Le and little Mai for the love and friendship and excellent food. To Ian Munro, best barman ever. To my friends in Cat Cat View Hotel, Sa Pa, Vietnam, for looking after me as I write. To Tom Greenwood, thanks for the always interesting insights into the manuscript in progress.

A special thanks to Indica Nolan for being such a wonderful companion.

Thank you as ever to Sheila Drummond, of the Drummond Agency, agent and good friend, thank you for all the hard work you put into caring for your authors. Peter McGuigan of Foundry Media was his usual self—patient, funny, encouraging, and, most of all, he believes in his authors.

To all the team at Atria, especially Sarah Cantin, whom all work away quietly in the background, your efforts and hard work are much appreciated.

Most of all, I owe a huge debt of thanks (which seems such an inadequate word) to Sarah Durand, my editor. Sarah, throughout the most difficult year of my life, you showed me love, patience, encouragement, and never stopped believing this book would be completed. I could not have done it without you.

Finally to Hugh, light of my life, who never got to read the ending.

A Double Death
on the
Black Isle

A. D. Scott

A Readers Club Guide

QUESTIONS AND TOPICS
FOR DISCUSSION

1. Joanne and Patricia's friendship is based on their shared history, but no longer translates as clearly to their present. Look closely at their interactions. How does their relationship evolve over the course of the novel? What moments in the text serve as particular turning points?

2. Were you familiar with the Tinkers (or Travelers) before reading this novel? Are there other minority groups that you find them similar to?

3. Rob is offered a job at the bigger, fancier newspaper in Aberdeen, but he decides to stay at the *Highland Gazette*. Did you agree with his decision?

4. As Rob thinks through Joanne's excuses for her bruises, he hits upon the truth: "*Joanne, it's simple. Take him to court, have him locked away.* And to his almost twenty-year-old thinking, it *was* that simple." To the narrator and Joanne herself, however, it clearly isn't. What do you think?

5. Family loyalty is critically important in this novel. Discuss the instances in which the actions or decisions

of various characters are directly tied to a desire to protect their relatives or family name. Did you think that the lengths these individuals went to were always justified?

6. On p. 194, Joanne is suffering through another sleepless night when it occurs to her: *"I can't go on like this. I am allowing Bill to win. I will no longer let him win."* In what ways does Joanne change her behavior after this moment in the text?

7. Compare Mrs. Munro and Joanne, and the relationship that each woman shares with Patricia. In what ways are they similar, and in what ways are they different?

8. Place is a very significant concept within the novel and is tied very closely to character. On page 27 Scott writes: "The Black Isle . . . was an island of the mind rather than geography." What is she saying here about both the physical characteristics of the Scottish Highlands and about the people who inhabit it?

9. Joanne recognizes in herself "that trait that seemed to be one of mothers and women in general, that catch-all phrase used when help was offered—I can manage. Yes she could manage, but only by being first in, last out." Though much has changed for working women since the 1950s, do you think this has?

10. There are multiple mother-daughter relationships depicted in the novel, and while some are quite loving,

others are more fraught. What is the role of the mother in this book and in the society that Scott portrays? Consider both birth mothers and those women who serve as mother figures for those who are not their biological children.

11. Hector's photographs are an important aspect of the revamped *Highland Gazette*. Consider the role that the written word plays in the novel in comparison to the photographic image. How does each help tell the stories behind the novel's unsolved mysteries?

12. In one of their candid conversations, McAllister says to Joanne, "It's the nature of the job . . . we are part of the town but apart." What does he mean by this? Do you think this statement applies to all journalists?

13. Scott depicts domestic interiors with great detail. Find the moments in the text when we are taken inside a character's home. What do we learn about their personalities from the descriptions of their space?

14. In their last exchange, Patricia says to Joanne, "Whatever happened to Sandy Skinner was an accident and I really don't care if you believe me or not." What do you think happened? Do you believe Patricia?

ENHANCE YOUR BOOK CLUB

+ If you haven't read *A Small Death in the Great Glen*, consider reading it on your own or as a group. You might also consider how your reading experience is affected by thinking of a book as a sequel or prequel.

+ Reread the May Day scene on page 72–74. Consider researching May Day rituals from other cultures or sharing with the group another memorable holiday ritual that you recall from your childhood.

+ Imagine that you are casting the film version of *A Double Death on the Black Isle*. Who do you imagine playing the novel's main characters?

A CONVERSATION WITH
A. D. SCOTT

This is your second novel. How did your writing process for this book compare to that of *A Small Death in the Great Glen*? Was one more of a challenge than the other?

Writing this novel was difficult for a number of reasons but mostly because with a second book, there are expectations—expectation (mostly self-imposed) that the book will be to the standard and hopefully better than the first. Musicians call it "the second album syndrome"—I now know what they mean!

How did your experience working at a newspaper inform your descriptions of life at the *Highland Gazette*?

I worked on a local newspaper for a year but as an advertising manager, so Mrs. Smart, the business manager of the *Gazette*, has all my sympathies. Also the paper where I worked was using an old printing press and so I was able to see the physical process of typesetting. "Putting the paper to bed" once a week was a real adrenaline high. That and the sense that the whole community feels they own their local paper is what I gleaned most from working on a small town weekly newspaper.

Were you already thinking about the plot of *A Double Death on the Black Isle* as you were writing *A Small Death in the Great Glen*?

The plots of the first three books in the *Highland Gazette* series were worked out from the beginning. I knew right from the start how the central characters and the fate of the *Highland Gazette* would progress, but in very broad terms. Alongside the development of the paper I also wanted to show the progression of the decade (the 1950s) as it moved on from wartime towards a new society. What I didn't know were the many characters outside of the *Gazette* that I would meet along the way.

Which of the new characters in this novel most intrigued you, and why?

Patricia Ord Mackenzie of course! Even now, I don't know her and am still intrigued by her. I feel that if I met her I would like her yet at the same time be slightly intimidated. Believe me, there are many of her ilk still living on country estates throughout the UK. Yes, the class system is alive and well.

Spatial relationships and positions are very important in this novel—where the Devil's Den is located in relation to the Munro farmhouse; where the Dores Inn is located in relation to the Falls of Foyers, etc. How do you keep it all straight when you're writing? Do you create maps?

First, this is my home. This area is where I was born and brought up. We used to holiday on the Black Isle and I couldn't count the times we crossed over on the ferry, the old Eilean Dubh (Gaelic for Black Isle). I married on the Black Isle, had children, and my son went to a local one-teacher school there. But, as an aide-memoire, I have an original and very detailed map of the area printed in 1954. The map has great detail and the topography is shaded in beautiful colors.

Of all of these characters, whose voice comes to you the most naturally? Whose requires the most crafting?

Hmmm, that's a tough question. I find it most difficult to write Joanne as I too want to shake her and say, "Have more confidence in yourself!" But the most naturally? That's easy. Don MacLeod. I want a best friend just like him.

Tell us about your inspiration for the May Day scene. Was this a ritual you ever took part in as a child?

Yes, it is—in parts. My mother and my grandmother had so many superstitions and rituals that, as a child, it never occurred to me that not everyone saw faeries and bogymen and ghosts. It never occurred to me that standing stones were unusual, that not everywhere were there castles and ruins and fairy wells. The May Day ritual of washing your face in the morning dew was fun. Hanging a cloth at the Clootie Well was fun. Picnicking at the stone circle of Clava was fun but creepy too. It is a strange place indeed.

There is such electricity between Joanne and McAllister! Will it ever be realized?

Wait and see!

Issues of class are very important within the novel. For those readers who might not be familiar with Scottish history and culture, can you give us some background on what the socioeconomic structures of Scotland looked like in the 1950s?

It would take a huge volume to explain that. Back then, everyone knew their place, "The rich man in his castle, the poor man at his gate."

One thing we have lost is the pride and status the workingman had in his employment. If you worked on the railways, for the postal office, or on the farm, there was a pride in those essential jobs that seems to have disappeared. As for the Lairds, very few of them left too. Nowadays, the estates are mostly owned by insurance companies or rich people from Europe.

In one particularly evocative passage, McAllister thinks to himself, "The lochs, trapped in the long narrow glen by bleak and beautiful mountains, ended in an equally

grand manner on the west coast. They could not be seen, but their presence, their geography, made the town what it is. And the people what they are." Can you elaborate further on this idea? Do you think every person's character is influenced by the physical landscape that surrounds them, or is there something unique to the influence of the Scottish Highlands?

I absolutely believe we are shaped by the landscape of childhood. I believe that throughout our lives our physical environment influences us. But even in the bleakest of circumstances we can find inspiration, be it in a flower, a cloud, a shaft of sunlight. As for the Scottish Highlanders, we are shockingly sentimental about our Highland home. The Bard Rabbie Burns put it best, "My heart's in the Highlands, my heart is not here . . . my heart's in the Highlands wherever I go."

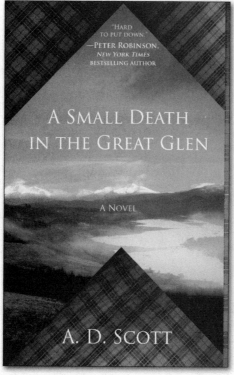